Don't Work Too

SALT

Isabel Zuber

SALT

Picador USA
New York

Picador® is a U.S. registered trademark and is used by St. Martin's Press under license from Pan Books Limited.

www.picadorusa.com

Selections from *Salt* have previously appeared in *The Sandhills Review* and *Shenandoah*. The poem "Empty Glass" from *Wildwood Flower* and the quotation from *Searching for Salt Woman* by Kathryn Stripling Byer are used with the permission of the author.

Sources for epigraphs and verse are on pages 351–352.

Library of Congress Cataloging-in-Publication Data

Zuber, Isabel.
    Salt / Isabel Zuber.—1st ed.
       p. cm.
    ISBN 0-312-28133-1
    1. Women—North Carolina—Fiction. 2. North Carolina—
Fiction. 3. Mountain life—Fiction. I. Title.

PS3626.U24 S25 2002
813'.54—dc21

                                                          2001054892

First Edition: March 2002

10   9   8   7   6   5   4   3   2   1

For Jonathan and Elizabeth

EMPTY GLASS

Last night I stood ringing
my empty glass under
the black empty sky and beginning, of all

things, to sing.
The mountains paid no attention.
The cruel ice did not melt.
But just for a moment the hoot owl grew silent.
And somewhere the wolves hiding out
in their dens opened cold, sober eyes.

Here's to you
I sang, meaning
the midnight
the dark moon
the empty well,

meaning myself
upon whom the snow fell
without any apology.

—Kathryn Stripling Byer
Wildwood Flower

SALT

. · . . · .

FAITH, 1932

The moles, he noticed, had made a progress and left ridges between the graves, even tunneled right over them. His grandfather would have been out with castor beans and poisons, his father with his steel trap jammed down above the little animal runs, set and poised to fall like a miniature portcullis, spiking the unwary. Roland smiled. It amused him to think that in this case the moles were having the last say in the matter.

Other than the mole runs, all was in order in the cemetery, grass cut, weeds pulled, markers upright. All that could be done was done. He could go. His mother had once commented that the place seemed a gracious, inviting spot and that it made her think of music. He had no idea why she would feel that way about an ordinary graveyard. She was a mystery to him.

Roland lived in town now, was married, and taught at the college. But he was one, as his acquaintances and relatives would tell him, who had not gotten above his raising. His visits to Faith were fairly regular, first to the cemetery, then to the store, then on to other calls as his quest or an invitation took him.

Sherwood, the longtime store owner, sat in a morris chair by the front window, so bulky and seemingly immobile that Roland could picture him sitting there all through the night watching the road for wrongdoing and misadventures. The man was past remembering all of the community happenings to tell Roland and repeated some of those he had told him before. Still he would usually think to say, "It's too bad about John, your dad," though sometimes he forgot that too. His elderly niece did nearly all the store's work now while Sherwood observed comings and goings. Her reactions to Roland were not predictable. She could nearly fawn over him. "And how is your dear lady wife these days, why don't you bring her to see us?" Or she could scowl at Roland and look sour when he came in and if there was no one to serve she would go into the stockroom and stay until he left.

Today Sherwood did remember something.

"Eli's boy has something for you. Told me to tell you to stop by."

This was to be a scowling day. The niece's expression seemed to say, You will have to tell him. She headed for the stockroom.

ELI'S "BOY," CARL, was the age of Roland's father but still running the post office, as his father had before him.

"But maybe not for much longer," he told Roland. "They've gotten to consolidating everything, schools, post offices, and who knows what else, maybe places themselves. We could lose our souls." He picked up a stack of the circulars, calendars, and catalogs that his patrons left behind and moved them from one end of the narrow table under the window to the other. The table and just such a stack, the mailboxes, and all of the post office supplies had been in the little low room on the Younces' porch for as far back as Roland could remember. Carl was a puttering-around man like his father, but he seemed far less sly.

Eli Younce, Roland's father used to say, had hidden out during the war from the rebels and Union folks alike, especially the Confederate Home Guard. He had a secret hiding place dug out under his house that couldn't be seen even from the cellar and he'd hole up in there with a jar of water, or something much stronger, whenever recruiters were about. As a child Roland had thought of that frightening gravelike place as being built exactly like a coffin and under the floorboards of the post office room he himself trod, though of course it would have been at the earlier Younce house.

"There was no fight in him," John Bayley would say. But there seemed to have been plenty of deviousness.

"HE HAD THEM squirreled away," Carl said. "I didn't find them until long after he passed. There was some more mail besides, but I don't know what's become of the other folks." He looked over Roland's shoulder. "Didn't seem right to throw them out, you being so close by and here so often."

"Thank you," said Roland. "I wonder why he didn't forward them."

"Maybe he didn't know your address after you moved."

Fifteen old-fashioned small envelopes, nearly square, addressed to his mother and postmarked years earlier. As he handled them Roland wondered if they had been steamed open and resealed. *Did not know the address?* Letters had come to them from Faith. No way not to have known. He thought his hand might shake. He'd not expected anything like this.

"Or maybe he thought she'd be back and he'd give them to her."

I bet. "Anyway, thanks again. I appreciate your holding on to them and letting me know.

"I thought you ought to have them but I don't want no danger to his reputation. You understand? Our being cousins and all?"

"Of course."

THINKING ABOUT ELI and his odd craftiness, Roland wandered off, following Cove Creek down to where the man had once lived. It seemed an appropriate place for secrets.

The Younce family's old homesite on the creek bend was marked now only by two stone chimneys, the low foundation wall, and the cellar hole. No house had been rebuilt on the place after the fire. Eli had long before moved closer in to the community when he became postmaster and let the place out to rent. Tall weeds and a tree or two were growing within the crumbling masonry.

The house had been burnt down when Roland was a boy by a storekeeper rival of Sherwood's who was a stranger to Faith, an odd soul who never did well there. The man had also stolen Roland's father's horse but was never caught and punished for either the theft or the arson.

Below the ruin was a narrow wooden footbridge across the stream. Roland sat down on it, dangling his feet over the brown water. He opened the envelopes.

They contained love letters to his mother, postmarked from two places out West he had never heard of, signed only with the initial *M*, letters from a man who, though he tried to joke and make light of trials now and then, was clearly lonely and unhappy to the bone, making his way by himself.

I know you said not to write, would not even give me your address. All I know is the name of that little place where you once lived. Perhaps this will reach you if they send it on. I cannot help it. I am without companions here and think of your sweet face all the time. Heaven and earth would not be too great a price if we could be together. . . .

I think of you fondly. Yours, in the sure and precious hope that we shall meet again to be parted never. M.

He had no idea who had written them. Possibly someone his mother had known when she lived and worked in town before she was married, someone who had loved her long ago.

Would she have wanted to see these foolish things? Should she have seen them? There was a great deal he didn't know about his mother.

The letters were much the same, and all ended the same way, except the last.

None of my letters to you have been returned to me and I have sent my address. I have no way of knowing if you ever received any of them and I've not had one from you. I write this last time to tell you that I'm to be married to a Mrs. Bonham, Ellie, a homesteader in her own right, with land that lies next to mine.

She is a widow with two small sons. So it seems I shall be a family man after all.

I remember you with great fondness. Yours in the hope that, since probably not again in this world, we may meet in the next.

Roland looked at the water for a while, then tore the letters into little squares and watched them float away downstream like a laundry of tiny handkerchiefs.

bread and salt

. · . . · .

On a bright, breezy day children run up the mountainside through the tall sweet grasses, cross circles of soft ferns, run so hard it takes their breath, so fast their small bare feet scarcely touch the ground. They scream back at the hawks overhead, waving their arms. They sing to meadowlarks nesting among the weeds. They wave stem swords and stick flowers behind their ears.

They have been running there always. Look for them.

. . . . . .

FAITH, 1877

Perhaps his father could be in hell. His spirit had come back from the dead, stood at the foot of John's bed and asked him for a deck of playing cards.

He wore the brown coat that he had been buried in two years before and had a puzzled, rather pained expression. Eternity, the spirit said, was very dull and he needed something to help pass the time.

Time?

But there was no time in heaven. John was only ten but he knew that a thousand years in God's sight were but as yesterday when it is past. Could his father not be in heaven after all in spite of the good words preached at the funeral and the things that his mother said? But surely not in hell. Hadn't his father been a decent and honorable man? He woke to wonder how he could get the cards without his mother knowing and how he could pass them on to a ghost. He went about dream-troubled all day. He knew he could not speak to her about the visit since there was a chance such a confidence might provoke one of her spells of agitation. Was there something between heaven and hell he knew not of, and who on earth could he ask?

He missed his father, thought of him nearly every day. The man had been thin but, until the fever, strong as anything, and the hardest of workers. He called John "my boy," might swat him on the rear, but never beat him. In a good and playful mood he would pick up John and wool him briskly, or he might walk around the yard carrying his son upside down by his ankles. Moving through the world with the sky at one's feet was a marvel, but all the blood in one's head was quickly too much. John's cries to be righted were always heeded with a laugh and a hug. His father had never done those things to his sisters. They were too little. Already those little girls didn't remember much about their father at all.

If his mother, Hannah, would stop long enough for him to ask her without saying why, she would certainly tell him that his father was in heaven and he should never, ever doubt it. But she was so busy trying to do everything he could hardly ask her anything at all, much less discuss eternity with her. Most of the time it did not even seem she remembered that, according to his father's last wishes, John had been left the head of the house. His mother went with him to the gristmill, the sawmill, the store, letting him go alone only to school and the post office.

"Always buy the best you can afford," his mother would say, which seemed odd to him, seeing as how they could afford very little, in fact, almost nothing at all.

"Cheap is dear."

"Yes, ma'am."

"Don't let them ever sell you spoiled hay, warped or knotty lumber, or seed grain with a nose to it. And watch out for short measures." His mother did not actually shake her finger at him but he felt as if she did. "There're honest men and there are those that will cheat you blind, no matter how deserving you may be. I get down on my knees at night to pray you'll grow up to know the difference."

SHE CRIED AT night as well as prayed. He heard her.

But by the light of day she neither cowered nor mourned. She stepped right out. She would walk up to a group of men, not hanging back at all, and talk to them in a loud, forceful voice, the way she sang at church, making them talk to her. When the piece of land they had to sell off was surveyed she walked the line with the survey crew, inspecting every stake, its placement down to the inch.

"It's from the ash to center of the big sugar maple on the ridge and not one bit more," she said, "certainly doesn't include the spring. It wouldn't be worth my while. I'm getting little enough as it is. You know what's agreed."

She also told off the hired hand, letting him know what she thought of his parentage and his mental ability. At that John cringed, afraid the man wouldn't come back to work anymore, but he did.

He was of two minds about his mother. On the one hand, she had usurped his rightful place, but on the other, he was often grateful for her strength and protection.

She was teaching him and at some point his managing duties would begin. He was learning all the time.

And then she went and married the Widower Shull with no forewarning at all. One day she and their neighbor, whose wife had died of consumption in the spring, drove into the county seat and came back wed. John hadn't suspected a thing, not even when his mother went off with her hat on instead of her scarf. Everything changed.

The families were brought together and John was not to be head of the house after all. Perhaps he and his sisters had lost what little inheritance they had as well.

One day he was beaten for the first time. Somebody left the gate open and, though only two of the cows wandered but a short way and were quickly reclaimed, John was punished for it. He was not even sure he was the one who had failed to close and latch the gate.

"A little hickory tea is good for the memory," said that man Shull who wasn't Widower anymore.

YES, I WILL *work as I am told. But I will also watch and wait, learn what is needful. A time will come and I will know it.*

And he would make sure when he had land that he never had to sell any of it.

. · . . · .

DEERFIELD, 1883

Thinking of something that happened when she was very small was
to her like finding a jewel in the grass; better even, since jewels in
the grass turned into nothing more than flecks of mica and drops of
dew. But the thoughts were colored crystal windows. You picked
one up, held it to the light from whatever source you had and a tiny
scene leapt to full-sized life. All at once there Anna was beside her
father, riding high in the swaying buggy on a green and gold day.
She was so short-legged her feet didn't touch the floor and every
curve around the mountain moved her toward or away from her
father.

In the valley the road ran straight and open, the earth dark with
damp, with new-leafing forest to one side and to the other a grassy
bank and meadows edged by rail fences of fresh split wood. A
spring wind with the coolness of a shower promised, or just past,
blew across their faces. Where they were going and when they
would arrive she did not remember.

T. A. Stockton, Anna's own papa, sat tall and dressed in his best
suit and white shirt, not a hair or dust mote to be seen on the hard-
brushed black wool, not a single scorch mark on the bleached linen
though her mother used an iron hot enough to raise steam from her
testing spit and the sprinkled clothes. He wore his red silk kerchief
tied around his neck and drove as always, holding both the reins and
the whip. He would not put the whip down, would never put it in
the socket. He might have been saying something serious to her. She
had forgotten his words, not having heeded them. Perhaps they had
only been about the early flowers that were blooming beside the wet

ditches. He ought, he often said, to know the names of all the plants and what they were good for. His mother had tried to teach him, hoping he might make a doctor. His mother, he would tell her, had been a fine horsewoman and an herbalist of note, more practiced in both than her mother, Tina, could ever hope to be. Tina did not know enough of the true English names for such things and never had advantages like a well-trained saddle horse. His mother could "kill or cure," he would say. It always sounded backwards to Anna.

Shouldn't it be cure or kill? she wanted to ask, but did not, knowing how he would have looked at such a question, turning and glaring down at her challenge, his thick eyebrows nearly meeting. His face was always fierce, cut across twice, once by his eyebrows and again by his mustache. He would look like the man with the pistol in his belt, Major DeHaven, her mother's first husband. Major DeHaven actually was much younger, but he was frowning that way in the picture her mother kept in the paper-covered box, along with the letter from the major's commander and a strip of fern-sprigged muslin from a wedding dress. He had been an officer. Her father, who had carried a rifle, had had no real rank that she knew of, only his fierce upright carriage and his anger. She wondered, if Major DeHaven had lived, would he have frowned at her like that? Or would he have smiled and told her funny things? But if the major had not been killed in his very first battle, she would most certainly not be who she was.

As her father spoke, a strange, lively glow had played over everything. So their journey must have been after a rain. The light was the sort that follows water, making all colors change, evergreens darkening and the sky yellowish. Heavy bright grasses flowed down the bank, thick and straight, like hair newly brushed, ready to be braided. He had been telling her something she couldn't remember. Maybe he was leaving again. She didn't know why he had taken her out riding alone, without her sister Nell. Had she forgotten something necessary to her very life? Or had it been nothing more than a short drive through the country? How could she forget when she needed to remember everything?

Light and swift, Anna ran straight up the lane behind the house as fast as she could go. She would run as far as the first big chestnut on the ridge, one of those that she and Nell and the two of the neighbor girls all holding hands together could barely reach around. But partway up her chest began to hurt and she had to stop.

Oh, I have never felt so happy. I am seven years old and I will remember this always for I may never have such a happiness again.

Even with her breath coming ragged and sharp, she felt glad enough to sing the way she and Nell did when they were out together, only she didn't quite have the wind for it. And there was no reason for this feeling that she could put a name to.

She pulled down a limb of the service tree and actually found a few of the sweet rosy berries the birds had not gotten to yet. When she had her breath back she would run down again to the house, hoping she wouldn't fall. But so what if she did? She already had a big dry scab on her left knee. It was a fine one. Tonight she would scale it off carefully all in one piece and pretend to throw it at Nell who would shriek and duck under the coverlet, nothing showing but her wide, long-lashed eyes. It was probably worth a fall to have a great scab like that. Perhaps she should have kept her scabs and put them all in a box, the long thin ones from briar scratches, the bigger rough ones from her knees and elbows, the oval one from the split on her chin cut there when her brother Dan had pushed her so hard in the swing that she fell right out on her face.

"Good god have mercy on us," he had said as she bled all over them both, and had tied up her whole jaw with both of his bandannas.

The scabs would have served to remind her of those times when she bravely flung herself against things that would not yield. Nell should envy her for such as that in the way she envied Nell for being older and knowing things first.

. ˙ . . ˙ .

T.A., their father, claimed he'd been much mistaken about their mother before they married and he worried them whenever he said it. He told Anna and Nell that when he first saw her she looked far more settled than she turned out to be, by which they figured he meant quiet and obedient, perhaps even sorrowing, which, it seemed, would have been all right with him. What with her being widowed in the war and all, he said he had felt he had the right to expect something altogether different. And, the way Tina didn't curb them, they, his only daughters, would grow up so untame and foolish that no man in his right mind would want either one of them. Running off from the house the way they did, out in all weathers, in the sun with no bonnets, they'd get brown as those Old People. What good man was going to want some squaw? And that wasn't the only thing either. They could get snakebit, or attacked by bears, or gnawed by rabid coons. They could fall off a cliff.

Tina, coming in from the garden with a basket of damp beans beginning to get rust spots, heard him. "Or carried off by eagles, sucked dry by leeches," she teased, but their father was a hard man to get at that way. "Come on, Mr. S., first you're afraid no husband will take them off your hands, and then you turn around and think in horror of all the things that could happen even before they come to a marrying age." She dumped more beans on the newspapers on the porch table for the girls to string and break. A strong scent came up from the ones already broken in the big bowl. Anna leaned over to sniff them. Beans smelled better raw than cooked.

"You well know that, in my view, it will make them hardy to get out and go some. From what I can see they're learning what they ought to learn, helping out as need be." Tina was stirring the pile about, not looking at him. Then she pulled up her skirt with the hem all muddy, scraped and retied her high-topped boots. "And besides, I like getting outside myself." She did not add "of this Stockton stockade," though they had heard her call their place that more than once.

"He'd like to close me up here behind some barricade of his own making," she would say when T.A. wasn't within hearing. "I'm not about to let him do that." The times she talked like that were the times when their father left to go stay with one or the other of their married brothers.

"Your mother may be a good woman," he would tell them, "but she does have those faults." Always taking off after some weed or other to concoct with when if she'd stayed and worked like she ought, they'd have money enough to pay for doctoring or to buy medicines that would do better than her mixtures. Anna and Nell listened, knowing all the while that grateful neighbors paid their mother in both trade and money for her ministrations and that the extra income raised their family's living above what it might have been on such stony land. Tina never bothered to remind him of that.

Before he could complain any more about his daughters' unseemly freedom Tina took up the emptied basket and headed back to the garden. "All this rain is about to ruin the crop before the beans are big enough to be shelly and tasty," she observed on the way. The heavy wet hem of her dress slapped her ankles, dropping little clots of mud as if to mark a trail by which she might intend to return or to bear witness to her exertions.

"She's trying to make me out a sluggard," T.A. said to no one, to the open air, to the big gray boulders in the yard, "showing off how hard she's working while I must nurse my feet lest these blisters get infected." A man had to look after his feet, he said. He learned that in the army. Of all the pairs of boots he took then he would keep only those well broken in. One never knew when one would have to run. It was getting new boots that had done this to him or he'd be out there in the field right now. Their brother Dan hadn't sized them carefully enough when he cobbled them. Next time he'd try store-bought.

"You," he said to Nell and Anna as they stood quiet and still on either side of the table, looking at the pile of beans they were string-ing instead of at him. Their plaits pulled their eyes so wide they felt they looked surprised, when they had actually heard all this before.

"Get that mess of beans broke before your mother gets back in here with more. Hear me?"

T.A. HAD FIRST seen Anna and Nell's mother as he came down the Shenandoah Valley through Virginia on his way back to Deerfield from his part in the war that was being lost. It had been early fall when he got to Carroll County, he told his daughters, with the creeper on bluffs and fences already scarlet and pretty as could be, but he was trying to make it home well before snow and had had lit-tle time to stop and admire. People with that windy, open, rolling land up there, if they had managed to hold on to it, were in a lot bet-ter shape than he knew he was going to be, coming back to a bony old mountain farm.

Then his horse threw a shoe and delayed him. He had stopped at Tina's father's blacksmith shop in Meadows of Dan to have it seen to and he was waiting, none too patiently, they could imagine, when Tina appeared.

"I took some notice," he said.

Anna and Nell could not think why he'd ever thought of their round, pretty, bustling little mother as a settled somebody. The way he described the girl coming from the house with lunch under a linen napkin, out of mourning, wearing light blue, with white ruffles on her apron shoulders and her gold hair coiled on her head with little ringlets coming loose, shouldn't he have known? Even he had said she had looked like a fairy sprite about to fly off at any moment.

Not far north of Jefferson his horse was stolen. As soon as he reached Deerfield he borrowed another mount from his brother-in-law and rode straight back to the blacksmith's where he proposed to the twenty-year-old Christina Tesh DeHaven and was accepted on the spot.

"She still had that heavy German accent then and half the time I didn't know what she was talking about."

Sometimes he would say he'd really struck it lucky. "She may be only a bit of a thing yet, but I've got three sons and you two girls of her. And if you set all the flowers, the gatherings and the dryings, those infusions, tinctures and salves, and whatnot to one side, she still does up the house, cooks and preserves, and sees to the animals and the gardens." He twisted his mustache and laughed.

"I could have done far worse, I suppose, especially after having gone for the South when most around Deerfield that weren't scouters and outliers went for the Union. It might have been hard to get a wife from amongst any of their kin."

He fumbled in Tina's workbox for her scissors to trim the ends of the mustache. "But there's times I regret she ever learned any English."

IN THE MIDDLE of the night Anna swallowed a knife. Monroe's knife, the smallest ivory-handled one, which her brother used for his fine carving work, was lying beside her on her pillow. She picked it up, touched it to her tongue to lick it, taste it, and suddenly down her throat it went, smooth as anything, and slightly salty.

"Mama, Mama." Something terrifying, so wrong! How could she have done such a thing? Her mind felt blank of reason.

"Oh, Mama, please come quick."

And Tina was there almost at once in her gown and the old gray wool wrapper that barely met over her bosom. The candle lit the kinky little curls all around her face. "What is it? What is the matter? Hush, now. You'll wake Nell."

Don't wake your papa. That went unsaid.

"Roe's knife, the littlest one, I swallowed it. I don't know why. Do something. Please."

"Lie still, very still. Tell me quick, was it open or closed?"

Anna tried to remember and could not. The knife had been on her pillow. What was it doing there?

"I don't know."

"Ein Brechmittel? Nein," murmured Tina. "No, bread, bread." Then, "Don't move," she said more loudly. "I'll be right back with bread for you to eat. It will help. Then we shall see. Do not be afraid. Don't move."

Her mother took the candle and went away. Anna lay there in the bed beside Nell, as rigid as she could make herself, only curling and uncurling her toes against the tightly tucked sheet and moving her eyes, watching for Tina's light as it moved through the house, visible around the edges of the doors, at places without moldings where the walls did not quite meet the ceiling, and here and there between the planking of those walls. Fine running lines of light spun out and laced their home together. She had seen this weaving before since Tina was known to check on her children at night and had once dropped hot wax on her son Dick's shoulder causing him to wake in the middle of a vivid dream of hellfire. Sometimes the light even flickered through the ceiling itself, when Tina went up to her attic drying room for some soporific herb in the small hours. Usually it made Anna feel peaceful, safe, as if the whole house could be threaded on strong cords and would swing her to sleep as if it swayed back and forth in a great tall tree. But tonight she was too afraid for any such ease. Open or closed? Why hadn't she noticed? She tried to feel with her mind to where the knife was now. Oh, if it were open it could slice her stomach and she would bleed and bleed inside. She might even die in spite of all Tina could do. Tears were running into her ears though she had not even realized that she was crying.

Eventually the light from the candle came wavering back into the room. It had taken a long time to find the bread. But Tina held out her hand. There was no bread. Monroe's little knife, solid metal and ivory, lay in her palm.

"A bad dream, mein kleiner Bär, that is all. The knife was still with Roe. No need for bread or Brechmittel. You will be fine." She kissed Anna's forehead.

"Get quiet up there," said T.A. from the front bedroom downstairs. "You all won't let a man get a good night's rest. Come back here, Tina."

But her mother fetched an extra quilt from the chest, gathered Anna up in her arms, though Anna was already more than half as tall as she was. She wrapped her in the quilt which smelled faintly of cloves and must and took her to the rocker where they sat rocking in the dark until it was time to build up the fires.

WHEN TINA SET them free from their chores they went as they would. Anna and Nell were eight and ten when they first started roaming so far away alone that not even their brothers working in the highest-up fields could have heard them if they had cried out for help. They were thirteen and fifteen the last time they left together on their long wanderings. Then Nell stopped courting too many and settled on Rush Hardy. And by the next summer after that Anna had gone to work in town for the Albas.

They argued sometimes, "like Papa and Mama," Nell said, about where they should go. Anna was usually for exploring all over, "to the back of beyond."

"Let's look for someplace different, see what else can be seen." An exceptional view, a fresh washout of stones on the hillside to pick through, a recently exposed layer of clay in the creek bank that was a new color and a new texture.

The kind of rain that rotted Tina's beans opened up the channels of mountain streams and revealed things hidden, white quartz, a granite stone the size of a hand that the Old Ones had shaped with two horns on one end and a long groove on the other, and layers of wonderful new slick gray-white clay earth buried for who knew how long.

When Anna touched that clay it said things to her. *Use me, use me,* it begged. She took handfuls of it, made markings on her face, triple lines on each cheek, a dot on her chin, and a zigzag across her forehead. She smeared each arm with the clay, arranged moss, lichens, and twigs on the sticky surfaces. She stood with her feet covered in the sand and muck at the stream's edge, the water rippling and speaking to her. She swayed and waved her arms as if in wind.

"Whisp, whisp, wisp, wisp," she sang softly.

"Anna, have you taken complete leave of all your senses? What about your shoes? They'll be ruined completely."

"Didn't wear any, remember? I'm a tree, a tree that must not be cut down. I have my face to the storm."

Nell shook her head, probably thinking of baths and laundry. Anna was all over gray with the creek dirt. Her hair and clothes would have to have a good scrub and Nell would probably have to do it and wouldn't want to. Anna knew getting the heavy clay out of her thick curls would not be easy. Maybe she could try to dunk herself all over in the creek before they went home. She did hope she hadn't torn her dress anywhere, but Nell didn't understand how important it was to do this special charm just this way and to do it this minute. At least she was strong enough now that Nell couldn't stop her, but she didn't want to upset her sister. They were so close their mother would call them by one name, Nellanna or Annanell, as if they were one person, not Eleanor Louise and Anna Maud.

Nell herself didn't do charms. She had a preference for visiting places they had been before, those that seemed familiar and home-like, especially the clearing in the rhododendron like a little room carpeted in small hemlock needles and little burrs from the beech tree at one end where she carved her initials with those of first one boy and then another. She called it her chapel and prayed there for a sweet-tempered, hardworking husband.

Nearby was the grave of Cotta, the gray tabby tomcat who had been Nell's practically from the time she could walk. He had been one of the few they had tame enough to pet and was the only cat Tina ever allowed in the house. When he was stepped on by one of the cows and quickly got so bad off that not even Tina could cure him, T.A. took him out and shot him. Though she knew it had to be done, Nell could not forgive her father, and when Anna would talk about how much she loved him, how tall he was, his brave soldiering, Nell would say, "But he didn't kill your cat." She took wildflowers to Cotta's grave and sometimes a few of Tina's yellow roses and sweet william.

"I KNOW," SAID Anna, her clay markings beginning to crack and flake off her skin, "we can climb past the sacred spring of poison and promises and on to the home of the mysterious Beast."

"The Beast is not that mysterious. He's a prince in disguise, under a spell. That's the way it always is."

"No, this Beast is far more mysterious than any who is only a prince. He is the real true Beast with magic powers. He is able to make drawings on a sheet of paper come to life."

Anna could almost, but not quite, see him, a man-animal with tawny skin, at work in his laboratory, grinding and mixing his compounds. He had the darkest eyes in the world.

"You said someday scientists would be able to do that, not the mysterious Beast. Why should the Beast do it?"

"Because he is lonely. He wants us to come visit and draw him some pictures to bring to life. He is the greatest scientist there is and he lives in a house with golden windows to match his fur and all the wood of it is black."

"Oh, Anna, Anna, what am I to do with you?" Nell fell to tickling her, poking her armpits and ribs till neither of them could stand up for laughing, the dried clay flakes falling to dust around them.

IF THERE WAS danger as they rambled they usually ignored it. They knew how to avoid snaky places and when they got leeches on themselves in the boggy streams they pulled them off each other and threw them back in the water. Tina did not use leeches so there was no need to carry them home. They were never afraid of getting lost, for if they climbed up high enough, they could always see their house and know which way to head down to it. Only once or twice did a soft fog come down on them so swiftly they were suddenly unable to see their way, the damp of it quickly plumping up the mosses and widening the lichens on the trees. Even then they simply struck out downhill, making it back only a little more slowly than usual. They were too surefooted to fall and too sturdy to give in to hunger or fatigue. They saw no bears, only crows, hawks, vultures, and smaller birds, and squirrels that screamed at them, also the watchful groundhogs, and the creatures of the damp, crayfish, frogs, snails, and salamanders.

Once they saw a whole family of foxes with the kits playing on an outcropping of stone on the opposite hillside. Anna wanted to go capture a kit and tame it, but they were too far away to reach the babies before they ran off.

"They've got fur like sunrise and the prettiest faces in the animal kingdom," she told Nell.

"Hen killers," said Nell. "And there're lots of animals with prettier faces."

"Name one."

Nell couldn't right offhand.

The worst things that happened were thorns and sharp twigs in their feet, itch from nettles, and bee stings. Being Tina's daughters, they knew to chew plantain and put it on a sting to give relief and keep down swelling, only sometimes deep in the woods, away from cleared ground, they couldn't find any. One day Nell almost walked into a hornets' nest as big as a teakettle. It was hidden in waist-high grass up on one of the balds and would have hit her right in the crotch. It frightened them both. Many bee stings could kill you, but even one hornet sting hurt worse than several from honeybees. The good bees in their hives and gums were said to have sympathy for people and needed to be told when someone died.

They climbed granite cliffs past the low twisted thorn bushes and the tall spikes of fragrant white flowers that did not grow lower down on the mountain, watching all the while where they put their hands.

"We are sheep. We are goats. Wild ones. And we never, ever fall." Anna leapt from one ledge to the other, her short checked skirt flying up above her knees, but Nell, who would soon be letting her dresses down, wanted a hand to help get her across. At the top they sat in the sharp, clear, open sunshine of the bald, ate biscuits they had brought with them and huckleberries they had picked. Out over Nell's shoe toes and Anna's dirty scratched feet the mountains went on and on in waves, growing paler and paler, thin as blue glass, till the most distant ridges went away into the sky.

"What's beyond the mountains, do you think?" Anna asked.

"Flat country and the ocean sea to the east, flat country and desert the other way till you get to more mountains and another ocean."

"No, I mean what is really beyond mountains? Is it God? I hope it's not God for I don't know what he'd make of two such savages."

"Oh, Anna, if it's God, wouldn't he see us anyway, beyond the mountains or not? But what do I know? Be a good girl and tell us a story now that we've climbed all the way up here. How about the Great Bear that helps sick people, or the one about the warrior plants?"

But Anna looked out into all those shades of blue. "Not today." She was quiet for a while, then brushed the crumbs off her shirt-waist. "I need another story," she said, "a new one." Maybe something about the stars, the heavens. Monroe had showed her the phases of the moon at the dining table, using the lamp, the sugar bowl, and one of the saltcellars. T.A. sat at summer, Tina at winter.

"And this is a total eclipse," Roe had said, demonstrating.

The moon pulled the tides of the ocean and that she would see for herself someday.

"I WENT TO my window," she sang along the upper path and when she finished that song, went on to the one about maids and Maying.

What precisely did people do when they Mayed? Probably it was love and flowers, being virgin, all mixed with those things that made her warm and sticky when she thought about them. It was fall, with May months away, plenty of time for her to find out what she needed to know.

She and Nell were on the mountain doing some of the last gathering of the season for Tina. By now their mother trusted them to pick and bring back the right plants. Anna was looking in the wet wooded places for the broad rough leaves of the old nettles, useful for curdling milk, but not so good to eat as they were in spring. "Grasp them quickly and firmly," Tina would advise, "that way they'll not sting." Anna would try but usually bandaged her hand in her handkerchief to protect it when she picked. Tina's little hands must be tough as leather. With her bare fingers she could take breads out of the oven that Anna could scarcely bear to touch, even after they had been sitting on the table for a while.

Nell had gone out into the sunny open meadow to cut goldenrod to dry for tea.

"Hallo?" Anna called, for Nell was nowhere in sight.

"Hallo," Nell answered faintly so that Anna could go farther off by herself.

When she remembered what had happened as she strayed away, and she was to recall it often, she tried to think if there had been any sort of signal or warning at the time. Surely something must have hinted at what was to come. In view of what came later a portent or a promise should have been required.

But there had been nothing. She had suddenly turned around and found herself face to face with a strange man who was walking up the path toward her.

His dress coat was longer than any she'd ever seen, except for slickers and overcoats, his watch chain huge, and his beard as bushy as the very bushiest in Deerfield. His shirt was pink and the tie under the beard was a knot of many loops of multicolored strips. He was no traveling man, for he had neither case nor valise, only his hat and a walking stick. He was short, lively-looking, but not handsome, with a peculiar lumpy forehead and little round glasses that glinted in the light coming through the trees.

When he saw that she saw him he stopped. His expression when he looked at her was something she could not make out. He seemed kind, pleased even, but somewhat bewildered. She could not tell if she was someone he expected to see. Then again perhaps he was only lost and in need of direction. He certainly seemed out of place. They stood looking at each other. "Show no fear in the face of your enemy," her father would have said, though, for all her admiration of him, there had been times when she had wondered if he was up to his own admonition. She was not at all afraid of this wondrous, outlandish man with his odd, friendly face and fine silver-tipped cane, yet she was trembling. She started to speak without knowing truly what she would say, perhaps to ask what he was doing there, what he wanted, but before she spoke a word, he was gone.

His absence frightened her as his presence had not.

"Nell, Nell. Hallo!" She bolted, but took care not to cross over the place where the man had stood, running to one side of the path just there.

"What's the matter?"

"Tell me quick, did anyone pass you coming up the hill?"

"Not a soul. Are you all right? What's the matter?"

"Nothing. Nothing's the matter. Just thought I heard something, that's all." She knew then, without knowing how, that even if the man were standing there at that moment, Nell would not see him. She was probably losing her mind and would have to be sent off to Morganton.

"Probably just a skunk or squirrel or something. Maybe the guineas. You know how far they'll wander."

Nell thinks I don't know a guinea when I hear one? But if I look as weak as I feel, she may only be trying to reassure me.

"Probably. Let me see your basket. What a big bunch of goldenrod! Enough to make all of us sneeze all winter."

ONE OF THE last times they were supposed to wildcraft together for Tina, it was Nell, not Anna, who wanted to go farther afield.

"The Episcopal church at St. Jude, near Valle Crucis. You know the one." Nell shifted her basket. "Papa has driven us by there, but I want to see inside."

When they could be spared, T.A. liked to drive his daughters about in the buggy to show them off, going as far as Zionville and Trade in one direction and Boone in the other. From these outings Nell and Anna knew a good bit about the county.

"I hear say," Nell went on, "that it would be a most beautiful place for a wedding, white plastered walls, stained glass in the windows, and an altar. I want to see."

"Who says? Sounds Catholic to me. They might have things like graven images and incense. Are you sure you want to go? It must be six miles at least, maybe more."

Wait, are you thinking of getting married?

She could not ask aloud because she did not want to hear the answer. She and Nell to be separated now and forever? Were they not heart-joined sisters?

They went, Anna not knowing what to say most of the way. They walked to Valle Crucis mostly on the new turnpike, which twisted back and forth upon itself. After T.A. drove that road for the first time, he spoke of hoping that people's buggy and wagon brakes would hold. Many went over it walking or on horseback because of the curves, but some were both as bold and careful as T.A. and dared it with two or four wheels. On foot Nell and Anna had no worries over brakes and did not have to pay any toll either.

The day was hot and tall thunderheads had formed in the west by the time they stopped for water at a traveler's rest where a spring was piped out of the bank by the road. They drank from their hands, the water tasting of their own sweat and the oak pipe. No one had provided the usual cup, or else someone had carried it off.

"We're going to get wet," Anna said. "I wish we'd brought something to eat. I would have if I'd known it would take this long."

The rain caught up with them and the downpour began just before they got to the church. They made a run for it, jerked open the door, and slipped inside, not forgetting to wipe their feet.

The church was all that Nell had said and more. The missionary who built it and had the stained-glass windows brought all the way from New York was buried close by.

"Why do they call this church St. John's when it's in St. Jude?" Anna watched the colored windows growing darker in the storm. They would be prettier in sunlight and she wished she could see them that way. Nell didn't answer her question.

They sat on a back pew in their damp clothes, too shy to approach the altar at the front. Water dripped from the eaves onto the river stones that made a path around the building. Then in the hush of the church, to the sound of the rain, perhaps moved by something that made her even more serious than usual, Nell said all that she had ever done. And Anna listened, listened to everything about Rush and the others, where they had put their hands and what they had said when they wanted it so much they shook.

Nell flushed and trembled with the telling. Anna considered that perhaps her sister thought confessing everything might in some way lead to herself here as a bride, one clad in a white satin dress with a train, though she knew, and Nell should too, that neither of them would ever have such a dress. Nell, with a wreath of flowers on her head, standing in this same aisle, someone shadowy waiting at the altar with a ring. A proper wedding leading to a proper marriage bed, though that might be more than some hot girl going after it in the woods and haystacks had any right to expect. And this all seemed to be flying together in Nell's mind somehow, though any wedding for either of them in a place like St. John's was out of the question. Nell took Anna's hands. "You are the only one who could understand. Well, perhaps you don't understand yet, do you? But you will. It feels a little like this."

And Nell kissed her. On the mouth.

Anna had been kissed behind the schoolhouse and again on a walk home from church when she and a classmate reached a place where the road curved and everyone else had gone on ahead out of sight. But it had been nothing like what Nell talked about. This was only a sisterly kiss and sure to be innocent on Nell's part, but Anna was stunned by the way it made her feel. At the kiss she felt a falling away, as if she had stepped off the side of the mountain and was tumbling through the air with no idea of who or what she was. She thought of her own self at the altar, in white, someone kissing her, later a man's hands undoing her dress, uncovering her breasts.

Too soon, too soon. Perhaps someday . . .

But it happened that Nell went on ahead and left Anna far behind.

Spilt salt is never all gathered.

· · · · · ·

Remember, remember. Remember it all.

A special smell of leather, dust. And a soft ruffling sound of pages turned, creamy white paper, the spiky ornamented black letters different in pattern from any other words in the house. Her mother's Bible from Philadelphia, from the German printing house there. Anna sits in her mother's lap as Tina reads to her. Spoken, the words have a harsh, strong, lively sound, as if they have an embodied existence of their own, separate from English, hanging out there in the air all by themselves. God, Anna was sure, spoke German and she would never be able to understand what he wanted.

. . . . . .

FAITH, 1883

He would never forget, nor would ever want to, even if able.

It had been late afternoon, fair, mild, and growing cooler. The bright edge of his hoe had come down across a clod still a bit too damp, dividing it into two smooth shiny halves and he had thought, not for the first time, *Out from under, out from under,* but that time the idea was most emphatic, insistent, and his plan, his serious and determined looking about him for the way, had begun right then.

He had been standing in the field he worked, and it was not his, nor would any part of it ever be, no matter how hard he might hoe, chop, and cultivate, no matter how sharp and forceful his strokes, how quickly he came to a row's end. He did this, and much, much more, for that man who was not his father, a man with his own blood children to consider, that man who had married his mother and didn't hesitate to lay a belt to her only son now and again. He had been thinking of all this, carefully. Had his hoe struck bone, or a worked flint, he might have tried to figure out why that particular stroke was of such importance, but he only divided an ordinary clod into two slick parts and changed his life.

"Don't stand there dawdling, John. When you finish with the corn, drive the cows down to the barn and see to the chickens. That hawk has been back lately. An owl's around too."

His stepfather had ordered as if he had the right, forever and always, to all of John's labor, every muscle, to his very breath, and ordered as if John did not know already what had to be done. And as if there were not others to shoulder a part of it. Any wish of his own that John might have, any yen to roam and wander, or even read, did not enter his stepfather's consciousness. John's own father would never have treated him so, he felt sure of that. Allowances would have been made.

"Owls keep down mice," he had muttered so it couldn't be heard. He remembered thinking then that it might rain again later in the evening.

Seeing to chickens was women's work and it was not as if there were not enough women and girls on the place to do it, five of them, counting his mother. His stepfather's oldest daughter was married and gone, but he had two full sisters and two half-sisters, all fully big enough to carry feed buckets and water the fowl. That man Shull spent his time thinking up things for him to do when there was no need, setting him chores that someone else could have looked after, a plot most likely to keep him home so he couldn't hire out and earn any money for a place of his own. John knew he was the best and strongest worker in the family, outdoing his stepfather and both his stepbrothers. But he was being used up making an inheritance for someone else. His own mother did not, or would not, understand.

He unlatched the gate beside the barn and headed into the field to call the cows down. At least he wasn't expected to milk them.

What had he seen in the wet mud surface of that particular clod? Nothing he could name. Not his future surely, written on dirt. But that one violent cut, the hoe biting like a sword, and he had told himself he would make everything different. Soon.

The next season he would go to work for the Widow Miller.

HE LEFT HOME on foot, with his clothes in a thin bleached meal sack and with his lock-box under his arm, making a move and taking up an employment frowned on, it seemed, by everyone except himself and the widow. But weren't they the only ones to whom it should matter? Why did everyone have to have a say?

He had made the box himself and he kept the key on a bootlace of groundhog leather around his neck, determined no one should look in it, not his mother, and especially not his stepfather. The box of curly maple was well finished with all the craft he could muster, which was considerable, for he loved to work wood, but there was very little in it, not much more than a new daily journal of weather, signs, plantings, and prices in which he was just beginning to make entries and an English novel, the legacy from a schoolmaster who had told him he was bright and could make a scholar if he would apply himself. The schoolmaster had been young and frail and much teased in the classroom with tricks and tauntings in which John had taken little part because he pitied the man. It was no way to have to earn one's bread, powdered with chalk dust and yelled at by children who wanted to be anywhere else but in the cold room with narrow windows and hard benches. When the old couple with whom the teacher was boarding fell ill of the fever sweeping the valley, he had nursed them with great care. The old man and his wife recovered, but the young man took sick and died in a few days. Most of his things were burnt, even though the fever had not the same contagion as consumption in the public eye, but the book escaped, probably because he had said specifically that he wished John to have it.

"The hero has the same first name" was the reason the dying man gave for his bequest to John Bayley, though he had had at least six pupils named John.

Instead of admiring the gentle care and sacrifice of the schoolmaster, some in the community wondered what might have been wrong in his heart that the Lord would snatch him away like that. Why was he being punished? John always considered that the ways of the Lord were far more mysterious than any mortal totting up of virtues and misdeeds, else why would his own decent father have been taken so young, leaving his only son in such a fix? In honor of the departed who had left him the gift, John read the book, a small one with wine-colored covers and tiny print.

He walked to the widow's partway down the valley, his stepfather not having offered to loan him a mount, much less give him one. The first thing he would buy when he had money would be a fine saddle horse. He had his heart set on a large bay stallion with no blaze.

AT THE PARTING his mother had her say.

"Young men need be wary of such women, John. They could be lying in wait, as it were," Hannah told him. "She might use you, might want to take advantage. And you only sixteen. But well set up and good-looking like you are."

She did not specify the kind of use she meant, but John had a good idea of what might be involved. The Widow Miller was still young and rather pretty, even if she did have red hair. Plump, but somewhat delicate, and older than John by five years.

"I figure I've been used and taken advantage of here. What's the difference?" But there was a great deal of difference, in both of their minds.

And I hardly think I'll be getting any beatings in that situation.

His stepfather had wondered aloud why the Millers had had no children. "A barren tree maybe. Or maybe touchy and she wouldn't let him near her as much as a good wife should."

John did not admit to either of them that he was considering the widow and her connection to his possible future, but it was not offspring he was counting on. It was the land.

"Maybe she resented he never built her a proper framed house when there was plenty to do it with, just kept on in that dark little cabin," Hannah had put in. "And you know the talk about what happened, the way it happened, to her husband, I mean."

The husband had been found dead in the woods, a wound in the stomach from his own shotgun. An accident, the sheriff ruled. The gun must have gone off as he climbed over a fence. So it was said. And much more was said too.

The body was come across on the Preslars' side of the fence and there was an old family anger, as everyone knew, between the Millers and the Preslars. Miller was counted to be deliberate and careful when he went out hunting and few agreed with the sheriff. Suicide? It could be, in spite of the awkwardness of it. And for that there was a possible motive, or so the community reasoned. Perhaps

Julia Miller kept her husband from her bed and he, unable to rule her, had given up on everything and called a bloody end to it.

These things were not directly repeated to John, but were said loud enough for him to hear when he was on errands for his new employer at the store or the mills. He minded none of them. The Widow Miller might live in a small cabin, but she had title to many acres of good, cleared land, more in timber, and several all-weather springs. Talk was cheaper than a productive farm.

The talk he minded was not his mother's, nor any of the others, but that of his friend Rufus Colvard. Rufus was hardest on him and, as usual, closest to the truth of John's mind.

"I'd be a bachelor and live at home all my days before I'd let myself be ruled by gain the way you are in this case."

"How do you know that? I look upon this situation as an opportunity to leave and assist—"

"Yes, but not just to leave home and help someone out. I know you too well. You aim to seduce, probably marry, and profit."

"An opportunity, like I said. And what's so wrong with that, if all parties are agreeable? Happens all the time."

"You know practically nothing about this woman, John, except how much property she has. And God knows what really happened to her husband and maybe not even he knows what happened in their bed."

John had started to say God knew all and that he had some doubts about his own ability to seduce, not having had all that much experience beyond some tentative tries and a general idea of how to proceed, but he kept his counsel.

"WALK WITH ME," said the widow. And he walked beside her to church, down the lane to the main road, west on it beyond the turn at Kilby Hollow, then on up North Fork to Cherish Church. She came up only to his shoulder and panted as she tried to keep pace with his much longer stride. Her black faille was tight across her breasts and the knot of auburn hair showed under her bonnet in the back. He wore a suit she had made for her husband who never even had a chance to try it on. It had taken little altering but the wool was scratchy around the neck and wrists because he was outgrowing his own shirt.

We look like two black crows. She should have a dark forest green dress to set off her hair.

He had mentioned something once about that color, but she'd said it was luckless.

"Sit with me," said the widow. And he sat beside her, across the aisle and in front of his own family whose eyes he could feel on himself and the widow all through the service.

Just like husband and wife. Well, why not?

HE DID NOT know how. She taught him.

It was not like Jacob and Rachel. He worked only one year before they were wed, but much sooner than that he had left his pallet in the barn loft, gone to her bed and learned more than he had ever thought possible to know. The coupling of animals he'd often watched for the stirrings it gave him, but that was nothing to this.

It amused him later to think how the community had marked Julia Miller down for a cold woman. She burnt and consumed him to the point that sometimes he wondered how he would have time and strength for the other work she required about the place. Her small, quick hands, which never grew rough and hard, knew all about everything having to do with bodies and pleasure and she showed him. They spent so much time in bed, even sometimes on the Sabbath, that he thought his mind would go soft as his rod got hard. Good women, his mother Hannah might have said, had no business knowing and doing such, but he gloried in it, didn't mind where it was going, or wherever she might have learned, and counted himself a lucky man.

For a while she wouldn't let him come inside her. She had been so sure with her first husband that she would die in childbirth that she had had him withdraw every time, never able to overcome her fears. After a time John would stand for no such thing any longer and now they had two healthy baby boys to show for it, Robert Owen and Arthur Grant Bayley, and another baby on the way.

But it was true that she was frail. At first she had been able to do all that was necessary. Then when the second pregnancy proved difficult John had to bring in a neighbor girl to help, something they could barely afford and managed only because the girl was poor and as eager to leave home as he had been. By the time the third pregnancy followed before Arthur was even weaned he found that he was serving both his wife and the hired girl, nothing he had planned, but nothing he resisted either. He did take care that Julia would discover nothing, but he felt no real pangs. After all, as she neared her confinements she always denied him because her childbed terrors made her fear that his entering might cause something to go wrong. What was a man expected to do in such cases? It was one sin or another. He was twenty-two, at the height of his powers. The situation was not poor Julia's fault. And the hired girl was no better than she ought to be. Girls like that knew to expect such things, didn't they?

Who was it said that we are all of us as God made us?

Thou shalt make proof how the bread of others
savors of salt, and how hard a path is the
descending and mounting of another's stairs.

. · . . · .

BOONE, 1891

They sat together on the parlor settee in the Blackburn Hotel on King Street waiting for Anna's life to change. The horsehair upholstery was hard and unyielding as if to let them know they were not wanted. Perhaps no one was supposed to sit on that particular sofa. Certainly neither of them wished to be there. Tina said hotels were only for traveling men and their tarts, entertainers, and lawyers with business before the courts at the county seat. Decent people stayed with friends and relatives or else did not travel. She was embarrassed that Mr. Alba had elected to meet them in such a place and was provoked that he was late. She never liked waiting.

Anna could feel her mother's discomfort through her arm in the sleeve of her worsted traveling coat, saw it in the motion of Tina's hands on the bag in her lap and in the way she settled her black and green feathered hat yet again on her head.

Tina was over her change of life, glad, she said, to be through with all of that, the mess, the care. Nell's life had changed completely when she broke the bond between herself and Anna, got engaged to Rush and made ready to move out West as soon as she was married. Anna's life was to change, but she was to be hired out away from home, to eat and sleep and live among people she did not know. She might even have to miss Nell's wedding.

She tried to turn her mind to one of her favorite escapes, that of seeing herself on a bright, cloudless day standing at the top of a cliff with a brisk wind blowing in over the crashing sea. But Tina was talking again about Mrs. Alba, how Anna was not going to be with complete strangers. That her mother would not have stood for, however necessary this situation might be. Mrs. Alba was a class-mate from Tina's school days in Virginia.

"I know her folks and they're plain country, like you and me. They never had much when she was young, were land-poor because her papa spent everything he got for more and more acreage, timber-land mostly, not fit for farming. It paid off when no one thought it would. That's how she met Mr. Alba, both their fathers being in the lumber business and having gotten successful. So Addie married well and it may have gone to her head, having money, that is, in these hard times. But there's much you can learn in such a household, a better class of speech, for one thing." Tina felt for her hat pin again.

"And Mr. Alba, he's not a bad sort, in spite of having inherited something he didn't build up himself."

"Mama, you know you've told me all this aready."

"Already." Tina went on, hardly pausing for breath. "The girls, I hear, are nice enough, though quite freckled. That must put sand in Addie's craw, to have daughters with speckled faces when she'd probably like them to be pale and spotless as lilies."

But lilies have marks upon them. And there's a small blood-red rare one that grows in marshy places and is more beautiful than all the others.

"You must remember to wear your bonnet and stay out of the sun while you're here. The son is reading law in Raleigh. I forget all their names. Addie told me but I don't remember. The boy's David, I think. Where could he be?"

She meant Mr. Alba, who was to meet them, not the distant son. Tina was getting breathless and nervous with the delay. Her talk went on nonstop because of it.

I'm the one who should be in a panic, I'm the one being hired out like some servant for the good of the family, because my papa's gone off again. It's not her facing this. My own mother never had to do this.

Anna looked out the window onto the boardwalk.

"Mama, is that him?" But before her mother could get up to see and make answer, Mr. Alba was bustling into the room.

"Most apologetic," he said, "accept them please—my apologies, that is."

Meeting them and then escorting them to the house instead of having them appear on the doorstep like strange tradespeople had been his idea. More gracious, he had written, befitting the situation in which one old friend was helping another, not an ordinary hiring out of some orphan or castaway.

"The canary," he went on with no explanation, waving his arms, perhaps in imitation of a bird flying. "Right there in the cage last night, we thought, all wrapped up in the shawl Mrs. A. knit for it so it wouldn't take cold. They're tropical, you know. Is this all of your luggage, my dear?" He reached for the valise.

"There's a trunk in the wagon that my son Monroe will bring by later." Tina answered for Anna. After dropping them at the hotel Roe had headed for the Farmers' Hardware where he was to buy a keg of common nails and a new crosscut blade, and where he would probably spend most of his time looking at a knife display in the glass case.

"Anna can carry that valise herself."

"Oh, wouldn't hear of it. I'm glad to help tote. We'll have someone to unload the trunk. Anyway," Mr. Alba went on, "the poor little bird was gone, missing. And they can't survive in this climate if they get outside. Because of being tropical, as I said."

They knew canaries were yellow and went down into mines.

"Mrs. Alba was truly having a spell. I simply could not leave till the little creature was found, but we had looked everywhere. Then Gage had the idea of closing all the curtains and getting very quiet to see if we could hear it. Sure enough, when we got Mrs. A. to stop taking on and listen, well, flutter, flutter from under the corner cupboard. Gage crept up, slipped a towel over the little thing and, well, it's back safe in the cage where it belongs. Great relief to all."

"Gage?"

"Our daughter Eugenia. Eugenia Gage, for my mother's maiden name, though sometimes I tell her it's short for engaging."

Mr. Alba had startled Anna on first sight. No, he was certainly not the strange man she had seen on the mountain, but there was a resemblance. Mr. Alba was also short, with a large head and small hands and feet. He wore glasses, had a high forehead and a close trimmed beard streaked with gray. But Mr. Alba was dressed very quietly in a dark suit, not the way the stranger had appeared to her with his loud colors, his checked waistcoat and the bright striped tie around his neck. She was much relieved, she decided. Whatever could you say to someone you have dreamed or seen in a vision if you suddenly met them? Yet there was something in the eyes of both men, a kindly expression of concern and bemusement, that was most like.

Once outside Mr. Alba trotted quickly ahead of them up the street, then took the turn toward the mountain above town, swinging the valise vigorously all the way.

"Not far," he called back to them, "not far at all."

Anna hoped her things wouldn't be too jumbled. She had to unpack as soon as she was shown to her place so that Tina could take the luggage back home. It had been borrowed from her brother's wife.

"You'll find our little home in a very healthful location. We're uphill from most of the drainage. The water is quite good and safe, even in summer."

He looked back at Anna. "I hope you are going to like it here," he said, sounding for all the world as if she were a guest or some traveling tourist and not the new hired girl.

The Albas' "little" place was large, gabled and turreted, with a veranda along the front and sides of the house. Lightning rods and a weather vane in the shape of a man standing on one leg and holding a staff ornamented the roof.

"My father built it. With his gains from the war, I'm afraid. He took the trees off near a quarter of the county. No, an exaggeration, but still a great deal of timber. Quite a folly of a place when an East Indian bungalow would suit me better. But Mrs. Alba likes it. Come in."

The hall was tall, wide, and shadowy, the floor on either side of the carpet painted dark blackish red and the wainscoting varnished almost the same shade. Grillwork spanned the space from wall to wall below the high ceiling, pendants hanging from it like pointed teeth. It smelled of dried flower petals and spice. At the foot of the stairs a tall clock with brass weights ticked away. Would it stop short, never to go again, when Mr. Alba died? Anna wondered. Obviously it hadn't stopped when his father died.

Tick, tick, this hall, tock, tock, could swallow, swallow, swallow them all.

A girl in a dark rose skirt and yellow shirtwaist came down the stairs. A square of sunlight from the landing window seemed to descend with her, though, of course, it could not actually have done so. She was tall, had a head of thick black curls and pale light eyes in a sharp, pale face. And, yes, freckles.

"My daughter, Eugenia."

"Hello, Anna," The girl extended her hand. It was thin and cool, but strong. "I'm Gage. I'm glad you've come. Let me show you your room."

HER WORK TURNED out not to be physically hard, nothing like what she was used to on the farm. Kindling for the kitchen stove arrived by wagonload, already split, seasoned and dry, scrap from Mr. Alba's furniture factory. And there was an icebox indoors instead of a separate springhouse. The fireplaces had grates and the coal for them, though dirty and smelly, was lighter and easier to handle than firewood. She had to take out the crunchy, dusty cinders, pour them on the carriage drive and pack them down with a mattock and her boots every day of winter, even icy or snowy ones. In summer a small garden stretched across the back of the lot, mostly herbs and flowers since the Albas could afford to buy the truck they needed or take it in on trade. She was to keep the garden weeded, flowers in bloom properly staked, then cut back, and to shoo Gage's enormous longhaired gray cat out of it. The outdoor chores away from Mrs. Alba's watchful eye she minded least of all. But there was almost no opportunity to roam by herself.

"I miss you, our rambles," she wrote to Nell after her sister moved to Kansas with Rush. But a married woman like Nell probably got no chance to ramble either.

"Always sieve the starch before using it. Even if you don't see the lumps while it's cooking, there will be some. Check the iron with a drop of water to see if it's hot enough and test it on the sheeting scrap to make sure it won't scorch." Mrs. Alba would see fit to trust her with some of the ironing once she was trained.

"Spit on it?" That was what Tina did.

"Heavens, no, child. Who wants spit on their clothes and linens? Use the water from the tap. And put a thicker pad under the napkins, then press them from the back. That way the embroidery will stand out."

To Anna's great relief, Mrs. Alba liked to do much of the cooking herself and was good at it. Anna did not realize how great her dread had been until it was lifted. She had lived in terror that she would have to prepare an entire meal, serve it forth, only to have it rejected, or, worse, make someone ill with it. Instead she helped Mrs. Alba in the kitchen at mealtimes, set the table, served, and did the washing up afterwards.

In the evenings she darned and mended while Lucille did her fancywork, Gage drew or wrote, Mrs. Alba knitted and Mr. Alba read to them all. She loved the evenings, especially loved the words, the stirring mystery and joy of them.

The setting sun, and music at the close,
As the last taste of sweets is sweetest last,
Writ in remembrance, more than things long past.

Mr. Alba had over half a wall of books in his study, collecting what he called "the finest." His special favorites were Shakespeare, Tennyson, Scott, Longfellow, and Mrs. Gaskell. Sometimes he indulged Mrs. Alba's appeals for something from the Holy Scriptures, but not Gage's sly request for the Song of Songs. Newspapers he left them to read on their own, if they so chose. "Ephemera," he said.

The feeling and intensity in the reading could even make being in Lucille's sour company bearable. Anna loved being told in Mr. Alba's light, clear voice "to strive, to seek, to find, and not to yield," but she was concerned by the prospect of being held "something better than his dog, a little dearer than his horse." The force of passion fascinated and frightened her.

Nell. Why do I never seek consummation the reckless way she did? What holds me back?

These evenings were one thing she would dearly miss when eventually the time came to leave. She might have no freedom to roam the mountain behind the house, but other horizons expanded. She tried to explain to Gage.

"I never thought . . ." She could not finish.

"Oh, yes, you did," said Gage. "Everyone can see what you think right on your face."

And she would miss Gage's playing the flute, not so much when she played "as written" to Lucille's accompaniment, but when she sat cross-legged in the window seat, bending low over her silver instrument, forming whatever notes and phrases came into her head. That wild and wailing music would take Anna straight to the highest open places she had ever climbed where the wind never stopped blowing. One could take a flute up there, hold it out over the cliffs and let the wind play it for itself.

BUT SOME THINGS were so painful they stung. She had to endure a hard separation from all she knew, but more difficult still was the unspoken assumption that at the Albas she was being done a favor, given experience and advantages she would never have had at home, and that she had nothing to bring into the bargain except her labor. Even in the Albas' kindnesses the feeling that her background was naturally inferior was never questioned, except perhaps by Gage, and Anna was not always certain if that was the case.

I need to have a brave and stalwart soul. I thought I did but I don't know where it's got to.

She longed for her mother's letters, the connection they made. Nothing in them more than ordinary news, but she always took care that Gage never saw anything beyond the address on the envelope. Not that Gage's own handwriting resembled the model she set for Anna. It was, in fact, not much better than Tina's. Yet Anna feared Gage would think her mother's childish and unformed. Tina's writing slanted first one way, then the other, with erratic punctuation and spelling and many extra capitals. Gage might have said "how individual and original," while thinking something else. Anna kept the letters to herself, reading them over and over. They were home.

Dick's are all well. Tomato plants are Big enough to transplant and chickens big enough to frye.

Walter Crawford has just come right in the yard and had a great big knife in his hand and cut my Choice flowers and took them off he was So drunk he could hardly walk.

The corn looks well but apples are cracking open and wn't be worth Anything. Dan's Gracie is fat as a pig and weighs 16 pounds.

And in the formation of the letters, the shape of the words she heard the sound of Tina's voice, urgent and vital, faintly accented.

Write to me, she heard Tina say on the page. *I'm oft alone.*

Yes, I will write. Always. I promise.

AND THEN THERE were Mrs. Alba's constant corrections, both public and private, for Anna's own good, of course. They would sit down to a meal, Mrs. Alba having "dressed for dinner" by taking off the apron that covered her head to toe. From the foot of the table she inspected everything.

"Oh dear, Anna," she would say, but not say why. So Anna, in dismay, would have to get up, and none of them could do anything, not touch a bite, until she had walked around the table, discovered what it was that Mrs. Alba had noticed and fixed it—a napkin with the corners facing the wrong way, a knife with its blade edge outward, or a glass not placed precisely at the tip of the knife. Ridiculous, she thought, for none of that would make a bit of difference the second they began to eat.

When they went out to town or church or school programs she would be told that her hair was too untidy, that she must do it up again, or must tend to her boots, which would be muddy or dusty before she'd gone fifty feet. Or remember next time to lace her stays tighter. All this when Gage's curls stuck out in every direction, there was cat hair all over her cloak where her indulged kitty had slept, and she often managed to leave off her stays altogether. Gage was so flat-chested that not even her corset could give her much of a figure.

"I don't know why Mother wastes her time with you." Lucille wore the same kind of look she had had when she caught Anna looking at herself in Lucille's triple mirror. One would have thought Anna could have ruined the glass itself, gotten herself stuck in there forever when all she had done was swing the silvery panels closer together to see herself going on and on, getting smaller and smaller till she vanished.

"It's very likely you'll end up doing something foolish, like marrying the wrong man for what you think is love." Lucille settled herself on the piano bench, propped the hymnbook open, and began to practice on "How Tedious and Tasteless the Hours," which she would follow with "I Was a Wandering Sheep, I Did Not Love the Fold."

"Then all you've learned here"—she struck two loud chords— "that is, if you're able to remember any of it, will be for naught."

"I'M SORRY, ANNA." Gage said.

"What for?"

"That they're like that, so stupid sometimes."

They were in Gage's study, the uppermost room of the turret, with drawings spread out all over the floor. Gage drew wicked little satirical pictures of people in town and odd romantic things, like unicorns with wreaths on their horns and dragons holding roses in their claws, gazing at them intently. Some of them illustrated her poems, which were as peculiar as the pictures. Anna was fascinated. Though she knew she did not understand every reference, she felt the possibility of a keen delight in making such things.

"You're like a governess in a book, Anna. Equal in most ways, but with no money. I wish you didn't have to take it the way you do. I wish you could turn and spit on them. Stop that, Cleopatra."

The cat had quit chasing a ball of paper and was chewing the tips of Gage's bootlaces.

"Spit on your mother?"

"I would, if she did that to me."

"Well, I can't. And I can't be the governess. You and Lucille are older than me. Besides, I'm the one supposed to be learning, not the teacher."

"It's 'older than I am.' "

And learn Anna did.

For someone who had had four children and who loved food so much Mrs. Alba was surprisingly slim and light. When preparing a meal she floated around the kitchen in her long white apron, singing brightly to herself, livelier songs than Anna would have expected. Even in summer when the stove made the room blazing hot and Mrs. Alba's face was all red, with sweat running off her nose and her black hair kinking up, she sang and turned out beautiful, special things for them all. She was very partial to watercress and went out to gather it herself in earliest spring. She knew which mushrooms were poisonous and which were not, something Tina would never try to teach Nell and Anna for fear they might get it wrong and wipe out the whole family. And she taught Anna how to separate eggs, whip the whites to a stiff foam for an angel food cake and turn the yolks into boiled custard flavored with dried orange peel, maple syrup and the scrapings of a vanilla bean. No extract in her house because of the alcohol. She and Anna spent more time in the kitchen than anywhere else.

"Prick them."

Anna was daydreaming a man's face in the steam from the boiling kettle.

"What?"

"Prick them," said Mrs. Alba. "The potatoes. See if they're done. They were old and going a bit soft to begin with. Ought to be done."

"Yes, ma'am. They're done."

The steam was only steam and Mrs. Alba was humming as she debated between popovers and spoon bread for their lunch.

Mr. Alba called from outside the window.

"Oh, my angel of culinary delights, behold what I have brought thee."

He opened the little low square door in the wall that the iceman used for delivery and thrust in a small bouquet of mallows, trillium, and flags.

"Hodges, that good fellow, and I were out looking over some property when I saw these, thought of you, and had to rush home with them. I'm afraid they need water."

Anna could imagine Mr. Alba as seen from outside the house, bending over, his coattails up, his bottom in the air, round shiny places showing on the seat of his pants because, even with the money he had, he believed in wearing his clothes completely threadbare, a principle that upset the yardman who was an equally firm believer that those who were well-off should even things out by handing goods down well before they were ruined.

Mrs. Alba took the flowers, stuck them in the front of her apron between her breasts. "Ah, Ralph." She grasped Mr. Alba's hands in hers and kissed them.

"Oh, my dear Adelaide," said Mr. Alba. He was silent for a moment as she held his hands. "Please put the posies in a vase or something. I fear they are beginning to droop."

DAVID ALBA CAME home for a month in the summer, getting out of the Raleigh heat, he said. He had ridden his own horse all the way, taking several days doing it. His trunk arrived before he did and he had, to his mother's dismay, a sunburnt neck.

"You could have gotten the train to Wilkesboro and the stage from there," she complained. "That way you wouldn't look like some sort of vagrant. And you would have more time at home. You're too far away to eat up the days in slower travel."

"I'll take the train at Christmas, I promise. But you have no idea how good it was out on the road in the open after more than six months in a city law office. I felt an absolute gypsy wanderer."

The Gypsy Davy, thought Anna, though no one looked less a gypsy than the ruddy, blond boy, who was much like his father.

"You could have been robbed." The idea of vagabondage was hardly an appealing one to Mrs. Alba.

He squeezed her waist lightly in sympathy, but laughed, mocking her fears. "Yea verily, killed even. But, Mother, that can happen on the train and the stage too, don't you know?"

"MY SON, THE lawyer," Mrs. Alba would say, though there were some months ahead before that would be the case. Without doubt David was the family favorite, with great things expected of him in the legal profession and perhaps in politics. Everyone doted on him except Lucille, and even she seemed to tolerate him easily. It was a wonder to Anna that he was not even more spoiled. True, he whistled in the house, would put his feet on the furniture and interrupt conversations, but he was kind like his father, hearty and sweet-spirited, like some bright boy let out of school which, in a sense, was exactly what he was. He and Gage were close, teased and romped with each other as if they were years younger than they were. To Anna, used to her more serious, hard-driven brothers who had all seemed old to her from the beginning, the play and high spirits were a revelation.

"Is he always like this?" she asked Gage when a truce was called after a brief fight with the parlor cushions. "Or is he just glad to be home?"

"Like what?"

"Like . . . fun."

"Oh, that. He's always fun. But make no mistake, there is a steely mind in there behind that beardless baby face. I imagine he will be all the more formidable an attorney because his manner and looks will disarm people. It's Mother, as you may have noticed, who is very ambitious for him. He could have read law right here in town but she wanted him to meet people of influence in the capital. Father is just pleased that he's been such a good boy and done everything she's asked him to do."

And you, Gage? Do you do everything you're asked? Will you?

WHILE DAVID WAS home there were special evenings when company came, those of the town's younger set whom Mrs. Alba considered it suitable to entertain. Lucille played the piano. Gage her flute, and Anna handed around Mrs. Alba's lemon bread and beaten biscuits. And there was dancing some evenings, not only the reels and squares Anna already knew but also polkas and schottisches and, once in a while, a waltz. The rugs were rolled back and David carried the upholstered chairs on his head to the upstairs hall. For a small man who worked in an office, he was sturdy, strong, and muscled.

"Indian clubs, my dear," he told Anna. "Have a go at them every day. Good for the constitution. Lots of walking and rowing on the lake too."

"I am not his dear," Anna said to Gage as she moved some of the breakable china ornaments to the higher shelves. He almost certainly meant nothing by it, but David both interested and concerned her. She put the framed deathbed ferrotype of Albert Dashwood Alba, Gage's departed baby brother, behind the vases where she wouldn't have to look at it.

"Oh, that's just his way." Gage seemed to consider something Anna didn't want to think about. "But in point of fact . . ."

Anna had a tight little chill. The stories of employers' sons and serving girls were all too clear in her mind. No, not that. But she knew that David was watching her, that he listened when she spoke and spoke for her to hear. She only prayed that Mrs. Alba had not noticed.

He danced with every girl in the room, as befitted the son of the house, then asked Anna for a waltz. She said no, that she did not know how.

"Then I will teach you and when I come home at Christmas you must save all the waltzes for me in gratitude for the instruction."

"You're making fun."

"No, Anna, I am not."

AFTER THE DANCING was over one evening and the guests had gone home Gage took them into Mr. Alba's study. She took her father's papers off the writing table, something not even Mrs. Alba would do, and brought out her cards to tell what their futures would hold.

"Hey now, gypsy sister," David chanted as he marched around the table. "Tell unto me what my lot in life shall be." His eyes were bright in the lamplight and even Lucille was drawing in her breath quickly.

"Oh, do sit down and be quiet. I have to concentrate. I'll get to each of you, but I'll do you first, David. Before you lose your nerve," Gage teased. She shuffled the cards as calmly and expertly as if they were sitting down to a game of hearts in the parlor.

David was to be successful, much admired, and the lieutenant governor of North Carolina.

"What?" David clutched the front of his shirt, pretending a terrible distress. "What? Not governor? Mother dear will be crushed!"

Anna did not believe Gage saw any political office in the cards, that she made it up for amusement. Yet it was troubling to her to try to raise the veil on what was to be. The familiar room felt odd and insubstantial, full of shadow, without mass. Not the place of the beautiful and exciting words, but one of vague threat. Laying out the patterns on the polished mahogany should have been only entertaining, not to be taken seriously, but she feared what Gage was doing, the use of power that was not in fortunes as told, but in Gage herself and in the disconcerting pictures and symbols on the cards.

Mrs. Alba certainly would not approve. She couldn't think where Gage had ever gotten such a deck.

Lucille would find her true love, but there was some obstacle. It could not be seen whether or not she could bring herself to accept him.

"Anna?"

"No, I'm sorry. I'm not sure. Maybe later?"

David looked disappointed. "Be a sport," he said, "It's only a game. Please."

"While she makes up her mind I shall do my own," said Gage.

She shuffled the cards and started the tree of life pattern, her face eager in the candlelight which was all they had allowed themselves for the readings. Suddenly Anna wanted to know. Everything. Even if there was danger in it. She was thrilled and could hardly wait.

Gage laid out a few cards.

"Hmm, I'm artistic." She had placed only a little more than half the cards for her pattern when her expression suddenly changed. Anna, sitting across from her, was more frightened by what she saw in Gage's face than she had been at the possible revelation of her own fate.

With a wide brush of her hand Gage swept the cards off the table and into a pile in her lap. She gathered up her skirt, rose, and dumped the cards in her father's wastebasket.

"That's enough," she said. "Bedtime, past it."

She left the room. "Good night, all."

DAVID CAME TO Anna's room the night before he was to leave for Raleigh. She heard the knock, said, "Come in," automatically, thinking it was Gage from her study across the hall. But David strode into the room. He was barefoot.

She was stricken and speechless. No. He must not close the door. He must not sit down on the bed. It would not do. If she were to fall, it could not be here in this house, not with her family counting on her, not with Gage possibly expecting too much. He seemed to be instantly aware of her discomfort. He did not close the door and remained standing, but he did not go.

"Look at this," he said. "I came to show you what she got me for the trip back." Anna did not have to ask who "she" was. He was holding a broader-brimmed hat than the one he had worn home and a long white silk scarf. "She's determined I'm not going back looking like some dirt farmer."

He laughed but Anna felt herself flinch. He seemed unaware of the difference he had set up between them, she being the daughter of just such a person.

"No, it's not what I came for, really, just an excuse. I wanted to ask you, Anna . . ." He paused. "Will you write to me in Raleigh? Or will you answer if I write to you? What I have actually brought you is my address. Surely you have some idea what it would mean to me to hear from you."

"You know your mother wouldn't stand for it," she said. "There's no point to it." But thinking of that lady and her ways, she suddenly decided on a measure of defiance, reached out and took the address before sending him from the room.

She wrote once and was disappointed, but not surprised, to receive no reply.

ON CHRISTMAS MORNING there was a tree. The Albas thought it would be the first Anna had ever seen but Tina had always had one decorated with paper chains, popcorn, folded fans, and candle stubs. The Albas' tree was more elaborate. It glittered with glass ornaments and tin icicles. And there were packages. A garnet brooch and earrings for Mrs. Alba from Mr. Alba. Books, silk parasols, and kid gloves with four buttons each for Lucille and Gage. Mrs. Alba gave Mr. Alba a leather business case and a deep yellow sateen vest Anna felt sure he would never wear, much as his wife might like to smarten him up. Gage and Mr. Alba together gave Anna a book of poems by Tennyson, including her favorite, "Come into the garden, Maud," and she got a pen wiper from Lucille with button stitch around the edge and an *A* in the corner. She had neither pen nor ink, wrote her essays for Gage and her letters home on a tablet in pencil. Mrs. Alba reminded Lucille that the proper initial would have been an *S*. "For the last name, dear, not the first."

"Open your package from me, Anna." Mrs. Alba was putting the new earrings in her ears.

She did so. Inside were a pair of woolen mittens knitted in rows of bright colors made from scraps of yarn left over from an afghan. When she had seen Mrs. Alba working on them she thought they were for the poor box at church.

"Thank you," she said.

"Merry Christmas, Anna. I made them for you myself. I know you saw me but I bet you didn't ever guess they were for you. You're most welcome. Now clear this away. There's much to do. David should be getting here by midafternoon and the party is this evening."

David brought his sisters and Anna gold earrings. His mother was displeased with a gift of jewelry to her, Anna could tell, but Gage was excited and offered to pierce Anna's ears for her. Lucille said that her earrings were heaviest, with the most gold in them, and that Anna's must be the lightest.

"I think they're all the same," said Gage.

"I WISH SHE'D let me spike the damn stuff," said David. "Might help liven things up a bit." The conversation from the parlor was low with many pauses. Anna had come back to the kitchen for more ice for the tea-based punch and stood at the sink, chipping off pieces into a bowl. She turned to carry it in to the sideboard but David barred her way.

"You never answered my letters," he said.

She knew then what had happened, felt her color go with the knowledge. He noticed.

"Never got them, did you?"

She shook her head. He took the bowl out of her hands, set it down, and kissed her. "Damn it, Anna, let's thwart the old biddy together. Say you'll marry me. I've been half-crazed over you. If you had gotten the letters you'd understand. Gage knows and is all for it. Say yes. Say 'Yes, dear David, I will be your wife.' "

She was hot and confused, her lips burning, but not too swept away to notice she had not heard him say he loved her, sensed that this had more to do with some rebellion than with her, that anyone his mother might object to could attract him.

She let him kiss her again, then slithered out of his arms and grabbed the bowl. "I must take this in before it melts."

She banged the swinging door open with her hip.

"I'll send your letters inside of the ones to Gage," he said.

She ran out and dumped the ice into the punch. When she got back to the kitchen he had gone in to the guests.

SHE WORE THE mittens to the church services in the winters because she knew she was expected to. They looked so childish and she was sixteen now. As she walked back with the family on a gray late-January day too cold even for snow, Gage signaled her to drop behind. The wind had turned even Gage's pale nose bright pink, causing some of her freckles to blend in and disappear.

"Give me your hand. No, without the mitten."

Gage had taken off her kid glove and put out her narrow hand with its stubby, bitten fingernails. She was holding something. Anna took Gage's hand in her own, warm from the mitten, and felt Gage slip David's letter into her palm.

"You're cold as ice, practically frozen."

"Ah, see. Things can fool you, can't they?" Gage put her glove back on. "Take good care, Anna."

THEN IN TIME everything changed. Gage was in love. She never admitted to anything, but Anna saw, knew it was so, and that it could not end well.

It was not the mayor's son. That would have pleased Mrs. Alba.

She invited him to every musical evening. He came and never made the mistake of trying to inject any frivolity into those staid hours. In fact, he did not seem to find them staid. He clapped as if he had to applaud every single note that Gage and Lucille had played and he begged on each occasion to put Gage's flute away, accomplishing this task with motions that could only be called fondling.

Gage responded by adding him to the sketchbook she kept in her tower room, making his incipient mustache droop to his chest in a manner he would almost certainly never be able to grow.

"Your mother likes him." Anna examined Gage's latest foray into caricature.

"As well she might. He's more her sort than he is mine."

"She might think you ought to marry him."

"She might just think again. Now sit still. I want to try you once more. I never can get you right." Gage turned the leaf of the sketchbook.

"If you'll hurry. It's almost time to put out things for supper."

"Oh, dinner, dinner. You're in town, remember." Gage busied herself, biting her lip the way she did when she was intent. "Anyway, I'm not sure I want to marry at all, certainly not anytime soon. There's so much else, an education, you know. We've talked. I mean a real one, not 'finishing.' Put your chin up a tiny bit. Just a quick sketch here. A husband and babies and you end up like Mother, concerned with nothing but the daily. Did you know that at one time she wanted to be a singer? I wish she would give you some lessons. You have a fine voice too."

"I do?"

"Yes, you really do. Didn't I just tell you? And don't I always say how it really is? Sit still."

ANDREW HODGES WAS something else altogether.

Anna did not understand it at the time but from the first she feared it. He kept books for Gage's father and lived in a little room Mr. Alba provided up the stairs from the furniture displays in the

King Street store. He was not from Boone but had walked in one day, described what he could do, and had gone to work immediately on a probationary basis. He was soon indispensable. He was probably thirty or more, not handsome, with stooped shoulders from working over those ledgers, Anna guessed. He had longish hair, a long face, and very beautiful hands.

"The hands of an artist, not a clerk," said Gage. Her face went a little pink and her eyes were bright. She bit one of her fingernails.

"But that's what he is, isn't it? The way I'm a servant."

"Hush that."

Even after the comment about the hands Anna did not really see how there could be anything between them. Then one day, by accident, she saw them standing together in the street, Gage looking up into his face, he gazing down at hers, and there was no possibility of mistaking what had happened. Anyone could have seen it. If she had laid herself down on the boardwalk and invited Andrew Hodges to do as he would with her, it could not have been plainer. Somehow she knew Anna knew, and it was the end of confidences between them. Gage became secretive, locked herself in her bedroom with the cat for hours, avoided the tower room and everyone in the family except her father.

Anna wanted to say how worried she was, but all she managed was to ask Gage if she was all right.

"You can mind your own business, thank you."

If Anna knew, then who else knew? Mrs. Alba? She did not even want to imagine what Mrs. Alba might do. But all of them soon found out.

"WHERE IS THAT girl, that misguided creature? You know where she is. You know what she's been up to, don't you?" Mrs. Alba had left the door open when she ran into her husband's study with the long white envelope that had just arrived by messenger. She was almost screaming.

"Well, I know something that you don't." She waved the envelope in Mr. Alba's face. "But you should have known. I made inquiries and found out. Why do I have to do such things for myself?" She paced in front of Mr. Alba, the writing table between them. "It's so demeaning. He's married, but has deserted his wife and child. What do you have to say about that? What have you allowed your daughter to get herself into? Where is she?"

"But . . ." said Mr. Alba.

Then Mrs. Alba, with her umbrella in hand, although it was not raining, marched downtown to the Alba store. She crossed the display room, tapping the umbrella as she went, and mounted the backstairs to the bookkeeper's little room where she made Gage pull her shoes out from under Andrew's bed and put them on. She did not look at Andrew as she told Gage what she had learned about him.

"I already know, Mother. It doesn't matter to me. I don't care."

"Shameless!"

"You don't know what he's been through, what he has borne."

"I know enough to know that you cannot excuse immorality with particularities."

She took Gage straight back home without Andrew Hodges ever having uttered a word.

ARRANGEMENTS WERE MADE the following week for Miss Eugenia Gage Alba to enter Miss Barbee's School for Young Ladies in Lenoir at the beginning of the next term. Andrew Hodges was packed and gone from Boone and the furniture business in less time than those arrangements took.

ANNA WAS IN the garden deadheading the Shasta daisies when she heard the scream. Mrs. Alba ran out onto the back porch and into the yard. She threw her arms about Anna, holding her tight, shrieking over and over.

"She's gone, oh, she is gone."

Anna knew immediately that she meant Gage, but she thought perhaps Mrs. Alba was saying she had run off, perhaps to meet Andrew somewhere. For several weeks Anna had seen her going paler each time her mother picked up and went through the mail. That Gage had waited for some word from him, she felt sure.

But Gage was truly gone.

AN UNTENDED TEAM of horses had shied at something and bolted on the steep part of King Street, bearing down through town with a heavy wagonload of coal. The driver, who apparently had not tied the horses up properly and who should have been with them, was instead out behind the Blackburn Hotel, talking to a friend and having some refreshment from a stoneware jug with a cork in it.

No one knew quite what happened. Perhaps the Alba girl bravely stepped out to try to grab the reins and stop the team, overestimating her abilities and underestimating their speed. Or she might not have heard them coming. Or she might have seen them after all.

That last thought was never spoken. All anyone knew for certain was that a wagon wheel crushed her chest and Gage Alba bled to death in minutes within a few feet of her father's store.

FOR THE FIRST night Gage lay on her own bed, her mother locked in the room with her, pacing and wailing. All night long Anna heard the cries, the sound of endless footsteps.

"Why you? Why you?"

She did not sleep that night. Mrs. Alba walked and walked and told them to tell callers that she was completely prostrated.

Mrs. Alba had already decided that the local burial practices were not good enough for her daughter. The young messenger boy who had brought the investigator's white envelope about Andrew Hodges was sent to Lenoir to fetch a real embalming expert who could make the dead "look as if they were only sleeping."

Before the visiting hour Anna saw the results of his labor. In his restoration of Gage's broken body the undertaker had padded her to a voluptuousness far beyond anything she had possessed in life. Anna burst into hysterical laughter, then broke down completely. The doctor was called. She was given drops and put to bed where she had nightmares about all that could happen to one's own self when one could do nothing about it.

DAVID TOOK HER aside after the funeral. There was something more in his distress, she sensed, than Gage's death. She too was shaken, had, for some troubling reason, thought of him with true desire for the first time at the graveside. Now he wanted to know her feelings for him.

"You have met someone," she guessed.

He flushed. "I made you an honorable offer," he said, but it seemed to make him uncomfortable to say.

Someone your mother would approve of, the least you could do for her after this.

"David, you are dear to me as Gage's brother and a friend. Remember, I never accepted and you have no obligation to me. And if there were anything to release you from, I would do it if you so wished." How controlled and grown-up she sounded as she told him, when she was not at all.

Gage. I will despair over this as far forward as I can see.

He took her hand and kissed it. She thought of Mr. Alba on that spring day, thrusting the early flowers to Mrs. Alba through the little door in the kitchen wall.

Ah, you're a good man, David Alba. Many a woman could be happy with you. Who knows, a time may come when I'll wish I had loved you. And that you had truly loved me.

SHE STOOD AT the kitchen window, looked at the mountain that rose behind the house, remembered the mists that nestled down along its sides on fall mornings, the rime that fretted the topmost trees in winter, and how the shadows of clouds moved over its cleared fields in the light of summer noon like a straggling herd of great shaggy beasts in a gentle migration.

She watched. It was beautiful. But it was not home.

Not the fine house in town, not Gage's good but lost friendship, not the wonderful library and Mr. Alba's kindness, none of it was home.

LUCILLE WENT TO Miss Barbee's in Gage's place. After she left, there were only Anna and Mrs. Alba in the house in the daytime. Both of them, for different reasons, eventually found the situation unbearable. They were such reminders of loss to each other. Anna knew Mrs. Alba wished her to leave.

Anna's brother Monroe, back from his latest stint of charcoal burning, came into town to fetch Anna. T.A. had finally returned to Tina. There would be renewed quarrels and strong words at Deerfield no doubt, but at least Anna's wages were no longer a necessity. Roe took her back home.

. · . . · .

Long ago in winter she and Nell had gone to the millpond when the ice measured five inches thick. All bundled up, they went to slide but stayed close to the pond's edge for safety's sake.

"In places where it's this cold for most of the winter people skate on silver ice skates with blades as thin as table knives." Nell was picking herself up from the first of several tumbles.

"No, you couldn't do that. You wouldn't be able to stand up."

"Yes, you can. Even the little children. And they have races for prizes and go like the wind." Nell had wiped her nose on her mitten. "I borrowed a book about it. I'll show you. You'll see. Really and truly, not just a story."

Flying feet skimming away, cutlery somehow lashed to the soles of their shoes, going fast as anything over a cold and polished surface. Surely the world was full of wonders, things Anna never had thought could be.

Nell gazed over the glassy greenish surface. "Some girl fell through millpond ice once in a winter like this and they never got her out till spring. The water was so cold that most of her was still there."

"Hereabouts?"

"No, somewhere up in Virginia. I heard about it."

Anna tried to look down through the mirror-smooth surface. No reflection of her own face caught there. No mirror to the fate of those who had had to die cold and alone. But, surely as there had been many, many winters, there had been those other countenances lost in eternal chill, beautiful and stilled forever, some perhaps never found.

Ah, water. When one drank from any stream one could drink of lives past, long past, and never even know it.

Before you trust a man,
eat a peck of salt with him.

DEERFIELD, 1897

"Who lives in that first house at the bend, just back over the rise, you know the one, the spruce, well-kept place?" John asked as soon as they were well beyond it on their way up Beech Knob. He and Rufus had an agreement to measure and mark a tract for the lumber company and then join the timbering crew later. It had been Rufus's idea to take on this job. He said some change would do John good after the long dark times he'd been through.

"Oh, you think it looks trim now? You should see it in the summer. Flowers everywhere. Big garden. Belongs to T. A. Stockton and his wife, Christina, but they fight a lot and he's not there half the time." Rufus shook his head over the problems and difficulties of married life. "She's German—well, he is too from way back—but her people are lately settled in Virginia from Pennsylvania. T.A. met and married her as the war was ending, after he'd been out rebelling. Brought her down here then. She's a worker, that Tina is. She's the one who keeps up the place. Can't see why he doesn't make more of an effort to get along with her. I would."

Rufus shifted the pack on his back with all of his gear. "Tina Stockton sets a great table, would be near the best meal you ever ate. And if you were to get sick she could physic you. She knows everything there is to know about plants. I know her sons Dan and Monroe. Could get us invited for dinner if you want so you could tell her yourself how much you admire her husbandry."

"You do that," said John. "Good idea." But it was not Mrs. Stockton's gracious table, or her farming abilities, that interested him. It was meeting the girl he had seen in the woodlot there yesterday.

HE WOKE ANGRY nearly every morning these days. And all alone, that is, except for the boys, Roby and Art. The unfairness of it smote him. The Almighty, it seemed, had it in for him for some trespass he didn't know enough of to ask forgiveness for. *Boils next,* he thought bitterly, *I'm being tested like Job.* Since his second bride, Belle, was taken by consumption, he was cold as ice in his bed, winter and summer. Even his sons had each other for company and comfort, but he had buried two wives now and had no one. This time he did not have his usual inclination to go looking for release with some other woman, and no hired girl on the place for consolation such as he had had when Julia went in childbed with their fourth. His mother, Hannah, helped out some with the domestic chores and with his boys, but that rankled too. He had no wish to be beholden to anyone of his stepfather's household, not even his own mother.

Widowers abounded, as well he knew, widows too, but he took it personally to have lost one wife after only five years and the second in less than two. He felt keenly that he tried harder, worked harder, than most men, had done so ever since he was left as the man of his house at the age of eight. When his mother remarried some knocking about by his stepfather showed him how far he had descended from that rank. The injustice festered.

That long-ago death, watching his father die in the dark of fever the way he did, being given the charge to look after everyone, had left sores on his soul that not even the richest bottomland, the most bountiful of crops could completely heal. It had pushed him into early marriage and early loss and that too was dark. He had prayed as strongly as he could for his father to live, on his very knees he had made prayer and supplication. But the Lord had not listened, had left him alone, bound by promise to do more than any son could. Yet he still prayed. Nightly. And he feared and hated God for his power and for his need for such prayers.

HE WOULD TAKE care, this time, not to unite himself to any sickly, ailing, or fragile wife. Two deathbeds, two burials were enough, far more than enough. And nearly three years with naught but dealing with those private cravings in a way that was an abomination before the Lord. That sin must end. The tall girl splitting wood at the Stocktons' as they went by, swinging the double-bitted ax so easily, looked both strong and healthy. John took note of that, and more too.

She had a head of thick blond curls, a pretty, open face, rosy from her chore. She was of a good figure, but with large, work-coarsened hands. Not that John was put off by the latter; rather, he thought it a good sign, certainly for his purposes.

They were all day on the mountain, marking off the boundaries of the tract and getting the lay of the land, blazing where the logging trails would go. On their way back down to the boardinghouse, they passed the Stockton place again. The girl was going out to milk with her stool and bucket.

"Anna," called Rufus.

She waved and went into the barn.

Next morning as they began to climb back up the mountain Rufus stopped in to pay his respects to Mrs. Stockton. He was going to mention how he had worked with her son Dan over at the forge before he took up surveying, timber estimating, and working with the crew. It wouldn't be the last thing Rufus took up, John figured, game as his friend was for anything new. He walked on slowly, expecting the visit to be brief. Rufus was such an engaging, oily-tongued rascal that he probably could get them an invitation to dinner. And he would meet Anna. And then what?

He knocked the pods off some milkweeds, already dry and splitting, with the stake he carried for surveying and had to remind himself not to use as a walking stick. He struck again and again, breaking more and more of the pods until the fine down filled the air. Then, suddenly, through the mist of floating white, he saw her walking down the hill toward him.

She was carrying a splint basket nearly full of chestnuts, faintly furred, brown, and just out of their prickly burrs. She had been on a useful errand then while he was being boyish and silly. He had no idea if he could get anything to come from his mouth.

He tipped his hat. "Morning, ma'am."

She looked right at him, her green eyes clear and steady. He liked young single women to blush and flutter, but he felt his own face getting hot. Something in her cool, straightforward gaze was unsettling.

"Good morning," she said, and walked on. Her voice was rich and low. She was well-spoken and sounded educated. She would be above him. She would pass him by. A sudden terrible disappointment. Then, almost immediately, he was all the more determined to have her.

"Anna was out early," said Rufus when he caught up with John.

"Guess you have to be to beat the squirrels and such to any late chestnuts. Rufus, I'm going to marry that girl."

Rufus stopped in the road, looking at him. John looked back at Rufus but instead of seeing his friend's face it was as if he saw ledger sheets totting up the assets and liabilities of the matter. In the plus column, John knew, were the farm up and working, livestock, his own strength and good health. He knew his own business and some others too, knew he was a good manager and would do even better. He was willing to truck to as far as Lenoir more than once over the summer instead of taking one big load in the fall the way most of the others did. Those long, hard trips had been worth it in ready money.

In the debit column, there were several things to be overcome. His father dying so young and leaving him with no standing, with nothing but to be raised in that mixed family with half and step brothers and sisters and his own sisters, no inheritance at all to speak of, what little his father had long since absorbed into his stepfather's holdings. And he had turned thirty, two children—no, make that four in all, though it would hardly matter about the daughters since he wasn't doing the raising of them. But the drink, his vice since Julia died, that drink had gotten even worse since he'd lost Belle. Yes, the bad habit, those two graves, and that twice-used wedding ring, the dark, run-down shack of a cabin with its awful memories and the feeling it always gave that the sun had just set. If Anna could see her way to accept him, he would moderate the drinking and build her a new house, a frame-constructed one, clean and fresh, for her very own, make a cradle for their child, would carve a beautiful design for a fireboard, cut decorative shingles of a tapered design he'd seen on a fine large house in Lenoir.

"That was fast. You ain't even spoken to her."

"Yes I have." *Barely.*

Rufus shook his head. "I hear she's turned down a lot better than you."

"She's not going to turn me down. I'll take care to see she doesn't."

AT DINNER AT the Stocktons' he said little, and let Rufus, Mrs. Stockton, and Monroe, the son still living at home, do the talking. He listened to what was said in turn, getting his bearings. The chicken and ham, potatoes, gravy, fried apples, kraut, and pickles went round and round the table, along with talk of crops, new ventures in the country, and items from the papers.

"Have some more light bread, Mr. Bayley. Anna made it. Learned how at the Albas'. She's kept her sourdough starter going from that time to this. I'm one for quick breads and dumplings myself. But you can use the starter in those too." Mrs. Stockton was a tiny, quick woman with a faint accent, German, as Rufus had said. She was so small, in fact, that John could not see how she could keep the place up by herself, what with a wandering husband and all. Wandering or not, Mr. Stockton had been home enough to father five offspring. Rufus had said they were married and away now, except for Monroe and Anna, who were at home. Their brother Dan and his family lived close by, but the third son had gone to Tennessee and the other girl had married and moved as far out as Kansas. Probably the near ones helped.

"Albas? In Boone? Would they be connected with the Alba Cabinet Shops and Furniture Store?" John took some of the light bread. "Yes, ma'am, this is excellent."

"Yes, Anna lived with them for nearly four years. A great opportunity for someone so young. Adelaide Alba is a friend of mine. We were at school together." She laughed. "If you can imagine a grownup widow woman going back to school. It was English I was still learning. Addie helped me then. Have some of the currant jelly. Anna made that too."

"Yes, that would be quite an opportunity." He knew the Alba house, that great one a quarter of the way up the mountain with a tall tower on one corner, lording it over everything else in town. He began to wonder if a new frame house, even one with an elaborate incised and ornamented mantel, would be enough to impress someone who had lived in that place.

Then, to his surprise, he found that his eyes were smarting a little, almost with tears, and that he had a great new wish to please this girl, to bring a smile to that face that had looked so sad and serious during the otherwise cheerful meal.

HE SAW HER as often as work and opportunity would allow that fall, stopping by the woodlot or the chicken yard if he noticed her there, and, when he found his tongue, told her a great deal about himself, beginning with the farm.

"For such steep upland it's producing well. I think there's real money to be made in grain and produce, livestock too, though there are lots of problems there. I mean to have, not just enough to manage, but some to save, to put by." *For some good bottomland.* "I want to do the best I can by my children." He included in that thought, though he did not say so, any that they might have together.

"My boys are fine little chaps, lively, but smart, good boys. I want all my sons to have a lot more from me than I got from my dad, which was near nothing." He didn't speak of the problem he was having with Roby's slipping off any chance he got. Not that Roby was a bad one, but there was some of the wild in him that John had not been able to get out yet. If Julia had not had all that red hair and Roby not turned out so blond, he'd have wondered about some old blood somewhere, the boy was that keen for the wilderness.

"How was that? What happened with your father?" Anna asked.

"Oh, nothing that was his fault nor for want of trying." John didn't want Anna to think he'd been disowned. "He was a great worker but he just took on too much too fast. He wore himself down for us and the fever got him."

He remembered the dying man, how in one of the moments between agitated ravings his father had gripped his hand so hard it hurt. John knew he picked at that memory like an unhealed wound, but he could not help it.

"Not that I myself wouldn't work hard, but there's also such a thing as good careful planning." He was back to the farm again. "With the best agricultural practices I can grow more than any family could need, load up the excess in the wagon and cart it to Boone, or to Lenoir. With all the industry down off the mountains now and those factory jobs, folks don't have time to garden, let alone farm. It would be a service to them to carry stuff in." He knew this to be so. In truth he had already done it several times and had some money in the bank to show for it. The money he didn't mention, nor his plans for a new house. Not yet. This time he'd not rush things or put them on the wrong footing. Nor did he speak of dead wives, and daughters sent to live with relatives, or the nightriding ruffians from just over the Tennessee line. And there were still fevers in the summer and winter lung troubles in his community, none of which he mentioned either.

"Faith's a fine Christian place. Folks like the religious meaning, talk about living and dying in Faith."

She, for her part, wanted to talk about growing herbs and flowers, singing the old songs, those mournful trials of love and death, and some of the lively, funny ones, to discuss who the best fiddlers were in Deerfield and how they might compare to the ones in Faith. Did anyone play the banjo there? Her brother Dan had a mean lick on the banjo. It was not her favorite instrument played by itself, but it sounded well enough with a fiddle and mandolin. Did people get together to make music?

Music? Oh, yes, some seasons of the year there were gatherings almost weekly. Playing, singing, some dancing.

And drinking. A good bit of that.

"Folk take turns, go to one another's houses."

But not to his, a bachelor cabin now, and much the worse for it.

And he did not tell her how on one such music night, near blind drunk, he had staggered out to puke in the bushes at the corner of someone's yard and afterwards encountered a woman's hand in the dark.

He had been almost falling to his knees and somehow she had pulled him up. For a few seconds, still in his alcohol fog, the music coming out of the door seeming distant, he thought Julia had returned from beyond to solace, protect, and pleasure him. A strange, deep comfort from that momentary thought, even when he quickly realized his mistake, had led him directly into another marriage, sudden and unwise. Belle was quiet and sympathetic, but consumptive. She gave out on him in less than two years, leaving him with yet another infant daughter he was powerless to care for. Unfair, unfair. He was owed a wife like this girl now beside him.

"Does anyone there own a piano?" Anna was looking at him closely.

No? Well, what about a pump organ? And what did people read in Faith? Books? Did he take a paper, get catalogs?

"The agents have sold subscriptions to the *Toledo Weekly Blade* and the *Watauga Democrat* all through the hills and when it comes to reading books I myself think highly of Mrs. Craik's novel. Halifax can be an example to us all, when you look to what a man can make of himself, not what he's born into." That lady's book was the only one John owned besides the Scriptures, an almanac, and a daybook, and it was almost the only one he'd ever read through.

But if you read one and knew it true, shouldn't that be enough? He kept the novel under lock and key in his box with his whiskey and the pistol.

How had the vote gone last election?

The county was pretty well still evenly split, he told her, hadn't been mostly Unionist, like Deerfield. It made for some lively discussions at the store, but women did not take part in them. Why should they when they couldn't vote?

She asked many questions, but she also said enough of what she did day by day for him to learn she was a worker and a good one. They were coming to know each other. Years at the Albas' had not spoiled her as a helpmeet for an up-and-coming farmer, even if she did seem to have too much of an interest in music and in reading and politics. And he figured she was the sort to want a man of experience to love her, one who would not fumble. Yes indeed, she would be Mrs. John Bayley, the next Mrs. John Bayley.

He said nothing either of the ugly drunken rages, when Roby and Art dashed out of the cabin in terror and ran all the way down to his mother's. Those were behind him now, brought on by a despair at things he could not control, deeds he could not call back, lives he could not save, and the terrible undeserved judgment that had come upon him. His own life was about to change greatly, and for the better. He was even aware that he stood straighter and frowned less. He felt his morning angers beginning to subside. Perhaps God had smiled. Anna was younger, stronger, and healthier than either Julia or Belle had been, and, much as he worried about how her experience at the Albas' might affect the two of them, he saw how that contact could be of benefit to his children. He was determined, and nothing short of her being taken in adultery before his very eyes could make him change his mind. He had an image of her all at once, with somebody else, and felt sudden fury. Who were those men she had known before, the ones Rufus had said were better than he was? Then he reminded himself that she couldn't be taken in adultery because they were not yet married yet. *Maybe I'm presuming too much,* he warned himself, but his assumption that a wedding would take place eased and comforted him anyway.

"I HESITATE," HE said, "to speak to you of my feelings. There are so many..."

He started to say "graves." But looking down into those young green eyes meeting his, he reflected that the eyes closed forever in those graves had also been almost as young. It was the wrong word at this moment.

"... years. Too many years between us. And it's more than just the number, I'm thirty, feel sixty. For all your seriousness you can laugh sometimes. I don't anymore."

He knew himself to be gambling, maneuvering, playing for her sympathy. He stated what had been fact but was fact no more. Already she had changed him. He took to wearing his hat on the back of his head like a young man so his whole face would tan and his neck would not. When he passed by her house in the mornings he cried out his halloos for the entire mountainside to hear and it was, it seemed to him, with the voice of a boy.

"G o o o o d morning all!" he would call out, loud as he could.

Anna had made the years fall away. The excitement, the power of the lust he felt watching her move so quick and graceful, was growing daily. If he had to deceive her, charm her, play for her pity, so be it. He knew he had to have her.

MID-NOVEMBER TURNED painfully sharp and cold. Hoarfrost was heavy when they went up to start the logging, and the smoke from every house in the valley below them stood straight up in the clear morning air. Sometimes the cold was bitter all day in spite of sunshine, and the small fire they had to warm their hands and feet didn't help that much. Jim Dotson cut off the end of his middle finger and it scarcely bled, his hand was so cold. They wrapped it in nearly every extra piece of cloth they had.

"Since it's my left," said Jim, "I can wait till we get back to Deer-field to see the doctor about any stitches."

Two days after Jim's accident the temperature was up a bit, right at freezing or a little below, and clouds had begun to come in. As they gathered up their tools, the axes, saws, mauls, and wedges, John saw that the sky was solid gray-white and he could feel a damp-ness in the wind. "Snow," he said to Rufus. "It's been too cold for it up to now."

"I hope it snows a whole damn foot and we don't have to work tomorrow. We need a break. It's being too cold that makes for acci-dents. Bad as it's been, we're lucky to lose only part of a finger."

By the time they passed down the road by the Stockton place the wind had let up, but fine icy pellets were beginning to fall, sticking to their clothes and faces. There was a lamp in the window though it was not yet dark. He did not see Anna.

"IT'S BUCKETING DOWN out there." Rufus had gotten up and, with his hands up to the glass around his face, was looking out the dining room window of the boardinghouse onto Deerfield's main street. He returned to his place and slapped John on the back. "What do you want to bet there's a foot out there tomorrow? And no work!" The thought made him smile.

"No work means no pay."

"Oh, we're doing well. We can afford a day or so off, can't we? What'll you bet me there's a foot? Oh, yeah, I forget. You're not a gambling man."

"I'll bet if it's a sure thing."

"That's not gambling."

"That's right."

IT SNOWED SIXTEEN inches by the yardstick stuck into the white covering of the backyard.

They had counted on the crew not having to go up the mountain in such a deep snow. Rufus had gone down to check in the wee hours and was so encouraged that they slept late, missed most of breakfast and had to make do with toast and cold potatoes midmorning.

Jim Dotson was in the kitchen soaking his hand in salt water that their landlady had gotten so hot she was practically scalding him. The stub of his finger looked red and angry where the doctor had pulled the skin over and stitched it. Infection had set in.

"She aims to draw it to a head, then lance it." Jim looked philosophical about the whole thing. "That is, if she don't cook me first. I hope it won't lead to blood poisoning."

Steam was rising from the pot he had his hand in. John wondered if something would be cooked for their supper in that same pot, maybe some of the establishment's famous rabbit stew with dumplings.

"Blood poisoning's not likely, hot as she's got that water. Anyway it's not bad swollen and you've got no red streaks."

"Sure hope I don't get blood poisoning, or lockjaw," Jim said again as they finished with their food. John and Rufus left him there soaking, got into their boots and coats and out in the white world.

"Something about snow makes the plainest place pretty."

"And Deerfield's a mighty plain place, that's for sure. No distinction around here whatsoever." Rufus had left off his hat and his hair was still sticking up from the previous night's sleep. Obviously he didn't expect to meet anyone of importance to him. Under his hat John's hair was combed and still a bit damp.

"I didn't know you could get poetical about snow, John."

They walked around, checked on the horses in the livery stable to find that all was taken care of, nothing needed to be done at the moment. They stopped at the Deerfield Mercantile, where trade was good in coffee and in vanilla and sugar for snow cream. And snow shovels. The storeowner had stocked the first in that part of the county, figuring now that they had the boardwalks they would need to keep them clear in the wintertime to hold off rot.

"Look at the size of these things. Two of them could make a

cowcatcher for a train. If a snow was wet and heavy a man could give himself a hernia trying to use one."

John was calculating how long it might take to clear a path the half mile to the Stocktons'. To Rufus's surprise, he bought one.

"Let's go back to a good fire, see if we can scare up some fellows and have ourselves a card game." Rufus was trying to catch flakes on his tongue, but it was snowing only lightly now.

"Is that what you wanted to lay out of work for, a card game?"

"You got any other ideas?"

"Going to play for money?"

"That depends."

"You can count me in if it's just for the sport of it." John considered that Rufus was not, and never had been, married. It could make a man careless to be a bachelor at his age, still living at home with only his father there.

The snow had almost stopped as they neared the corner the boardinghouse was on. Coming up behind them was the sound of muffled hooves and laughter, shouts and singing. An ox team came struggling up the unbroken street pulling a big sled piled high with straw and full of people, waving, making noise, and carrying on as if winter were the most glorious thing ever. One of them threw back her blue-and-white shawl, revealing blond curls piled up on her head. It was Anna.

"Oh, John, come with us, oh please." She held out her arms.

He handed Rufus the shovel and went straight to them.

SHE SMELLED OF soap and snow and clean fresh straw. They sat close and touching, from shoulders to thighs, and she threw the end of her shawl up around his bare neck. "Somebody should knit you a nice warm muffler." She smiled. Her tone made him wonder if she had the colors and pattern already picked out. He had never heard her sound so pleased and happy. Her smile and her eyes were bright and warm.

Even near hot enough to melt this snow?
He figured then that he was winning.

BY THE NEXT day it had turned milder. The snow melted in the sled ruts and cold water dropped off the eaves and down people's necks as they went in and out of houses. The crew was back on the mountain by the following day, but in the meantime John had been with Anna in her parents' barn, following her in there at milking time.

She was fully as eager as he was, trembling even before he reached for her.

"I've wanted and wanted," she said.

That was good. He didn't hold with the idea that a woman had none of those urges that a man did. From experience he knew better. Even so, he bruised her lip and her thigh while she left no mark on him. They lay in the loft over the heat of the cows and moved against each other so strongly that the beams creaked and hay dropped down through the cracks onto the beasts below. He met her like that once more before it turned off so cold again that when they were together they could only kiss and stroke each other. Then the logging was finished for the season. It was time for Christmas, and he had to head for home.

"New Year's," he told her, "For sure and certain, no matter what. Come blizzard, cloudburst or ice storm, I'll be here."

ALL THREE WEATHERS came in for New Year's, first a coarse, icy, blowing snow that slashed the cabin's small west window, then rain that fell on top of it, froze, and crusted it over. John reckoned himself a fool for even starting on such a trip. She would not expect him, he argued to himself, even as he was saddling the horse. His mother had taken the boys again when he wanted her to, this time not asking why.

The journey was worst at first. He had a fear of his horse's slipping and falling, pinning him underneath, an honest dread of dying of exposure, but he had given his word. And even more, he wanted her, he wanted her. It was a long time before he remembered that at first she had said she wanted, but not that she wanted him.

"Why, girl," he said aloud to himself, "you really have me. I'm damned lost over you." And if she were as lost over him he would soon find it out. He had to know.

The footing was difficult in spots, but the horse's hooves broke through the thin ice surface into the snow and he went on. No one else was on the turnpike. He saw folks outside their houses here and there, seeing to their animals. Roby, his oldest, but only eleven, would have to walk from John's mother's, climb the hill tonight, and do those chores at home. Except for those chance dark forms going about their business by lantern light at their own places he was all alone. And, if anything happened, done for. No way he could turn back.

SHE LOOKED STARTLED, frightened even, when she opened the door.

"John, what on earth . . ."

"I said I'd come. I gave my word. God is my witness. My word is always good."

He hugged her tight in spite of his cold and sleety clothes, and quick before anyone else came in, grabbed for her hips and breasts, felt her shaking against him. Her lips were quivering under his. He felt certain now that he had her. All that remained was to get the words said.

There were four of them for New Year's Eve supper. Dan had been by earlier with his greetings and a jar of hard cider for Monroe, who shared it with John. Even Anna and her mother took a little.

"Only two more years to a new century! Let's drink to nineteen hundred!"

"Let's," said John.

HE AND ANNA stayed up by the fire after the others went to bed. He sat in the rocker and she on the little stool at his feet, her head on his knee. A log popped in the fire, the chimney gave a puff, and some fine gray ash fell on her skirt. Was it midnight yet? He stroked her hair and asked her.

"I'm not sure I want to be married," she said.

The answer stung him like a sudden whip smart. He hadn't taken her for a tease. Surely she wasn't that. But what was she trying, the tricks of a whore?

"Then what have we been at this while? I don't see how I could have been mistaken that you care for me."

"You're not mistaken. I do care. Very much. But I think . . ."

She looked up at him with something in her face he knew he did not want to see there. A German mother, the Albas, her reading—something had made her too proud. Love him she might, but she had too much spirit yet for a good wife.

She turned and looked back into the fire. "There're things I want to know about. It may not be possible, but I do want to try. To read books, maybe see a real city, hear an orchestra, perhaps playing a piece with a flute in it. Probably I'll find it's only something to dream about, but I know nothing like that will happen with a husband and babies right off. I want to wait. I'm just not ready to marry, not now. Even though I do care, believe me, I do. And I've not cared for anyone else. Please understand."

"I don't know as I believe you, don't know as I believe you at all."

He got up, jerked her to her feet and pushed her against the wall by the chimney. In his disappointment, his anger and determination, he yanked up her skirts and thrust into her almost at once. She began to moan and he covered her mouth with his. In a moment she was kissing him back, twining her arms tight around his neck. He did not withdraw as he had before but let her have it all.

"Oh, Anna, I thought I should never be a happy man again."

"Happy New Year," she said, but she didn't quite sound as if she meant it.

When she went upstairs he could hear her pacing back and forth over his head. Trying to get it to all run out, he supposed. After a while she stopped walking. She must have given up and gone to bed. He had planned to sleep by the fireside, but instead he went out and got his horse. He could get a place at the boardinghouse and let her wonder and worry where he'd gone for the night.

The wind had risen again, but the clouds were beginning to break in places. Now and again a partial moon shone through overhead, giving enough light to guide him. Without it he would have had to stay in the barn till daylight. As he got on the road he thought he saw a small group of people in dark robes standing under the hemlock tree at the far corner of the yard. Then it seemed that they were slowly moving away from him.

"Halloo," he said as he got to the tree. But there was no one there. A trick of the moonlight and the wind in the moving branches of the tree, no doubt.

WHEN SHE MISSED the second time she sent him word. They were married the next month.

· · · · ·

DEERFIELD, 1898

When Mrs. Alba had let Anna go home because she could no longer stand the way Anna reminded her of Gage, she had given her some of Gage's clothes to take with her. Anna accepted them for the sake of peace between herself and her friend's mother although she knew she would never be able to put on anything she had ever seen Gage wear.

Once she recognized Anna's resistance to this gift, Tina made the skirts, shirtwaists, jackets, and underthings into a parcel and sent it to her son Dick, now settled near Elizabethton, because his family was having times harder than any other relative's. But not Gage's old dark blue cloak, the one that caught every hair and dust mote and had to be brushed constantly. That, Tina hemmed up and kept for herself. Serviceable and warm, she said, even as Anna wondered how she would be able to stand seeing her mother in it.

And Tina also kept the ivory silk.

"We could never afford anything near so fine. Hold on to this. You can be married in it. Look at that lace! Much fancier than what we had for Nell."

"It's a party dress, a ball gown. Low on the shoulders and the bust. I couldn't go to church in that. Wouldn't be fitting."

"We'll see about fitting. There's remedies for every problem. I can make you a church-decent dress with a touch here and snippet of material there. You'll see. You can be a lovely bride. I'm not sending this dress to those Tennessee folks. They wouldn't know what to do with it. That Dick, poor boy, he's married to no sense and less grit."

"They might appreciate it. God knows, they've got little enough beauty in their lives. Besides, I like Polly. She's good-hearted and can be funny, in spite of everything. I could have worse for a sister-in-law."

"Polly wouldn't know root from rot on a plant cutting. I doubt she'd have any idea of the value of silk. Anyway, I want this lovely thing for you, Liebchen. Beauty? Don't you deserve some beauty, something fine for yourself?"

But it had been Gage's. Though, unlike the cloak, Anna had seen Gage wear it only once, the ivory silk was still a dress of the dead.

AT HER MONTHLY time right after New Year's she had spotted only, but would not let herself think it was anything but regular. She knew John wanted her desperately for a wife. She wanted him too, and felt heat, the urge to touch him if she even thought about him. But was she desperate for a husband? What of all she had told him?

Remembering Gage, the talk of art, books, travel, so different from the debates about faith and works by John and others around her, she was not certain she wished to be a wife, maybe especially not John's wife, in spite of the passion between them. There might have been a time when she wanted nothing but a husband and children, but not now. Could it be that in some way she wanted to make amends for what Gage had been denied? Were those genuinely her own needs? It troubled her. John, with his terrible will to subjugate the land, his daybook, the figures in his head on weekdays, sermons to be discussed on Sundays. He'd read only one book that she knew of, outside of the Scriptures.

All that aside, something in him still wrung her heart in spite of faith and figures, called to her to hold him and tell him the past was past and would not come again.

Then the second month she missed completely. She took Tina's hand mirror to her room, looked at her parts, saw them purplish blue, and knew. She found herself afraid.

Far enough up the hollow that Tina couldn't see the smoke she built a small fire, boiled dried pennyroyal in a tin, drank cup after cup. It did not have any immediate effect. How long did it take? She worried about laboring. Could she bear it? Maybe it was only fresh pennyroyal that brought it on, but there was none of that in mid-winter. Perhaps the oil was needed, but that she knew could be deadly. This risk she was taking for the sake of dreams that might never come to pass anyway. Could she give John up forever, have him marry someone else, as he surely would?

Then suddenly she sensed the stranger nearby. She did not look around, did not see him, but even in the extremes of her conflict and anguish it came to her that his silent presence could mean the babe was supposed to be born. A mysterious, charged feeling made her flesh tighten and tingle, something beyond herself alone. Perhaps she could do it after all, bear the child, and the change, the loss, that such a marriage would bring. Perhaps she was meant to and always had been.

The Star is set. That was what Tina would say, if she knew.

She gagged herself quickly and retched up all of the herb that she could.

The naked trees stood around her like spears and she covered the fire with snow.

AFTER SHE TOLD him, Roe, as if he couldn't trust himself to speak, gave her a letter although they lived in the same house. "You don't have to," he had written. "We look after our own. He's much older than you and has wore out two wives already. It need not be." He laid out on the narrow tablet sheets the dreams he knew she had, reminding her. He had had some dreams of his own, he wrote, and, through the nights he sat in the forest while charcoal burnt, had seen things, what used to be, and what might be to come. Their father, T.A., called Monroe a poet, by which he meant a ne'er-do-well.

"Marry him if you feel you must, but oh, sister, I grieve for it. I truly grieve. These are tears that stain this page."

JOHN GAVE IN to her wish not to have family or guests, though he had wanted both. But otherwise he seemed highly pleased at the way things had turned out. It crossed Anna's mind more than once that she had been trapped, but then there was that feel of him, the roughness and strength, all that called to her. She found she could hardly wait till the next time they were to have each other. He knew what to do, was no tentative innocent like her classmate and nothing like others she had had to do with. And David. No, nothing like David at all. But with David there could have been everything else.

GAGE HAD BEEN as tall as Anna, but not so full-figured. Still the dress fastened even though she was into her third month. With her corset partly laced it pulled across the bust, pushing her up. On the day she and John had set she took the ivory silk from Tina's chest, rolled it up carefully, and carried it in a basket over to Dan's, where his wife helped her adjust the laces, hooks, and buttons and picked her some ivy, early jasmine, marchflower buds, and witch hazel for a bouquet. Anna wished for Nell. It should have been Nell's hands pulling at her back, Nell's hands picking the flowers, such as they were, a poor sight but a sweet fragrance. But Nell was out West, in Kansas, with two babies of her own already.

She held the flowers against her not yet very swollen belly as the preacher spoke his words of obedience, love, and honor. She stood on a little hooked rug with a design of lilies on it, red lilies, petals folded back, the stamens pointing at her feet. The preacher married them in front of his fireplace, his wife and daughter as witnesses since no one had come with John, not even Rufus, and Anna had sent Dan back home. The preacher's wife's hairpins were all awry.

Gage's dress had not been made fitting for a religious service after all. Anna's breasts rose brazen above the stays and the tight fabric, and a mole on her shoulder showed. Did it matter since it was no church but only the low-ceilinged little parlor of the minister's home?

And as the words were said, promises made, she felt as if there were a widening stain on the front of her dress, a patch of red that started between her breasts, spread over her chest, blood running down her arms and her front. Her heart seized and seemed to stop. She looked down, saw only the curves of her bosom, white skin against ivory. Still she felt sickened and faint. And she was cold.

Perhaps if she had gone out to draw the new water in silence on that New Year's Eve, drunk it the next morning as one should, perhaps if she had done all that and not stayed alone with him beside the fire. Perhaps.

But the Star was set.

Then John leaned down, was kissing her, his mustache scratching her lips, and it was done.

. ˙ . . ˙ .

FAITH, 1898

The bride touched the ruffle of her traveling dress at her throat,
touched her earrings. She surveyed the cabin, looked upon her new
stepchildren, and they looked back at her solemn as could be. She
opened her trunk, took out the carved walnut clock, wound it,
guessed at the time, set it on the mantel, then unfolded a new bride's
quilt and spread it on the bed. Behind the golden cranes in their bul-
rushes on the clock's glass door the pendulum swung, *Too late? Too
late?* went the tick.

The bride looked at the two stools in the room. There were no
chairs. She sat down on the rounded top of her trunk and wept, an
action she was not often to repeat.

She wiped her eyes and looked at the two boys. She smiled at them
then and held out her hands. They did not reach to take her hands,
but they smiled back, ducked their heads and ran from the room.

THE IVORY SILK dress she put in her trunk. She would redo it into
something else, for someone else. She would never put it on again,
but Tina was probably right. It was too good to waste.

. . . . .

If he had thought of the wheels of the universe, great and god-given, moving smoothly together forever and ever it would not have been any more beautiful and right than John felt his and Anna's first months together to be. He moved as if within a miracle.

His luck, it seemed, had finally and completely changed. Spring came early, mild and breezy, and stayed on, with no false starts, bitter cold spells, or late frosts. They got the right amount of rain and no late snows the way they had them some years. He did not have to plant anything twice so he already had his extra seed for the fall garden. He tried to remember the second of February for that year, to see if the day's prediction had come true, but the date had fallen when Anna had been worrying about whether or not she was pregnant, whether or not she would marry him if she were, and he had not noted the auguring weather. And then that letter written against him by her brother Roe, which she had accidentally mentioned, had been such a worry. For a while he thought she was swayed by it. Weather, for once, had not been much on his mind.

Feeling fortunate, even blessed, when the marriage did take place, he put in more garden than usual, planted things he hadn't planted in years, cantaloupe, watermelon, okra and sweet potatoes, warm weather crops all.

"DON'T GET TOO glad you're living," his mother, Hannah, said, looking over the garden plot and then into his face. He knew he was standing there grinning like a fool at her, but he couldn't help it. Why shouldn't someone be glad, even too glad, to be living? He had never understood that old sour expression of hers. It smacked of superstition, as if one could be struck down for nothing more than happiness. She omitted the rest of it but he knew it ended "for the Lord hates a dead'un." And that he didn't understand either, nor try to. His own rage at the Almighty was fading away like sky clearing after storm.

Anna had taken the spoiled hay he usually hauled to washouts and spread it between the rows to hold down weeds and keep the earth moist. She seemed to delight in the garden, in this wonder of a growing time, as much as he did. Her worries too seemed to have lifted and blown away.

"What's all that stuff?" asked Hannah. He explained the purpose to her, feeling, not for the first time, that he was on the defensive with this formidable woman. He could still be awed after all this time by the way she had taken over when his father went. She had outdone her dead husband at farming, then remarried and raised a healthy brood of nine in all, six of whom had a father of their own until they were grown. Awe, and resentment too. He and his sisters had been used and pushed aside too early. She had let it happen. He would take care that Roby and Art were not treated the way he had been. But then stepmothers were different from stepfathers. Anna would love his boys, not keep her distance from them the way his mother's husband had done from her first children. And she would never beat them. He would do that when necessary. It was a bad thing to be beaten by someone not of your own blood.

"It's something German she learned, I think, using hay this way. That and the raised beds."

"Maybe she should unlearn it. As best I can tell she's just planting more weeds. Too many seeds in that stuff. Nothing beats cultivation and keeping the ground loose."

"We'll see, I guess." Privately he thought Anna's methods would beat Hannah's cultivation anytime.

Hannah turned to walk back home.

"Oh, yes, about the boys coming to stay with us when you have your tea party. Of course they can. When did you say Anna was due?"

"Late November, early December," he lied quickly. When the baby came earlier than that and looked full term she would be sure to know. Perhaps, guessing from the look she gave him, she knew already. He wondered if she were fishing for him to tell her the truth. And he also wondered why he cared enough to lie. Babies that came too soon were common enough and easily accepted. But care he did. He felt he had a woman a cut above most in the community, certainly one who was used to better than many of them had. He didn't want her put down as a loose one.

THE MULCH WORKED well in the kitchen garden. In midsummer, Anna wasn't hauling water as some of their neighbors were. He never mulched any of the field crops though, preferring to send the boys out to bust clods and chop the weeds.

Melons rounded on the vines. Anna rounded too. She had left off her stays early on and filled out quickly.

"We're going to have ourselves a little tea party," she would say and pat herself, using Hannah's silly phrase for what her own mother, Tina, would term "your expectations." He didn't like for her to call attention to her swelling figure in front of Roby and Art, but it was getting so obvious they could hardly help noticing for themselves. The plain cotton shifts she wore out to the garden hit her ankles well above her bare feet and she rolled her sleeves all the way up on her shoulders, letting her arms go brown. But she wore her bonnet, lest she freckle, she said. John wondered at this since none of her kin that he had seen had freckle one. He didn't know about her sister, Nell, already married and gone to Kansas, the one who wrote so many letters she must not have enough to do. Somebody had put it in Anna's mind to care about freckling though she did not seem to have overmuch concern for her appearance except for those spots, the cleanliness of her hair and her teeth, her gold earrings, and the whiteness of her underwear. He figured a woman should have some of those little vanities, but not too many, to help keep her sweet for her husband.

When he saw how long and hard she could work, tasted the food she could cook, he thought again how charmed it all was.

Easily the best field hand I've ever had, he thought, but didn't say it publicly. He wasn't sure what folk would say if they knew he was letting a pregnant woman work as hard as she did, and he had his standing in the community to think of. He worried sometimes she might miscarry from going at her work with such vigor, thought once or twice that perhaps she might even want to, then discarded the notion because she seemed so delighted with the baby's kicking around inside her.

The look of her out on the land, tall, brown, big in bosom and belly, with her hair a crown of gold in summer sun when she pushed back her bonnet or took it off. It fair took his breath. But most of all he loved the look and feel of her beneath him when he had her every night. They always waited until Art and Roby were asleep up in the loft, and it was during those waits that he decided she was right. He should carry out his plan. He did need to build a new house.

Sometimes during the day they didn't wait, but left the boys hoeing in the corn, ran up into the woods and made love quickly on a big sun-warmed rock in the clearing. At first he had had some fear that Roby would take off on one of his wild treks while they were gone, but the boy didn't leave Art alone. After those times Anna laughed all the way back down the hill. She sang about unclouded days and seemed to have forgotten all about books and travel and the like.

LATE AUGUST AND September they weren't running off to the woods anymore. She was large, carrying the baby low like it was a boy, so low her walking was affected. She was drying, canning and preserving at the cabin now in addition to doing the gardening while he framed up the new house as quickly as he could, hoping to get it closed in before cold weather, hoping that the baby would be born in it.

She went to bed with a bad backache. She had cleaned the cabin, boiled up the wash in the morning and hung it out on the fence.

John had said he would string her a proper clothesline when the house was finished. He had no time now, hurried as he was. All he had done outside of building on the house was to make the cradle that stood waiting near the fireplace. It was of cherry, and by the time it held the last of their children it would be a beautiful dark red. They could pass it on, see their grandchildren laid in it.

After the wash she had picked the very last of the beans, then strung and threaded them to dry. She chopped up the pumpkins that had worm holes, and threaded the sound orange chunks to dry above the fireplace too. Then she cooked supper for the four of them and washed up.

In the early morning hours her water broke. She woke up to find a warm jelly puddled between her legs.

John gave her the towel she asked for, then woke Roby and Art. She watched from the bed as he hustled them into their clothes and out the door. She knew that if she had only had a few labor pains he wouldn't have to be in such a hurry, but she wasn't sure what to expect when this sudden flood happened first.

"I'll stop at Uncle Eli's and get Louisa to come stay with you till I get back with Ma. She'll get the other women to come along later. Boys, do you have a clean shirt each, just in case?"

"Yes, they do," she said, "I washed this morning." Then she remembered that she had not brought in the clothes. They were still hanging on the fence because she had been too tired to think of them. They would be dew-damp and cold. Art and Roby went out with just what they were wearing.

At the door John sent the boys on and turned back to her. "Since it's your first, nothing's going to happen for a good while. The women who are coming will know what to do. Louisa's midwifed dozens and so has Ma."

She felt panic rising in her. She did not want to be alone for any time at all. "The doctor," she said. "You told me I could have the doctor."

"You won't need any doctor unless there are complications."

"I have a complication aready, already. A dry birth is a complication. Don't treat me like I don't know anything." But in truth she felt she knew very little.

"Dad?" said Art, somewhere out in the dark. He sounded as frightened as she felt. John came back to the bed, kissed her quickly and left without another word.

When he was gone she got up, changed the bed and her night-dress. The pains were not bad yet, but she was afraid and alone.

Isn't it some divine joke that we are given love so we will bring children into the world, swing low toward death, then, if lucky, up again?

She went and barred the door. She could undo it when Louisa came.

BUT LOUISA HAD fallen that afternoon on her cellar steps. She was lying flat on boards stuck under the bedtick, her back so wrenched she could not move without screaming.

John stopped at Dr. Campbell's because his house was between John's and his mother's. It would cost him but he didn't know what else to do.

"Her first? Then it will be a while. I'll be on up to your place soon as I've had a bit of breakfast and saddled up Hippocrates."

John's mother wanted her breakfast too. And she had to get her things together, had nothing much ready as yet because he had said Anna was expecting as much as two months later in the year. He sent Roby and Art out to hitch up the buggy so they could get back quicker than walking. Even so it was well after sunrise before they turned into the lane up to the cabin. He saw the doctor's horse standing there. And the doctor.

"I can't get in. She's got the door tight fast. I thought I heard something, but she doesn't answer."

John kicked the door down.

Anna lay on her back on the bed, pale and completely still, a dark stain of blood to either side of her hips and thighs. On her belly a naked red infant squirmed and mewed, the cord still attached.

John bit into his fist so he would not scream.

Hannah began to cry. "If only I hadn't stopped to eat."

"Get out," said the doctor to John.

Anna opened her eyes. "It's a boy," she said. "I'm so tired."

"SHE'S FINE." DR. Campbell rolled down his sleeves. "All I delivered was the afterbirth. I'd say only half my fee, wouldn't you?" He laughed. "Lucky for her, labor is like this sometimes. Less than two hours for any delivery is precipitous and those for later pregnancies can be even quicker. I would advise you for the future not to take her on any jolting buggy rides when she's well along or you might find yourself delivering your own offspring."

"How is . . ." *Roland, that was the name finally agreed on.*

"The baby? Little and scrawny, but seems healthy enough. Developed. I think he'll make it."

"GOD FORGIVE ME." he said, "I thought you were dead. I thought I'd gone off and left you to die alone."

"I'm glad you changed your mind about my needing the doctor after all. I know you have my welfare at heart. Sorry about barring the door, it getting broken and all, but I was afraid."

"Don't worry about it. The new place is so near finished I may not even need to fix it."

She opened her shirtwaist to feed Roland. She giggled. "Your mother thinks he's a seven months baby because he's so thin." She wiped sweat off her forehead on her sleeve. Hannah's obsession with Roland's prematurity caused her to keep a roaring fire in the fireplace, even through the hottest part of the day, lest he get cold. She was overheating all the rest of them.

"You didn't tell her any different, did you?" she added. "Don't you dare."

SHE WAS BARELY over her birth pangs and into wondering how to get Hannah out of her house, though she herself could not really take care of everything yet, when help arrived. They appeared on her doorstep with their babes, their bundles and baskets, and filled the cabin like a band of angels, a migration of bright birds, but with sweeping skirts, full sleeves, and flyaway hair escaping from twists and knots. John called them a flock of chickens and stayed out of their way.

Alice, Bina, Tempe, and Maggie. By now Anna knew everyone in Faith by face and name from church, school, and store, and she had spoken to these young women. But they had never invited her to their homes and she had never asked them to the cabin. John was too ashamed of it now to ask anyone not family inside in spite of all her cleaning and ordering. Anna still had to cook in the fireplace when few did anymore.

These angels had not waited on an invitation when a young wife gave birth alone without even her mother nearby. They had some neglect to make up for and they set about doing so as soon as they came in the door.

Anna could imagine Tina giving a sly wink had she been there when Alice and Bina plumped up the pillows and the tick and ordered her daughter back to bed.

"Well, I was always up and doing within hours after every one of mine," Hannah told them. "Bed rest is rated too high."

"But I bet you're tired now," said Maggie, "having to do for everybody here and at your house too. Why don't you let us take care of things for a while?" One could not say that she and Tempe practically shooed Hannah out the door, but they did put her things in her basket for her and assured her over and over they would make certain that the cord had been buried under a rosebush and that they would let her know when Anna's real milk came in, all the time telling her good-bye.

Then they each admired Roland. Maggie said that he had a fine forehead and perfect ears and Alice confirmed that, no, he was really not too thin after all and predicted that he would fill out quickly. Tempe had crocheted him a cap with ties finished off with pompoms, tried it on him, and said that he was adorable in it. Bina let Roland grip her little boy's finger.

"Babies notice babies," she said. "Look, he's trying to focus his eyes."

From the bed Anna watched them all, the first guests not kin in her home. They were making her stay put while they set out supper for her family. Alice got the plates down from the shelf and Anna felt a bit of ridiculous pride that her dishes all matched for now. Probably when she had been married as long as Tina she would have only bits and pieces of various sets too.

Maggie had gotten Roland away from Bina and had rocked him to sleep in spite of the bustle and chatter in the room. Maggie was childless herself but said she loved to tend everyone else's babies because she could hand them back if they got cranky. She put the sleeping child in the bed with Anna and he did not even wake up to nurse the way he usually did as soon as he smelled Anna's front.

"You're not to worry that he's sallow. It's not all that dangerous and he's likely to grow out of it soon." Maggie smoothed the baby's dark hair.

Anna felt her first stab of mother fear in spite of the advice. She had been proud of Roland's skin color, thought him prettier than bright pink and red babies. Maggie, with no babies of her own, somehow knew more than she did. Perhaps if she had been the first of Tina's children instead of the last she would have the common knowledge that she needed. Tina had told her more of plants than people, more of balm than babies.

But now she had help to call on.

Anna was warmed in her soul from more than the fire, the pile of quilts, her sleeping son by her side. The terror she had felt in labor alone in the dark would not afflict her again. She was connected now. By pin and needle, hook and shuttle, they would be threaded together. She would have friends.

She had had reason to wonder if she had any luck or talent for friendship. Nell, sister, friend, had gone so far away by choice that

Anna would be fortunate if she saw her once or twice more in their natural lives. And Gage? Gage had been lost to her well before the accident, something that had made her death more difficult to bear because it canceled all chance, all hope, of reconciliation. But these new friends of her age, her time, her place, who tended to her so carefully and spoke so kindly, she might well grow old with them.

TINA CAME TO stay for a few weeks. Roland's skinny little body concerned her. And she was angry that Anna had delivered alone.

"Why didn't you stay with her until someone else came?" she railed at John. "Birthing is difficult enough with all one's friends gathered round. I can't imagine going down into that valley with that risk, that danger, all alone. You could have sent the chaps on by themselves."

"But it was pitch-dark outside and no lantern working. And two stops to make before they got to the Shulls' to fetch my ma." He didn't say the stop for the doctor had not been part of the original plan. That would have made Tina even more furious. She had still to forgive him for having the wedding on the sly and not giving her the chance to bake a bride's cake and have the neighbors in. She held their virtual elopement against him although it had actually been Anna's idea.

"Come on, Roby's a big boy now. What is he—ten, twelve? He could have made his way easy if you'd had it all planned out for him."

Of course he could have. Roby knew every landmark for miles around, probably every tree. But it was not the time to say that.

"It took us by surprise, the baby coming so soon."

"Ha," said Tina, and covered the ashes from the breakfast fire.

WHILE TINA WAS there John and the boys slept on pallets in the new house. The subfloor was down and the outside weatherboarding in place but the fall nights were chill and cold came through the walls and up from the ground beneath. Rufus and two of John's cousins, Eli's unmarried sons, had been helping out with the building, but John put out the word that he was in a hurry and could use some more hands. The house was done enough for winter in short order, complete except for some of the finish work, the shingles around the front door and the carving on the mantels he had planned.

Anna's friends came to help with the move. Tempe and Maggie carried the trunk down to the new house, one at each of the ends with the leather handles, Tempe dancing along backwards and Maggie, strong and solid, with more than her share of the load. Alice and Bina carried the ticks, quilts, and other bedding. Alice had a folded pile of linens on her dark little head and flitted along so quickly that Anna was afraid her clean sheets and pillow slips would tumble onto the dusty path or off into the grass. Anna carried the baby and the clock, one on each arm, the ornate pendulum weight safe at the bottom of her pocket. She held both tightly and walked carefully. She was loving Roland so fiercely these days that sometimes she clutched him hard enough that her teeth clenched and she found herself watching her friends to see if any of them did the same with their infants. He was her treasure, the treasure of her womb. She might bear and bear, making up for other losses.

After John, Anna, and the baby were moved into the new place, Tina left and was back home in Deerfield before the first snow flew. For Christmas John bought Anna a cookstove that made her cry when she saw it.

.　·　.　.　·　.

How they rioted and rollicked! Friday nights, music nights. A week to work, a day to market, a day to praise the Lord for all his goodness. And the Friday nights in spring and fall. There were more clean shirts in Faith those Fridays, John said, than any other time, even the Sabbath.

The gatherings had always gone from house to house, a different front room each week near bursting with folk and noise. "Red Wing," "Shady Grove," "When You and I Were Young, Maggie," "Wildwood Flower," "Old Joe Clark," those and many, many more. Singing, playing the banjo, fiddle, guitar and mandolin, a harmonica or tin whistle sometimes, and now and again a cousin from over the mountain would put in an appearance with her accordion. John himself was good on the harmonica and could sing loud and on pitch, if not sweetly.

Once the new frame house had popped up in the pasture, John could play host as he never could in the cabin. For one thing, there had to be at least two largish rooms, one for the musicians to play in and another for the babies. Now he had four rooms and all the babies, except for Roland in his cradle, were lined up on his and Anna's bed, where they were bundled tightly together with pillows, bolsters, and rolled-up quilts all around so they could not fall off. Usually the infants slept through it all. Older children were less welcome. They were either left at home or, if they came, had to stay outside on the porch to amuse themselves or listen.

"REMEMBER WHEN MAGGIE had a mite much to drink, went in and picked up a baby?" Alice brushed back her dark bangs. Her little pointed face was all pink from dancing, her round brown eyes too bright. Alice might be talking of the babies, but those eyes were for the men in the room. "Nearly went home with Tempe's least one."

"Babies can get switched. There's accidents, changelings, and those gypsies that take infants. It's serious."

"I wasn't really going to take him home," Maggie defended herself. "He just looked so dear I had to pick him up. And I don't believe in changelings. That's from fairy tales."

"May be an excuse for people who can't make their children

behave," Anna put in, but she didn't like the way this conversation was going.

"And the Indians," Tempe reminded. "Don't ever forget how those Old People carried off children to raise as their own. Those they took were ruined for civilization for all time." Anna looked at Maggie when Tempe said this, thought she saw a flicker, a swift shadow cross her face. Maggie was born a Kilby, and all the Kilbys were dark enough to have some of the old blood in them, probably did, for none of them ever sunburned. Was Tempe about to imply that Maggie was Indian enough to steal a baby, having none of her own?

Oh, friends, please don't accuse and quarrel in my house, especially not about what we are and cannot help but be.

JOHN WAS FOND of having her sing when company gathered, especially on the Fridays. He paraded her out whenever he could, he was that proud of her voice. Strong, clear, and pure, he said, more adjectives than he usually put together. A part of her resented it, thought he was showing her off for his own benefit and glory, as with a possession, a new gun with a carved stock, or a fine foxhound, but another part reveled instead of resenting, loving the audience of attentive listeners who would weep at a sad song, smile, laugh at a merry one, and wring her hand when she finished. The compliments were warm and, she hoped, genuine. But she was most gratified by those who brought back songs for her from other places, like souvenirs of travels in foreign parts. Wanderers away from Faith would hear a song somewhere, memorize the melody, take down the words and bring it home. Then they would come over shyly to give it to her, would sing it slowly and carefully over and over while sitting at her kitchen table till she had it by heart. On rare occasions there was even sheet music. The next Friday night they would come and expect to hear their prizes from her mouth.

"That's my song. I got it off a driver in Wilkesboro. Good one, ain't it? I bet there's a sight more where that came from. Anna ought to go hear them for herself, but she does fine secondhand."

"You don't hear them like that in singing school. Though, of course, that's real fine music too. Music, I love all kinds of music, the old and the new."

"And the teacher down at the Seminary, don't forget her. She's got some good songbooks too."

ANNA USUALLY SANG first, while everyone was still sober enough to listen. One night right after Anna, little Jenny Sherwood, that skinny little thing just barely old enough to be there, got up and sang a lively, suggestive song. Everyone laughed, including John, but Anna was not quite sure what Jenny meant by it. She knew what the song meant, of course, but not why Jenny sang it where and when she did. It might have meant she thought Anna was too high-flown for them, or getting too much attention for someone new in the community. It worried Anna at first since something about Jenny seemed to her sharp and underhanded, even weasely, but she later decided she was probably concerned over nothing.

The dancing did not begin until all the men had had a good amount to drink and some of the women as well. They clogged, they did reels and squares till the floor shook and the dishes rattled in the kitchen cupboard on the other side of the wall. Some of the older women got red in the face and had to sit down, but the dancing went on until late.

John's oldest stepsister was usually the only woman who could really drink and not show it. "Fill me up again, John. I'm raring to go," she would say and hold out her tumbler. She did not say where she was raring to go to. Then to prove something or other she would set the tumbler on her head and do a remarkably steady turn without spilling a drop.

"Good thing there's a heavy bottom," Bina whispered to Anna.

"You mean the glass, or her behind?" It was mean, but she couldn't resist.

Bina laughed. "You're a good one, Anna. She does have one big fanny."

One Friday night, Anna and Bina, who was pretty and round but also light on her feet, gave the musicians a special request and danced a schottische all around the parlor, out into the hall, into the kitchen and back again. It was something Anna had learned at the Albas' and taught Bina. They had practiced till they could do the turns nearly perfectly. The others clapped and whistled, but as they swept out into the hall again Anna saw that John was standing by the door, scowling.

"That's enough," he said.

A little later Tempe's husband played the farewell tune on the fiddle, "Brethren, We Are Met to Worship," an odd selection for such occasions, Anna thought, but it had a sprightly rhythm and was certainly a better choice than the "Old One Hundred." Their guests left soon after, with her wondering, not for the first time, how some of them were going to get home in the dark. They all seemed to make it. John would joke, "We haven't lost one yet."

But tonight he was not joking. He was angry.

"There will be no round dancing in this house. It's unchristian."

"What?"

"You heard me the first time."

It crossed her mind to ask why round dancing was more unchristian than square or, for that matter, than drinking moonshine and other hard stuff, or singing vulgar songs, but his look was so dark she thought better of it, something she was finding she had to do from time to time.

"It's unfitting, two women, two people, holding on to each other like that."

What on earth would he think of a waltz?

"Must be more of the foolishness you got at the Albas'. By god, no daughter of mine is going to hire out and get notions like novels and round dancing in her head."

More unchristian than swearing too? And as for novels, didn't he himself bring up Mrs. Craik from time to time? It crossed her mind that John, for all that he was an excellent manager and was making money when others were struggling, was not the most consistent of mortals in his ideas. But she had other things to worry about. She thought she might be pregnant again.

· ˙ · · ˙ ·

FAITH, 1902

If John could have seen the face of his pocket watch it would have shown the time to be half past eleven. Stars of the moonless night gave some light, but his vision had gotten sharper hour by hour until it seemed to him that he would be able to see in almost no light at all. Most of the shakes were in place. All that he had to determine absolutely was the edge of the roof, the line between shakes and space, and that was as clear to him as the margin of a page. A few more of the shakes tonight, tomorrow the ridge cap and the thing would be done. None too soon. A man with four sons and another on the way now needed to take care of such things quick as he could. Damn, and two daughters too. Father to six, soon to be seven. And likely to be more. The bastards he didn't count.

No man has ever stood on the peak of his own barn, on his own land, on this spot since the beginning of time.

He stood at the very top, one foot on the decking of each side of the roof, so high it seemed the faint night wind could have blown him off, but he never even swayed.

This is mine, what I have done, the frame I raised and sided, the shakes I've riven and fastened. And I swear by these labors of my own hands. I shall make a good of it. I shall prosper and increase. My wife shall never go in rags. My babes shall not be hungry and I shall leave a husbanded place to my sons after me.

I will have more stools and chairs made so that everyone can sit down at once. We'll have a lamp for the parlor and I will buy Anna the blue paint that she wants for the rocker and for new straight chairs.

In time to come I shall look up from the ground at this barn, see the roofline against the sky, remember this night and what I have sworn for me and mine. You stars, be witness.

I am the true first here. Those that were before count no more. They built nothing to last, knew no civilizing ways. Their spears, axes, arrowheads I trample underfoot, or throw aside. I plow under the bones and dust of their dead. Even the bones of what may have been beautiful women.

He thought suddenly of his first wife's long-gone and seldom-remembered husband who had built an earlier, much smaller barn farther up the hollow. But that hapless departed was one with the Others in John's mind, to be displaced in accomplishments as he had been replaced in his widow's bed.

The valley was a bowl of darkness full up to the trees along the ridges. Lights in the other houses were out, their shapes and angles blurred and blunted. He thought of his hammer, its ringing shocks echoing off the hills on the other side of the valley, keeping all of Faith awake in their beds, everyone lying there waiting for him to strike again. It would have been a decent courtesy to stop and let them fall into their deserved rest, but he was obsessed. He must fasten the last shakes, finish all the way to the top. He could not stop now, so close to the end, so close to doing it all.

He yelled to Roby to bring him another bundle of shakes. They'd hear that up and down the creek too. Night air carried everything.

His son's face appeared at the top of the ladder, pale and in space a little way off. It opened and divided strangely in the gloom and John realized that the boy had yawned. He wanted to say, "Go to bed. I'll finish up," but it would mean taking longer, going down the ladder to fetch the shakes himself. And he had this strong feeling that he must stay where he was, that if he went down, if his foot touched the ground he would be down for the night, would not be able to climb back up again. Not that the work couldn't be finished up later, but no, that would not do. He must go on. He kept Roby with him.

HE WAS PROBABLY helping to keep Anna awake too. Although she was no longer getting up to nurse Leonard. This latest pregnancy, her third, was not going as well as the others and she likely wouldn't be sleeping soundly anyway. That Roland, he could sleep through anything. John hammered on and the heads of the nails almost shone in the starshine. Beneath him there would be a stall for his stallion Rocket, for Roby's new mare, for the draft animals, for the milk cows. He had already come a long way from one mule and one cow and he would go further.

Tear down my barns and build greater ones?

Looked at in those terms, suddenly his pride, his own arrogance, put a fear in him. What kind of soul had he, should the Lord require it this very night?

"Roby," he said when the boy brought up the next bundle of shakes, "go on to bed."

IN SPITE OF all that had gone well he still had days when he felt that everywhere he stepped there was an open grave right in front of him. And a long memory of pain went in stripes down his back. True, this happened less often now, but not all of the past could be assuaged. It was a feeling Anna could know nothing of, and he was not about to tell her. But it was the reason he needed to, had to, do those things that brought him back to life. Take a drink with the men at the mill. Build this barn, the intensity of the work, the shaping of wood under his hands stirring him. And, of course, those other sweet women. Jenny, the girl at the store, with her tiny bosom, perhaps sweetest of all. He was waiting for her to be ready.

He hammered the last of the shakes Roby had carried up. Now he would have to go down the long ladder himself. He jerked the smaller chicken ladder to move it to the very last section and, as he did so, dropped the hammer. He grabbed, missed, almost lost his balance. The hammer landed on the ground on the back side of the barn. In the dark. Where he would not be able to find it till daybreak.

A sign, he thought, to quit after all. He climbed down and went straight in to bed beside Anna, taking off only his shoes and his pants.

. . . . . .

The doors slammed. Roby felt them in his mind now and again, how they had suddenly swung to, cutting him off in ways and for reasons he could not understand. Stop it, he cried silently to himself, but he had found no way around those barriers.

Slam. His mother had died. She lay gray in the coffin a neighbor had made of wood so unseasoned that the resin dripped down with the fluids from her body. His father had been angry about that coffin, the workmanship, or lack thereof, angry about everything.

"Damn, damn, goddamn," he said, and threw things.

Roby listened, heard the cursing, heard the drops that fell at intervals into the saucers under the coffin all through the night before his mother's burial. The little unfinished baby was strangely nested, not in her arms, but curled up in her red hair.

His father married again, suddenly. Slam. His stepmother had one baby and coughed for nearly two years until she died too, leaving a tiny girl to give away.

His father drank and beat him, beat him and drank. Roby would get Art by the hand and drag him away from the cabin before their father could do the same to the smaller boy.

"Come on, come on," he would urge his brother who was sometimes terrified, but more often than not still full of sleep. They might go all the way to their grandmother's, but usually they fled up the hill into the woods and sat on a great cold flat rock until morning.

Then the day came when his father took him out of school to work the fields most of the time and he knew he had to find a way around what was happening between them.

He'd always been one to wander and now he began to slip away ever more often, anytime he could, moving off silently, letting the deep forest close softly behind him like a different dark door of excitement and protection.

On the upper slopes the trees told him which of them were the wood of weapons. The oak, the poplar, and ash whispered. "Not yew," they said, "but we will do. Make a bow of us."

He tried, but his hands, lightning quick at some things, lacked his father's skill with wood. He made a short flat-limbed bow which Mr. Green, the schoolmaster, had told him about instead of a long-bow, but it was not strong enough. The ash from which he took the wood was wrong about its qualities. It didn't last, went brash, and put splinters in his hands.

The arrows he had fletched were even more clumsy. He carried off a pair of dress-making shears belonging to his father's new wife to cut the cock and hen feathers to go on the spruce branches he had shaped.

"Ask before you borrow," said Anna, then went down to Sherwood's and bought him a small pair of barbering scissors of his own. She had said it was high time he learned some useful things, that everyone in the family she had lived with in town knew how to sew on their own buttons and she considered that an excellent skill for anyone. She kept her own pincushion at the ready, as her employer had, stuck full of needles threaded in almost every color.

"So there's no excuse not to put those buttons right back on, or, better still, tighten them before they fall off."

"Did you stick yourself with them?"

"What?"

"Did you stick yourself with the scissors? Grandma Hannah says if you give anybody something sharp you stick or cut yourself with it first. Otherwise it's bad luck."

"That's foolish. But if it will reassure you . . ." She took the scissors and drew one tiny drop of blood from her thumb. "There. Satisfied?"

HE NEVER MADE a truly successful arrow, but he learned how to put a one-handed knot in the end of the thread by twisting it around his forefinger and rolling it off with his thumb, how to reattach buttons and even how to fashion a buttonhole. It amused him to take up such skills, partly because Anna was teaching him and partly because he kept his knowledge a secret from his father who, he was sure, had no notion of how to do the like and would be angry if he knew that his firstborn did.

After the failures with the bow and arrows Roby began to take his rifle with him, reluctantly, for he hated the way the sound of gunfire stopped the other sounds from the high branches or from under the black earth that he wanted to listen to.

Now and again he went off unarmed except for a knife, on into the dense and tangled laurel, searching for water by the sound of its rushing. In this way he located the wildest streams, would lie on the stones overhanging their banks just beyond the places where the water fell full force from one deep green brown pool to another. And there he learned to judge right and move quick enough to take the brown and mountain trout with his hands.

He was always amazed at the beauty of the fishes' sides when he pulled them out of the water, the silver, the colors, and the sheen. Of course they were dark on top for protection, only fish shadows when seen from above to keep them from birds and bears. Their beauty, then, was for their own kind. Or saved for the eyes of those who managed to kill them, a reward to the taker. Not only their bodies, but their movement as well, fascinated him. He would sit feeling all that smooth swimming strength twisting and writhing between his hands before he bashed their heads and strung them on a willow twig to take home for supper.

If he came home with enough for a meal nothing much was

said of his absence. But if he returned empty-handed it meant a beating.

"This will teach you to do right," John would say, raising the belt.

Roby preferred to take this to mean that he should hunt and fish right. It gave him considerable incentive to sharpen his skills. When he brought down a young buck with only two shots John shared the venison with family and neighbors, nailed the hide to the shed wall and put the antlers over the cabin's front door.

"Now how's that for a lad only thirteen years old?" his father would brag to anyone who came by and took a look. He would clap Roby on the back.

The venison was good the way Anna fixed it, soaking it first in cider with onions, black pepper, and cloves, but Roby thought it would have tasted much better if he had shot the deer with an arrow.

Somewhere he had seen a picture of a stag with a cross between its antlers. If he ever saw that he wouldn't shoot at all.

AND THERE HAD come to be other doors besides the one to the forest and the wild. The first one had opened when Anna walked in.

She had been a wonder.

He hadn't been able to take his eyes off her. He and Art couldn't speak, didn't take her hands when she reached out to them. But he looked at her and felt himself smiling. He knew then some things would change.

She could dance. Lightly as grasses in the wind, soft as kittens playing. When she wasn't pregnant. She sang. She knew a great deal. At first he wanted her to be his mother. If he had had such a mother everything could have been different for him.

"I would have learned and read, been smarter," he told her.

And beaten less. I shall never raise my hand to any one of my own children.

Anna did not stop the beatings altogether, but after she came they were fewer and less crazed and wild. And, just before he met

Mecie, who opened the perfect door, he could have loved Anna. His father would have killed him for it, might have killed them both, but he could have done it.

EACH NIGHT I go to her is like the first night in the world, not always soft and warm, but always so new I shake with it.

After they've all gone to bed in the big house I leave Art in the cabin up the hollow. I don't know or care if he's sleeping. He knows where I go whether he's asleep or not and we don't talk about it. When there's some-one for him like Mecie maybe we'll discuss it but for now it would seem like bragging and I can't see that. I have to leave the door unbolted because I can't lock him inside. Anything could come, push it open in the dark where he's lying there defenseless, but it never does.

I take the path down past the house to the barn. In the house. She sleeps with him in the house, beyond the windows I pass, and may they both get what pleasure they can out of it. She's got over me, I reckon, what little moment there was to that. I wonder if she knows how close a thing it was.

In the barn nothing makes a stir. King doesn't even bark. Everything knows me, my step, my smell. And I know every step, every smell, the floor soft with shavings, hoof-cut dirt and manure, the threshold of the stall only a little barrier for my mare to step out over the minute I've got the bridle on. I imagine that she's excited too, that the shake, the short hard breath is on her too, but of course it's not. She's only happy to run in the cool dark, the warm dark, with no wagon or buggy behind her and, of course, would be even happier without me on her back. She snorts only once, her breath full of a gassy hay smell.

I lead her down the lane in the turf between the wagon ruts. The grass muffles the sound of her hooves. Pretty soon, often as we go, we may wear that middle down to dark road earth and then how will I sneak or without noise? At the foot of the hill I mount bareback. The night is full of din and noise, all the tiny things courting, singing of little loves before winter.

. · . · · .

FAITH, 1904

She looked up as he came through the back door.

Roby should shave.

He was sunburnt and the dirt and blond hairs showed against his reddened skin. He was much fairer than any of her boys and his beard was heavier these days. In her own sons her fairness was diluted a bit by John's black hair and sallow complexion.

Roby and Art stayed in the log cabin up the path between the white rocks, the cabin in which their mother and first stepmother had died and where Roland had been born. When the new house had been finished, Roby had been nearly twelve, Art nine. John gave them their choice then of half the upstairs in the new place or the cabin, and they took the cabin, bad memories and all, sleeping and keeping their clothes and belongings there. They had meals with the rest of the family instead of trying to cook for themselves in the old mud-daubed fireplace and came in to sleep by the stove in the kitchen on those nights that were so cold an open fire would not warm the log room fast losing its chinking.

"Will supper be long?" he asked, not looking straight at her. "Do I have time to wash up?"

HE HAD NEVER touched her again since that night John walked in and found them dancing in the kitchen. Roby had been most taken with the schottische she and Bina had done one music night and told her so.

"Do you think you could teach me? I never saw the like."

She was just getting her shape back after Spencer's birth and, feeling suddenly young, daring, and free, she had tried. They had been galloping around the table, holding on to each other and laughing when she turned and saw John coming from the hallway, his narrow face pale and furious. She and Roby had flown apart like two birds startled in a thicket and Roby went white around the mouth. With his fist John had knocked over the tin of coffee beans on the cupboard, spilling them all, then made her pick them up, one by one. When Roby had offered to help her, John had ordered him out.

As she was gathering the beans she had glanced at John. He had met her eyes and seemed surprised at what he saw there.

I have spaces of my own, she had been thinking. *I hold and hoard them against you as I must. Enter at your peril. You won't like what you find.*

"NOT LONG, BUT you do have time to clean up."

And, to be honest, she had not wanted Roby to touch her again, at least she didn't want it often, only once in a while, like now when he was looking so young, fair, and handsome, under a strain to be sure, but still handsome. It disturbed her that she wanted it. There were probably good reasons not to trust stepmothers. He had been a boy, gawky, rather pretty, when she and John were married. He was not a boy now.

She put both hands to her back where it hurt with her tiredness, then was suddenly conscious of what that did for her figure. No, he would never pull her to him again. She would never again feel those hands holding her. As was proper.

She wanted to say something to him of importance, something profound, that he could remember. She thought of saying, The blood of the world is one with the juice of the berry. But that would sound ridiculous. It was ridiculous. And yet it was somehow close to what she meant.

How do I make my work, the jelly and such, truly mean something? How to tell them it does mean something that I take fluid from fruit, set

it to drip from the bag into the pan, turn it into clear, quivering jewels,
gorgeous rubies that sit quaking on the table and are spread like blood on
snow white bread? How can I make them see it is all connected, all of
importance?

She wanted to tell him to pay attention to the things of this world,
by which she meant not "worldly things," not figures, acreages,
monies, all in columns in daybooks, account books, and who knew
where else. Those were John's obsessions. Not that such things were
of no importance. She herself had gotten into the habit of counting
her canning jars, her hams, sausages and bacon sides, the cheeses and
dried herbs and medicinals. But the jelly was more than the number
of jars all paraffined and paper-covered. It was sweetness and a
beauty. And the trees that carried the wind up the hillside were more
than board feet. And the panther, the scream of the panther, was no
evil thing. But men did not listen to women and did not notice what
they did. This also she had learned in six years of marriage.

"And isn't the wild a garden too?" she had asked John when he
spoke of clearing farther and farther up the slopes. She was remembering all that she and Nell had gathered for Tina, none of it
planted or tended by hand.

"Yes," he had said, "the one that's full of snakes."

Now she wanted to say something to help. Roby's distress these
days was plain and frightening to see. He had said yesterday that if
anything happened to him, he wanted Roland to have his hunting
knife. Art already had one, didn't need it, but Roland did—that is,
he would. It was as if he wanted to give it away.

"Go on now. It won't take me much longer. You stink like a horse."

He sniffed himself and gave a little laugh. "Horses don't smell
this bad." It was an old joke with them, only this time she thought
the laugh sounded forced.

SOME MONTHS AFTER the interrupted dancing lesson in the
kitchen, Cousin Solomon's daughter Sally had named Roby the
father of her baby boy.

John, Anna could tell, had been of two minds about it. On the one hand, he seemed to have a perverse pride that his firstborn was a man now and had proved it, but on the other, he didn't want him tied to Sally on any kind of permanent basis, whether married or making payments for the upkeep of a bastard. Sally's father, he said, was a no-good layabout, even if he was kin. It was told on him that a rat had died in his spring and he took no notice of the stink or the taste for weeks. Solomon could do nothing for his daughter, or with her, dried-up little fellow that he was, nothing left in him at all but some spite. And Sally, well, she was no better than she ought to be, and a bit dim besides.

John took steps. By the time he was through, four other boys had said they too could be the father of Sally's child. That made it look to the community as if Sally had named Roby because it was well-known his father turned a profit every year. She was painted a slut and opportunist and left to raise her bastard by herself in her father's low-built little cabin.

Anna knew what he had done. It didn't seem right, she told him, that the girl should be treated so. John reminded her of the drowned rat as if it were justification for his actions.

"Dirt, vermin, filth. They don't know the name of clean."

"Oh, it's always easy to slander those we have injured."

JOHN THEN SET about to cure Roby of further temptation.

He worked the boy all day, every day but Sunday, in the fields, the woodlot, and the barn until Roby was sweaty, shaking and ashen-faced, about to drop, or, if it was hot, as scarlet as if he were about to have a stroke. He worked Art and Roland too, and some-times her, but not the same way he drove Roby, day after day. While John waked, Roby had no time to hunt or fish, no time to go anywhere except on to the next row in the field to be hoed, the next stall to be shoveled, or to the next log to be split. It was as if John were trying to get all the urges out of the boy and bottle up his juices for the future.

It troubled Anna and it didn't work. Roby, she knew, would not live so bound. She feared it might come near to killing him. Sometimes at night after they were all abed she would hear faint sounds from the barn, then hoofbeats going away into the distance on the dry road, not to return till deep in the night, or close on to morning. "It's a girl," she whispered to John's heavy, hot back in the darkness when she knew he was too deep in sleep to hear her.

It's a girl. And there's nothing you can do about it.

. ' . . ' .

Some told how he had seen her first in the yard of a house where she was visiting on a Sunday and had followed her home without her ever glimpsing him, trailing her through the woods, looking down at her from along the high ridges like some soundless blond Indian. And so Anna could see him each time he took the horse and rode away into the dark, could fancy him crouching low on the animal's neck, looking to each side when they picked their way under the trees, over the rises, the rough and stony parts, then throwing his head up, his hair flying, letting the beast all out when they came to the open stretches near the sandy creek bottoms, going like a hot wind in the starlight.

Anna shuddered with fear and excitement. The girl was a Thomas, of a family known for brawls and shootings, along with a lot of hard self-righteousness, no safe choice, but then the danger was probably part of the attraction in it.

She listened to the water splashing in the basin on the back porch. Roby came in, his hair water-slicked, his shirt damp. They gathered for John to bless all that she had prepared and credit the Father with it.

"Rufus and me are going up on the mountain tomorrow. Time

for Harv to round up his sheep. They want me to come and bring the King."

It's "Rufus and I." Would their boys ever speak the way she wanted?

Harvey Mast, Tempe's father-in-law, called for help with the sheep twice a year, once at shearing time when the shorn sheep had to be driven up the mountain to summer pasture, and once in the fall when the creatures, by now nearly half-feral, had to be fetched down again well before winter. Two of Harv's unmarried boys lived in the shepherds' hut in the gap over the summer with the blundering sheep, and when they came down they were half-wild too, full of tales of bear, catamount, even wolves, though everyone knew the wolves had been bountied out of the territory years ago. And the summer storms on the mountain, they told of those too, terrible storms with lightning so bright and fierce it lit up everything, and even at night they could see into Tennessee, Virginia, and Kentucky, maybe as far as Georgia. The sheep probably could have wintered it, if they could be kept out of the laurel, which would kill them, but the men could not have stood that season's high, cold fury.

Harvey said he loved the sheep, the smooth, greasy way they made his hands feel when he petted them, the lumpy, fluffy way they looked at pasture, like soft boulders. He hated having to kill off the young males in the fall.

"It doesn't pay to have balls in the kingdom of domestic animals," he would say. Mostly he missed being up on the mountain himself, he said. He had done it till he had some boys big enough to take over, couldn't do it now with all of his responsibilities, especially those to the community, making sure that outside ideas were judged right. But his sons were certainly correct about one thing. It was something passing grand to stand in the doorway of the hut and watch a great storm sweep up over the mountain like God's justice.

"I may be gone overnight, maybe two nights. Depending . . ."

"Depending?"

"Depending on how good the dogs are and how stupid the sheep have got."

Harv paid in the spring with fleeces and in the fall with mutton. It was worth a day or two. "But don't be thinking you've time off because I'm not around," John reminded them all. "You boys get to the field right after school, and Roby, I expect the cornfield chopped once more by the time I get back."

"Yessir."

"Do you have to take King, Dad? You said last time he near got snakebit. He might really get bit this time, might die." King was Roland's favorite. He had learned to walk pulling up on the ears of the big soft woolly dog. Death—he knew what death was now and it frightened him.

"King's one of the best. Why, he even tries to herd those geese of your mother's when the other dogs run from them."

"Wanna, wanna," said Spencer, who was beginning to babble some sounds. He kicked at Anna's lap from where he sat in the high chair while he ate what she had mashed up for him.

"You're a ninny." Leonard reached over and began to move Spencer's little plate and cup around, shifting their positions ever so slightly. Anna was feeding him but he liked to stick his hand in the food too. The movement of his plate and cup provoked Spencer to tears of frustration and anguish. Art put Spencer's things back in place.

"Just like they were," he said, but Spencer was still crying.

"Boys," said John.

Roby sat looking down at his plate, eating little and saying nothing. There were dark rings around his eyes and his open shirt collar showed his collarbone sticking out. Anna wondered why John didn't seem to notice. Or was it part and parcel of his "cure"? If so, was there something she could do, a word she could say?

EARLY AFTERNOON THE next day she took the fresh butter out to the springhouse to cool. Art was in the cornfield already but she did not see Roby there. When she blew the horn for supper Art came in but Roby was not with him.

"He's gone. He wasn't here when I got home from school," Art said. "His rifle's gone too."

Probably taking advantage of John's absence to hunt, she guessed, but it made her uneasy. She hoped for his sake he had finished the cornfield before he left and dreaded John's return if that task had not been done.

That night neither John nor Roby came home. She was not worried about John off with the group of temporary and likely drunk sheepherders, and she told herself not to be concerned about Roby either, that he often roamed in the dark and would be home by the next morning, surely.

But the next afternoon Roby was still not home. John and Roby could both be angry at her for a lack of trust in them if it all turned out to be over nothing, but she knew she had to act, and on her own without waiting for her husband's permission. She hesitated to rouse the whole community yet, but she sent Art to Rufus's for his hounds, hoping there was still some trail for them to follow.

Art and Rufus lost the trail at the first big stream. Though they went up and down the banks for considerable distances they could not pick it up again. John gave her no blame for her action when he came home that evening, and if he blamed himself for Roby's absence, she couldn't tell. Every able-bodied man and boy in Faith went out looking the next morning and the sheriff was called. The search went on for five days.

One of the mornings there was an unusually early frost that went straight to her heart. Even if Roby was alive he was likely days without food and had worn no heavy jacket. Her hope was flickering away and she tried to prepare herself and the others as best she could.

Alice brought over an apple pie with latticed pastry and sat with her long enough for coffee.

"When will Roby be back?" asked Roland. "I want him to swing me around in the yard."

"Soon, we hope, soon. You mustn't worry now. We'll see." And she thought how it had been awhile since Roby had swung any of them, driven as he had been. Oh yes, driven, driven away.

They will have to give up soon.

She mourned as she did the noonday dishes and swept the kitchen floor. She opened the back door to brush out the leavings and Art was standing right in front of her on the doorstep.

"He's back," he said.

She had felt that, if Roby did return, it would be in such a way, quietly, no one the wiser. Early each morning she had gone to the cabin, peeped in at the tiny window nearest the bed to see if he had come back in the night and she had watched the edge of the woods, the open fields.

"I think he's in a bad way," Art said.

SHE STOOD A moment outside the cabin, holding her breath, fearing to push open the door and enter. When she gathered her nerve and did so, the first thing she saw was the rifle on the floor, its stock scratched and muddy. Roby lay curled on the bed, silent and still, a pile of quilts over him.

"Roby?" She made her voice low.

He opened the eye that was not purple, bruised and swollen shut.

"I fell," he said.

Later he would tell her what had happened. But first she fetched a cup of hot broth and a basin of warm water. She fed him, stripped him down, washed and changed both him and the bed. His feet were turning into farmer's feet already, she noticed, hard and beginning to show the lines that would someday become almost too deep to get the dirt out of. And on his back there were old marks, of which she knew the cause.

Most of Roby's wounds were superficial—bruises, small cuts, and scratches which she cleaned and salved with comfrey and goldenseal. But a puncture wound on his thigh just above the knee and a long cut on one wrist were red and beginning to fester. They would have to be watched, probably drawn, and treated carefully. His left foot and ankle were swollen, the leg black and puffy almost to the knee. She guessed then that he had used the rifle for a crutch as he made his way back. It was beyond her skill to tell if the ankle was broken. Without waiting to ask John's permission, she sent Art for the doctor.

"YOU DID WELL. Sister Bayley," said Dr. Campbell. "Couldn't have done better on most of those places myself. The ankle's badly sprained, but not broken that I can tell. He's got to be off it awhile."

John will hate that.

"Use hot and cold compresses alternately and put a pillow under it. Let me know if he gets a bone ache. We'll splint it if he does." The doctor looked as if he were about to pat Roby on the head. "You hear that, boy. Your mother does well by you. You owe her."

I'm not his mother and I don't want to be owed.

"Watch out for blood poisoning," the doctor whispered to Anna when she walked him out to his horse. "Use the hot compresses on the infected places as well. He could lose that leg, maybe the hand too, if things go badly. Hope for the best and call me if there's a fever or a change."

HE HAD GONE far, Roby told her, really far, farther and higher than he had ever been, to the tallest cliffs that could be seen from any-where around, climbing up the treacherous rock falls, well beyond any trees, only some blasted shrubs growing among the boulders.

And all alone.

"The wind. The wind up there's so strong it blew me right off," he said. "I couldn't even catch myself. I think I was out cold for hours. You know, someone camps on the ledge near the top. There're bones, hides, and a fire pit." Roby shifted on the bed and winced. "They're recent too. I kept wondering if someone of bad intent was going to find me." He tried to move his leg. "You have no idea how far a man can crawl if he has to."

She was silent, imagining it all. It was a wonder he was not worse hurt.

Roby propped himself up on his elbows. "Dad is killing me. Can't you do something, make him stop?"

"And what do you suppose that would take?"

"Get him to let me marry Mecie. Mecie will save me. I know she can. I kept seeing her the whole way back. I thought she was guiding me."

She set Art to watch him while she milked and fixed supper. After she and the little boys had eaten, she took Roby milk and his meal and sent Art back down to eat the food she had put in the warmer and to look out for the others.

"You mind Art," she told Spencer, with no idea that he really understood her. Spencer was the only one who might be a problem, the baby who might want his mother there instead of a more lenient older brother who would probably let the other two stay up past bedtime and get into the molasses with a spoon.

After the warm day the night turned cool. She smelled fall, leaves, the coming nights of frost, another year going, dying, another year coming. She built a fire and sat between it and Roby. She did not light the lamp and the shadows in the cabin were dark and full of the past. Roby lay on the bed in which John had fathered him and the others before Roland. A cramped piece of a place, one room with a loft and the two tiny shed rooms John had added years ago. She looked into the flames and pondered why women did not have something better to do in this world than to save the men who wanted them.

"Mother." She had thought Roby was asleep. And when had she become Mother, not Mama, not Anna?

"You know, the truth is, Sally's baby could be mine."

"Don't be bothering yourself about that now. You need to rest and get better."

"Sally's not really a bad sort, unless wanting a little bit of a good time is all that bad. Now Dad has gone and ruined things for her completely. Why did he want to do that?"

"He was thinking of you and your future, I guess." *And of his own good name.*

"I don't want him to think of me, or for me. I just want him to let up on me and let me marry Mecie."

"So she can save you."

"Yes, so I won't end up like . . ." He didn't say who but she had a good idea he might well mean his father.

"I'll do what I can. But you know him. No promises."

He held out his hand and she got up, crossed the floor and took it in hers. "Now you make a promise to me," she said. "No more foolishness like this again. Ever."

"Right. I hurt everywhere, can't even twitch a toe without a pain. But, listen, thank you, Mother." He shook her hand. "I wish you were my mother."

His words stung. She did not want to be his mother. If she were she would be dead and fourteen years in the ground. She pulled her hand back. "You're welcome. Now go back to sleep."

She meant to stay awake and watch as she had promised but fell asleep herself sitting upright on the stool. She woke only when John slipped in and lightly, surprisingly, kissed her on the back of the neck, pulled her up by her shoulders, took her place, and sent her off to bed.

ROBERT OWEN BAYLEY and Lamecia Jane Thomas were promised at once, but John made them put off the ceremony until the spring, perhaps to prove they didn't have to get married, the incident with Sally apparently making him sensitive. There was a real wedding with a preacher in the little church at Forest Grove. Wildflowers decorated the pulpit and the bride's head. Mecie was small and golden fair, almost as pretty as Roby. The Thomases set aside their cantankerous, prickly natures for once and rose to the occasion. A bride's lunch, complete with a frosted wedding cake, was served on the grounds. Then the couple went off in Mecie's father's buggy to a new cabin on the farm John was helping Roby buy.

Art would not stay in the old cabin by himself. He moved down to the frame house to share the upstairs with Roland. John piled extra hay in the old place, not even bothering to take out all the furniture. It filled with snakes and vermin and later, when John swapped houses with Rufus, the cabin went to ruin. The roof fell in and Rufus had it all torn away except for part of the chimney and the hearthstone.

After Roby's wedding, John set in on Anna about another baby, and she bet that by harvest time she would be in her big smocks again and walking slow. At night in bed she whispered to the back that rose along beside her, between her and the rest of the world, "It will be a girl."

. · . . · .

FAITH, 1905

When Yale Leftwich moved into Faith there was none who could ignore it, though many may have wished to, especially Ben Sherwood, who had owned the only store up to that point. For Leftwich aimed to set up shop and provide, as he said to most anyone he met on the road, a bit of competition.

One had to wonder how competitive he could be. He was not related to anyone thereabout. His wagon was patched and peeling, his old mule so near worn-out that it died before the next spring. And he took up residence in the decrepit Younce place that John's uncle Eli had grown up in and moved away from quickly as he could, a house right on the creek bank and not a stone's throw from the cranberry bog, an unhealthy place if ever there was one. Small wonder it was empty, waiting for something peculiar to move in and squat.

"Yale? What the hell kind of name is that?" The men at Sherwood's store pushed their Stetsons back the better to see the strange, shabby conveyance with the flaking remains of odd designs painted on the sides and its even stranger driver going back and forth on what Leftwich called his "expeditions." All their foreheads were white above their eyebrows.

"Some school, university, up North's called that. Damn Yankee, that's what kind of name."

"Hey, mind what you say." One of the men there had gone for the Union and sometimes did not take kindly to slights, even though his cause had not been lost and even if the slights were not directed toward him. On the Fourth of July, he and a handful of others donned their blue and marched with the men who wore gray, all of them together right down Faith's street, moving to the fife and the beating of the drum. They all knew the same songs.

"Ain't Leftwich a local name though? Seems I've heard of some over near Beaver Dam. Wasn't it a Leftwich that one of the Burketts married?"

"No, that was a Leverton, good solid family.

"And he's none of the Virginia Leftwiches for sure. Don't talk like any of them. They're alright."

But Yale Leftwich was odd almost beyond belief for Faith. First, he wore no hat, instead had a kerchief tied around his head.

"Like a pirate," someone said. "Sort of Moorish," someone else put in without much of an idea what Moorish was. "Or you think he might be a Catholic?" What sort of man didn't wear a hat? He wore his hair to his shoulders under the kerchief. "Curls like Custer, only dark," another said. But he was like no hero, being short and overweight, yet big-shouldered, and with a small trimmed goatee. He often hid his mouth with his hand when he spoke as if his teeth were bad, but they were no worse than most. Winter and summer he dressed in a long rusty coat because, it was said, he had no shirts. It was also told on him that the collar that could be seen was nothing but a false front.

When Anna first saw him driving down the road she thought, *gypsy, tinker,* and wondered whether, if she saw him up close, he would be wearing an earring.

"Maybe a renegade, fugitive. Even a robber." John had no romantic ideas about criminals or wanderers. "They're swearing down at Sherwood's he's got money somewhere, that something's not right. How could he, with no visible means, stock a store anyway? And why here? Unless he's hiding something, or hiding out from something. Faith's not exactly on the beaten track." He took the almanac off the shelf to consult on late-summer storms. "They're talking at the store about going over there when he's away and poking around in the yard to see if he's buried his own little treasure."

Anna started to say that would make them worse than Leftwich, if anything, for they would have intent to steal for certain, while any mischief or thievery on his part was pure conjecture. She thought better of it. She was not sure why, contrary to her impulses, she should not take his part openly, only knew that it was so.

"I don't want you giving him any trade. Loyalty, that's what's important. People like that have to be shown. Ben Sherwood's got everything that we need, you know, and a new hat special-ordered for me every year, everything. Top quality." He put the almanac back. "Besides, Ben's got to support that little bit of a niece of his, along with his own. And he's a second cousin once removed on my mother's side. Bet you didn't remember that fact, did you?"

Being a cousin hadn't kept John from acting against Solomon's Sally, and the only cousins of his he really liked were the Olivers. Still he would say, "Kin's kin," every chance he got.

"I believe you've mentioned it." Loyalty or no loyalty, she couldn't see Sherwood's as first quality, the stock of fabric not much more than bolts of fading, dusty calico, alpaca, and black faille gone brown. Some pins and needles for sewing and knitting perhaps, but, except for staples, there was little else she would use, need, want, or afford.

YALE LEFTWICH HAD gotten permission to stay at the empty Younce place, saying he would do some fixing up in exchange for rent. As

Anna approached the house after she had doubled back along the creek bank she saw that tar had been applied to rusted places on the roof and a large pile of rubbish, most of it the newspapers off the walls, lay in the backyard waiting to be burnt.

Leftwich had put a bench on the front porch like the one the men sat on at Sherwood's, but no one was sitting on it that day, nor would they ever, she felt sure. A cord hung by the front door with a sign, "Pull for Assistance." An attached bell rang somewhere in the house and she heard steps coming to the door.

Without the kerchief his hair showed thin, but clean, and he was beginning to lose it. He smiled at her, pulling his upper lip down oddly over his front teeth. She also noticed that he was much younger than she'd expected, not much over twenty-five, if that. Perhaps there was something behind the strangeness of his going into business here after all, but what it was she couldn't imagine.

Still smiling, he led her into the front room. He moved with his big shoulders well back and had a striding walk in spite of his short legs.

Some of the tacks that had held the newspapers in place were sticking out of the wall boards but everything had been white-washed and the floor swept and scrubbed clean.

"Why take the newspapers down?" She thought of her own walls carefully lined with the *Blade* and the *Democrat*. Roland, when a wee thing, had taught himself to read on those headlines and pictures, and later read aloud to the others from the columns and stories. "They're a big help against the wind," she went on. "It comes down this valley in the wintertime like you wouldn't believe. Snow too, keeps the snow out as well." She could see daylight in places through Leftwich's walls, like Tina's light in her old Deerfield home before Dan put in beaded ceiling and moldings for his mother.

"Oh, they're dirty, harbor bugs and vermin. Besides, they were crumbling anyway. I like the simplicity of the plain white wall, especially in a showroom. Shows off the merchandise better without all that clutter behind it, don't you think?"

A showroom? The stock was displayed on boards resting on

sawhorses and shelves nailed onto the wall. There was a table with one drawer, perhaps for an account book, and one small glass case, not rows of them like the stores in Boone and Deerfield had. Even Sherwood had more glassed-in display space than this. It was sad, wishful, wistful, hopeless. She had no idea if he had ever even had another customer besides herself. Something in his efforts touched her. She began to look around for something to buy to aid and please him.

The stock took her by surprise. Leftwich had some fine and beautiful things—kid gloves, India shawls, silk hose, cameos, coral bracelets, gold earrings. Obviously he had a sense of style, was offering for sale things that even Mrs. Alba would not sneer at. But who in Faith would be able to afford them? Fabric and notions too, of course, eyelets, lawn, batiste, lace, braids and buttons, fancy buttons, not the underwear variety that Sherwood carried. And there were pieces of china with gilt trim and pictures on them.

What sort of man picked out such stock to sell? There were whispers about that, she knew. She picked up a pair of the gloves. Four buttons. Like Gage's. An old pain, loss, the ache of it, came over her when she looked at them. She tried them on.

"How much?"

The figure surprised her, more than she could really afford, but less than she had expected.

"Will you take some down and the rest on account?" What would John say, and where could she wear such things? They were too fine even for church in Faith.

"Why not have your husband buy them for you for Valentine's? Gloves are a lover's present."

And not what a lady should have to buy for herself? Was that what he meant? Not a chance in a million John would ever give her such. She was provoked and embarrassed.

Then she saw the books.

They were in the corner near the window. Of all the people she had known, only Mr. Alba and Mr. Green, the schoolteacher, had more. Five whole shelves of books. First the gloves, then the books, reminding her of the paneled study at the Albas and the permission she had had from Mr. Alba to read whatever she wanted, a rich, rich time, as long as she could hide her reading from Mrs. Alba. What kind of an omen was there here in this odd place?

"My subscription library."

She recognized a few titles, but most were new to her. On the second shelf was a row of small books quarter-bound in blue leather, with marbled paper on the covers and gold on top of the pages. There must have been fifty of them. She took down one to look at it. "W. Collins" was printed on the spine in tiny gilt letters, "Collection of British Authors, Tauchniz Edition" on the half title, "Wilkie Collins" on the title page. Narrow little green silk ribbons were sewn in them for marking one's place. The author's name seemed to mean something to her though she could not remember ever having heard it before.

"Published in Leipzig. Lots of different dates. Some are more than forty years old but in perfect condition. That European manufacture, you know, quality. Collins is—was—quite a writer, a bit sensational, but still most enjoyable. No longer with us, alas. I wish I had some Scott and Dickens, or perhaps Eliot, to offer as well, but they've not come my way. I collect and read anything of quality that does." He touched one of the shelves with two fingers. "Wordsworth, I've a great admiration for Wordsworth. And Keats."

"Not for sale then? A subscription library, you say? What does a subscription cost?"

"A penny a volume. You pay, sign the little card in the back of the book. I keep the card so I know who has each one." The shelves were full. Had anyone taken anything to read? she wondered. She would likely be the first, the books sitting there just for her. She put back the volume she had looked at and took the very first one in the row. She would read them all the way through from the beginning, fifty cents, one penny at a time. She gave Leftwich a quarter on account for the gloves and a penny and her name for *The Queen of Hearts*.

She went back again and again, going almost every month for more than three years, even when Maud was an infant in arms, gently, carefully taking down one volume at a time, returning it and getting another. She went almost up to the time that Leftwich disappeared, stealing John's horse, firing his store and goods, all those lovely books burnt, the ones she had loved and the ones she had not yet gotten to, precious, wonderful stories, gone to smoke and ashes. How could he ever have done that?

· · · · · ·

John bought the molasses mill outright and had it partly set up without even telling her. Often he did not consult her but usually he at least told her what he had decided and bragged about his upcoming new ventures, like the extra land he and Roby had taken on for more wheat. That way she got to give her opinion only when it was too late.

"What's done is done," he would say. "It will all work out well. You'll see." There would be little or nothing she could change. That was the way it had gone with the shares in the oil well to be drilled in the creek bottom down at Mast. He had bought into a small stock company gotten up among the residents all along Cove Creek. The casing was already sunk when she asked why anyone would think there might be oil in the mountains. He gave her the explanation from the prospectus, put in words like *shale* and *sediment*.

"And it might make our fortunes. Horseless travel, something tells me that's a coming thing, not just a novelty. Oil will be used for a lot more than greasing mill machinery. This drilling? It's opportunity come knock, knock, knocking. Besides I didn't put more in than I could afford to lose and who knows . . ."

"I thought you weren't a gambling man."

"Little things, little things, bets and cards, those things you know I don't do. But any crop you put in the ground is a gamble, if you want to look at it that way. A farmer can be your very worst man to gamble."

Knock, knock was the noise the drill made day and night. John would turn to her sometimes in the dark, the sound faint and far off. "Listen, it's opportunity. Opportunity knocks." He would chuckle to himself even when she did not respond.

The opportunity turned out to be for the outsiders who had come in, organized the company, and sold the stock. After months of drilling with no results and no profits the demand for the stock stopped completely and there was talk of asking for money back, of people being intentionally misled.

Whether it had been intentional or not no one ever found out. The organizers took all the capital and left the state, gone no one knew where. They must have had most of the money still intact, for the investment in the casing, drill, and pump was apparently so little that they could afford to leave it behind. It sat and rusted in the creek bottom for years.

None of them had the nerve to call the wreck "Opportunity" in front of John, though that was how they referred to it among themselves.

John nailed up the prospectus and the now-worthless stock certificates on top of the newspapers on the front room wall.

"There," he said to Roland, "you're so keen to read. Learn all those words, options, common stock, preferred stock. Might do you good one day to know them. Save you from being a fool."

BUT THE MOLASSES mill seemed a great success for a while. He had gotten it "for the community," John said, and they were uncrating and assembling it down on the flat below the house before she knew a thing about it. Alice's husband had talked of setting up such a mill but John had beaten him to it. Alice had married up and her husband could have afforded it more easily than John. Anna hoped it wouldn't be a difficulty between herself and her friend. Her other friends seemed very pleased with the mill and said they would bring their cane down to the flat.

It was a shares proposition, more straightforward than drilling for oil. John had bought the mill, would build the shed, furnish the mule to walk round and round the track to grind the cane, and the firewood to boil down the syrup. He had Roby and Art build fire pits to fit the evaporating pans and rigged up his own skimmer by punching nail holes in a pie tin.

After that folks were on their own to bring their own cane and do the work. He would get the spent cane to put on his fields and he was asking only one quart in ten which was a lot better than taking cane by wagon all the way to the mill at Vilas and having to give up one in five. It made sense that it would be a success and a service too.

At first the wood held out though Roby had to make trip after trip down the lane with the barrow. The house was full of smoke and sugar scent day and night and Anna couldn't open the windows on that side to air things out. Bina and Maggie visited at the house when they came with their cane but Tempe's husband was drinking again and hadn't planted any sorghum. Without saying Anna knew they would all share their molasses with Tempe and she would repay them with her herbs and salves.

John got enough gallons out of the syrup made to make it worth his while. He sold some and the jars that were left gleamed in the pantry like rich old oiled wood. Anna gave her mother more than John wanted her to when Tina came to visit. She made gingerbread and molasses cookies with hickory nuts, boiled some down for brown sugar. John's own mother's family, the Shulls, he made go on shares like everybody else.

The word had gotten out that one could do much better at Bayley's with sorghum cane than at any other place around. The folk at Vilas had to cut back on their shares or lose all of their custom. Wagons were sometimes lined up in their road and Anna feared for their winter wood supply. She could see now that the boys would be out felling trees into cold weather and that was always dangerous. It seemed to her that the woods were in fast retreat up the ridge.

"That much more land for pasture or a new buckwheat field," John would tell her.

He had built two more fire pits and bought additional evaporation pans to handle the increase. It took two mules now, one spelling the other. At night the flat below the house glowed red with the coals from the fires and shapes moved among them making shadows. When she looked down there in the dark, it was like a mouth of something that could eat a person. The late summer had been moderately dry and the brush on the bank behind the mill was enough like tinder that it could catch, flame climbing to the barn and then to the house. She remembered a long-ago nightmare of being trapped upstairs in a huge room with a high ceiling and fire all around, no way out. Gage had told her how the grandmother of a friend was burnt alive when she set her sleeve afire with the candle while sealing a letter. The death of Joan of Arc could obsess her, as it had when she was a child. These things she thought of, standing by the window, feeling a dread in the night of something fated to happen. So it was that when the screams came they horrified but did not surprise her.

THE OLIVERS WERE distant cousins of John's. When they drove their cane over from Beaver Dams they left the two oldest at home to chore and brought the young ones along for an outing. Mary and A. R. Oliver took turns tending and sleeping under the wagon. They got water from the Bayleys' spring, as nearly everyone did, and Mary cooked their meals on the edge of the fire pit.

"It's like a picnic, an excursion," Mary told Anna when they met in the springhouse doorway, brushing by the broom corn hung up inside to dry and shed seed. Mary was tall and thin, with a tanned face and happy, expectant eyes.

Yes, you might see it that way.

Mary and A.R. sang and whistled at their tasks, Mary's mellow alto voice carrying all the way up the hill. Anna wished, not for the first time, that the Olivers lived closer by and could come to music nights. She and Mary could do duets, their voices complementing each other's. She hadn't sung duets since Nell moved west.

No, since Gage died.

"Your springhouse is so nice. Reminds me of a traveler's rest on the way to Mountain City. They've built a shed cover, have a log pipe just like yours. Like John's. And the cup hanging on a nail, so any passerby can take refreshment. Thanks for everything. The children are having the time of their little lives."

Then in the middle of the night the Olivers' four-year-old got up, left his mother's side and somehow fell into one of the evaporating pans. Screams woke the valley, the child's and Mary's.

The little boy was carried across the creek to Eli and Louisa Younce's house where he cried and screamed all the rest of the night. By noon the next day he had fallen asleep, and he died as the sun went down.

Anna, standing on her front porch with her hand at her mouth, wondered at first why he had not been brought to her instead of to the Younces, John being the Olivers' kin and all, or why she was not asked to come to the bedside, given what she knew of relieving pain. Then she understood that, of course, she was divided from them by the fact of the mill itself, John's ownership of it. The wives of coal mine owners likely felt this when stretcher bearers carrying crushed victims of underground explosions passed their doors, not one person looking toward them. How did they stand it? And mill owners' wives in their fine houses that had been bought by missing fingers, hands or arms torn off, and worse. Did they want to run, hide away from wrong, give it all up? She felt guilty, shaken, and distraught.

"It's my fault. It truly is. I went to sleep when I should have been watching," A.R. explained to John. "Don't blame yourself. You were running everything right."

John said he would forgo his one-in-ten share in this case but A.R. said he could have it all, that the Olivers would not eat molasses for a while.

Anna could not either. John and the children mashed the syrup together with butter into a golden paste and spread it on her biscuits. She could not touch a drop. The jars sat on the shelf and were the color of burnt blood.

. · . . · .

The snow and rain were both sparse again the next year. The first sign of how it would be was a spring that got hot too quickly, then alternated with late freezes that killed fruit in bud and stunted gardens. The wind came hard, not small, out of the west, pulling moisture from the ground and carrying it away. Progress of a horseback rider or ox-drawn sled on the road below could be read in dust that lingered long as a morning fog might, and heat lightning, rare in those parts, danced behind the mountains almost every evening in a terrible teasing.

By summer the water in the log pipe slowed to a trickle, then almost stopped. John redug the upper spring twice, but each time it settled away into a muddy sink. He moved the pipe to the lower one for what little flow there was.

Anna was early in her fourth pregnancy, sick as soon as she got out of bed. The heat made her feel swollen and bruised, blood puffing up her eyelids, lips, and nipples. The finger of her own hand admonished her in the mirror. *Take care,* it said. *Take good care.*

Mothers, she among them, greeted their children coming in from work or play by lifting their damp hair and kissing them on the back of their necks, no matter how sweaty or dirty. The fever test. They looked into eyes that reflected back their own with fear and dread.

Word of illness could spread quickly down the string of hamlets along Cove Creek with the talk of enteric fever, "the pink stage," red rashes, delirium. At the news of the first case Anna began to boil their milk and all their water, even what they washed up with. But it was already too late.

The second case was Roland.

He was six weeks in bed and out of his head much of that time. His hands and feet were coated with meal. Red ants crawled up the door which was covered with crocheted net. Robed people were coming down the road.

"Must be a dozen of them, in the brownest brown you ever saw, and with hoods."

Then down through the ceiling came the trunk and tusks of an elephant, next the head, and, without a single sound, the whole animal descended and stood beside his bed. He reached out to touch it and seemed to encounter something. It had been there, he told his mother. He'd touched it.

The corn was just coming up when he was taken sick and what had survived the drought was in tassel when he got his mind back. Anna had kept him away from the other children in one of the little rooms upstairs under the eaves. Each night she slept beside him on a pallet on the floor. John thought she ought not to in her condition, but Roland was her firstborn, only eight years old, and nothing would do but she stay by him. Late into the night she cut selected poems out of the *Blade* and other papers by candlelight, then slept fitfully, hearing one very early morning those Tennessee rowdies passing below the house, but not stopping. Roland didn't seem to hear, thank God.

She sponged the child off every few hours, dosed him with willow-bark infusions and medicine that Dr. Campbell prescribed. When Roland's hair started to fall out from his own heat John barbered all of it off, wrapped it in paper, and put it in his box.

"They're praying for him over at the church," John told her, "him and the others."

She thought of Brother Harbin, who had wanted all the men to sit to one side and women to the other, children on the front rows, not families together as they had been used to in church, how that cranky little over-righteous stick of a man irritated her. What did the eternal powers care about how folk sat at Cherish? But for the moment she set that aside and was grateful to know her son's name was a word spoken in kindness on other's lips.

The rain returned the same night John carried Roland, shorn, pale, and wasted, but on the mend, down the stairs to supper for the first time since he had gotten sick. The worst for that year was over, but one of Harv's boys, Maggie's niece, and two of the youngest Wilson children had died in Faith, and one more who was abed would go before all danger had passed, if indeed danger ever truly passed.

In the nights she had slept upstairs she had dreams in the heat also, a night or two even took off her shift and lay naked in the dark, wondering if she dared sponge herself off with the water she kept by to cool Roland's fever. She dreamed of storms and rain and once had thought herself in a great wood with the wind rushing through the trees, but that time, instead of rain falling, blood dropped on her from the tossing branches. Some fell on her hands and when she tried to clean them she accidentally tasted it. With that taste she understood what the trees were saying. They had a violent, malignant hatred of the human race and of other plants as well, were trying to shade and crowd them out, or, failing that, drop limbs to crush them. She thought of the dream next morning and of how the kingdom of green growing things could truly be a cruel one, full of poisons for people and animals, perhaps even insects unwary enough to eat the wrong thing, walnut trees tainting the earth for other plants, dodder smothering, vines strangling, and many other wars and battles going on she knew nothing about, defenses she could only dream of.

And well they might hate us, our coming to cut them all down, to pull up their very roots, to clear and destroy and burn.

She smiled to herself grimly.

It sounds like a story I might have told Nell. My dreams are near as crazy as Roland's ravings.

When the child's hair grew back after his illness it was far darker than it had been before.

An egg, a pinch of salt, and a penny
or a sup o' milk

. ˙ . . ˙ .

FAITH, 1907

He was there at Maud's birth, came into the room right after and
took up the infant, saying, "This is the bonniest babe that ever was
born." He smiled at Anna. "You've fair outdone yourself this time."

He allowed it was time they had a girl in the family. He was
going to carry her outside at once, let the sun shine on her eyes to
give her a bright outlook, an old superstition, to be sure, but a happy,
admirable idea.

"It's the middle of January," she protested. "Too cold."

"Oh, she'll be warm enough." He took off his coat, wrapped the
baby in another flannel and laid her inside the coat. He carried her
away with the tiny face barely showing.

Anna smiled at all his joy. A daughter, a daughter. She was
exhausted, but warm, sleepy, and satisfied with herself. And John?
It was not like most men to take on so over a girl. Then she thought
to herself how this babe was not the first girl in John's family after
all, that John had had two daughters before this one. And as she lay
with the blood seeping onto the cloths between her legs she wondered if he'd come into the birthing rooms of the other wives and
declared their baby girls the bonniest ever. Had he swooped down
on those other children of his, carried them off too for some ritual to
bring happiness, long life, success? And a pain smote her, as it not
often did anymore, that she was not the first, not the first he bedded,
not the first to give him sons, not the first to bear him a daughter.

But oh, this one is remarkable, yes, most bonny.

She took the infant back from his big hard hands. A neat little
round head covered in the finest of white hair, not dark like that of

most babes, but like the down on a mullein leaf. The tiny little slit of her, the wee behind, fatter and more rounded than any of the boys' had been. Somehow they had all seemed unfinished, like tadpoles, she'd thought, but this bit was done perfect. A daughter. Every woman needs a daughter, her friend Maggie had told her once, to keep her humble. "With a daughter there'll always be someone younger and prettier in the house," an odd thing for Maggie to say since she had no children at all, only a self-righteous husband who prayed over her nightly, asking the Lord to show her the error of her ways without saying what he thought those errors were.

John's first two wives had not lived long enough to be thus humbled. And perhaps their daughters would not have been prettier than they. It was a certainty they weren't pretty now. She minded Roby and Art's sister, staying on at the Shulls', her pale, plain face, high forehead and the eyes too big below it, the chin small and pointed, her frame thin and skinny, the only beauty there in her thick dark hair. And the younger girl, Belle's only child, living with her mother's people, quiet and chunky and solid. Surely they looked good enough for everyday, but she'd gone and had a Sunday girl this time, a rose to bloom in her garden for aye.

SHE SLEPT SOUNDLY most of the night, nursing the baby only twice, and not hearing Hannah rise to do breakfast. She missed her own mother, but it was too far for Tina at her age to come for a winter lying-in. A rattling clatter in the barnyard finally woke her, John and Roby readying the team to go harrow the fields they had leased together near the mill, since it was just barely thawed enough for it. And John was singing, full and strong above all the noise. He didn't sing that often anymore, though he knew many of the old songs and had a good voice. Decidedly he was a happy man that day. Increase, increase, around his table and on it.

He too called the baby a little rose, and talked so much of her one would have thought she was his first and not his eighth. She had only half that number, could never catch up and didn't want to.

"Shall we call her Rose? Since you keep saying that?"

"No, I want to name her Ursula."

"What?"

"Ursula. After Ursula March. In Mrs. Craik's book."

"What about Maud?"

For me, my middle name, for my favorite poem.

Mr. Alba. His kind, gentle voice, how he would say as he opened the book to read it, "And this one is for our own Annie Maud." And didn't Ursula have something to do with bears? A bit foreign-sounding and outlandish for a place like Faith.

"Ursula Maud?"

She nodded. She knew she could call the baby Maud and have it stick.

How had he behaved, she wondered, when he got Roby, his first-born? Was he so pleased then? He had not been much more than a boy himself at the time, only twenty, with a wife older than he was. Anna imagined that her being older might have made him more serious and fearful that first time, though she had no way of knowing for certain. Perhaps not. However that had gone, he seemed to have no fears this day, this second dawning day of a new life, just pride.

And his bastards? He was already given to slipping off now and again, and she suspected there were some though no one would tell her. How did he feel about those others of his begetting? Increase, increase?

Sing and strut all you will, John Bayley, but I think this could well be the last babe you'll ever get from me.

And Nell wrote, "So now you have a little girl! You'll find out how it is. They're so sweet and good for you. I bet she's a peach. Send me a picture please."

"Don't get too glad you're living," John's mother, Hannah, would say. But why shouldn't one get too glad if one wanted to? Where was the harm in it? Everyone wanted her humble and she was proud, proud, proud.

. · . . · .

She woke suddenly from a dream but could not remember it, only
an impression of something terrible and ordinary, farm-lot butch-
ery, disposing of extra cats, perhaps. Or had she struck someone
because she was commanded to when she meant to resist the order?
How easy in this world to unintentionally afflict the weak, even in
one's sleep. She lay quiet, trying to hear if there were anything
abroad in the house or yard. John breathed heavily beside her and
she eased away so she could hear something besides his breath, listened for the creak of the house timbers, possible rats in the kitchen.

How strange and trusting folk were to all go to sleep at the same
time, daylight creatures giving themselves over to dreams at night-
fall and not even setting a guard.

Bundled in the cradle beside the bed, Maud was snug in the
snowflake-pattern blanket Tempe knitted for her, a wondrously
good baby, already sleeping through. Across the room the two
youngest boys lay in their bed against the wall, their covers slipping
sideways toward the floor. Oh, angels, it was cold as she slid out
from under the heavy pile of quilts. The floor felt as if it were lay-
ered with frost. A little later and a little lighter into the morning and
she could have seen her own breath in the air.

She often did not sleep through the night. She would tell them
the next morning, "I woke in the night and couldn't go back to
sleep," and they would look at her as if she spoke in an exotic language, one they hoped never to have to learn. John would drop off
when his head hit the pillow and seldom rouse. She woke to prowl
the house alone.

She dragged the covers back over Leonard and Spencer. Their
sleeping faces were only dim disks in the darkness. Spencer's hair
was damp. Another illness? Please, no. He was the most ailing of

her children, would hang head-down over the kitchen stool with a pain in his stomach for what seemed hours at a time. She wormed him thoroughly, but it didn't seem to do any good. A chill crossed her shoulders and went down the back of her neck. But her little son's forehead felt cool and her alarm subsided. She thought of seeing to the others as well, but Art and Roland slept in the overhead eave room now and her step on the stairs was likely to wake them— well, wake Art anyway. Roland slept like his father.

In the front room the fireplace smelled of damp ashes as if cold had entered the house by dropping down the chimney. Clock ticks were sharp in the silence and she felt rather than saw the golden pendulum swing behind the golden cranes standing one-legged among the gold reeds on the glass door.

Tea, she thought, and went back to the kitchen. Chamomile, with honey and milk to help her sleep. But under her hand the lids of the cookstove were so cold her flesh seemed to freeze to them and the kindling box was nearly empty. She took a match from the box on the wall anyway, thinking perhaps to light the lamp, warm her fingers by it. But a light in the house could be seen from outside.

In all the dark and drowsing valley she was the only one awake. Or was she? Another night she had seen far down below a light flicker from room to room at Leftwich's, a poor light, as from an ill-trimmed lamp wick or a guttering candle. Did he too prowl his house at night, counting and checking his small store of goods, noting how very little he had sold?

As she moved her gown caught between her thighs below her belly not yet flat after Maud's delivery. She passed again through the front room on her way back to bed and took up her shawl from the chair where she had left it.

Then something said to her, plain as speaking, *Go to the window.*

Under clear, icy starshine and a three-quarter moon the familiar valley stretched away, following the stream in its course to where it curved off in the distance and was hidden behind the farthest slopes. She brought out one of the heavy stools from the kitchen table, set it by the window and seated herself on it, pulling the shawl tight at her chin and resting her elbows on the sill. It was so cold outside and in the room her breath barely fogged the glass.

She gave herself to the night's beauty, stark and indefinite all at once. And terrifying. The snow that still rested in places on the upper northern slopes seemed to move and quiver like a drift of white birds about to rise in flight. The narrow valley floor had a dark meandering snake line where Cove Creek slipped by, thick in places with black bulges of willow bushes and elder, as if the snake had eaten.

The heavy woods seemed to be sliding downward with their weight of shadow, while the cleared fields, edged in brush rows or jagged fences, were motionless and still. She was looking too hard, she told herself. That was what was unsettling the landscape, making things seem to move when they did not, causing her to be uncertain whether or not she saw something dart by on the road below. Only she and other live things and the stars wheeling by were truly on the move. She looked upon their brilliance. In school she had heard of celestial navigation and the workings of a sextant, ways to use the stars for the profit of man, but that did not tell where they came from or what they were really for, if indeed they had any purpose beyond being. Latitudes and calculations to the sixth part, they could take one around the globe and never reveal anything that was an answer.

Somewhere in the night a fox was on his way home over the hills, carrying in his mouth something still warm that had been unwary enough to stir forth into the dark. He was taking food to his mate to nourish the kits stirring in her. She saw no fox but knew he had been there and was now moving away from her. She sighed and shifted. There are little murders every night, she thought. And she thought of men and women and their terrible hungers for one another, how, in spite of anger and arguments, John could still make her tremble, remembered the vague pleasures she gave herself when he was not there, thought how her own children had moved inside her.

And there was something out there. It approached. Coming in darkness and the palest of light. Something with no shape, no name, no sound, only presence, still out there beyond the bend, but roused, perhaps by her watching, and on the move. She turned away quickly from the window. Her legs were heavy with the sudden fall of blood away from her heart. They did not want to carry her weight.

Her eyes accustomed to the outside, she could hardly see at all in the darker room. She made out the gun on its rack above the door, useless against what she sensed. She fled back to bed, where she shivered for a long time against the angle of John's shoulder and his strong body.

"I could scare myself to death," she whispered to his back.

She dreamed and told herself a story. And with no Nell there to hear it, no Gage for whom to write it down.

FOX WOMAN WAS tall and very beautiful. She had a great cape of night sprinkled with stars and fringed in lightning. Seeing a creature so beautiful and so adorned it was hard to remember that she was such a killer.

"But we must eat," said Fox Woman.

Fox Woman and Fox Man lived in a large den with white sand on the floor in summer and lined with leaves and tufts of their own fur in the winter. They raised many fine kits there who grew to hunt and bark and roam the hills on their own after Fox Man and Fox Woman taught them how.

Fox Woman and Fox Man hunted together except when Fox Woman had kits to feed. At those times Fox Man hunted and brought food to her. One day when her time was nearing Fox Man went out to hunt alone and did not return. At first Fox Woman was not concerned but when he did not return by the following morning she went out and barked for him, heard no bark answering hers. Her kits were born during the next night.

Fox Woman fed her kits as best she could. She nursed them and left them only for water and short hunts on which she found little. Fox Man still did not return. At length she saw that the kits must die and she must

*die if she did not leave them to hunt and that if she did leave she would
live and they die. She went to hunt to feed herself and one by one the kits
mewed and starved, shivering without the heat of her body. When Fox
Woman had carried the last of them gently away from the den she went
to look for her mate Fox Man.*

*She sought him and sought him, up the creeks and over the hills and
through the forests, barking, listening for barks in reply, searching for the
sight of a copper coat among the trees, or for eyes glowing back at hers in
the dark. She found nothing.*

Then the raven told her, "I saw him in the village of the people."

*Fox Woman put on her cape of stars and slipped without sound to
where she could see the village and its two-legged creatures going about
the strange things they did during the day. She thought perhaps they had
Fox Man captured and tied as they were wont to do with foxes, wolves,
and the like. Perhaps when they went to sleep she would be able to rescue
him.*

*Finally she saw him and her heart rose in gladness. And then it sank
so far down that ever after she thought she had no heart. Her husband
came out of one of the houses. But it was not he. It was only his beautiful
skin, his thick and red-orange fur and his great bushy tail hanging down
a human back.*

*That night when all the people were at rest Fox Woman searched
around the outside of the village and found the bones of her husband. She
gathered them together and wrapped them in a net of cobwebs. This she
carried to the top of the mountain and hung the net carefully in a tree so
that it swayed in the wind and she could see it afar off.*

Then she went back to the village.

*For three days and three nights Fox Woman stayed hidden in her
starry cape. She neither ate nor drank but mourned her family and
watched the people. She saw that the hunter who wore her husband's skin
had but one child, a boy just between childhood and manhood.*

And Fox Woman plotted her revenge.

· ˙ · ˙ · ·

She lay on her back in the grass in the bright morning sun and all around her were six empty chairs. Painted blue.

The ground was warm, the sky perfectly clear. She had only to turn her head to see the green trees on the hills all around. Six blue chairs. She smiled up into the boundless light.

The chairs had come all the way from a maker in Jefferson, highly crafted ones, not the ordinary mule-eared variety, but made with tapered legs, front rungs and posts with turned decorations. The paint John got in Lenoir, real oil paint. No whitewash this time or buttermilk and iron oxide. A true and beautiful color, her favorite. Azure, she thought, azure, azure.

The chairs and paint were to celebrate Maud's being six months old. For some reason John had in his mind that if an infant survived for six months it would live to grow up. Since it seemed fact in his case she could not shake him in this belief. Obviously it was not true, as a trip to any cemetery would attest, but if he wanted to think thus, and she was rewarded with real chairs with backs to them and sky-blue paint, so be it.

It all delighted her, the grass, the sky, the chairs. If she had a smooth board and some whitewash she would paint a scene with such a blue sky, rub the grass itself across the surface for leaves and field, use charcoal for the fence rails and tree trunks. And some birds, hawks maybe, high overhead. If she could make such a picture then she would be something more than a look-after woman standing in the cellar, measuring the duration of winter in half-gallons, pints, and quarts. Something more than the worn-down soul running a house, making a garden, minding the fowl and the milking, nursing a baby, and chasing three venturesome little boys, Spencer at four already clambering after the others. But there was hardly any paint left, perhaps not even enough for a patch of sky.

She had been asking for chairs, actual dining chairs, for years. Since all of the children had stood to eat in his stepfather's house, John had no vision of a family seated around a table, nothing like that to recall the way she remembered meals at her mother's and at the Albas'. When they were first married there had been only two stools at the table. She and John had sat at the head and foot, Roby and Art standing on either side though they were both already half-grown. She had prevailed on him to make two more stools right away and a high chair when the first baby came, but all the while the wish of her heart was for chairs with backs for the class and the comfort of them. John prided himself on his cabinet work but somehow he never got around to making any more chairs.

The day the wagon rolled up the lane with all those chairs piled in the back she hardly knew what to say.

"Well?" he asked as she stood silently stroking the turning at the top of one of the posts. "What do you think?"

She nearly cried from the pleasure of it all.

The paint, and a small brush too, John bought with some of the bean money. When she had stirred down through the brown oil on top and brought up the precious pigment, mixing it all thoroughly, she found every brush stroke pleasing to her, and even the drops on the grass, the stains on her apron that would never wash out. When she had finished the beautiful chairs stood all around her. Her table would be glorious.

JOHN, WATCHING HER lying out in the yard, the sun on her hair, a smile on her face, blue paint all over her hands and clothes, knew that he had at least once more made her happy. It brought to his mind the look of her beneath him in their first year together. For a moment he was content. But what, he thought suddenly, if he had gone and gotten her in the way of expecting such niceties? What if she would want him to do those little things again and again? Had he done the right thing? Surely this should be enough for a good long while.

AZURE, AZURE, I will tell them. You are seated, I will say, upon my azure chairs.

· · . . · .

Perhaps they couldn't help themselves. It could have been their nature to take to nightriding the way their fathers had gone in for bushwhacking during the war. The boys were from Trade, that well-known wild place where Tennessee sticks into its eastern neighbor as it shouldn't, and maybe they liked to think they were living up to its reputation. They were all young and their history made them feel free to ride over into North Carolina, do whatever mischief came into their heads, and then scoot back across the state line before anyone could catch them. Mostly it was only mischief, yelling and shooting into the air in the middle of the night, turning over outhouses and spattering stores and schools with rotten eggs.

"Halloween pranks," John said. "They lack imagination, thank God."

They rode through the communities strung out along the creek as far down as the cheese factory in Sugar Grove with their general meanness, but churches they left alone, even the boys from Trade having some lines they would not cross.

Then came another hot summer of near-drought, with everything fraying out in the heat. Anna began to boil their water and milk again even before there was notice of any fever, making the kitchen steamy all day and into the evening and herself even more tired than usual. A good winter storm was what she longed for, when all that absolutely had to be done was to stay warm enough and feed themselves and the animals.

How ever had her mother done it, the sewing, the wash, the meals, and so much else? Her father, before he stopped trying to get along with Tina, and all her older brothers in the dining room, in from the fields, big, red-faced, and full of loud talking, singing, whistling, joking, a great business with the cutlery, large hands on the heavy-stemmed glasses, rivers of milk and mountains of food disappearing from the stretch of oilcloth. Throughout the work season they came in to meals like a tide, swept everything away, then receded back to the fields till the next bell. Tina did it all.

Her tiny mother, by miracles hardly to be guessed at, had produced all that food, from seed to plant to garden to stove to table. Even her bread rose up to call her blessed. Tina, fairy mother in her light blue dress with the white apron, braids twisted around the top of her head like a straw-yellow halo so light that the strands going white hardly showed, flying about, now and again stomping a little foot in its black buttoned shoe about things she didn't like, such as the burning of the hornets which she said were beneficial, and T.A.'s poisoning the moles in her yard and garden too close to her crops.

In this harsh season the boys from Trade finally went too far. When they fired the Warrens' fields in the dead of night they almost burnt the house down too. It was luck Bina heard them, saw the glow of the fire coming toward her home and raised the alarm. She and the children stood in the creek while her husband and the neighbors beat out the flames with wet blankets and the backs of shovels.

Bina said later that she had arthritis in her ankles from standing in the cold water with the heat all around and that she had seen Jesus' mother coming toward her from the flames of the burning field. The Virgin had promised her that she and her children would survive and, sure enough, they did.

But when she had tried to thank Mary publicly in church, Brother Harbin declared that the Virgin Mary did not appear to good Protestants and that what Bina was saying was clearly close to idolatry. Christians one and all should concentrate on the Trinity. He called on Bina to renounce her "so-called vision." She told Anna that she could never disown that kind and reassuring face, but she never mentioned Mary in public again. And she never said a word against Brother Harbin.

"THIS IS AS bad as living next to a border town."

"Which in a sense we do."

"Thank god there wasn't any wind with that fire. Who knows what else might have gone."

"They think they're like a bunch from the Black Patch. Good thing there's no coloreds around here. Somebody could get hurt. If they'd fire a crop, they might could take it in their heads to burn . . . well, you know, a person."

"Nightriding in the interest of the public morality is one thing, for pure devilment quite another."

Harvey Mast made that last observation, but it was John who stood up in the schoolhouse and said it was time to see about some real law to stop them, even if it took procedures of extradition. And if that didn't do it, then there were other ways, and they all knew what those were.

"But I wouldn't want to make them mad, have them against me. They're mighty good men to have on a bear hunt."

"There's not enough bears left to make much difference." John could not see how some folk were so short-sighted. Nearly the whole of the Warrens' wheat crop was burnt down to blackened stubble and his neighbor Will Wilson was talking bear hunts.

"I still wouldn't want to make them mad. They can be mean as hornets," said Will.

"They've made *me* mad. They come over here again and I can't answer for what I might do." John gritted his teeth. "It is high time they were stopped and stopped hard. They need to be horsewhipped and all their goods confiscated."

WHO TOLD WAS anyone's guess. maybe one of those still angry about the molasses operation taking a child's life. Or someone stung by John's successful objections to the woolen mill coming in because he said he drew the line at manufactures that would take people off the land. It could have been anyone. Then Will Wilson brought back the word.

The boys from Trade had heard about what John Bayley had said and claimed they'd been challenged. The part about confiscating their goods truly riled them. Being wild, young, and single, they cared for nothing on earth more than their horses and their guns. Those were near all they had and they were not of a mind to even think of losing either. They would be riding over again to make him sorry he'd ever said a word, or drawn a breath, for that matter. They would fix him and his, fix them good. Come Saturday night they would be there, without fail. John Bayley could count on it.

HE WORE HIS revolver in his belt all that week in case they took it into their heads to come over early. On Saturday he made ready. He cleaned his guns, and even Art's .22, borrowed Roby's, loaded them all, then lined them up against the wall on either side of the front window, rifles to one side, shotguns on the other. The barrels gleamed in each row and his hands were smeared with oil. His and Roby's pistols he laid to either side of where he would kneel in front of the open window behind two of the rolled-up bedticks. Roby came over from his place and wanted to take the bedroom window but John wouldn't let him.

"Suppose they come around the back?" Anna said. What would she have to defend herself with if they did? John had all the guns, including the one she had used for intimidation more than once when his drunk friends brought him home and wanted to come in the house. She had waved both barrels at them and told them to leave her husband on the porch. She could have boiling hot water to throw in case the nightriders tried to come in the kitchen door. During any fever season, she was quite a hand to boil water. "What do you want me to do?"

"I thought of the rear of the house. But they're not all that clever." He began to line up additional shells on the windowsill. "That would be an Indian trick. These fellows will go for the direct frontal assault, Pickett's charge, or some such nonsense. They think they can ride right up the steps, in at the front door, and into the parlor, guns blazing." He grinned, tightly, without showing his teeth.

We're here in the house with him. It can't be that he looks forward to this, is enjoying it.

But she knew that he was. She could smell a wolfish sort of exhilaration on him, along with the gun oil.

Her older boys were thrilled. "They'll remember this all their lives," John had said. The preparations excited them feverishly.

"I can't wait, can't wait." Leonard ran in circles around the room until Roland caught him and wrestled him to the floor. "You'll wait," he told his brother.

Spencer cried. "Will Dad be hurt? Will they shoot him? Will they burn up our house?"

"No, boy, of course not. Everything will be fine. You'll see." Roby picked up Maud and tickled her till she cooed at him. But Anna had no idea he would be right, that anything would be fine. Art and Roland watched her, she saw. They were certainly more than old enough to figure out what was really going on. Could they not see through the bluster and bravado and into the danger? Through the afternoon she could hardly get her breath.

Men and their hot, bloody thoughts, the demons that beset them.

John made them go into the kitchen and lie on the floor behind the tables turned on their sides, the chairs and bedsteads and the rest of the ticks. When they left him in front of the open window she wondered if she would see him alive again, if they would all make it through the night. After she had settled the children she went out briefly into the backyard and threw up before she joined them.

ALL NIGHT HE watched and listened, thinking even against his will how it would be to be one of them, riding unleashed and free in the night, excited and dangerous to the social order, instead of holed up behind mattresses defending hearth and home. He had gotten married too young, taken on too much responsibility right off, a father at twenty. He had had to forgo the pleasures of a misspent youth. Even before that first marriage he had worked hard so his stepfather could not reproach his mother for himself and his sisters. And besides all that he had completely missed the war, hadn't even been born till it was over. Oh, he could still get liquored up with the men from time to time, but he hardly ever fought anymore, hardly ever had, did not even beat his wife—wives—had seldom even hit them, or any of his other women, only the boys for their own good. Black looks, tongue-lashings, and breaking things were what he generally allowed himself to keep women in their places and then only if they provoked him to it. True, he forced Anna once in a while but that was only for his due.

This night, this wait, the outcome, could make up for a lot of deprivation. He wasn't all that worried about himself. The nightriders would be drunk. He was cold sober and a very good shot. Anna and the children would be all right if they stayed put and kept their heads down.

The moonlight gleamed on the shell casings on the windowsill, moved across them from left to right. By three o'clock, he was wondering. By four he was afraid they were not going to come. He drowsed off for a few moments, woke to think bodies lay all over the front yard.

By the time Anna's mantel clock struck five-thirty he was sure the boys from Trade weren't going to show after all. He got up off his knees. He had rested them on the end of the tick but they were still stiff and terribly sore. The nightriders had let him down. He was angrier at them for not coming than he would have been facing them in hot and cold blood with all of his guns.

He stomped into the kitchen. They were all asleep, Anna and the children curled together like a heap of puppies on the quilt behind the tabletop, Art and Roby sitting leaned against each other with their backs to the wall where they had been waiting in case he needed them.

"Could ye not watch with me one hour?" he muttered, then thought that they probably had watched far more than one hour. But he was still furious. An ashy musk filled the kitchen, the stove standing there cold, unlit and it already past five. Feeling deprived, he lifted a stove lid, then banged it down.

"Dad?" said Roby.

"Did you shoot them all?" asked Leonard.

"I didn't get to shoot anybody," he said. He wondered what had caused such ill luck.

After breakfast he shaved, dressed, and went to church.

THE BOYS FROM Trade had started out all right, and fully as drunk as John had expected them to be, but just over the state line in Zionville were a group of Faith's and Zionville's finest, who knew all about what was intended for John Bayley. They were as drunk as the boys from Trade and more than spoiling for a good fight which they proceeded to have in the church cemetery.

It was a highly satisfactory brawl on both sides. No guns were fired, but a number of eyes were blackened, one wrist broken and several ribs stoven in. Monuments were overturned and graveside plantings crushed. It ended when one of the boys from Trade crashed against the tombstone of a Revolutionary War veteran and suffered a concussion. He was taken to Dr. Campbell's where he lay unconscious for a week and after he went home he was, by report, never really the same and given to fits.

· · · 161 · · ·

"I WISH YOU had told me you were fixing to take my part." John surveyed Rufus's split lip and the bruises on his knuckles and forearms.

"We didn't tell you because you would have said not to, that we should let them come on down to you, that you'd take care of it."

"I could have too. Or I might have gone up there with you then."

"We didn't want that either, John. You weren't quite in the spirit of the thing. You would have killed somebody."

John thought of the sheen on the gun barrels, of the row of brass-cased shells along the windowsill in moonlight. Most likely. He looked at Rufus.

"I don't know if I'm obliged to you or not," he said.

. · . . · .

For Rufus pitched fights against nightriders were nothing, could be taken in stride, injuries and all, but when his father died he stopped coping. The Colvard house started smelling strongly of dirt, soiled clothes, farts, soured milk, and rotting food. True, it had not been very clean since Fanny Colvard died, leaving father and son to fend for themselves, but now it was noticeably so much worse that even John winced and wanted to hold his nose when he went in.

He tried talking to his friend, but Rufus barely seemed to hear him, sometimes even closed his eyes. Jack Colvard's death had been a shock, sudden, not like fever which gave some time to prepare. One day a father hale and hearty, the next writhing in terrible pain, and, on the following, gone. The doctor had said it was cramp colic and locked bowels, prescribed ice packs and morphine. When the little that was left of the pond ice stored in Faith had given out, Rufus had borrowed Rocket and ridden breakneck to Boone for manufactured ice which he brought back wrapped and tied in blankets and slung over the horse's flanks. Rocket was tender and sore for a week. The morphine gave Jack some relief but the ice, already melted down a good bit, didn't last long nor seem to help much while it was in place. Jack died in near-agony and Rufus went into a sort of stupor. During the preparations he sat all alone in his little photography shed, not making a sound as tears ran down his face. Anna, Tempe, and Alice had to do everything for the laying out and burial. Bina held his hand before they went to the church service and told him to think about Mary, the mother of Jesus, but he didn't seem to hear her. Rufus's older married sister didn't get home until the funeral was already over and she left after two days of gathering up what she wanted.

"She even took the most of Fanny's old quilts. I hope Rufus won't freeze come winter. I don't think she has a care in the world for her brother." Alice looked concerned, but they all knew she had other things to think about as well. The doctor said it might be twins this time and already she was huge, could barely move in the heat.

"My feet, my feet," she would say, "are they still down there?" And she tried to see them from the side.

"We'll get together and quilt him another, maybe two," said Tempe. "Doesn't look like he's going to have anyone else to do it, him being a confirmed bachelor and all."

"I SHOULD HAVE gone for more ice," Rufus kept telling John when he could bring himself to come back in the house. "A man ought to do everything he can for his own dad." But he hadn't even been able to pick out Jack's grave clothes.

John listened. An old memory, his father's face, a young man's face still, but distorted with illness. It had been hard for John to look at him. He pushed the image away. Rufus had had his easygoing father far longer than John had had his. And in truth Rufus had done everything that could be done. Blame was pointless. But he couldn't seem to get on with things. John thought how his friend had not lived alone before, had no one to look after now, and no one to look after him. The situation left Rufus lost and as aimless as a chip in a whirlpool. He should have been married long since. Then maybe the loss would not have hurt so, would have been more in the order of things.

John had never known anyone to withdraw as Rufus had. He neither bathed nor shaved. John had to send Art and Roland to do his chores for him or all of his stock would have perished.

"How are you sleeping?" he asked Rufus.

"Sleeping? Don't sleep. I don't even go to bed." He was, John learned, sitting up all night every night in Jack's old chair.

On another visit he noted that the man's shirt was sagging on his shoulders and his belt was over two notches beyond its usual worn place.

"God, Rufus, don't you eat anything?"

"Some, I guess. Nothing tempts me much. You know, don't you, I should have taken the wagon and gone for more ice, lots of it. If we could have kept him cold enough he might have made it."

ANNA WAS SIMMERING stew beef on the stove with potatoes, carrots, onions, and some of the weed stuff she was wont to throw into what she cooked. He wondered now and again if she might once make a mistake and poison them all, but her food did taste good. He grabbed up a dishclout, padded the bail of the pot and started out the door with it. Anna, coming in from the springhouse with the water bucket, caught him.

"Where are you going with that, John? It's our supper."

"Somebody needs it far worse than we do."

"I beg your pardon. I've peeled, chopped, stirred, and skimmed that stew most of the afternoon. And we don't get beef all that often, wouldn't have it now if Maggie's Jake hadn't had to butcher that steer. I'm not of a mind to have you give all that food and work away. It's not as if we have overmuch to spare."

Everyone knew Maggie's husband to be of an uncertain temper. He had been trying to turn a young steer into a working ox with fury and blows. He had alternately beaten the animal with a framing timber and prayed over it until he injured it so badly it had to be killed. Anna said sometimes she feared for Maggie and thought it might be fortunate there were no children in that household.

She reached out for the pot.

He had never actually struck her, having sensed that she would not stand for it, but he felt like swinging on her then. She needed it. Couldn't she understand a man was literally starving to death before their eyes? He had to save Rufus. How could she be so ungenerous?

"The Bible commands that we share. You are going against religion for selfishness' sake."

He yanked back when she touched the bail and the remaining hot grease from the top of the liquid went down the front of her skirt. He was so angry he hoped it was still hot when it soaked through to her skin.

Rufus ate nearly half the stew while John was there. It would have fed all the Bayleys. John put the rest in one of the Colvards' pots so he could take Anna's home, set it in the warmer for the next day. The stove was stone-cold and he wondered if Rufus had cooked for weeks. He could have gone for a while on leftovers from what folks brought in for the funeral, but that wouldn't have lasted too long.

"You're a most lucky bastard, John, to have a wife who can make a stew like this." Meat juices and broth were running down his chin. "It could sustain one's very soul." Rufus smiled. "I was about to famish away, wasn't I?"

After he ate Rufus actually got up to get a towel to wipe his face. He rubbed his beard.

"Think I'll shave in the morning."

"I NEVER FIGURED a man could be saved by food alone," John told Anna, "but that stew wrought a miracle right before my very eyes. Good thing I carried it over there."

She had changed her dress and still looked furious.

"You and your crazed, loony friends," she said.

They had cornbread, greens, and milk for supper.

. · . · . ·

FAITH, 1907

Rufus was on the mend. He scythed down the grass in the yard, even raked it, weeded the garden and did the wash. He opened his photography shop back up and took pictures of Alice with her new twin babies, one on each arm, and of Tempe and her three, as thanks for their help at the time of Jack's death. He asked Bina about a portrait as well but she said she didn't want him to take a picture of her, that no one should look into her eyes when she could not see them. John turned Art and Roland back to their usual chores since Rufus was looking to his own animals again.

THE HOUSE SWAP took place when Rufus said he had had enough of death, of being haunted.

"It comes down to this. I want to live in a house no one has died in."

John thought of the cabin up the hollow. Death inside a dwelling, the way it clung, he understood. And Rufus wasn't the farmer John was. He had all his other interests, and little use for that good bottomland, the Old Fields, and a big house.

"Feel like coming back to life, starting over. The eight of you— seven, that is, with Roby married off—are busting out the sides of your place, but it would be just the right size, maybe even a mite too big, for a bachelor like me. Think Anna will agree? You built it for her, I know."

John had an image of Will Wilson's kids, the whole batch of them, from the farm next to his, coming into the feedlot, running through Anna's garden and drinking out of his spring. Lately they had gotten to him, provoking him the way some things did nowadays, especially the young without respect. They yelled back and jeered if he yelled at them. And he'd not forgotten that Will Wilson hadn't truly taken his part when the threats came over from Trade. But likely the Wilsons would not bother Rufus that much. And there were other reasons. He made the deal to exchange places without asking Anna. By the first of November it was arranged.

HE TOLD HER he was tired of the neighbor children climbing his fence and of every Tom, Dick, and Harry walking up the lane to his spring after he had put in all that work to bring water closer to the house from far above in the hollow. The spring at the Colvards' was right behind the house and he didn't expect to have the problem with folks practically coming in at the back door. And they could have a bedroom to themselves, without any of the little ones in it.

"Except infants, of course."

Anna did not believe those were the only reasons. She thought John had looked across the level fields of the Indian grounds that the Colvards had long owned and coveted them for himself. She even wondered if he had put the idea in Rufus's mind in the first place.

By agreement Rufus left his photography studio where it was, instead of trying to move it down the road and up the hill, with the understanding he could come and go there as he pleased. He seemed as keen on that little shop as any house-proud woman would be, truly fond of its tiny red window in the darkroom and the big skylight on the north side set to let in the right illumination for his portraits.

HOUSE-PROUD. THIS place that John had built for her he could give up as easily as anything. It made sense of course, better land, bottomland even, a bigger house, one with a whole second floor, not just two little eave rooms with no heat. The Colvard place had a fireplace or stove in every room.

But this house was hers. It had been John's dream for her when they were courting, so that she would not have to stay in the cabin much of any time at all. He had begun cutting some of the timber before they said "I do." She had never told him with what delight she had seen the framing going up that summer, how the cabin had oppressed her, tucked so far back in the hollow she could not see out. No breeze would come through and the place never seemed truly clean. With that and John's memories, the ones he seldom talked about, she had felt trapped.

Every night after supper that season she had gone down to the knoll in the pasture they had picked out for a house site and walked over where her floors would be, looked at the views she would see out of her windows. Fresh, clean lumber. She'd almost been able to smell it before it was back from the mill.

"Beaded ceiling?" she had asked. "Can we have that, not just planks? It's tighter." *And prettier.*

An east-facing slope had made the house open and cheery-feeling in the morning but the steepness and height of the land behind it to the west could put a chill on one by midafternoon well before winter.

All three of their children after Roland had been born in the new house. After nine years she still thought of it as "the new house." Now they were leaving it. As she was packing it began to seem small. And it was. When everything had been stowed and taken away in the wagon she walked the empty place, stood in the bedroom looking out at the springhouse. So much water, so much butter, so much milk. From that window she could also see down to the flat where the molasses mill still stood, the pits for the fires. That was one view she would not miss. In the front room she ran her fingers over the carving on the mantel that John had done when he still thought of ways of pleasing her, remembered Alice commenting on the clock when it was first set there, how she said it ticked just like a heartbeat. The china cabinet built into the kitchen wall with shelves John devised so she could move them up or down as need be, more of his skilled work. Her mother had never had anything that convenient.

Oh, the sand I have flung out on these floors and swept up till I made the wood nearly white.

Upstairs she found some seed corn left behind. She would leave it for Rufus or the mice and rats, whoever got to it first.

She stood at the top of the narrow staircase going down into the front hall, thought of herself pregnant and carrying the slops and basins up and down those steps all the days and weeks Roland had the fever. Those dents in the bottom steps. The awful noise the day they were made.

Leonard yelling, "There's a horse going up our stairs."

And one was. A skittish and scared animal that got stuck halfway up and was about to kick in the bedroom wall. Roby had to get a ladder, climb in the upstairs window and put a blanket over the creature's head before they could calm it down enough to back it out.

"Now how did that happen? Who's responsible?" John had asked, looking at the damage, the scarred staircase. No one said a word at first because no one wanted a whipping for leaving both the gate and the front door open. Then, after she got up nerve to tell him about the horse, John suddenly bent nearly double, he was laughing so hard. A bit more and she thought he would actually have rolled in the floor.

"Oh, I wish I'd been here. I wish I'd seen that. I wish I had a picture."

Spencer drew him one on a sheet from Art's tablet. One could tell it was intended to be a horse and where the stairway was supposed to be, but Roby floated above like some angel with the blanket for wings.

John had been pleased, put the picture up on the wall in the front room, and would point it out to company,

"My son Spencer drew that. Good for his age, don't you think? Did I ever tell you about that horse . . . ?" And in due time he had told them all. Spencer watched and listened every time, a smile on his little face.

SHE SHOULD BE getting on up the road to the new place. It was time, time for her to be putting another house in order. She picked up her basket with the tiny breakables and three of Roe's carved birds on her way out the back door, then turned and went back into the front room once more. Someone had taken down Spencer's picture of the horse on the stairs and also removed the oil-drilling stock certificates. John? One of the boys? The places where they had been showed less yellow than the rest of the newspapered outside walls. She shifted her basket to her other hand and opened the front door, then remembered she had left the back door open. So be it. She left the front door open too. If the foxes of the hills chose, deep in the night, to run right through the middle of her house, the house that had been hers, it was no bad thing.

FOX WOMAN BEGAN to follow the hunter's son. He was a gentle lad and often alone, so it was not difficult to trail him. She discovered that he went off to bathe by himself in a pool below the waterfall halfway up the mountain and that after he had bathed he would fall asleep in his nakedness on the warm rocks and sand. She saw that he dreamed then.

I will come to you in a dream from which you will not awaken, she thought. But when she stood over the sleeping boy, ready to slash the vein in his throat quickly, she found that she could not. His face was as beautiful as the sun and moon, and she wanted him.

The next time that the boy came to bathe, Fox Woman let herself be seen by him and Fox Woman with her cape thrown back was lovely to see. The boy was not frightened. She brushed his legs with her tail and looked into his black eyes. He was as in a trance.

"Will you lie with me after the manner of men?" asked Fox Woman. And the boy agreed. She wrapped him in her cape and, though it was not easy, they managed. Afterwards Fox Woman sprang away into the forest where the boy could not follow her.

The boy was obsessed by her beauty, the warmth of her fur, the smell of wildness and blood that was on her. He could think of nothing but Fox Woman. Each day he climbed to the pool to look for her to return. She never did. He called and called. She never answered.

At length the boy did not eat. He grew thinner and could hardly climb as far as the pool. One day his father the hunter followed him and heard him calling out to Fox Woman.

"What is this you are saying?" asked the hunter of his son.

"Oh, Father," said the boy. "I shall die if I cannot have Fox Woman."

"Child, you are bewitched. But do not fear. We will cure you."

The hunter took his only child back to the village where he was bound wrist and ankle in leather thongs. Powdered fox bone was put up his nostrils, burnt fox flesh was forced into his mouth, and the hide of Fox Man was stretched over him where he was left out in the night in the dew crying for Fox Woman. Within a week he was dead.

Is this my revenge? thought Fox Woman as she watched the thin frame of her human love being borne to its resting place. I had not thought it would be so bitter.

At that moment the seed of the dead boy took root in Fox Woman. She felt it quicken. And in the fullness of time she bore her children of both worlds, Fox Boy and Fox Girl.

She had fears for them when they were newborn, worrying that she could not feed them without a mate. But they seemed to need less than if they were all fox and thrived on more things than foxes usually eat. When they were little they could not control their shifting shapes and each time she came back to the den she did not know if she would find two furry fox kits or two naked human babies. As they grew they were better at it, stayed foxes most of the time and changed to humans only when they went down to spy upon the village, their father's home.

JOHN HAD SOLD the molasses mill to one of merchants at Sugar Grove who moved it behind his store and sold off most of his shares of the runs. The mules' track showed by the road at the Bayleys' first house for a long time, but since Rufus didn't use that corner of the property for anything, it eventually grew up in briars and vines.

· ′ · · ′ ·

It came toward her from the mountain, descending the steep slope in the night, not a single stone turning under its sure foot. She could sense its approach in her sleep.

John was not there.

My eyelids must open.

In near-total darkness something had waked her. She knew it was sound, not a dream. One of the boys talking in his sleep in the next room, Maud crying in her trundle, King barking suddenly? No, not King. King was dead. And there had not been any barking, though she realized almost at once she had heard a dog after all. In the starshine of the very early morning, she made out Gyp standing in his squared-off terrier fighting stance by the open window. He was growling low in his throat. No one outside could have heard it and he had not disturbed the baby.

Smart dog, thought Anna, and got out of bed, but she wished for King, his intimidating size, three times that of Gyp, though he had actually been much less ferocious. She was alone in the house with the children, John having gone off to Lenoir with a load of the first truck from her garden, the orchard's early apples and cherries, not to be back for two or three days. It would be well known in the community that he was gone.

She flung on her shawl, jerked down the gun hanging over the door, and went into the hall. The children were quiet in whatever dreams they had. Roland slept through everything, but Leonard and Spencer were of the restless, wakeful kind. She was always careful when she went about at night. It was June already but the floor upstairs still felt chill to her bare feet. Anna went down the steps, hoping they would not creak. Gyp brushed on past her, treading on the tail of her nightdress.

Her feet made no sound on the rag rugs as she slipped from room to room to peer between the curtains. Nothing, but Gyp still growled. Would any of her friends hear her should she scream for help? No, probably not even Alice who lived closest, but not close enough. Anna was often uneasy now being in another house, but usually nothing came of these alarms. This time felt different.

Carefully she unlatched the kitchen door, cocked the gun, and tried to move out in silence, but Gyp shoved and pushed by her again. He made his fierce rumbling sound and lunged toward the bigger garden plot up the bank behind the house. Over the dog's noise she could barely hear the rustling in the pea vines. Something after all.

"Who's there?" she called out, trying to make her voice as rough and harsh as she could manage. A bear, one of the last? Did bears like peas? She hoped she could frighten it off so she would not have to shoot. Perhaps it was only a small animal.

From behind the net of trellised vines someone stood up straight against the night sky.

A thieving neighbor? Possible, but unlikely. Perhaps one of those wandering, rootless men who came through Faith from time to time, knocking on doors with dirty, scarred hands, offering to work for food. Then as she looked closely in the dimness she thought the person in her garden likely to be much younger. She could distinguish no face but the figure was that of someone slender, with no hat or pack.

And with that figure, the youthful way it moved, the stance, though she saw little more than a faint silhouette, she realized who she might well have come upon, that wild runaway boy from up on the mountain who lived by his wits and his stealth.

"You!" she called out to her own surprise. "You come right down here."

The figure turned away, moved off up the hill soundlessly, seeming not to walk but to change substance and flow into darkness. Anna grabbed Gyp's collar, held him by her until the presence was completely gone, absorbed by the night. Then she dragged the reluctant, excited dog back into the house, not stopping for either of them to pee in the yard though she felt the pressure.

Whatever had she had in mind when she spoke? Taking in a half-feral child to tame him? Maybe. Or at least to give him a meal and a wash.

"No, I guess not," she told Gyp, as if he could understand. "That's one battle that's not really ours."

She latched the door, put the gun back, and slipped into bed. She pulled her gown down straight and lay there alone, chilled from the dew on her bare feet, considering lives of stealth and disconnection. And an absolute freedom, elemental, given to wind, motion, turbulence, lived on the run. How would it be?

Once when Roland was not even a crawling, pulling-up baby, she herself had left him in his cradle and suddenly bolted, dashed off up the ridge for no good reason that she remembered now. Perhaps she had sensed what life with John would be when their passion for each other was gone. Perhaps it was, or could have been, something else entirely. But she remembered her run, how she lost her bonnet and tore off her apron. It hadn't been in her to stay in the woods, not then. And she knew she could not do it now. How did one bathe and wash in such circumstances? In the cold, cold streams, rinsing out rags, watching one's own blood, the faintest of stain, run off downhill. She thought of baths in the big tub by the stove in the kitchen, with warmed water and soap scented with mint and comfrey, the rough knit towels. Oh, but she was spoiled. There would have to have been a toughness in anyone, going off that way and staying gone, and a kind of strength that, if she herself had ever had, she feared she had no longer.

Gyp growled again. "Let him be," she told him.

She turned her face into the pillow with John's scent on it. She wondered if he had taken the girl from the store with him to Lenoir, pretending it was a buying trip, saying they were economizing, taking a wagonload down, bringing one back. His smell of sweat and a faint sweet blend of hair oil and whiskey were mixed with that of the sun-dried linen.

She could not go back to sleep, got up and took one of her tinctures, being careful not to disturb the baby. The medicinal always gave her dreams. Long ago at the Albas' she had dreamed that Roe's carved animals came to life, not full-sized, but small as his carvings themselves, a roomful of little creatures running about. The tiny pale sheep made from holly gamboled over the furniture and baaed so high and faint they could barely be heard.

The dream this night was nowhere near as innocent. In it she felt wet black granite under her feet and a stormy wind whipping her skirts. Then the whole side of a mountain came crashing down. Boulders rolled past her. Out of the fissure created by the landslide horsemen rode forth in the rain, wearing brown cloaks and carved masks that covered their faces. They were naked and tattooed under their cloaks, their hair gleaming like the pelts of otters rising from streams. She wanted to cry out, "Take me with you," but let them ride past her into the mist.

She woke cold before she could see where the riders were going and turned to warm herself against John. When he was not there she pulled up another quilt.

· · · · ·

She marked her name off the card, returned *The Haunted Hotel* and took down the first volume of *Armadale* from the circulating library shelf. The joy and pure greed of it! At times she felt that if she laid her palm against the spine of one of the books her very flesh would cleave to the gorgeous gilt and leather, even to the words within, she loved them so. Not all the Collins novels were great works, of course, but she felt somehow a special connection to them that she did not quite understand.

"Writers are so lucky," she said to Leftwich who was once more rearranging stock no one ever seemed to disturb. "When they finish something they can still have a copy of it. I wonder how artists can paint a picture, sell it, and have it gone forever. Must break their hearts."

"Perhaps they hold everything they have done in memory. Could be it's like having a child, raising it to leave home, do you think?"

"Maybe." *Probably that breaks hearts too.*

"And now, which of my little treasure set do you like best?"

"*The Woman in White* and *No Name*. I like them all, but those two are the best so far. Are English laws still so unfair to women? About inheritance and all? Are ours as bad and I just don't know it?"

"About the law I've no idea, what with having little family and less interest. And certainly nothing to inherit or leave to anyone. But about the novels, as I suspected, you have a taste for literature and selected the best of Collins's work. It's a pity I don't have more to offer. As you know, some of the other volumes in my little subscription library are for quite a different readership. More on the practical and religious side. And then there's been stuff like that worthless school text I was throwing out that you wanted to take. For your clippings, you said." Leftwich gestured to the shelves. "Still, you have the rest of *Armadale* and *The Moonstone* to look forward to. You have my guarantee that they will not disappoint. How did you like Captain and Mrs. Wragg? Aren't they capital inventions? I could scarcely contain myself when the captain confronted the redoubtable Mrs. Lecount armed only with *Joyce's Scientific Dialogues*. What memory and audacity! Oh, Collins, no wonder they called him 'the king of inventors.' "

"What was he like? Any idea? I wish there was a picture."

"Know very little about him. Clever, of course, there's no doubt, brilliant even. Worldly and experienced, probably. I think he was a friend of Dickens and led a somewhat irregular life. Would you have time for a cup of coffee today? Won't take me a minute. The beans are already roasted and ground. We could discuss the Wraggs, personal favorites of mine."

"Yes, coffee." She tried to move from her own thoughts to what he was talking of. "Magdalen interests me. Such daring, so bold!"

"Oh, Magdalen, is it?" Leftwich chuckled. "Hmm, then you interest me, dear lady. Can't wait till you get to that redheaded adventuress Lydia Gwilt," he said, and went to fix the coffee.

While he was in the little back room that served him as a kitchen Anna looked over the rest of the stock, most of it still there, five or six books, maybe more, off the shelves, circulating somewhere to other souls bold enough to put their name to one of Leftwich's little cards. Alice? Maybe Bina who liked reading and once in a while had the time. Everything was always clean, neat and orderly, not dusty and jumbled like Sherwood's, but then Sherwood had a good deal more to jumble. She wondered how Leftwich lived, if it was true he had money hidden somewhere. In case it was not, she always brought something in her basket each time she came, bread, butter-milk, side meat, some pickles, sauerkraut, and jam. By this time he had a small garden and some chickens, but no cow. Did anyone else do the same for him? How did he keep up that weight? She never mentioned her trips to Leftwich's even to her close friends and they mentioned no such visits of theirs to her. She had a peculiar sense, not of danger to herself nor of impropriety, for which she would have cared little, but of something else entirely, the feeling that she or someone else could, perhaps by accident, do a terrible harm. She took care never to stop to talk to him in public, only to acknowledge him with the briefest of nods, the slightest of smiles, hoping he would understand why. Since he did not attend church, she had one less place to be so circumspect.

"Here you are, dear lady. Sorry to offer you no cream or sugar, but I'm fresh out." He probably had none to begin with. "And these are really teacups, not for coffee. Have you ever tasted China tea?"

She almost felt tears start when she saw that he had brought their coffee, not in the usual heavy mugs everyone had, but in thin, painted china cups with gold rims and fluted saucers. She thought of the beautiful things at the Albas', of Gage, and then of how no man had ever served her anything before, not ever.

And she thought how she had never in her life sat down to a table to eat or drink by herself that she could remember, though sometimes sitting with Mrs. Alba and Lucille she had felt as if she were alone. How was it for Leftwich, taking meal after meal with no one else there? He certainly didn't waste away as Rufus had when he was first by himself.

"Now," said Leftwich, stirring with a tiny silver spoon the cup which did not need to be stirred, "tell me more about your reactions to that bold girl Magdalen."

ANNA AND MAUD were both sick before Christmas with high fevers, congestion, and coughs. She wondered if it had to do with the move, something still lurking in the Colvard house in spite of all her scouring, the scrubbings she did until her knees hurt so much she could hardly sleep. She managed to dose herself and the child with chamomile and willow bark and by Christmas Eve they were past the worst, fevers broken, aches gone. The baby was playing, trying to talk back to her instead of crying and clinging to her neck, but she was still weak and dragging around the house. The season was upon them and she was not ready for it, no baking, no boughten presents. She did have some things put by, winter socks knitted for the boys, a merino muffler with dark red and black stripes for John to wear to church, a fancy needle case for Mecie, a rag doll with a dress and cape and some tatting for a new dress for Maud. John had bought oranges and stick candy, like Mr. Alba had sent to her family on her behalf at a Christmas she missed going home for long ago. All those oranges! A whole sackful! She would dry the peel behind the stove and pound it out for flavoring when she felt like baking again. It would certainly not be the Bayleys' worst Christmas, not like the year Roland was three, Leonard an infant, when floods and rains had rotted the oats, cabbage, and potatoes, and John made little corn or rye either. But she was not satisfied, felt as if she had to make up for something, but had no idea what it was or why she felt as she did.

"HERE'S THE MONEY, Ronald, and the list. I'm still too weak to walk all the way down to the store and back. Don't want a relapse here at Christmas. Now, the bandannas for Art and Roby can be either red or blue, whichever has the prettiest designs. A pack of needles in plain paper for Mecie for me to put in the case. Harmonicas for Leonard and Spencer. I hope Sherwood still has them in stock. We're getting to all this so very late."

"Leftwich's got a little china doll Maudie would love." Roland took the folded packet.

"You know she's much too young. She'd break it straight off. Anyway, I made her a doll already."

So he knew Leftwich's stock. Was he one of the library subscribers, a secret reader the way she was? She thought again how fortunate it was that all the Collins novels were the same color and about the same size. John surely thought she was taking forever to finish the first book.

"Now, what for you? I didn't put you down for anything on purpose, so you could pick out what you want yourself. Got your eye on anything at Sherwood's?"

"I'll find something."

He got everything she asked for. Yes, Sherwood had had the harmonicas, one with a slide, and they discussed who should get that, Leonard because he was older, or Spencer because he was more musical. He had even gotten some horehound candy for Maud with his own money.

"It will be good for her throat."

"And you. What did you get for yourself? Do I have to wait till Christmas morning to see what I've given you?"

The paper wrapping gave her a start. It was solid white, not newsprint, but off the roll she knew stood in the corner at Leftwich's, waiting for him to get a cutter on which to mount it. Roland unwrapped what he had bought and set it on the table between them.

It was a china cup, small, a child's cup, and he was ten years old. But she could tell why he had selected it. Pure white, straight sides, a strip of gilt down the handle and around the rim, and, in an oval on the front, no bigger than a quarter across, a whole miniature landscape with trees, fields, a river, and clouds in a clear blue sky.

"It's beautiful. A treasure for always."

"Yes, put it up in the cupboard where Maudie can't get at it. And these are for you." He handed her a tiny paper bag, folded over, with a Christmas seal on it. Inside were eight chocolate bonbons, the ones Leftwich carried. Sherwood had only licorice, sweetened wax, hore-hound, and stick candy.

"You shouldn't have spent your money on these."

"I didn't. They were a gift."

She did not have to ask who had sent them. Christmas morning she put one by each person's plate. When they asked where they had come from she said, "Santa Claus."

If the salt fall right against him
all the stars cannot save him.

. · . · .

They held the meeting about the boy's accusation at the school-house, as if to sanction what they were planning, the schoolhouse being the community institution halfway between the store and the church, the place where the oil drilling and the woolen mill had been discussed. But no Mr. Green was there to instruct and counsel, to hold them back in his deliberate, schoolmasterly way, so they got angry and almost of one mind in a hurry. And Rufus wasn't present either to talk against their plans as John was sure he would have.

John looked around the room, figured he knew something near as bad, or worse, on most of the ones there. The Scriptures said no jerking off and no adultery, for example, and which of them could claim to be free of either or both? Certainly not himself. He was trying to remember what was written in the Bible about what they were discussing when someone said the Lord God frowned on such as unnatural, a terrible sin to be rooted out and destroyed.

Oh hell, here we go. What if we are talking about bearing false witness?

Anna would say most folk read the Bible to name what other people's sins were and to find out what would reward themselves and discredit their enemies. She had a point, even if it did annoy him to admit it. He thought of his mother closing her eyes and cracking open the Good Book without looking, placing her finger blindly upon a verse to serve as the principle for guiding her life. "Judge not that ye be not judged" was what she had once lighted upon, to absolutely no effect on her behavior that he could detect.

And it was the same with the men he was gathered with. They were bound on judgment and reminding them of that admonition would do no good, might even be of some danger to himself. He left without saying anything.

"I GUESS WE get down on our knees and give thanks to God that it wasn't one of our sons he got after." John dropped the sugar from Sherwood's on the cupboard and frowned, the corners of his mouth lowering his mustache the way they always did when he tightened his lips to invoke the name of the Almighty. He had told her he was going to the store only, not to a meeting.

She was silent, felt dry-mouthed and sick. The talk was coming to a head then, and she was helpless. Harv Mast was bound to have been there and drinking, and Harv in his cups was no sane man. He could get vindictive and rouse others to be the same.

"They've got that middle Carlton boy down there in the school-house—you know which one."

Yes, she knew, a strange, crafty child. That was one she wouldn't want around her boys.

"They're asking him all sorts of questions. And getting answers, monstrous answers I didn't even want to listen to. Harv's got a jug. He says it's an abomination, confusion, deserving the worst. They're taking their time, trying to get him to say what Leftwich did to him, egging him on, I think, maybe to make up things. And they're certainly getting all righteous and likkered up for some action. Will's saying Leftwich stole all that stuff he has for sale from the dead, that no real man would deal in those things."

"Action? Will they call the sheriff? Over that boy's lies?"

"Don't think they'll wait for that. My guess is they'll try and get rid of him one way or another, clean house, so to speak. Harv and Will are mean enough when they're drunk for a two-man lynch mob. What makes you think it's all lies?"

Why ever should men choose to equate their violence with women's daily work? she wondered. And she thought of what Leftwich had said when she asked if he had ever been married, how he explained, strangely, she thought at the time, that he could care for neither man nor woman like that, that to him others could be friends, nothing more. "As we are, dear lady."

Lies? Lies.

She started for the door.

"Hey, where do you think you're going?"

"To warn him."

"The hell you are!" He grabbed her arm and slung her hard against the table. "Stop and consider. What do you think they'd do to you if they caught you there? They could be tempted to string up more than one, soused as they'll be."

"Then you go back. They might listen to you. It's wrong, wrong. At the least he should be warned. And you know it." She burst into tears. "Remember what Papa said about that awful time up in Virginia, what he saw, what they did to those black people in town? How could anyone . . ."

He looked at her. Then, to her surprise, he nodded, took his hat, his fast riding horse, and left.

"GET. YOU'D BETTER get. Just take what money you've got and get on out of here."

Leftwich stood in the doorway, looking blank and stupefied. Then said, "Won't you please come in and explain yourself? I don't know what this is about, you riding down here like the dam had burst."

"I'll bust your damn thick head. It's Carlton."

"I see," said Leftwich. "Come in."

Inside, right in front of John, he pulled up a board in the floor, took out his cashbox and dumped the contents into a saddlebag. Most of the things from the glass case followed, wrapped in the India shawls.

"Hurry," said John. "They're up there getting drunk as can be and nobody can answer for what they might do."

"This is what I came here to avoid." Leftwich fastened the buckles on the bags. "I'll not deny my tendencies, but I've seldom acted on them, and certainly never would in a place like this. For the most part I've lived a monkish life. But Carlton, he sensed me out, wanted what I wouldn't give. So what is he saying?"

"Everything you did."

"Everything he wanted me to do, you mean."

"One of you is a goddamn liar."

"And you don't know which, do you?"

"I ought to beat you to a pulp right here and now, save them the trouble."

"Why don't you do that?" said Leftwich, dropping his arms to his sides and closing his eyes.

John looked around wildly for something with which to strike, a stick of stove wood, maybe. He thought suddenly about the scalded, peeling body of the burnt child that they had tried to keep him from seeing when he thought that he, of all people, should know and remember. And that time in Lenoir he'd never told Anna about, when he himself had looked at the bodies of those two young black men, hardly more than boys, who had been killed so awfully. He had seen Roby and Art in his mind's eye then as if they had suffered there. The moment, his anger, passed.

"Why did you come?" Leftwich opened his eyes. "Ah, the dear lady."

"She's no dear of yours."

"A true friend, nonetheless. Listen, there is little time, I know. The books, those blue ones there. They'll likely destroy everything when they come. Save those. Take them to her, a parting gift from me. She loves them so and hasn't quite finished all of them."

"Books? All those . . . ?"

"Yes, please. Must go. And thank you for the timely warning." Leftwich struggled toward the door, carrying the heavy saddlebags. It was hopeless that way. John met his eyes. Leftwich knew. In his expression was a combination of fear and resignation that John recognized. He had seen it on his father's face toward the end when his father was giving up. And Leftwich's eyes. Something about them was like his father, though it was the only likeness except for the expression. His father had never run to flesh, never had enough extra to do so.

"You won't get far like that. Take the horse. Ride him down the creek, far as you can."

"Yes, right, good. Thanks, many thanks. Don't forget the books. Valuable, maybe worth a horse."

"I won't."

"I shall always remember you for this."

John thought of his and Anna's images in Leftwich's mind, mixed up with whatever else was in there.

I hope you don't remember. And I hope to God I never have to think of you again.

But aloud he said only, "Get going."

He watched Leftwich fling over the saddlebags, mount with difficulty, and ride down the slope. Then he prowled the house, noting everything, the neat little kitchen with its tiny stove, the low pegged-together bed with the threadbare blankets, a much-mended quilt. The place smelled of damp and something he interpreted as fear. And he had a peculiar feeling that someone was in the house with him, someone who for unknown reasons both approved and disapproved of his actions, what he had done and was about to do. There was no one.

From every room he gathered the kerosene lamps and anything easily flammable. In the middle of the front room he piled the blankets, the quilt, Leftwich's clothes, the kitchen stool, and all the books, the blue-bound volumes on top. He could hardly bear to think of Anna's hands on them. He poured the liquid from the lamps over it all, threw a match from the doorway, and watched till the flames jumped up the wall and halfway across the ceiling.

By the time he got to the yard the blaze had covered all of the window in the front room. When the others arrived the whole house was alight.

"You're too late. He's done took off."

"And what are you doing here, John Bayley? We thought you and your buddy Rufus didn't want no part in this." Will Wilson squinted at him.

"It's Rocket. He's got Rocket. When I got back to the house the horse was gone. I put two and two together, thought he must've got wind of something and stole him to get away on. Sure enough, look here at these prints. Those nicks there are from Rocket's front shoes. The house was already going when I got here. Must have just missed him. Goddamn horse thief."

"Goddamn degenerate horse thief. Hanging's too good for him. Maybe we should try something like this when we catch up with him." Eli Younce gestured to the fire.

"Who's going to catch him on Rocket? He's got a head start. And we don't even know which way he took off."

"West, he'd head west for sure."

"Naw, down the creek, no prints and no scent."

"Bet he took off up on the ridge so he could see us coming afar off."

"We could split up and start looking." Nobody offered to go anywhere. They were all looking at the fire, seeming to find it too interesting to leave.

"Damn, ain't it the truth? Damn. He's done us up good, boys. Who's got the jug?"

By the time they had watched the house burn to the ground most of them were too drunk to get home. John, who had had only enough to be sociable, and some of the soberer ones got a wagon, rolled the willing ones into it, drove up to their houses, and rolled them out again on the grass for their families to look after. The unwilling they left in Leftwich's backyard to get lumbago from sleeping it off next to the creek.

WHEN HE WALKED back home she met him partway down the lane, her face stricken. She had seen the fire, smelled smoke and drink on him, feared the worst, the very worst. She twisted her hands in her skirt.

"He'd fired the house by the time I got there. Then, while I was looking to see if there was any way I could put it out, he jumped on Rocket and took off. It's your fault I've lost my best horse. I've a mind to slap you."

She drew a long breath of cautious relief. "You couldn't stop him?"

"Stop a man riding Rocket? You might as well try to stop a full team and loaded wagon going downhill."

"Was nothing saved from the house?"

"Not a bloody thing."

"Perhaps he took some things with him."

"Probably not. Most likely he didn't have the time."

THAT NIGHT SHE listened to John's whiskey snores. Cold with terror and loss she crept up against him. In his slumber he slung his arm over her. She hid her face in his neck, cried briefly, and did not sleep.

John's stomach cramped on him so fiercely the next morning that he stayed in bed for the whole day.

. · . · .

To: John F. Bayley, Esquire
Faith, NC
My dear Mr. Bayley,

I believe that I am in possession of something that will interest you a large bay stallion, 16 hands with saddle and bridle. I received this horse of a gentleman in need of immediate transportation to points west in lieu of money for a ticket in all honesty it is a fine animal and worth much more than I am out for the swap. I am not justified in keeping it for that sum you may reclaim same by identifying yourself paying the price of the ticket in question plus any livery fees.

Your respectful obedient servant,
Hiram Easter
Southern Railways
Ticket agent

Included in the envelope was a small scrap of folded paper with a brief message in pencil:

Bayley, for a fat man a seat in a railway car beats one on the back of a horse any day of the week and twice on Sundays. Thanks. My best to your dear lady and may she long enjoy her books.

It was unsigned. John lifted the stove lid and dropped it into the fire as soon as he read it.

· ˙ · · ˙ ·

Saved. Married. Saved, but not totally changed. Anna had begun Roby's salvation. Grace abounding. Sometimes he wondered what would have happened to him if she had not come when she did. But she had come. Then when the time to love her safely passed, they had become the closest of friends, and that was best. Mecie was the darling of his heart, their little Janie a sweet delight. But even the room beyond Mecie's perfect door was not enough for everything in him. Still he left on his solitary journeys, off into the wild every chance he got.

It was not that he didn't get the work done. Mecie could have no worries on that score. He took care of that and then some, loving the dark brown earth, the dimensions of each field. He tended to every-thing as his father did, and prospered.

But now and again Roby had to leave.

Fall and winter he hunted. Spring and summer he fished. He had long since abandoned his barehanded methods and now bait-fished, wading upstream and then back down to where he had left his boots on the bank. The old injury to his ankle hurt in the cold water but he wouldn't have it any other way. Someday when he had the money he would buy new tackle and learn how to cast flies. He might catch less, but it seemed such a fine sport, giving the trout a fighting chance the way it did.

John thought his interests and his methods a waste of valuable time.

"There's quicker ways to get one's dinner. Now your grand-mother, not that I like to credit her overmuch, but she had the right idea when it comes to getting fish on the table."

Roby and his father had almost come to blows one time over Hannah's way of catching fish. She ripped tow sacks down the sides, sewed them together end to end and, with one of her Shull offspring on one side of the creek and herself on the other, she could fish out a whole section of stream in a matter of minutes. And she was too greedy to throw back any but the smallest of fingerlings. Roby could only hope that there were some wily old fish wise enough to swim away and escape her seine. That was the waste, to take everything away at once, leaving nothing to the future. One of the many rea-sons he wanted to fly-fish was so he could throw back the young ones he caught relatively undamaged.

He took many of the fish he caught to Anna who cleaned and cooked them, served them up with cornbread, slaw, and fresh cucumber pickles. She always invited him and his family to supper then and those meals when she brought out the big white platter with the dredged and peppered pan-fried brook trout on it were the times that his father said nothing at all about how wasteful fishing was.

· · · · ·

I yank the strap off the nail, step out the kitchen door onto the great square stone. With one fist on my hip, I throw my head back and set the dark curving horn to my lips. The horn is so old no one remembers the steer it came from, the ordinary violence of dehorning, a steer sure to have been eaten, its hide tanned, its bones ground to dust. With this horn I blast a summons out into distance. No tune, but they all know my call.

And at the mighty, ancient, rolling, echoing sound all my beaming bright-faced boys will come to me, dropping from the apple trees, tumbling down the hillside. Up from the streambed they will come, from green groves, tall grasses and the Old Fields, all of them come gathering home to me, home to my skirts, my arms, my pain that they will leave me again and again.

SHE TOLD HERSELF she was thinking, sat absolutely still in a sober, intense frame of mind, ready to concentrate. But the thoughts she wished to consider did not come. Duties, concerns, chores, all dodged and skipped about in her head, refusing to organize, arrange themselves, and then go away. What next? Change the beds next week. Order new ticking at Sherwood's. Render the fat. Renew the *Comfort* subscription, drawing for who will get the curtains. Get a cutting of that yellow rose from Tina.

Oh, ride off the edge of the world and never come back.

Consider John and the children's future, somehow more schooling. Roland, so bright, must not stay here, buried in this village, mired in this dirt, rich though it may be, the ways that don't change. Leonard, Spencer? Must see Maggie about weaving another coverlet. Maud, what was it she needed to consider about Maud? Oh, yes, ask the doctor about her eyes. Ask John for a galvanized washtub, lighter than the wooden ones. Answer Nell's latest letter. A place for a new lamp in the kitchen. More red felt to color the kerosene.

Ride away, ride away.

When was it Tina was coming to visit? Must make sure she and T.A. don't arrive at the same time. Paste the poems out of the paper in the scrapbook. Time soon to chop and salt down the cabbage.

A hundred things, a thousand things moved in her mind. And, besides those, music over and over, old, old songs she knew of betrayal, blood, and death, voices that had sung them before her. She thought of how she could feel the notes ringing inside her very bone when she sang full voice in a good room.

And then sometimes underneath, far beneath it all, she heard and thought of those from the years before any of her kind ever came here, those who were here long, long since. She looked out across their fields, the lands they had walked, streams they fished, and heard them faint and far away in time, but steady as a beating heart.

. · . . · .

Nine years between them but Art and Roland were close at the second house. They minnow-fished together, worked side by side as John directed on the straightening out of the creek's meander which was cutting into the field. They made a swing for Maud that they swung on themselves. When Art plowed Roland followed in the furrow, supposedly picking up the rocks but also collecting arrowheads, axes, and spear points that the share turned up.

At night they washed and sorted these treasures, laying them out on the dining table.

"Bones, why do you suppose we never find any bones?" Roland didn't know if he really wanted to find them, or only wondered why they were missing. Turning up the jaw of an old boar under the laurel was one thing, but to see a yellowed human skull before one in the dirt grinning in its mortality . . . People could die like King had. He would never get over it.

"They've been dead and gone too long. Gone to dust. Nothing left but things made of stone." Art felt the edge of a spear point and handed it to Roland. "Think you could kill a bear with this?"

It was glowing deep orange. If he held it in his hand until it warmed all through, would it quiver and tell him truths?

"With you to help me I could. Roby, he could probably do it by himself. With a knife. But wouldn't there be something where they buried people, teeth maybe?" Animal teeth they did find sometimes.

"Yeah, Roby could probably do in a bear with a pocketknife, he's that quick." Art took back the spear point. "Maybe they didn't even bury anybody. Nell's Rush said out West they put their dead people up in trees for the crows to pick at."

"Think they did that around here?" Roland thought of teeth scattered like seed corn on the ground in the forest, an army that might rise from them where they were strewn.

"Naw, you ain't seen any bags of bones up a tree, have you?"

"Haven't seen," said Anna from where she sat by the fireplace listening and mending in the lamplight.

THEY CLIMBED THE hill on their way up to Buckeye. Roland looked at Art's back in front of him. Would he ever be that big? Art was taller and broader than Roby, almost as big as their dad. And courting too. Not many as big and as old as Art would take little brothers along on such treks. He would be just like Art and kind to everybody when he was grown.

"Somebody brought some western bighorns up here. Thought to naturalize them in these mountains." Art held a limb out of the way so Roland could get by. "This ain't the Rockies. They didn't make it."

Isn't. "What happened to them?"

"Idiots thought they could winter over with no care at all. Even

Harv knows more about sheep than that. Sure enough, they ate laurel and poisoned themselves. You need me to cut you a walking stick to help you climb?"

"Don't need it. I can do it. Could we find one of their horns?"

Their horns curled up. He had seen pictures. That would be a better find than the boar's jaw and near as good as a spear point. You could blow one.

AND SOMETIMES IN the afternoons he and Art did not venture but simply sat together on the creek bank with Anna's cornbread and slices of onion and told each other no one could be happier than they.

· · · · · ·

FAITH, 1909

When Art married, he brought his bride home to live in the second house with his folks. It seemed to hurt him that his father had not set him up with some property the way he did Roby, but the bottom fields had flooded two springs in a row and had to be replanted each time. That did not leave much to invest in another farm. Nor did John much care to so invest, desirable land getting harder to come by in the valley these days.

It had nothing to do with the way John felt about Art's choice. Leah was a childless young widow, a strong girl, almost as tall as Art, and if the legal mess between her and her late husband's family about property got settled in her favor, she might be bringing Art enough to buy a place of their own without much help from John.

Since it was Leah's second marriage there was a small wedding for family only in the Methodist chapel at Amantha. Nothing in the circuit rider's peaceful reading of the service, or the pleasant wedding supper afterwards, prepared them for what was to come.

Late in the night John heard the voices, faint, as if trying to approach quietly. Flickering lights from lanterns and torches showed against the curtain. He got up to look out, and as he did so, the din began. They had washtubs and cowbells, and who knew what else. More than likely they were all drunk.

"Shivaree," he told Anna. "They're just teasing them. Letting off some high spirits. Maybe a little jealous tonight." He laughed.

The noise went on. Yelling increased, and before long it was clear that some of the shouts were curses. "Goddamn whore," someone yelled. "Fucking thief."

Suddenly there was a shot, the sharp crack of a large rifle, and a scream from the front upstairs bedroom where the bridal couple were.

"Oh my god." John sat straight up. A door was flung open and someone was crying. Anna threw back the covers and they both ran out into the hall. From a candle in the front bedroom, they could see Leah at the end of the hallway, her long white gown pulled up above her knees as she twisted the cloth in her hands. Her bare legs and feet were pale, seemed hardly strong enough to support her. Her heavy dark plait swung as she shook her head.

"No, no," she was sobbing. Art was right behind her.

"She was near shot," Art yelled. "There's a bullet hole not a foot from where her head was."

"Put out that candle," John shouted, not caring if he was heard. "Get her into the back room with Mama. We'll take care of those sons of bitches." It was like the boys from Trade, only this time they had really come. He felt the stiffening of violence in him.

"They're his brothers." Leah's voice shook. "Be careful. They can be awful rough."

"Whose?" asked John, then figured it out before she could answer.

This ain't no shivaree. They could do a murder, or murders, and cover it up as a mistake, an accident, could say a gun went off with no intent more than fun.

"Especially when they're drunk," she said.

Art shoved Leah into the back bedroom with Anna and Maud and got them all behind the bed and the chest of drawers. Another shot was fired but did not hit the house. John yanked open the door to the younger boys' room, yelled for them to stay quiet and get on the floor under the beds, then grabbed his shotgun off the rack over the door and snatched up some shells. He loaded in the dark on his way down to the front room.

He could make out six or seven men in the yard from their lights. Any more? Had Leah's dead husband that many brothers? At least it wasn't fifteen or twenty the way it sounded. And the size of the group confirmed, as he had guessed, that it was not a community teasing of newlyweds but something much more mean-spirited.

I don't care if I hit one of them. They'd be paid for.

He yanked up the window sash and fired both barrels.

He saw the flash, knew the shot had hit the ground in front of them. At the last moment he had lowered his sights so as not to wound or kill after all. The sound had an effect anyway. The men were on the run down the road in an instant to where he guessed they'd left their horses.

"What's the matter?" someone yelled in the darkness. "Can't you take a joke?"

John reloaded, raised the gun, thought to fire again, then thought better of it and let them go. He turned to stay Art, finally there with his pistol in his hand. Art had forgotten that he'd taken it out from under the feather bed for the wedding night, and had groped for it all over before remembering it was in a drawer.

After John got everyone back to bed he went outside with the shotgun, just in case. All was quiet. He nearly fell over a washtub left behind. Good thing he didn't trip with the gun loaded. It would have been an awful thing to shoot himself in the gut on such an occasion. The washtub was fine except for a few dents. He picked it up and carried it inside for Anna. She would be pleased to see it, he thought, and now could get rid of one of the heavy wooden ones which were even heavier when water-soaked.

THE SHOTGUN BLAST had torn a six-inch gash in the front yard. Leonard and Spencer dug for the shot but didn't find much. Art and Leah continued to sleep in the front bedroom where the rifle bullet hole in the doorjamb was actually two or three feet away from where Leah's head would have been, depending on how close she'd been to Art, and higher up on the frame.

Roland put his finger in the bullet hole when he passed by the front bedroom on his way downstairs.

"Mother." He pinched off a little piece of her cookie dough and ate it raw. "I don't think I want to get married."

It would be awful to get shot just for getting married.

She smiled. "All right, Roland, you can stay here with me."

He watched her put the little balls of dough on the black baking sheet. "You have a long, long time to think about that though," she said.

He did not want to leave, did not ever want to leave.

ART AND LEAH stayed on with John and Anna until the move to Tennessee. Her late husband's estate was finally settled largely in her favor in spite of there being no will and no children, but when the Bayleys left Faith, Art and Leah did too, settling first in the next valley over outside Queensburg, then moving on up North and staying so long that Leah's speech changed to the point that no one hearing her would have thought she'd ever even seen a mountain.

. · . . · .

FAITH, 1910

Anna looked down to see her work-rough red knuckles whitening on the back of the pew in front of her, she was gripping it so hard in her fury. The preacher was not going to recognize her, not call on her, would not let her speak, no matter what. All of their minds were made up already and nothing she could say would make any difference. But she stood determined to try to say it anyway.

"May I be recognized? I wish to speak on Sister Warren's behalf. Please hear me. You've heard everybody else." She thought how, given the nature of her friends, she should have been more likely to have been speaking for Alice instead of Bina. But then Alice's husband watched her like a hawk. With reason.

"No, you may not be recognized. Mind your place, Sister Bayley. Women are not to speak in church and that's from the Holy Writ. Saint Paul." Men were always quoting Paul, more than Jesus. They liked Paul better.

"If you have something on your heart, have some man say it for you, your good husband perhaps."

John? Good husband? Speak for me?

He was one of the deacons and as keen to see her friend Bina churched as all the rest of them, though when it came to adultery, he was in no way fit to cast the first stone. So Bina's baby had come a year after Eben went out to Montana, so what? He'd owned it when he got back, hadn't he? The child had his name. If he could forgive, shouldn't they? Until seventy times seven? Obviously a married man shouldn't have left to join sheepshearers in the first place. Wasn't there some wrong, neglect, on Eben's part? She had put these arguments before John, who hadn't listened any better than Brother Harbin. It was not the first time and surely not the last. They made nothing of bastards and first children who came too soon, but Bina was a high-spirited young woman they wanted to make an example of, even many months after the fact. And maybe Brother Harbin had never forgiven her for seeing the Virgin Mary.

A man had to be sure of his wife, didn't he? That adulteress! Some of them looked as if they could remember back to stonings and liked those memories. Brother Harbin had at least declared the fruit of her sin to be innocent.

Oh, noble of him, wasn't it?

"Sister Bayley, sit ye down and mind your brazen tongue. We don't want to be a-churching thee." Churching, they probably would not stop at churching, but might try to send her off certified to a state institution, they were that strong on their rules.

She was quivering now, felt her hat shaking on her head in spite of its pin. Men were sitting there pious and in judgment who she knew for a fact had plotted murder as a mob, perhaps one who had done or would do a killing. And maybe the arsonist who had burnt down the first church on this very spot. Making and drinking whiskey were nothing to them, nor fornication either, but a man must be sure of his legal seed, mustn't he? She remained standing, would stand there till she got to speak. Would stand till hell froze over. Where was the man at fault? Probably right there in the church this minute. And he wouldn't say a mumbling word, nor take any of the blame.

She remembered how she might have come close to knowing, completely by accident. She had taken Maudie one day while the boys were at school and walked all the way to Bina's to take her the set of number-eight wool cards Bina had said she wanted to borrow. Anna had had nothing in mind but a good walk with the baby and a chance to see her friend for the first time in a while.

But Bina would not let her come in.

She had come out of the house at Anna's knock, pulling the front door closed behind her and stood there holding on to the knob as if to keep it shut while she shook her head, saying no, nothing was wrong when wrong was plain on her face.

He, whoever he was, must have been there with Bina. Was it someone she truly cared for, or only a neighbor who helped out while Eben was away and took pleasure for his pay? Anna had no way of knowing. Bina never said.

Oh, Bina.

"Brother Bayley, would ye set your good wife down so that we may continue our business?"

Would John obey Brother Harbin? He'd been no good friend to the preacher since Harbin preached against deathbed conversions, which, he claimed, were a way of cheating. If one held that those were valid, why then a man could be the worst of sinners and delay and delay until the last moment, then attempt to make it all come out right with the final breath. How could that be fair to those good people who struggled against temptation and kept their slates spotless all of their lives? John had said that was against the Bible, which was plainly in favor of such, including forgiveness for the thief on the cross.

Thinking of himself, his own end?

But now John was right there with all the others. He stood up from his place in the front with the rest of the deacons as if to come and do to her as the preacher bade.

Too much, too much. No.

On either side of her Leonard and Spencer, who was only seven and certain not to understand, tugged at her skirt, trying to pull her down. They looked terrified.

"Never mind about churching me, Brother Harbin, I shall church myself." She moved past Leonard's knees and out of the pew. "Not you," she said to the boys who looked as if they didn't know whether to go or stay. "Come home with Dad. I'll be there."

SHE HAD THOUGHT she might cry once she got outside, but instead she felt exhilarated, strong. An illusion, she was sure, but a pleasant feeling. There was something liberating in the notion of never having to go to church again, not put on the stays, nor the hat with feathers and pin, not hear another dreary sermon that Ward Harbin would pull out of his dusty bag, punctuated by amens for sentiments few of the congregation chose to live by. The music. She would miss the music, the parts on the old hymns. Singing and looking up the hill to the little cemetery on the high slope under the sky. That was all. Would not even miss the cup they passed in close communion, remembering how the last time she had looked down into the red-purple blood of Christ there seemed to be a strange, blank eye winking there on the surface, looking back, but not really seeing her, looking at nothing.

With a little inward laugh she suddenly wondered if Bina would feel the same way when they got through churching her. What a good joke that would be if her punishment also turned out to be a great relief! She would go call on Bina again, both of them outcasts and sinners. Maybe they could sing together. They could hymn praises to God all on their own. She felt sure he would be in some other places besides the church in Faith.

Her mother used to read aloud to them all from her German Bible, never explaining a word, nor telling them how what she was reading corresponded to the King James. Monroe would ask but Tina would never say. Perhaps by that time she herself had forgotten what some of the words meant and was only guessing at how to pronounce them from what she did remember. Anna always loved the rich rough sound of the voice of God in German, but that her mother would not, or perhaps could not, teach her the language had made her fear back then for her immortal soul.

Did she fear for it now, at this moment? She thought not.

At the crossroads in front of the schoolhouse she became aware that someone was walking along beside her. It was he, in the open, in Faith, in broad daylight. He walked along haltingly, as if in pain, leaning on his cane, but his eyes were as merry and kindly as ever. She knew him by now for a ghost of someone, but instead of being frightened anymore she was immeasurably cheered. Who had he been, she wondered, and why did he come to her? Long ago on the mountain he had been drawn to her in some way, and now he was there, she knew, because of the trial she had come through. They proceeded slowly, silently, she not looking steadily at him, he leaning on his cane. At the turn of their lane he stopped, raised his hat to her and vanished.

THE CHICKEN HAD been soaking in milk in the springhouse all morning. After she changed to a housedress she battered it and, when the water drops danced in the skillet grease, threw it in. She fixed the rest of the meal and had it on the table when they came home. John did not speak to her. After she cleared and washed the dishes she took her poetry scrapbook out onto the porch and sat in the rocker reading all afternoon.

John went out again, without speaking, headed who knew where.

Down in the gully where the skunks came by night to scavenge, a host of tiny slate blue butterflies swooped and swarmed over the chicken offal, the head, its eyes and beak open.

Father, we have all sinned and come short of the glories. Where are those promised glories? John is unfaithful. The boys grow up willful, beset with idleness and dreaming. And I, have I sinned and fallen short? Perhaps I have always wanted more than my due. But cannot my longings be balanced against my afflictions?

Young, I wanted the great doors to swing open and possibilities to lie out there beyond like an endless, unpeopled, unclaimed land. I got a philandering husband, some saddened children for whom I was the third mother, babes of my own, bright, but taken with their own distresses and sickness.

And, oh, yes, I wished for a great wild horse to ride, like my father's mother had, earrings of jet and gold, a library of my own. But even my wedding ring is third-hand. If it is unlucky to marry twice with the same ring how can there be any luck at all the third time? But when you come to think on it, how all gold is likely to have been used, reused, made into money, made into rings again, it's near certain all of it at one time or another has been on some wife's finger. How lucky does that make any bride?

"YOU'RE NOT READY." He had tied his tie by the mirror over the bureau, even placed his Bible on the table by the front door and she was still at the dining table with a second cup of coffee, book in hand, her hair piled loosely, her wrapper open.

"I'm not going today. I have too much to do."

He took the boys and left. He would steam all through the service in that hot suit, she thought with some satisfaction.

"Your mother has too much to do," he told them when they asked.

By time for them to be home, the weekly miracle would have occurred. Breakfast would be cleared away, a bowl of zinnias and hydrangeas on the table, potatoes boiling, chicken frying, tomatoes sliced, beans cooked, pickles in their oval dish, pie for dessert. They would eat up everything, probably in silence.

SUPPOSE, JOHN, JUST suppose how it would be to have no names for days, no Monday, no Sunday, to feel worshipful or to take a day of rest whenever you felt like it.

WHEN SHE LOOKED at the church afterward she had the feeling that no way on earth could she enter that place again of her own free will, that she would have to be taken in by force and would lapse into fits the moment her body passed over the threshold.

Amongst friends much salt is eaten.

· ˙ · ˙ ·

FAITH, 1911

Alice came up the Bayleys' lane with her sewing box under her arm, walking in a hurry and swinging her mending stuffed in a pillow slip. She brought news that Jim Dotson had just dropped dead, fallen straight down in the field while plowing, his face in the dirt. The mules had walked on a piece, pulled the arm that had the reins around it straight up over Jim's head before the lines unwrapped and trailed behind them. What was first noticed was those mules standing stock-still in the middle of the field. By the time they got to him, Alice said, Jim was already gray and going cold.

What was it about awful happenings that folks liked so much? Anna wondered. John couldn't wait to tell her about Jim cutting the end of his finger off while on the timbering crew all those years ago. Enjoying bad news was certainly perverse, but enjoy it they did, for all that their faces were so long and tones so doleful. And she was no better about it than anyone. When the word went around that Jim had not had a moment's warning of ill health she and everyone else gave themselves light little shivers about being struck down in one's prime, but each one personally felt immortal.

And immediately they would all begin to think of what they could cook to take to the Dotsons', bad news always bringing forth the idea of food.

BINA, ALICE, TEMPE, and Maggie. This is my church now and they my congregation. We hold close communion when we pass the coffee and the gingerbread and the text for the day is opinion, gossip, and distress. And sometimes our joys.

"WHAT'S IN THE gingerbread, Anna, that gives it that special taste?"

"Dried orange peel." Christmas oranges, not a bit of them ever going to waste.

THEY HAD ALL been her friends since she came to Faith. At the first house they would climb the bank, hastening their young ones along with them to sit a spell on the porch while they knitted, embroidered, mended, and darned. They laid their infants on pallets, turned the toddling babies onto the grass inside the picket-fenced yard, and allowed the slightly older ones to jump off the side of the porch, climb back up the steps, jump off again, climb, jump, climb, over and over.

At the Colvard place they usually gathered by the parlor fire during school hours. They still brought work that could justify the time they spent together. During the afternoons they took turns, as they always had, reading aloud their favorite stories from *Comfort Magazine,* the news and editorials from the *Democrat* and the *Toledo Weekly Blade.* John subscribed to the latter two and the five women all subscribed to *Comfort* because of their lace curtain plans.

The Russians and the Japanese were having at each other again, and Mrs. Roff turned out not to be dead after all, but was discovered to be with relations in Germany. After that bitter, terrible divorce she had escaped from the hospital for the insane where her former husband had placed her, apparently because he wanted control of her fortune. A letter she wrote back inquiring about her property indicated that she was in full possession of her wits.

Lightning, Tempe had heard, struck a barn over in Beaver Dams, burnt it to the ground, the stock luckily having been gotten out, and Anna was prompted to tell, not for the first time, how Leonard had started over a barbed-wire fence on the way home during a thunderstorm.

"He had climbed over it but still had his hand on the top wire. It struck somewhere up on the ridge, not anywhere near him, but the current traveled down the wire, gave him a terrible shock and burned his hand. He hides under the bed now when it storms."

"My next-to-youngest, he's awfully afraid in storms too. He can cry just hearing one of Harv's boys tell about how lightning on the mountain makes hair stand up on your body."

They each had lightning stories, stories of drownings in millponds, of children falling out of apple trees, or being run over by wagons. Out of kindness to Anna they did not often speak of children being burnt, remembering the Oliver child. The accounts of little ones in peril were cautionary, to learn by, and were repeated for safety's sake, not for pleasure.

But at times Anna felt they could be less kind. Alice said she thought it was a terrible thing to marry for carnal love alone and that a woman should look for a good provider and good father to the children she would have. Alice was small and lithe as a limber twig, could whip about in a breeze and not break. But she could also turn and make someone feel the sting of her lash. It was a sharp thing she said in Bina's presence and, if they only knew, in hers too.

GAGE. GAGE STOOD there holding her cat in the middle of the damp garden path so I could not get by. And she told me one need not marry for love, that there could be advantages in not doing so. She spoke under strain, as if the words were not her own at all, or as if she could see how it might be for her without someone like Andrew Hodges. The cat squirmed in her arms and got mud all over the front of her skirt.

Mrs. Alba going in or out of a room, the way she lightly touched her Ralph each time, only the gentlest brush of her fingers. Where had Gage gotten such an idea and why did she feel she had to pass it on? More like

advice from Lucille than from Gage. Was she trying to make me recon-
sider David? Or was it something else entirely?

Gage never took such advice, nor did I. My choice was as carnal as
they come. Whatever the advantages of a practical marriage, neither of us
would know them. Even if Gage had come back from the dead with a
complete vision of the future, it could not have dissuaded me from that
first wild year. Oh, the great happy laugh of letting him inside then! The
great desire, the greatest desire.

"YOU CAN'T COUNT on it," said Tempe. "Those kinds of feelings
just go away. It's sort of a trick."

"Freida Ragan has run off from Dudley Gaither, or so he
claims." Maggie made her knot and bit off the end of the thread. She
took up another shirt to turn its frayed and worn collar.

"Wonder why it took her any time at all to pick up and go after
her mother died. That old buzzard is sour and bitter as they come.
But when you think on it," said Tempe, "some of the blame is at our
door. We shouldn't have left no fifteen-year-old there alone in the
house with a man not related to her. One or the other of us could
have taken her in."

"Oh, like hired help, you mean." Anna watched Tempe pull the
blue thread through a daisy petal on the pillow sham she was
embroidering. Unlike Alice and Bina, Tempe did not bring things
like her husband's socks to darn or her children's clothes to mend,
but always had some fancywork at hand. "You're showing off again,
Tempe," Bina had said when the sham was first unrolled.

"Yes, something like that. Goodness knows, there's aplenty of
work in any household hereabouts." But which of them, Anna wondered, would have wanted a slim, curly-haired young thing like
Freida under the same roof with their husbands?

"Hired girls? You have to watch them too much. They get
notions in their heads, and off away from family, their drawers get
so hot . . . Oh, Anna, sorry. Present company excepted, of course."

Bina blushed all over her pretty round face. She probably realized it was nothing she should be saying either.

Anna laughed to ease the strain. "Don't think I don't know about hot drawers. You're right, though. You do have to be careful, very careful in such a position."

The picture of Mr. Alba leaning over in his pants with the shiny seat came to her. It amused her, but there was never anything between her and Mr. Alba, certainly not. The way Mrs. Alba felt about her Ralph, Anna would have been strangled in her bed had she had a single thought in that direction, never mind how kind he had been to her with the books and all. But then there had been David. That thought returned unbidden now and again and it hurt, especially now, conscious as she was of all that was missing. What if she had listened to Gage after all and held David to his proposal?

"I hate to speculate," said Alice, "but Dud Gaither does have a lot to gain from her being gone. It's Freida's mother's place he squats on, after all. If he could do away with the daughter, and no one the wiser, well, wouldn't he be sitting pretty? You could say he might not have Freida's best interest at heart. Remember he never said nothing about it until she'd been gone who knows how long." She leaned toward the others in the group, her black eyes flashing in her pale little face. "I've heard talk at the store about lost children, their bones, a few of them anyway, being found later out in the woods, scattered all over the place by bears." Her thin voice went as low as it could. "Maybe Dud heard the same thing. Maybe he might have thought he could do away with her somewhere and blame it on wild animals."

Anna didn't want the girl lost or dead. "Both of you are probably way off. Most likely, she's down the mountain working at one of those hotels in Lenoir. Has a new career, if you know what I mean." She wanted to call back the words the moment she'd said them. All of them knew how often John made trips to Lenoir. But what had come into her mind as a fate for Freida was possibly even worse than the other.

But before the month was out all of Faith knew where Freida was.

She had been seen running with him, that stray boy with no name who roamed the mountains, coming down only to steal, then fleeing with whatever he could find to carry off. The men from the store organized a hunt for the two of them. Those who showed no interest in whether or not Freida had had to sell herself into whoredom in Lenoir were obsessed with finding her now, and perhaps more obsessed with finding the boy she was with.

"She'll slow him down, hold him back. Women can't keep up. We can catch him now for sure. It's as good as if we had put out bait."

"They can't get all that far on shank's mare."

"But what if they take it in mind to steal a horse or two?"

"Then hanging's too good for them."

When the first hunts were unsuccessful they put it down to the rains, decided to try again later.

The couple were not found all summer and fall. Those hunting told themselves, "When the snow flies, then for sure we can track them." Winter came. But the boy and Freida were never found.

Walking in the white drifts to the barn Anna thought of the wild young couple. Perhaps they had turned to bones so far and deep in the forest that no one would ever see the place. Or maybe they had gone elsewhere, leaving who knew what in their wake on lonely and desolate roads.

. · . · · .

It was Maggie's turn to get the lace curtains since she had pulled the shortest straw. After the drawing Alice filled out all of their names and addresses on the form from the back of *Comfort Magazine* and collected the money. One pair of curtains came as a premium with five new subscriptions or renewals and Alice and Bina already had their curtains from the first times they had gotten together to subscribe.

Anna sent Roland to the post office with an envelope, the form, and the cash to get a money order from Eli and send everything on its way. Roland never minded trips to the post office. When he was small he used to run down the hill and across the creek to get to Eli's before the mail boy rode up on his pony. Now that he was older he no longer had to go behind the corncrib to pee lest he wet his pants in his excitement and anticipation of the dashing rider rushing up with both legs on the same side of his mount, ready to exchange mailbags in seconds. But the errand was still one he did without protest, though he no longer had those notions of carrying the mail himself. He said now that he wanted to write plays and John made fun of him, calling him a good-for-nothing poet.

Maggie was beaming, a smile on her tan face that showed most of her nearly perfect teeth. She was very proud of her teeth. Not many had them as good.

"How long did they take to get here?" she asked Alice. "Do you remember? I don't know as I can wait." All of them had been pleased with the quality of the curtains, especially Alice, who was fond of pretty things and, whenever she could, sewed new dresses for herself, or matching ones for the twins.

Anna was disappointed with her long straw but tried not to show it. After all, her turn would come, and then her curtains would be newer than those of her friends who had gotten them first. And she knew where she would hang them, not in the front room to show off to any passerby on foot or horseback, but in the bedroom where she could see the earliest light through them in the morning and the moonlight casting delicate patterns across the quilts at night. She would take down those old domestic ones she had made for her first house and reused at the Colvards', now showing thin spots and tiny holes. And she would make real curtain rods for the lace curtains, no more nails and string, not for those wonders.

"You're not sharing," they would say. "We should all be able to see each other's places getting fancied up," and Bina would try to pull a long face at her. But not everything need be shared. The placing of the curtains was between her and the sun, the moon, and whatever strange and untame that came roaming in the night.

"Anna, Anna, Anna." Tempe was snapping her slim fingers in front of Anna's face. "Where do you go when you start looking like that?"

"Uh? Looking like what?"

"Looking as far away as if you were over the ocean sea or way off up the mountain."

"Oh, just woolgathering, I guess. Thinking of something that came to mind for a moment."

Being haunted, yes. Old Ones whose places have been taken coming back to me. Something like that. She probably had the same look on her face that Roland did sometimes. Did the wild and the Old Ones haunt him too?

Lace curtains. A cloak of stars.

Nell would love some lace curtains. Perhaps she and her friends would keep on subscribing long enough for her to get not one pair but two and send one set out to Nell. She felt sure things were stretched too tight for the Hardys to buy any extras like that on their own.

"I've six to do for now, plus the hired girl, and the neighbors that help out in threshing season," Nell wrote. And Anna could see her at work, on the go from morning till night, her face and arms probably now so tan T.A. wouldn't have wanted to own her. Rush had long since decided Nell was not going to melt out of doors the way he seemed to think when they first moved out West.

She and Nell had had their monthlies together as soon as Anna started. That had never happened again, not even with Gage, nor was it ever likely to in the future. With Maudie someday? No, probably not. She might well be starting to go through the change by then.

Her friends took their last sips of coffee, gathered their things and turned to go. There they were, all four of them, departing, framed in her open doorway, light defining them. The dear ones, next to kin the dearest.

"Good-bye," she said, but inside she cried for them not to go, for them to stay and join with her, guard her against what might be to come.

· ˙ · · ˙ ·

This time the move was her doing as well as his, though she doubted that John had any idea how much she had to do with it, as she doubted that it wrenched him the way it did her. When she thought of leaving Faith she felt herself a bone being torn out of its socket. Her friends, her friends. When they were all young with little babies, their practical advice and caring had stood between her and Hannah's superstitions. She could never have done without them. If anyone had asked she would have said, yes, of course, they would be old women together. Now they were parting.

I could see us sitting by the hearth, singing together in quavering voices, spitting juice into the fire. If I'd told them, one or the other would have said, "Now that would be interesting, seeing as how not one of us dips or chews." And I might have said "We could take up tobacco in our waning years. You never can tell."

There was nothing else possible for the children's schooling she had her heart set on. The Three Forks Association's academy, which would have been within riding distance, had failed for want of students, and sending their children as far as the one in Globe or Edgemont would have meant boarding them. That, as John said, was impossible.

"No way can we pay that amount of money and do without their labor at the same time. A public high school maybe I would consider, but, as you see, there's not one, nor is there likely to be in the foreseeable."

A public high school. She wrote a letter to her brother Dick in Queensburg.

Mr. Green in the Faith school taught subjects only to grade six and all three of the boys had gotten that far and all in less than six years, they were that bright. Roland had gone two terms to the Mast Seminary where they had elocution, art, and music and the only piano in those parts, brought to Shouns by train, then hauled over the mountains from there by wagon. Miss Hatcher played the beautifully carved square instrument for assembly, and another teacher loaned Roland "Rip Van Winkle" and "The Legend of Sleepy Hollow" from her own library, but he had already had all the subjects that the principal taught.

"Why can't I go back next term? I know it's two dollars a month but Miss Hatcher knows all those new songs. I could learn them for you. Did I tell you how one of the little girls threw up because her mother braided her hair so tight it made her sick?"

"It's only fair that the others should have their turn now. But don't fret too much. I have something in mind. And remind me never to do that to Maud."

"The *Christian Observer* that the teachers share, how are you going to do without that if I don't go?"

"Spencer and Leonard can borrow it for me. Now run on. Your father expects you at the barn as soon as you get home. You know that's why he has me send you off to school in your work clothes so you won't waste a minute changing."

DICK STOCKTON WROTE to John without telling him, as she had carefully specified, that he had heard from Anna. A place was up for sale not far from his that he thought John might like to know about.

"As soon as the hay is in, I think I'll go over and have a look. If it's half what Dick says it is, I could almost buy it sight unseen. Old man McCain is dead and none of the heirs wants to farm it or take the trouble to lease it out. They've all gone into the hardware business." John reached for his daybook, to calculate some, he said.

"Dick says they want all the money at once, but I can hardly believe how little they are asking. There must be a bog, a spring that fails, or mites in the beehives. I'll take Roby and we'll give it an A-1 inspection. He's got a good eye for small signs, that boy."

COULD SHE LEAVE? Had she set the right thing in motion? Her friends in Faith she had had for nearly half her life, and now she almost felt closer to them than to her own sister. And the house, she had made it her own. From the day she had taken lye and pennyroyal to scrub out the fleas left from Rufus's dogs, it had been hers. He had kept all his dogs inside while she never allowed more than one dog and one cat indoors and scrubbed them with the herb too.

That was the good use of pennyroyal. She had made bad use of it twice. First, she, who had never had any trouble carrying before, lost a baby without any trying in the fourth month. And the next two times she missed she drank the tea to the effect that she wanted. She was glad that it had not worked when she was pregnant with Roland, but now she wanted no more babies. If her friends had known they might have said Bina should have asked Anna what to do in her time of need. But probably Bina would not have taken such a remedy. She and Eben were both taken with the little boy and had become Methodists.

Four children were enough. She had those angry times when she threatened to burn their toys if they didn't put them away, could hardly bear the litter of their whistles, blocks, slingshots, and checkers, Maud's dolls and doll clothes. Enough, she thought, when he came to her, but she believed he would never leave off. Perhaps he sensed something, for in time he bothered her less and less and did not seem to think anything untoward when she miscarried three times in a row.

They still gathered in the parlor after supper, John with his newspaper, a farm journal, or his daybook, she with her magazine or book which she read while she knitted all those stockings, socks, mittens, caps, scarves, and towels. The children did their lessons around the lamp on the table, talking, pushing, and teasing one another. She saw visions in the fire sometimes of what could have been, then felt guilty for not loving strongly enough what she had.

Some evenings, when John was away, she brought out the cards and she and the boys played setback and hearts. She had taught them herself at home in preference to their going off somewhere else for entertainment. Besides, she had never had any idea that cards counted for a sin, no matter what was said in preaching. Nonsense. Those were good times, good, that is, unless someone trumped Spencer's jack of diamonds, a play that he could not stand. Her youngest son's temper was terrible to see and she suspected that from time to time the other boys avoided taking the card he thought was his alone. Spencer said he looked like the profile on the card and occasionally wanted his brothers to call him Jack. Surely they could all see the resemblance. He wanted to be told he looked like the king's son and that he would to grow up to marry the princess and have a beautiful life.

John came home unexpectedly one evening and found them just starting another hand. Daringly she showed off, shuffled the cards expertly as Gage and David had taught her long ago.

"Cut," she said to Leonard, and looked John straight in the eye.

"All you need," he said, putting his hat on the peg, "is a cigar and a shot glass at your elbow and you could be right at home in any bar or saloon there is." To her great surprise he grinned at her.

"Am I to be forgiven then for leading your sons astray?"

"I reckon."

．　·　．　．　·　．

Anna's father had come to their fireside recently when he and Tina
were feuding again, this time over furniture she wanted to give to
Dan. With only Roe left at home Tina felt they could easily let loose
of a number of things. It could be that T.A. didn't begrudge his son,
but, as John well knew, his father-in-law always wanted to have
absolute say and would leave home whenever he couldn't get his
way. He and Tina could not agree on what to give Dan so T.A. left
for a stay in Faith with John and Anna.

John realized that Anna did not find it easy to have him there,
especially now when they might be making ready to move. The old
man never turned a hand to help and the tales he told John and the
boys were endless, harsh, and cruel.

"The corporal said he wanted to go home, just wanted to piss one
more time without worrying if somebody was going to shoot his
pecker off while he was doing it."

John could let himself be overwhelmed by her father, the way he
had mastered both wounds and weapons, even imprisonment, knew
the smell of powder that killed men. He had been in the smoke, the
thick of it, gone most of the way through the war while John's own
father had been just a boy and Tina's first husband had been killed
almost immediately. An idleness that he would never have tolerated
in anyone else he ignored in T.A.'s character, perhaps for the sake of
the stories. The old man could be said to use his tales as currency to
pay for his keep away from home.

"On the day after my friend, my good friend, was killed, I saw
the general. And he came riding by to see us all, rank on rank. He
rode that big gray gelding and wore this wide yellow silk sash with
fringes, a hat with a feather, had a sword that shone in the sunlight.
Oh, he saluted and saluted because we had won the battle at New

Market, alongside those brave young cadets, most of them younger than your boys. And we cheered and cheered. My friend was near blown completely in two."

A man was surely foolish to regret being spared that, but a part of John envied the experience. Sometimes at night he pictured T.A. against the sky, in the smoke, firing, slashing, doing as a man should, in a role that likely would never be his.

"I got that horse I rode to Hillsville off a dead man, him just sitting there on it." T.A. had come across the animal stumbling along a backwoods path, a corpse leaning on its neck, feet still in the stirrups. The rider had been shot in the back. "A mercy," he claimed, "that I came along to relieve the beast of its burden."

John wondered why T.A. had not been mustered out with a mount. Had he been exchanged from the prison at Point Lookout or escaped on his own? It could be that he had never rejoined his unit at all, had just taken his leave and headed home. That, John knew, would have taken courage too, especially with the Home Guard marauding about at the time. Someday he would get up his nerve to ask the old man for the particulars. The gaps and inconsistencies in the tales were partly why he kept on listening.

"I took him down, set him on the ground, his back against a tree, turned out his pockets so no one else would disturb him with searching that way." T.A. poked the fire, took down a spill, and lit his pipe with it.

"You know, I'd seen all kinds of stuff, death every way you could imagine. But all I could think about while I handled that dead man and did those dirty, oily pockets was a bucket of cool water with a dipper beside it. Never been so thirsty in my life. Wasn't no spring in sight."

The smoke circled the head of the old man, twining past his thick white hair. "I prayed in the war like I ain't prayed before or since and many a better man, and some less so for sure, fell to my left and to my right. My wounds were never much and never festered. But somehow when those bushwhackers got onto me and took the horse, well, not much made me feel worse."

John watched the smoke rise farther and collect like a flimsy little shelf above the mantel. He had the urge to stand up and stir it away, but stopped himself.

"You were damn lucky to escape with your throat uncut," he told T.A. "Over on Green Hill they shot a man right in his own front yard of a Sunday afternoon with his wife and babies looking on. He was just standing there, hadn't done one thing to them, wasn't even armed. I've seen the vest he was wearing. The family kept it and shows it off. Big bullet hole right through from front to back. Now there's some pure devilment. I hope they all went straight to hell where they belonged."

"I don't know if it's right to curse about such deeds, it having been wartime and all." T.A. champed down on his pipe stem. "But I had prayed for that horse, or one like it. The Lord provided it for me, as with a ram in the thicket. I was due some recompense when it was taken, was I not?"

He didn't say what that recompense was, but John had heard this tale often enough to have figured out that T.A. meant a new bride, Tina. He didn't remind the old man that in the Bible the ram had been provided as a sacrifice to the Lord, that he would be getting it right back. Some things T.A. conveniently forgot.

A wife for a horse. Interesting how some folk evened things out.

There is salt between us.

· ˙ · · ˙ ·

John came back from Queensburg with his mind made up.

"You won't believe the house, the way it's been done up modern. It's big, brick, and old, but it has those things you know I've been wanting to give you." He had never thought of them before, but now he felt that he had, that he had always wanted her to have a place with electric lights, indoor plumbing, and a real separate bathroom. It was like his telling her Faith was called that because of the religious meaning, when it turned out to have been named for the wife of the first man in the valley with a land grant. For all of his usual insistence on accuracy, especially in others, he could sometimes come to believe things that were not so.

"What's the land like?"

"Couldn't be better, black and just loamy enough, rich. Even Roby—and you know how picky he is about cropland and everything else—even he couldn't find any fault with it. He's only ticked because he didn't hear of any good trout streams thereabouts. But there's a small creek, three or four good springs, and with excellent drainage. Bottomland and upland, more than forty acres cleared for cultivation and pasturage, and plenty of timber. Those McCains don't seem to know what they're letting go." He could picture her in the kitchen there, turning the tap for the water. Glory, in a place like that he could go all out and even buy her a sewing machine.

"Is there a high school, a public one?" she asked.

"What a school! Modern, everything up to date and the boys can walk there and back, Maud too, when the time comes. Our children are going to be educated!"

She turned away, looked as if she were about to cry.

"Did you hear me? Aren't you happy? It's everything you wanted."

"Yes, I'm happy."

"And the church, it's not much farther away than the school." He was hinting strongly that she attend. He didn't want her to be absent at the services in Queensburg as she had been in Faith. Even so, he knew she probably would not go. She said her Sunday mornings all alone were something precious to her. Perhaps. But he resented them. She was setting a bad example, perhaps even doing some evil.

THE BELONGINGS THEY were leaving behind were parceled out to relatives and friends. Anna gave Tempe the blue chairs because her friend had only benches and stools in her kitchen. It was hard to see those chairs rolling away in the wagon as she remembered the day John had come home with them, and how she had sat out on the grass, making each slat and leg and rung sky blue all by herself. The pungent, rich smell of the oil in the paint, the warmth of the sun came to her as she watched the chairs bob out of sight. And there had been something else that day, a longing she knew all too well how to put a name to, but had tried to set aside. Her yearning meant only loss, but not for anything she had ever truly had.

The tall cherry bureau with the split spindles on the front that Rufus had made for their tenth anniversary gift John sold to a cousin for five dollars. John's sisters got the cord beds because Anna was determined to have iron beds at the new house, no bugs lurking in the dark cavities of the rail slots or in the holes for the cords. And she wanted real mattresses, like the Albas had, no bedticks to empty, scrub, and restuff with new straw twice a year. John had said there would be less for her to do in the new place. She wondered if that were so.

The night before they were to leave she went out on the porch and sat in the rocker they were selling with the house. John had gone off somewhere and the stranger came, as she had thought he might, sat on the next to bottom step, his stick lying beside him, throwing pebbles out into the yard. They sat together that way for a long time.

If he spoke a few words, would I know him?

The pebbles made no sound when they fell and the next morning as the last things were loaded into the wagon she looked in the grass for the stones. There were some to be found but she was not sure they'd not been there before.

I should call him friend, not stranger. He is stranger to me no more.

The cradle that John had made for Roland that summer long ago, the one all of their children had slept in, was left far back under the house, sitting on one of the great foundation stones. John's hands carving the design of his own devising on the headboard, making the whole thing of fine cherry. Might as well leave it. None of her friends wanted it and there were not likely to be any more babies for her, given the way she felt and what with John finding his elsewhere most of the time. Was it with Jenny, the girl at the store, as she had long suspected?

THEY HAD NEVER held hands, nor danced in any circle, yet she saw them that way, whirling and turning together over the grasses, round and round again, as they came to bid her farewell, bringing the quilt.

That circle. She touched the hands that had stitched her friendship quilt, cooked food she had shared, soothed her children when hurt if they had been closer to them than she. She said good-bye and, as in the old game, broke the circle. The hands to either side of the break would join behind her, leaving her outside, somewhere running away from them and alone.

Was it a right thing they were doing? She had connived for it, for the schooling it would make possible. She could not bear to think of Roland's hands on a plow all of his life, on axes, hoes, and froes forever, the endless dirt and tiredness, his reading and writing nothing but almanacs and daybooks. John's thought was always the farm, the farm, his gain and profit. If she were on her deathbed she could bet that he would be talking to her of his crops, his hay and timber, his costs and plans for increase in yields, not of eternity.

There was more, had to be, the things Gage had talked of. At her age, with four children, she found she still wanted more for herself though she thought she had suppressed those longings years ago. Books to read, things to see, places to go. Elizabethton was not likely to ever have an opera or a ballet, and the Queensburg section right outside town would have still less to offer, but even so, there would be more than in Faith. There had to be. After all, Dickens and Bernhardt had toured; shows and circuses had even come to Boone.

Gage would have applauded this move. It would have appealed to her. And John, he had taken to the adventure and advancement of it. The uprooting, the distance, the journey, were nothing in return for the prize of a better farm in an area with a somewhat milder climate in winter, a fine brick house, indoor plumbing, and the electric lights he kept talking about. Never, she felt sure, would he have thought of moving for a high school alone.

She folded and smoothed the quilt her friends had made for her, recognized most of the scraps that had gone into it. The cream pieces with blue cornflowers were from Bina's summer Sunday dress, the wine stripe with wheat ears and ribbons had been Maggie's, a bright green with tiny multicolored flowers Alice had sewn into dresses for her twins, and bits from Tempe's traveling dress with the fine gray and white stripes were there too, all with their names embroidered. *Remember us, remember us,* it said in every stitch. *Love us now and forever.*

And in the upper center the block with the strange dark picture that Tempe had done.

"We didn't know whether to put it in or not," Alice whispered, "but after she had spent all that time on it . . . She traced it out of one of Mr. Green's books over at the school."

"Not anything I could do freehand, of course. Took more thread than I thought. I had to go back to Sherwood's twice for more floss," Tempe said.

Anna could imagine her sitting with her frame, wisps of her yellow-red hair fallen out of her bun and hanging on each side of her long white face as she took stitch after stitch after stitch.

The picture was on a solid white quilt block, but it was almost black with fine stitches that copied an engraving of a young man enveloped in a long cloak, leaning forward, a walking stick in his hand. It was difficult to say from the embroidery what the expression on his face might have been in the original engraving. Longing, expectation, exhaustion, fear, perhaps joy. But it was still obvious that he struggled on a tortuous path through a densely tangled forest toward a light shining through the trees from a house at some distance.

"Midwinter," said Anna, thought of *Armadale,* Leftwich, small blue books on the shelf, how she had taken them down eagerly in her hands. Whatever had happened to that friend?

"Looks more like November to me, some leaves still on the trees, but it's called 'The Wanderer.' See?" The caption was done in neat block letters across the bottom.

"Maybe it's all right after all," said Bina. "I guess you are wandering away from us, even if by wagon, instead of on foot through a dark wood." She kissed Anna on the cheek. "Think of us. Don't forget. And please write."

WHEN PACKING FOR the move Anna had found her wedding dress at the bottom of her trunk. Gage's ivory silk. After Maud was born she had been possessed by an unreasonable fear that when the girl was grown she might be tempted to clothe her in that gown, an act that could bring who knew what along with it. She remembered how she had placed the garment as far down as it would go, underneath everything else.

She pulled it out and stroked the folds of the skirt. The silk had not aged well, was already brittle, but the lace was still intact, though going yellow. She cut off all the trimming with John's straight razor, and put the lace in her sewing basket. The dress she rolled around her arm, carried it far off up the hill and hung it on a tree at the top of the ridge. It danced in the breeze like a ghost of someone hanged. As the wagons rolled out to their new home she looked back and thought she could see it waving good-bye in the wind.

· · · · · ·

QUEENSBURG, 1913

Water. Who would have thought that, after losing her friends, it would be water that she missed when she woke in the night?

When she couldn't fall to sleep again in the strange room, the new bed, she listened for the spring running. Hearing nothing at the new place she would get up only to turn the water on, to listen to it running in the night. It was not the same sound, was an action perhaps not even quite sane, but it was better than nothing.

If John waked he would curse. "Damn, you left the tap open again. You'll drain the tank that way. Can't you remember anything? You're not in the backcountry anymore."

Would that I were.

"Sorry, I keep forgetting. Can't seem to get used to it."

She would climb back into bed without going back to the bathroom and feign falling asleep at once. Usually John would nudge her until she got up again and turned it off. Or once in a while he would go close the tap himself. But on those nights when she was lucky he did not wake and she could listen, telling herself the lie that made it bearable,

It's the spring. It's the true old spring. Those waters of the mountains are born in the rocks themselves and gush forth in more clear, pure joy

than all the waves of the greatest ocean. You could worship them if you were a mind to.

And hearing the sound first thing in the morning she would get up before John woke and turn off the flow. The pump was never ruined and the tank never ran dry.

. . . . . .

John missed no springs at the McCain place. Free-flowing water he had aplenty. He missed Jenny.

He called her his "little Jenny Wren," though she asked him not to, said every girl in the world with her name probably had to put up with that. But she was like a bird, small-boned and thin, with round black eyes and flitting ways.

Of all the women he had had while married to others, Jenny was the only one who mattered much, though perhaps he could never have convinced Anna of that and, of course, never tried. Jenny was the one he sought out the night before the wagon left for Tennessee.

HE HAD WATCHED her for years, watched her grow up. But he had never been anything but distant and courteous, even took her on the trips to Lenoir and never touched her. Sherwood and his standing in the community put the fear in John and kept him from acting on what he started to feel and what he thought on far too much.

Then Anna tried to refuse him sometimes after her first miscarriage. Of course she didn't put him off every time. She couldn't do that and be true to her duty, but he couldn't force her every time he wanted. It was not the same, and both of them knew it.

"I have these pains in my back," she would say. "Could we wait . . . ?"

He didn't know whether the pains were real or not, nor if it was worth the trouble of an argument.

He knew Jenny was watching him too.

SHE MADE THE first move and after that there was no stopping. She was warm and eager. And young.

"I have always loved you," she said. "From the time I was little I said to myself that I would marry no one but you."

But he had not known. She had been much too young anyway. He had married Anna instead after Belle died, never having even considered Jenny for a wife, much as the sight of her might tease and heat him. It crossed his mind that now she was either light-headed or disremembering the fact he was already wed. Or she was ignoring it, was witchy, wishing Anna some evil so she could take her place.

But these considerations were quickly gone when she pulled up her skirts, sat in his lap, undid his fly, and kissed and licked his ear. She was not as strong and vigorous as Anna, but she moaned louder. Afterwards he would pick her up and carry her a good part of the way back from the moss and fern banks in the forest, or the high grasses of the field, her arms around his neck, her hot breath in the crease of his neck and shoulder.

SHE HAD A pure screaming fit when he told her they were moving to Tennessee.

"Don't you dare go off and leave me like this. I saved it for you. You were the first. You know it. And you don't love her anymore, if ever you did. We are the most important thing in the world to each other. And that you well know."

"It's for the boys' sake, so they can go to high school and all." He was not about to get into a discussion of his true feelings for Anna or the advantages of the McCain place. He could put his sons first with Jenny, but not his land greed or his wife.

She twined her thin little arm around his and took his hand. Her grip was tight and stronger than he would have expected. "You can't leave. I shall never let you." She looked up at him, her eyes bright and determined.

He decided then that this move would truly be a good thing. And for more reasons than he had thought of before.

THE LAST TIME they were together they lay in a real bed for the first time, the Colvards' lumpy old cord bed in Rufus's house, the house John had built, board by board, shingle by shingle. Rufus had set his parents' bed in the same corner where John's and Anna's had stood, and if he had stayed until morning, he would have seen the same sights out of the window.

Rufus was away surveying again. He had a new partner now that John didn't take on those contracts anymore. John had said nothing to Rufus about using his house, wondered if he would even notice that someone had been there when he returned. Rufus favored Anna. If he knew, he would not like it.

Jenny fell completely silent, not even a moan. When it was done she turned her face to the wall and, stiffened with rage and despair, would not look at him or speak when he got up to leave.

· · · · ·

Anna upset the fortuneteller from the caravan, but she had no idea why. The only bad thing the seer predicted was far away, concerned none of them, but she could tell when the woman left that she was distressed. And after Anna had given her all that food too.

THE QUEENSBURG FOLK had come by the McCain place complaining when John let the gypsies into the hay field to camp after the grass was cut and in the barn loft.

"We'll be stolen blind. You'll be sorry. We'll be sorry. If this is the same group that stopped over near Bristol, well, when they left there lots of chickens and at least three pigs were taken and who knows what else folks haven't missed yet."

They also suspected, but with no proof at all, that John gave the gypsies permission when no one else would to intentionally make more trouble between himself and his neighbors. John Bayley was not fitting in well in Queensburg. Already it was obvious he managed better than most around and they didn't like the way his wife talked either. Several of them said they wished they had known the McCain heirs were willing to let the place go so cheaply, that they should have been able to buy it and keep outsiders out.

They sensed one of his reasons, true enough, but not the others.

The gypsies were a scraggly bunch of people, dirty, strangely dressed, but they had marvelous horses. Great strong draft animals to pull their brightly decorated carts and fine riding horses for the men.

"Stolen," said the people of Queensburg.

People who appreciate good horses, and know how to adorn them.

Their saddles and harness, bridles, all of their leather work was finely made and well cared for. The art, the beauty of it. He was taken completely by it, obsessed almost, wanted it for his own. For an amount of leather work bargained for and agreed upon he arranged to swap the use of the campsite, water, and oats for the horses.

ANNA FORBADE THE boys to go down to the camp. She did not have to forbid Maud because Maud was terrified of the strangers and stayed in the house most of the time the gypsies were there. If the boys disobeyed her she didn't want to know about it. She wondered if she should ever have told them not to go. They were growing up fast and didn't one learn by new experiences? Gypsies were a new experience for certain, almost dark as colored, though not so featured. They put her in mind of her friend Maggie and those part-Indian-blooded Kilbys up the hollow from Faith. Their clothes were extravagant but dingy from long travel and dust. They washed some in the creek while in the encampment, but it did not seem to make the clothes any cleaner or brighter. Anna passed them as she walked to the store, or her favorite place, the library in town. She wondered if they had with them any little dogs that could dance on their hind legs, like in Collins's book. The children were pretty, with sharp features and black curly hair. Even the small boys and girls wore earrings.

She touched her earlobes, the holes long since grown over. After the pair David had given her were lost she had worn threads in her ears for a long time, in case by some miracle her earrings might be found. But Roland had put them on his fingers, worn them into the woods where they had slipped off and out of sight, those bright little hoops likely hidden forever under leaf mold and pine needles.

And all of the gypsies had beautiful dark brown eyes. She had wanted a baby with brown eyes, thought that with John having dark hair and an olive complexion she might have one, but all their children had grown to be fair like her and to have either blue or green eyes. And now with things the way they were between her and John much of the time she doubted there would be any more children, any chances for brown eyes.

JOHN WAS OFTEN in the camp. He talked horses with the gypsy men while the new harness and a saddle were being made. He told them about his horses, about Rocket, how Rocket had been stolen and how he had traced his prize mount and gotten him back, the lengths he had gone to. He told them this so they would know how he kept up with his own property and would guess he kept animals fast enough to track down any slow-moving wagons.

When he came back with some of the gypsies' stories to repeat

Anna regretted her prohibition because, if the boys couldn't go to the camp, then neither should she. She felt a little uncertain, but at the same time she longed to go down there anyway, to see and listen for herself. But when Anna did not go to the gypsies, a gypsy came to her.

THE WOMAN KNOCKED at the back door. She was not old but her face was lined and seamed with smoke and dirt. She wore a red fringed rag around her head and held a long clay pipe between her teeth. It was not lit. She apparently had a cold.

"For food," she said, and held up a pair of gold earrings.

Anna almost gave her the larder.

THE GYPSY WOMAN tied the jam, cheese, sausages, salt, and potatoes into her shawl and gave Anna the earrings. Anna offered her a jar of pickles, giving as a sample one from the pressed-glass dish on the table.

"No, thank you," said the woman, politely as any Alba.

Anna asked where the caravan was going. The woman said there was talk they might stay in Queensburg for a while. It would be good to stop, at least for a bit.

"And with your husband, a man of influence in the community, to speak for us, this might be possible."

Anna thought of John's real standing in Queensburg and felt that the gypsies had some misplaced faith if they were depending on him for their bond.

The gypsy started to leave with her bundle, then turned back suddenly.

"Your fortune?" she asked Anna.

Gage and her cards. Do I want to know now? At last?

She thought of the cards lying in the wastebasket long ago where Gage had thrown them, how she had taken them out as instructed to use to build the fire. But she had saved one, slipped it into her apron pocket. *The Queen of Wands.* She had kept that card for years. Where was it now?

"How much?"

"This is enough." The woman patted the bundle in her shawl.

Anna felt suddenly giddy with excitement and daring. She clutched the earrings. She didn't care if they turned out to be brass, or, worse, the earrings of the dead. They were the main thing. The fortune was really just for fun, wasn't it, as David had said so long ago?

She and the woman sat down at the kitchen table and she gave her red callused hand into the dark one. The gypsy woman looked oddly upset and that puzzled Anna. She did not really believe in such things as fortunes, had resisted crediting Gage's forecasts and would not believe in anything that the woman said, but she thought that all predictions were supposed to be positive because that was good for the fortune-telling business.

"A great darkness, across the ocean," said the gypsy.

What about me?

"A long and happy life?" she asked. There seemed to be a third person in the room, but only for a moment.

The woman stirred uncomfortably. "That I cannot tell. It is not clear. There is a journey . . ." She looked into Anna's face and her deep eyes were as blank as the eye in the cup of communion wine. Prophecy was perhaps a dark art after all, not to be taken lightly. A danger to the soul.

"Your children. I can see that they will prosper and honor you all the days of their lives."

Anna was disappointed then. It sounded so bland and ordinary. She had good children. Of course they would honor her into her old age, as she did Tina. Nothing remarkable in that.

Then the woman smiled as if relieved to be able to predict something else. "And you will have another child. I believe it is a boy. With brown eyes."

"I don't see how. . . ." Anna saw John coming down from the barn. She noticed as he approached that he was putting on more weight than she had realized. He was nearing fifty, losing his hair too.

She pulled her hand away.

"I don't believe you," she said. "I don't know if I believe you at all."

QUEENSBURG, 1914

Tina came to Queensburg when Anna went out to nurse Nell. Anna worried over it since Tina and John had never gotten on well together, but Nell was dying and had asked for her. Who could refuse?

For the sake of our childhood together, dear sister, I would see you once more, have you with me at the end.

The handwriting was still Nell's strong, looping scrawl. "It could be she's wrong about the end," John said when Anna showed the letter to him. But she told him it was a summons that could not be disobeyed. Maud was only seven, but already a busy, capable little body, well able to help Tina. He could see Anna was determined to go.

"I haven't the faintest idea what I will find when I get there."

"What if I keep you from going?" he said.

"Then I'll throw myself off the bridge."

"What will I do if something happens while you're gone?"

"The same as I do when you're away, the best you can. I'll telegraph you as soon as I see how things are."

"You're set to go off and leave me in pain like this?" John was in bed with one of his attacks of dyspepsia.

"It will pass. Drink the tea like I told you. It will give you ease. Mama can brew some more if you need it."

"She might take a notion to poison me."

Anna gathered her clothes and went into the bathroom where he could hear the tap running. He closed his eyes, staved off a spasm, and remembered how she used to bathe and dress in front of him. The water would splash from the pitcher, slop out of the basin and soak the toilet cover when she moved in such a hurry that drops went everywhere. She would have stabbed a few pins through the rope of her hair to hold it up while she washed her neck and arms. He had loved to watch her. Would still love to. Her hands had been hard and coarse ever since he had known her, but her arms were smooth and graceful. She would wipe them with the rough toweling, a morning glow from the window behind her outlining the fine hairs and letting light shine through flying droplets of water.

From the dining room came the usual sounds of the boys' discussions and squabbles. They were breakfasting on the meal Anna had set in the warmer before she started dressing for her trip. Tina and Maud were out already seeing to the geese and chickens and running around doing who knew what else. That woman could not be trusted to keep them all going. Roby would have to take time from his own place to keep the chaps hustling while he was laid up. Damn, it was a terrible time for Anna to take it into her head to go somewhere.

Nell. Anna had seen her only twice in more than twenty years. What kind of a claim of sisterhood could there be? Of course they wrote to each other, but it was not as if they were close anymore. He saw his own sisters oftener than that, sent them money now and again when they had troubles and reverses, but he thought it unlikely that either of them would think to send for him from a deathbed.

He had another attack as Anna came back from the bathroom. She took the cooling flatiron off his stomach, carried it to the kitchen and brought him a warm one wrapped in a flannel.

"Thanks."

As he lay on the bed watching her he thought of the way she looked and realized he didn't watch her often enough now. He had an unexpected wish to enjoy her dressing the same as a man might a woman's undressing, to appreciate the long, thin stockings, the narrow shoes with the strap over the instep, embroidered underthings, the slim silky burgundy dress, "lily red" she called it, with the high waist and the lace trim, the swirl of hair swept up as a cushion for her hat. While it pleased him that she kept up with fashion now, made stylish clothes on the new sewing machine, outfits that even the Queensburg ladies could not scoff at, and no longer dressed in the long skirts and shirtwaists, he also remembered fondly the volume and billows of petticoats, the ripping, shredding sound made when she pushed her arms through starched, fresh-ironed sleeves. Yes, he should pay her more attention, fine-looking woman no matter what she wore. Or didn't wear. He had the urge to grab her about the waist and throw her on the bed. Sometime, but not right now. His stomach hurt too much. When she returned.

She fastened onto her bosom the bar pin she used to wear at her throat, settled the turbanlike hat with its rose and iridescent wings on the pile of straw-colored hair. Likely, he thought, she would never show much gray.

When she stood there complete she seemed very tall, and of course she was well over average, as he was. And so strong, like the very first day he saw her. He stretched out his hand. Don't go, he wanted to say. He wanted to say, Please. She touched his hand briefly.

"Dick and Polly will be here soon to take me to the station in Johnson City. I mustn't be late."

He wanted her to say, I wish you were coming too. Wanted a kiss.

The bedroom door closed. There was a murmur in the dining room, a little rise in the voices, then good-byes. The front door opened and closed.

He must get up. He had the impulse to go to the window and watch her walk down their drive. He imagined the white shirtwaist, no, she had on the dark wine dress with all the tucks. And her hat, he could fancy her hat borne swiftly along on top of her hair, the last thing he would be able to see, going into the distance.

He did not look. It was bad luck to watch anyone out of sight. And he didn't want anything to happen on the train.

SHE DID NOT know what had made her so brazen before leaving, but right in front of him she had opened the linen drawer where he never looked and pulled out from under the all-white summer coverlet the gold hoop gypsy earrings and the four-button gloves that she had bought at Leftwich's and never let John see in all the years she had owned them. And standing before him she had put the earrings in her secretly repierced ears, pulled on the gloves, buttoned the buttons, slowly, one at a time, as he watched.

"But I thought the boys lost your earrings."

She hadn't answered him.

. · . . ` .

She had not ridden a train since the excursion Tina had sent her on to try to cheer her when she had come back grieving from the Albas. There were many modern things now, like those electric lights that had looked so harsh and shadowless the first time she saw them in houses as they came over the mountain on the move to Queensburg. She was used to them, and sometimes glad of not having to scrub black off of all the lamp chimneys. Trains. Rufus showing *The Great Train Robbery* in the schoolhouse back in Faith, running the projector with a little generator, and using a bedsheet hung up behind the teacher's desk. He had charged a penny apiece to get in, three pins for those who didn't have pennies. After he had paid for his projector from the Sears Roebuck catalog he had shows for free every other Saturday night until they had all seen all of the pictures so many times they knew everything by heart. Not even the bandit firing his pistol point-blank at the audience made them jump anymore.

That was the first time she had realized how utterly strange and changed things were going to be, already were, not just automobiles instead of horses, and mills instead of hand looms in weaving sheds, but everything, and realized that her children could not stay in Faith if they were going to get on.

Trains, however, had not changed all that much, at least not the one from Johnson City to Knoxville. The seats were dark red plush instead of horsehair but everything else was the same, the lurch and sway, the noise of the wheels, smoke and cinders blowing by the windows. She closed her eyes, remembering that earlier excursion. The towering hat with its huge bow that she wore, her first grown-up one, her long skirt and the shirtwaist with fullest sleeves, her gold bar pin, a present from her father to make up for one of his many absences. The picnic they'd had at a healing spring before they caught the train on its run back toward Boone in the afternoon. She had had her first picture taken that day, with the whole excursion group. She and her hat were so tall the photographer put her in the back row.

"But you really stand out," Leonard would say when he took the photograph down off the mantel to look at it. "My mama is a beautiful woman."

WHEN SHE OPENED her eyes, a man in a dark suit, white shirt, and a string tie was sitting opposite her. She had not heard him sit down. Had she been asleep? Why was he sitting there so close to her when the car was almost empty near the beginning of the run? She had never seen him before, she knew, yet something about him she tried to place. He took off his hat, laid it on the seat beside him, and smoothed back his black hair. He smiled and she saw that he was some years younger than she, had white teeth in a dark, tanned face. She guessed why he had sat down with her.

"IN THE STATION," he said later. "I saw you and wondered, Why does that pretty lady look so sad?"

His name was Martin Daniels. He was living out West and was now headed back there from a sorrowful errand of his own, arriving home too late to bury his father but staying long enough to arrange to sell the farm and auction the tools and livestock.

"I didn't realize much, I'm afraid. Poor old man, he'd let a lot go in his later years." He took up his hat and rolled it around in his hands. "I shouldn't have gone when I did. I should have stayed, at least a while. But my wife and baby had died, Pa and I weren't getting on at the time, and I thought I ought to leave. I think back now, he wasn't too well, even then."

"Your mother?"

"She died when I was twelve. I've a stepmother, but she's already thinking to remarry. I expected he would have cut me off, but he didn't, left me everything. She and my dad didn't have any children and I guess he wanted it to go to kin. I was his one and only." He rolled the hat around again. "I gave her half what everything brought, would have given her the whole place if she weren't going to be all right in a new situation. That's what she thought she was getting before they found the will." He grinned. "The old man stuck it in his tackle box. Doesn't that beat all? She found it by accident. Honorable woman to file it and have them get in touch with me. She and I didn't have differences, not like him and me. Lucky in that regard."

She almost laughed. "Sounds like a plot by Wilkie Collins."

"Collins? Like in *The Moonstone*? What a great yarn, a real mystery."

Oh, a title that she had not read, never got to before Leftwich vanished. She wondered where that book was, whether it had burnt or gone somewhere with her portly young friend.

"Have you read *The Woman in White*?" she asked. "That's a mystery too."

"I've missed that one. Not much comes my way, but I read everything that does."

Leftwich and his little library. Leftwich, he probably went out West too. She wondered if he was still alive, or if some other rope or fire had found him. Could he be out there somewhere with more stock and more books for readers as greedy and grateful as she had been? She took two quick short breaths. It might be no bad thing to journey with Martin Daniels.

"The women he writes about. Not like in most novels and stories." Magdalen with her talent for acting and disguise, the fabulous criminal Lydia Gwilt whom Collins said would have made a fine

lawyer if she had been born a man, but who instead made the ulti-
mate sacrifice for the man she loved. She told Martin about them all.
And then about the poems.

"I have a scrapbook and I keep the ones I like in it."

It was the old chemistry textbook that Leftwich had let her take
because he said it was too out of date for use or study. She had covered the pages, their peculiar and puzzling signs and formulas, with
poems clipped from newspapers and magazines. She knew they
were not all good, but at first she took anything she could find.
Later, as she rejected some, she would paste over them a new clip-
ping, another poem. The pages grew so thick the book would not
really close, but was fanned out permanently.

"I memorize some of them."

"Tell me."

She felt briefly shy, vulnerable even, not at all like a married
woman who had had four children, a woman who could handle a
team and plow her own field, or stand off with a shotgun those bul-
lies who brought her husband home drunk and wanted to come in
with him to do god knows what. Her face growing pink, she
smoothed her dress over the thighs. But underneath she became
steady and full of ancient knowledge. If she spoke, would he . . . ?
Yes, she felt sure that he would. The power would be there. She said
the words carefully and slow.

" 'O, Western wind, when wilt thou blow . . . ' "

THEY STAYED IN Knoxville for three days, not the single overnight
stay her train schedule had indicated. The agent did not want to
change her ticket at first and looked as if he wanted more of an
explanation than "pressing business, come up unexpectedly," but in
the end he gave in.

Their room had a true luxury, a private bath with heavy looped
terry towels. They registered as Mr. and Mrs. Daniels and she took
off her gloves to show her third-hand wedding ring. She did not ask
until after the first time.

"Why didn't you marry again? Most men do."

John certainly had. Twice. And twice had given off his daughters to be raised in other families. She thought, and not for the first time, how it was that he had let the girls go and kept his sons by him. A widow could get along with hired hands, but most men had to remarry, had to have wives to do what wives did, to one side of warming the bed. Yet when it came to children they could hardly see the use of little girls, while, it seemed to her, sons were sometimes prized beyond their merits. To be sure, John had been taken with Maudie when she was tiny but he seemed to have gotten over it. He wasn't even concerned when the little girl stumbled into things and had to hold her schoolbooks so close to her face that Anna knew she needed the glasses he wouldn't buy.

She loved her boys, knew she did, wanted them out and off the land, educated, making something of themselves, especially Roland. But they were all headstrong and difficult, John's harsh discipline cowing none of them, especially not Spencer who was given to furious rages.

Her sons. She had to fear for them always. There were the happenings in Europe. Sons went to war. The Archduke dead, and that Kaiser, the one who had had a tall gateway cut through King David's ancient wall of Jerusalem so he could ride in on his horse instead of walking like an ordinary mortal, was declaring war, first on one country, then another. Would John have laughed to see that ride into the Holy City? Germany was far away, to be sure, but folk already talked of getting into it with them, did terrible things to Germans in some places.

My own people, my blood from there.

There had been a newspaper in the hotel lobby with a headline about the British in Belgium.

Not my sons, please, not my sons. When mothers think on wars perhaps they should wish they had only daughters.

"Never found the right one," Martin said.

All night long it rained. The water poured down the windowpanes in sheets, lit by the streetlight on the corner. The storm had already started before they got there. They had been wet and shaking themselves as they came into the lobby. Her coat was splotched and spotted and the tulle limp on her hat. They were laughing and so breathless when they signed the register that the clerk asked if they were newlyweds.

"No," said Martin. "We just haven't seen each other for a long time." Right there in front of everybody, he kissed her. Even the clerk laughed as he gave them the key.

THERE WAS SUCH a hunger on his face when he turned to her in their room. It moved her profoundly, seeing a man look at her that way. And troubled her. She had been given over to John, who had the fiercest hunger of them all, by nothing more than the silly fight her parents had had over T.A.'s will, which sent her off to the Albas' and left her vulnerable. At the first John had devoured her, but he seldom looked at her in that way now. His little bastards here and there. Had he looked at their mothers the way he used to look at her?

Afterward she thought of that expression on Martin's face every time she looked at Milton, but she was never to know what had happened for sure and certain.

THEY MADE LOVE three times during the first night, sleeping curled up together in between, waking to love again. He had thick curly black hair on his chest, a mat she could dig her fingers into.

"I admire your chest," she said, laughing.

"And I admire your thighs. Love me?"

"All I want," he whispered later in the night, "is your immortal soul." He sounded half serious.

"I don't know if I have one." She laughed, but thought perhaps she really did mean it.

And no, my this-one-time dear, you want too much.

All night long it rained, not stopping until shortly before dawn.

MARTIN DRESSED AND went out early. She sat on the edge of the bed, thinking what she could do if he never came back. How would she pay the hotel bill when she had money for only one night, not two?

But he did come back.

He was carrying two box lunches and a large umbrella. "Just in case," he said though the weather was turning off fair and breezy.

He had leased a chaise for the day. She learned later that the hotel manager had offered to loan them his new car, to show off probably. She had never ridden in one. It would have been an adventure.

But Martin had refused. "I was scared to death I'd damage it in some way," he said, but she guessed he really did not know how to drive an automobile.

With the horse he was expert. They drove almost to Morristown, found a great broad spring that overflowed an old stage road and had a picnic. After they had eaten and were sitting on the stone bench beside the springhouse he reached inside his coat pocket.

"Can I show you these? I'm a bit bashful about this, since you're the connoisseur, the collector, with the scrapbook and all."

The pages were plain, unruled, creased and worn around the edges, the ink faint, not anything he had done recently but obviously something he took everywhere with him. They sat under the trees beside the bright water while she read them all, he watching her the whole time.

"My hawks cry only to one another," and "I've set tongues of wood and made them sing.

"May I copy these? For my book. What does it mean, 'tongues of wood'?" Something like those little pointed shingles set around the front door of the first house? A memory of John sitting by the fire, finishing and smoothing the rough cuts of each one by hand with his pocketknife, throwing the shavings onto the glowing logs. She did not want to think of John right now.

"I was just writing about building a house. They're not as good as anything printed. I've stopped doing them."

"But they are good. I think they are."

"You would say that, of course, because of us. Which reminds me, what about us?"

"You know that already. After tomorrow there's not anything about us."

"You will write to me, won't you? Let me know how you are?"

"I don't know."

"What if I say I can't bear not knowing? What if I say I know I will see you again?"

"I still don't know." She looked down at the papers in her hands. "I love you and I love your words," she said. "Isn't that enough? I hope so, because that's all there is."

THEIR LAST MORNING she woke to find him out of bed and sitting at the table by the window. On hotel stationery he was copying out the poems in the little packet. When he had finished he put them in one of the envelopes on the table, sealed it and gave it to her.

"I'm honest about this," she insisted. "You should have these printed."

He shook his head. "I wouldn't have the least idea where to send them."

HIS TRAIN LEFT first. She had pulled off one of her gloves and given it to him for remembrance. After he was gone she sat perfectly still in the waiting room with the poems inside the bodice of her dress and the umbrella he had insisted that she take beside her. She never even wiped her eyes.

. . . in a salt land and not inhabited.

. . . . .

BURDEN, 1914

Nell was dying in Kansas. Nell when newly married. Nell writing of "doing for six." That kiss so long ago, meant to teach Anna some of what she should know. Oh, what she had learned since! Sisters have the longest bond, someone said, but that had not been, would not be. Strange, she thought, how grief and desire lay down together, the dead complete, alone, the living twined in each other's arms. Yet perhaps it was not strange after all, death calling for more life that way. She thought how she had stood in the cemetery at Gage's funeral, well apart from the family, but so placed that she could see David. How she had wanted him then, far more than she ever had when he wanted her. More than when he kissed her. She had looked at the edge of his jaw, his neck above his collar, wanted to hold him to her, put a mark just there. And there. And there. All the while Gage was being buried under earth, her lightness, the quick fanciful dragons, the lilting floating music to be weighed down by sod, marble, and yews. And Anna had been thinking of bedding David, their clothes off, gone somewhere nearby, out of the way.

Her clothes had been in such a heap on the chair and the floor in the hotel room it was a wonder she could look decent the next day.

Nell dying in Kansas. Never to run the mountains again, never to sit in her green chapel in the forest. She and Rush had left all those years ago happy and confident, Nell young and all smiles under her new white bonnet. "I've turned into an old woman before my time," she had written not long since.

Martin leaving, surely as lost and gone as if he too were dying. But by the time her train was finally called she was completely dry-eyed.

NELL HAD BEEN right. She looked like what she was, a woman fixing to lay it all down and never get up again. The marks, pallor, the sunken forehead, were on her. Anna saw it immediately. Her sister was far beyond any remedy skilled nursing or Anna's preparations could provide, beyond doctors too. She tried not to let Nell see what she knew, but Nell was not fooling herself.

What Anna did not know was that her sister did not even want nursing from her now, had changed her mind and wanted something else entirely. She wanted Anna to take her home.

"You came to try to lift this curse off of me, but you can't. Nobody can. Not even Rush, blessed, caring, praying soul that he is. But there is this one thing you can do for me. Get me back there so I can see Mama and Papa one more time, Dan, Roe, Dick, everybody, the house, all the old places up on the hill, the schoolhouse, the church. I want to be buried in that churchyard, not out here on this prairie. I never belonged here, no matter how good Rush has been. I should never have left the mountains. I think about them all the time. I dream their shapes." She pulled at Anna's fingers with transparent hands. Her eyes glistened.

"Who knows," she said. "The mountains are good for consumptives, aren't they? Maybe I will get better. Maybe I should have done this long before now. Believe me, I have my heart set on it. Don't deny me this, Anna. Please."

"IT WILL KILL her," the doctor said.

"Well, that's for certain anyway. What I want to know is, can she stand the trip?"

"Can't say. That's in the hands of the Almighty. She might make it home, barely. Still, it's hardly fair to other passengers, is it? A woman that sick on board."

"But it's what she wants."

"Don't I know it. It's all she's talked about since you were sent for."

ONCE THE DECISION was made Nell seemed stronger. She got up and dressed, moved about the house, giving instructions to Rose, the girl from the farm next to theirs who was going to look after things "while I am away." Anna, hanging out the clothes, watched her pinching back the plantings by the porch, picking the dried heads of the flowers to save seed for blossoms she would never see.

Rush's shirts on the line made Anna think of Martin, how he undid his tie, his buttons. She knew she could never have gone off with him, though he did beg, but that did not stop her from thinking, wondering how they might have gotten on together, say on his ranch, or a small farm somewhere where no one knew either of them. She could have started her whole life over again and touched his face above hers in the dark night by night. Would she have missed the mountains as passionately as Nell did? At least from Queensburg she could still see them, their distant forms, long for them.

Regret, oh, yes, regret. The children were getting on well at school, all the boys taking to Latin as their secret language. That was one good thing, even if John couldn't see the use of the dead words he didn't understand. But the house was not yet hers and she doubted it ever would be. Too many McCains there for too long and some of them still around, up there in the family cemetery on the hill. She had lost her home, her own friends, to take some strange woman's place in strange rooms and be gossiped about by the neighbors. All for a good cause, for the children, of course, but it was a bitter thing to bear, especially since so much of it was of her own doing.

Martin. How much stranger could it have been with him?

ROSE'S BROTHER CAME to drive them to the train. Rush couldn't trust himself. He was near to breaking down. He and Nell went into their room and closed the door. They stayed for a long time. Then Nell came out all dressed and ready. She closed the door behind her and hugged the girls. The older children, who knew what was going on, looked both blank and stricken. Edith was nearly grown, but she trembled like a terrified child when she put her arms around her mother. The little ones almost ran out of the room.

"Mother is going home to get well. I'll be back when I'm all better. Be good girls and mind Daddy and Rose till I see you again. I love you."

Rose's brother picked up the bags and took them to the wagon.

"I'm counting on you, Edith," Nell said.

ON THE TRAIN, as soon as she sat down, Nell said, "I've given him over to Rose. It's for the best." She took off her hat and jabbed the pin through it. "The girls love her. She's known them since they were born. I couldn't ask for a better stepmother." She smoothed the wrinkles in her lap. "I've been so happy with Rush. He's a fine, good man. I have to spare him this last. Leave him with other memories."

After that she was near silent, sat looking out the window, tears hanging in her lashes. She never sobbed or brushed them away. Spots of hectic red color appeared on both her cheeks.

"Remember how Mama used to say that her flowers missed her when she was away, that they knew when she was gone?"

BY AFTERNOON THEY were into more low, rolling hills. The land bumped along gently, the fields seeming to be stitched or knitted on with delicate embroidery rows, animals like toys decorating the slight slopes and soft meadows, some lakes off in the distance. Here and there were houses of brick. There seemed to be hawks on every fence post, looking for prey.

They were far away from seeing actual mountains but Nell began to look for them. Her mind seized again on recovery.

"I do believe that fresh mountain air, rest in my old room and Mama's cooking can cure anything, consumption, even cancer. You wait and see, Anna, I'll be well before you know it." Then later, "It was all that dust from the fields, the crops, the constant wind, the heavy air. I know that's what made me sick. I'll get Rush to come on back home when I'm well. We never should have left."

She was in good spirits by evening. "Oh, Anna, it will be so good to be home. I am so happy you came out to take me back. I've missed you so."

Nell adjusted her waistband. The dress hung on her like a sack. "You don't remember, I'm sure, but I do, what a determined, fearless thing you were when you were little. I couldn't believe how you did. I can remember you toddling after our mother, calling yourself by your name, saying, 'Anna go milking with Mama,' or 'Anna go with Mama to get the geese.' Not asking her if you could, but telling her what you intended to do. You were just a tot but you weren't a bit afraid of those great hissing, honking creatures and they plumb terrified me." She laughed and began to cough.

That night she had a small hemorrhage. Her forehead was blazing hot and she had constant thirst, said her tongue was parched. After they changed trains in Kansas City the conductor moved them to a sleeping car, had the bed made up, and called for a doctor at the next station.

"It's not much more than a few days, may not be more than one. I can't tell you if she will last out the trip or not. I've given her something." This doctor was more than a little angry. "The two of you should never have been allowed on this train, but since you're here . . . Well, make the best of things, do your best. It will not be easy."

"I thought her will would carry her through the trip, help her to make it home."

"Ha," said the doctor. "You give the human spirit a lot of credit."

Anna was not surprised to see the man sitting in one of the coach seats as she made her way back to Nell. She had known he would be with her. His bushy brown beard was shot with gray now and he wore a patch over one eye. He did not smile but raised his hand in greeting, gave her a steady look of warmth and sympathy.

Words. If only she could hear his words.

"REMEMBER," NELL SAID in her fever, "up in the hills, how you said not to worry if we got lost, that the mother bear would come for us? If it was summer she'd feed us honey and berries, you said, and if it was winter she would take us to her den and wrap us up warm in her fur."

"Did I say that? No, I don't remember that one."

"Oh, yes, you always were a good hand to tell stories. After that I always cried every time I saw a dead bear."

Anna thought how there would be less reason for that kind of crying now that most of the bears had been killed off in their part of the country. Wasn't there an old story about bears taking pain away, being able to cure human ills? Did folk sicken as the animals were exterminated?

As the doctor's drug began to take effect Nell claimed she felt like a young girl again, standing barefoot in the snow wearing only her shift. But her forehead was hot as fire. She fell asleep from the medication soon after Anna got back from the ladies' room where she had vomited as quietly as possible. During the night Nell turned and said quite clearly, "Please, can we go home now?"

The journey went on with the specificity and confusion of nightmare, jumbled details searing Anna's mind. The coffee laced with something strong that the porter brought in a heavy mug. Scrub pines and marshes outside the window where Nell thought she was seeing mountains. A pile of stained towels in the corner. Anna had thought the last blood would never stop coming, found herself praying for it to be over.

They will have to throw them all away, burn them maybe, fumigate the whole car.

Nell was conscious almost to the end, at first frightened, wanting Anna to hold her. She was unbelievably light. Then, just before she faded, very calm. "It's going to be well with me," she told Anna, "I know it is." Anna could not tell if it were a final delusion of cure in this world or a vision into the next. She was grateful Nell asked her nothing about God and heaven. She didn't know what she would have said.

Nell died very early in the morning just outside a sagging, sad little town. Anna opened the window, then went to the door at the end of the car, stood out in a chill wind looking down at those terrible huge wheels that could cut one to pieces.

In her last letter, Nell had written, "Didn't you once say up on the mountain that God wouldn't love us because we were savages? But I've not been savage. Who does God love?"

Anna did not remember saying such a thing. But was it true? The way he let those termed *savage* be destroyed. And what of the destruction of the unsavage? She made herself think of being on horseback somewhere far away, Martin by her side, riding under an enormous sky.

In the afternoon she dozed and in her sleep dreamed that John's dead wives were with her in the car, accusing her with their looks. Both of them looked very ill and coughed. She woke, went to the ladies' and was sick again.

She continued the journey with a coffin sealed by orders of the health department.

ROE DROVE HER home to Queensburg from Deerfield where she had left Nell, not in her old room after all, but first on two sawhorses draped in a sheet in the front parlor, then in the churchyard, as she had requested. Anna felt death on herself, in her hair, clinging to her clothes, felt far worse than when Gage died, even with the bloodstains she had had to scrub out of the carpet then with water so cold it chapped her hands. Gage had been friend, the close and dear friend of her youth. But Nell was kin, blood kin, her only sister. Blood. When she lighted from the buggy she was so worn she nearly fell. John was there and caught her.

"My poor little girl, my dear one. What a terrible time you've had." He took her in the house, undressed her as if she were a child and put her to bed. When he joined her there that night he loved her like one of the first times, as if to prove to them both that they were still alive.

TINA HAD GONE back home as soon as Anna's telegram came and a neighbor girl had been in to stay till Anna got home. Anna found one of her hairpins when she made their bed the next day.

When John asked where her other glove was she said that in all the confusion she had left it on the train.

It was not long after Nell was buried at Deerfield that Anna realized she might well be pregnant.

．　·　．　·　·　．

When she'd been young and with Nell, running up and down the hills, standing in the wind on high granite cliffs, or leaping among the flood-tumbled rocks of Elk River, she had thought of herself as destined for air, for lightness, for flight. "Higher, higher," she had called to her brothers as they swung her long ago. But now her path seemed to incline downwards, to the earth, to the simple dirt she stood and worked in. She looked at the clods at her feet, felt heavy, sorrowful. The breeze ruffling her hat brim did not speak to her, flat-footed there in the furrow, bound to and bound on the ground.

It was an autumn day, still bright, intense in late afternoon. Everything should have been suffused with great meaning, but she could not determine what it was.

Then suddenly at the far end of the plot an errant little dust devil appeared, not large, not powerful, but magic whirling energy. She watched as he danced, gathering to himself an inverted cone of dry golden particles, then lifted and carried them away.

Oh, Martin. His mouth on hers.

What does it feel like? Nell all those years ago at St. John's. Nell had kissed her full on the lips, but nothing more, that kiss in reply to a question never asked. In the little white church with colored windows. She knew well now what was more than any kiss, but she could not say what good it had done her.

What was good? Common dirt, said her back and shoulders, even in their soreness, common dirt hath more mercy than rain or sky for it accepts death, any death, all deaths, and brings forth life. Common work, day by day.

Her heart and soul struggled. Had she let Martin uproot her after all, like a rosebush transported to bloom in another clime, could she have flourished in that kind of love, with that kind of cost? No, impossible. It never could have been.

Far off to the northeast something towered huge, massive, taller than the hills. She looked and thought for one moment that a mountain was coming to her, moving slowly in majesty. She caught her breath. But it was only a great gray thunderhead. Still, for that short time, her spirit thrilled.

· · · · ·

He would always think first of the new bridge over the river at the edge of town. Each time his father announced that he would be away for any time at all Roland could already see himself coming back across it, laden down.

John would hardly be down the drive before Roland was off toward town on foot, swinging his empty meal sack. A few hours later he would be back with the sackful of books from the library, bringing them carefully across the river and up the hill. They must not fall into the water or be dropped in the mud. If it was raining he brought home fewer volumes, only the number he could fit up under his coat.

When the family first got to Queensburg he had been rash enough to let his father see some of the library books. After all, they had moved to further his education and that of the others.

But John was of no mind to put up with wasteful pleasures. Schoolwork and school texts only, the things that would get his off-spring ahead. He took himself into town and demanded that the library check out no more books to any of his children. He did draw a line, made an exception, and didn't mention his wife.

"It is not the policy of the library to censor anyone's reading," the librarian said. "We encourage young people, everyone, to broaden their minds."

"I'll broaden you," John muttered. He scowled like an angry dog and the librarian tried another tack.

"Perhaps if you looked around you might find—" she ventured to suggest.

"There's work to be done." John slapped his hand flat down on the counter. "And reading in idleness doesn't do it." He turned and stalked away from the desk, making his every step sound on the tiled floor.

HIS FATHER TOLD Roland what he had done and declared any more books from "that place" and "that uppity woman" would go straight in the fire. He picked up the stove lid to illustrate but the fire was out and the stove cold.

"Right in there," John said anyway. Iron rang on iron as the lid fell back into place.

But Roland wasn't about to stop going over the bridge to that other world. It was unfair to ask him to. He'd have to be more cautious, that was all. In the future he would wait until his father was well out of the way.

But even so he was always afraid. Not of the beatings. John could no longer beat Roby, and Art was gone. Soon, very soon, he himself would be too big for whipping. What he could not bear was the thought of any of those books destroyed. In his nightmares he saw scorched and muddy pages, covers torn away and chewed by rats. He nearly could have cried.

His mother said nothing about his reading, not even when he was late getting his chores done, said nothing either when he burnt a lamp deep into the night and was about to ruin his eyesight. She took books out of the library too and she would not forbid or criticize, would even have checked out things for him if John's attempted prohibition with the librarian had worked.

Roland knew his mother could see the square of light from his window out on the lawn until all hours, and of course she would know why he didn't use the electric light and run up the bill in a way that would be noticed, but all she ever said was, "I don't know if he'll pay for another pair of glasses or not. You know how hard it was to get those for Maud."

His father was expected home the next day. Roland went through the kitchen on his way out to take library books back before that return. His mother was at the table, already in her big smock, drinking a cup of peppermint tea to calm the nausea.

She smiled over the steaming cup and took a small sip. "Must you hurry? Do you have time to read me a little something, something you found that you like?"

"Of course." But what to read?

Sohrab and Rustum? That was his favorite. He opened the book and glanced over the pages, seeing much that stirred him but nothing that seemed appropriate to read to her. She had already listened to his reading of "Dover Beach" and that might do to read again. Then he took up a collection of another poet, found a short, simple poem and read it aloud.

"Here is the ancient floor,
   Footworn and hallowed and thin,
Here was the former door
   Where the dead feet walked in.

"She sat here in her chair,
  Smiling into the fire;
  He who played stood there,
  Bowing it higher and higher.

"Childlike I danced in a dream;
  Blessings emblazoned that day;
  Everything glowed with a gleam;
  Yet we were looking away!"

His mother shivered though it was warm in the kitchen from the fire she had built up for the tea. She looked down into the cup for a long time.

She drank the rest of the tea, stood up and carried the empty cup to the sink.

"Just imagine," she said, "a day emblazoned with blessings."

Why was she having another baby now? Maudie was nearly eight. God, what if she were to die in childbirth? He needed her, needed her to stand up and champion him in the things he wanted to do. She could hardly expect him to contend with his father alone. But an infant in arms would take much of her attention just as he needed her to help him make his way. The beginning of the curve of her belly under her smock upset and even angered him.

She ran the water over her hand and into the cup. She always ran the water longer than necessary. "Oh, son, be happy, enjoy," she said lightly.

But as he went out the door he saw that her eyes were very bright.

He will not accept any food you give him,
unless you join salt to the rest of your benevolence.

· · · · ·

"Come with me," he said and told her what to bring, what was needed.

"Who? Is it them?" she asked, though she should have known that it was not, not after all this time, not in this place, not the runaway Freida and her wild young love, now miles away and years back. Something else, somewhere else, had happened to those two. They were not the objects of this sudden righteous community charity.

ANNA'S BROTHER HAD found them.

"Dick said they must have sneaked into that old shed he's never finished building, doesn't even have all of the roof on. Sometime last night. She birthed the baby there without anyone on the place hearing a sound. At least that's what Polly thinks happened, the little thing looking not even a day old. Pol only got one peek at it before the mother bundled it away again. A woman couldn't walk up the hill and get in there right after being delivered." He fastened the last button on his coat, loose on its threads from being buttoned over the stomach he was getting.

But maybe down the hill, not climbing up it. Maybe out of the forest instead of off the road.

He showed her the button. "Can you fix this when we get back?" She nodded. He took his hat.

"Get your coat and shawl," he told her. "It's nippish out there."

Frost likely and a young couple with a newborn in an open shed. No, the pair would not go down to Dick's, get warm by the stove. He'd offered but they had refused, would not move from the pile of hay and old clothes they had found somewhere. The woman had the baby inside her dress, so close she was like to smother it. They would not have even known what she was holding if she hadn't taken it out for a moment when it mewed like a weak kitten, there being no trace of birth in the shed.

"They're ... well, you'll see. It's like they're wary, on guard against something or someone. And so pitiful. You'll see for yourself." Usually John thought folks should look out for themselves, but this was somehow different, as if the pair were almost a strange species that couldn't cope, even with the ordinary.

He had one of the blankets, a couple of old quilts, the larger basket of food, and a flask tucked in his pocket, a small one. He didn't want to be overly generous with his best whiskey. Anna had the other basket with cheese, cold biscuits, dried apples, and jam, as well as warm clothes, including some of the baby flannels that she had kept though she had said she might never use them again. Now she would probably need most of that store herself. John was rather pleased that another child was coming along after all this time. It confirmed that he still had it in him. Among the baby clothes she had put in a handkerchief knotted around some of the little cash she had. He saw her do it and was touched by her gesture. He thought about how it could make women sweet and good to be pregnant.

"When Polly moved toward her, to check on the infant, you know, she let out a scream as if Pol was coming at her with a knife." John took Anna's basket so she could unlatch the gate. "A howling cry, Dick said, and she put out her free arm as if to strike or ward off a blow. She barely let Polly see it was moving before she tucked it away again."

SOMEONE HAD BROUGHT in a lantern but the couple had moved back from its light. The food that Dick's neighbors had brought lay in a half circle round them like bait put out for wild animals. He both looked and tried not to look at them, how they were crouched in the one corner of the shed that had a bit of roof over it. They were probably neither one as old as twenty, and thin, both with long dark hair hanging lank and oily on either side of their pale faces. Dick, he had told Anna as they walked over, had offered the man work for their keep in better quarters, but they'd said no, it wasn't wanted, in hoarse, croaking voices.

"Like they didn't much know how to use their tongues, had forgotten how to speak. Anyway, that's according to Dick."

The woman's face was a pasty pointed wedge in the lantern light. John wondered if she had been tended to at all, and what had happened to the afterbirth. She was bundled up now in a heavy shawl that he recognized as one belonging to the doctor's wife. Then perhaps there had been a modicum of medical attention after all, though, given what he'd heard, he doubted it. And the baby was somewhere underneath the shawl where none of them could see it. Had the poor thing been properly cleaned up and dressed warmly or simply swaddled in whatever was at hand?

One of Dick's neighbors from up the creek stepped out of the dark and offered the man a swig from his flask. John knew him as the one who had gotten angriest about the gypsies camping in the flat and had threatened to fight John over it. Not a big man, but years younger and able do some serious damage. The threat had excited John, made him feel the way he did getting ready for the nightriders, but, as in that case, nothing came of it.

The pale stranger took a drink, not more than a sip really, and thanked the neighbor in a soft, cracking voice. John had been bested, lost the generosity race. But he'd get to keep all his whiskey.

Then he surprised himself. He knew enough to mistrust some of his motives. Not that he was incapable of kindness. No, not that. But what was an openhanded impulse, what calculated show? Did he see himself in this strange frail boy, too young, too much on him? Or he could even tell himself perhaps that the good folk of Queensburg might come to say, "That John Bayley! He'd give you the shirt off his back."

Whatever the reason, he took off his coat, the heavy oiled canvas one, the one into which Anna had sewn not one, but two, flannel linings. He gave it to the man who held it up to his chest for a moment before putting it on. It was far too large, the sleeves hanging down over the young man's dirty hands, but he did not give it back. The man looked directly at John, but said nothing.

Anna would think, *Sure, give it away, and he never had to sew one stitch of it.* And she would consider how he had said nothing as to work for the couple, or a roof, anything lasting, the way Dick had.

The people smelled. The shed smelled. Rank, feral, a condition from the other side of an invisible line. It was beyond pitiful. It was frightening, a reminder of what could happen to anyone who slipped and fell, who made a mistake, who crossed someone they shouldn't have, or who came into this world wronged to begin with.

And they were only a little older than Roland.

Anna stumbled away from that place into the dark. He heard the hoarfrost crunch under her feet. He followed her outside quickly. She staggered and he caught her.

"If she had looked like . . . oh, if that, I couldn't have stood it." She sounded afraid, a strange response for her. He was not at all sure whom she was talking about, but he held her. They clung to each other for a moment before they turned to walk home.

"He acted like it would hurt him to say 'Thank ye.' " He kicked a bunch of frozen grass in his way. Damn, he was going to be cold.

The young man's face, narrow, high-boned, with something of the Old People in feature, if not in color. The proud who have suffered in shame, disease, and displacement, and been murdered for their blood.

"Maybe it would have," she said.

"The drink, I guess, was man to man. That coat could be seen as man to beggar."

Anna put her arm around his waist.

"But it was kind and generous of you," she said.

He suddenly felt anger in himself, cleared his throat. "You know, don't you, that sometime or other, somebody's going to find the bones of that baby in a ditch somewhere. No way those two can take care of it." He shook his head, put his arm across her shoulders and they jostled each other in the narrow, rutted lane. Dick never could keep his road up. He was shivering without his coat. Anna shivered too, perhaps from what they had seen.

Or perhaps no one would ever find any bones. The thought of what such a child might grow up to be was even more frightening than death from neglect. A lost child, either way.

. · . . · .

She dreamed one night that she left, that she took Roland's little china cup, some books, a pair of scissors, and five spools of thread, wrapped them in her shawl, and found herself outside, standing in a peculiarly glowing dusk on the edge of a limestone wall.

Soul, stretch arms and fly.

And she flew and soon was on the road far below, where it lay clear and white as creek pebbles and leading straight west.

Wait for me in Oklahoma. Don't leave till I get there. It is so very far to walk and dangerous.

There were leftover men from the war lying in wait, as there had been when she was a child. She clutched her bundle and the road itself seemed to move her along. She stood in one place, legs and feet like trunks of wood, but the road bore her on, taking away any chance she had to turn back. She must go on. She must reach him. The pale white way turned to the ruins of a city and she was climbing over jumbled blocks of stone and broken columns. He was in some safe, secure place and she must hurry to join him. Something had happened to her bundle. A dog began to bark.

But you rejected him. You! You did it to yourself.

She heard Gyp barking loudly outside. He was up by the barn and, judging from the fierce terrier sound of his yaps, probably after a rat.

She let go of the covers she found herself gripping, smoothed them over her aching breasts.

Why is it that I have stood between myself and the things I want?

THE FIRST OF the bitter winter winds was moving the tree branches like grasping arms, gray against a gray sky. Soon the end of December and the first of snow. The baby would be due in June if she had calculated things correctly.

She cut two sad poems from the previous week's newspaper and put them in her book before filling the kettle and adding more wood to the cookstove. She would warm up the leftover coffee for herself, hoping it wouldn't make her feel sick, and have some hot cocoa for the children when they came home from school.

WHEN SPRING FINALLY came she was well advanced, due in a few weeks, but she rode into town in the buggy wearing one of her old, out-of-fashion smocks, the need for some diversion was that strong.

The wheel struck a rock, the buggy tipped, but John righted it. Nothing had changed. She still had all her old griefs, felt them inside as heaviness and pain, a soreness in the ribs just under her armpit, in her lower back, the weight around her hips pulling her down. She closed her eyes, felt ill, nauseated. The swaying buggy seat seemed to have come free, seemed to be a flying swing in motion thorough the air, a wild feeling with a fall at the end of it. As in her dream.

If only she could convince John to let go of enough money to get an automobile, a conveyance with more comfort to it, assuming that ease was true the way the advertisements claimed.

She opened her eyes upon the dazzling spring day. It glittered, the bright water in the valley, hillsides sifted with dogwood. She must bring something up to happiness.

"Oh, the beautiful river," she cried out in hope. "Oh, the flowers."

Perhaps the heavens did declare glory. Perhaps not. But the earth did speak, through every vein of rock, every dust mote, each frond and leaf and vein, it spoke. Indeed to the careful listener it chattered incessantly, or murmured lovingly, depending upon one's point of view.

BEFORE BABY MILTON came she made up a song, picked it out on the pump organ when everyone else was out of the house. There were words to it, but she never sang them aloud.

. ˙ . . ˙ .

QUEENSBURG, 1915

Down the road in the early mornings, the factory girls came in their long, slim skirts and their crisp starched shirts, walking close beside the house. The way they carried their heads, not looking down as they walked, as if there could be nothing in the roadway that might possibly trip them up, as if they had been born and raised to move forward, nothing to bar their progress! It was a marvel.

"It's the earning of their own money, don't you think?" Anna asked Mecie as they sat out on the porch boxing the strawberries that had cooled in the cellar overnight. As soon as they were done John and Roby would drive the boxes straight to market. "Gives them that kind of pride, that carriage."

She and Mecie were sorting out the best berries for sale from the gathering buckets. Culls they could keep for jams, pies, and short-cake, though once in a while Mecie dared to sneak a fat first-class beauty into her mouth. John was very particular about his berries, raising them on the field where the gypsies had camped so he could irrigate from the creek. He would not even let any of the children except Roland and Leonard pick in the straw-mulched rows. Roby's girls, he said, were much too giddy, would step on the runners and pull by the berry without holding the stems. Their fingerprints would begin to show on the sides of the fruit before he got to the buyers if they picked that way.

He had Anna and Mecie arrange the berries to show the finest at the top of the little wooden boxes. All this care made strawberries one of his best cash crops.

WHATEVER WOULD I do without you, Mecie? More than stepdaughter-in-law, like my sister, dear friend.

Queensburg had proved no kind place and it had been good to have Roby and Mecie close by. They were hardworking, helpful, and so happy and fond of each other that often she had a pang of jealousy. All their pretty little daughters growing up around them, Jane a bright, laughing, cheerful playmate for Anna's more serious Maud. She hoped for as much happiness for Art and Leah, but they were too far away for her to know about, gone up North to factory jobs over such strong objections from John that they now addressed their letters to Anna alone. Those letters sounded pleased and satisfied, but who could tell from letters? Hers to Tina were seldom all of the truth.

"Most of those girls probably have to give their wages to their folks for their keep or extras around the farm. John would say they're just a bunch of lintheads, no matter how they walk." Mecie looked around and ate another berry. She didn't care much for John.

But some of the factory girls had such style, such dash. One in particular Anna had noticed, a small yellow-haired girl who wore a boldly checked black and white shirtwaist and, on some days, an outrageous hat with cherries on it. She'd be willing to bet that girl went to those scandalous street dances in Elizabethton that she was secretly longing to attend. Then she had to laugh at herself, the idea of being out there on the paving listening to the caller's chant, doing the figures he commanded, and her nine months gone. Oh, for just one music night back in Faith, one breathless whirling turn around the room with the fiddles scraping loudly in the doorway. No one there, except possibly John, would have cared in what condition she danced.

"What sort of person," John would ask, "could give up the lands of their fathers to work in a mill?" Probably he thought of Art and Leah as well as assorted lintheads. Back in Faith he had opposed the idea of building a woolen mill in the community for just that reason. Those in favor had argued that a mill would bring jobs to keep youth in the community, but John prevailed when he said how it took people off their land, took away their independence. And for what? Paltry wages and lungs full of dust. Better to work one's own fields, hard as that was, than to take orders and jump when a whistle said jump.

"Perhaps some don't care that much for the lands of their fathers. Perhaps, for some, one boss is the same as another. Maybe one better than the other if it means ready money."

He had pretended not to hear her and she thought of how she worked like a field hand, had ever since they were married, pregnant or not. Way back when Nell was first married she had written that Rush wouldn't let her work outside. He seemed to be afraid she would melt, she said. John had always known well and good Anna'd not melt. She'd been put to that test often enough, but had not a cent to show for it beyond what she got for what little she could sell and the tiny housekeeping allowance.

"We could make collars and cuffs at home for cash, the way they do in some places," Mecie had suggested when she and Anna talked of ways to earn besides selling their eggs and butter. "Or roll cigars," she added with a wink. Not serious, of course. John would not hear of it, they knew. He and his son supported their families. Anna tried to think of something she could do and read at the same time besides the knitting.

"Those girls get too high and mighty with their bosses," Mecie said, "and they'll bring in some foreigners to replace them, or some from so far back in the sticks they can be cowed by the least little thing. They wouldn't have to read to the foreigners at lunchtime the way they do now."

"Oh, Mecie, we're from the sticks and you don't see anybody cowing us, do you?"

But how long had it been since she had really held her chin up, since she walked the way the factory girls did? Mills or no mills, John was always sure they would flourish and prosper. She had never been certain that was the case.

She picked up the flat full of beautiful little boxes. The fragrance of the fruit said that summer had almost come. She leaned over the flat to draw in the smell and a pain struck in her lower back, like iron stays with spikes suddenly cinching around her hips.

"Oh, Mecie. Just now, just now."

. ˙ · · ˙ .

Roby often wished they had never moved. Oh, yes, he had to agree with his father that the McCain land was as good as it came and that the milder weather was beneficial to everything they planted. But he sensed . . . what was it? Something off, not as it should be. The honeysuckle in Tennessee was sweet-smelling, but it seemed pestilent, as if it were concealing a secret but signaling danger.

While she enjoyed the space of a larger, more convenient house than the one they had had in Faith, Mecie was not happy to be a whole two days' travel from all her kin and more than anything he wanted her happy. She also disapproved of the hold John had over him, feeling they should be more off on their own in spite of the hardship she had to know that would bring.

He was caught between his duty to wife and to father and had nights when he sat up all hours in the dining room weighing the matter. Sometimes he saw Anna's light on in the kitchen down the hill.

"What were you doing up so late?" he would ask her the next day, knowing well it had not been anyone else in the kitchen.

"Couldn't sleep," she used to say, but now it was, "The baby. He has colic bad, you know. I walk him and walk him." At least she had something she had to be doing, would have the kettle boiling for soothing steam and flannels warming for the baby's stomach, leaving less time for grieving over her sister and for those dark thoughts of an insomniac which he guessed she had.

He wondered if she rued the choice of this place, a decision that had in truth been hers. Anna did not seem as happy with her fine brick house as Mecie was with their more modest frame place. But he knew she was highly pleased with the schools and gratified that the boys were all bright and excited over their studies. Even Maud didn't mind going. Not a reluctant scholar among hers or his and Mecie's. What else was it had kept her awake in the middle of the night before the baby came?

He had Mecie's homesickness for her family and his father's needs to worry over as well, but his own deepest inner anguish was for what was missing. This land over the mountain had been cleared for so long that game was scarce and unpredictable. If a groundhog as much as showed his furry little face or rump there were enough men out with guns that they were likely to shoot one another.

And all the waters were nearly fished out.

There was that talk of fish hatcheries and of stocking streams and having fishing seasons. He could scarcely stand to hear it. In all likelihood practices around Queensburg similar to his grandmother's seining out every creek that she could walk to had contributed to the dearth. It took the sport away. Worse, it took away the right and balance of things.

Even the wet could come to be desert.

He wanted the wild water with fish that were born there. He wanted the fly pole in his hands, wanted to hear the faint *whiss* as the line went by his head. A strike, a strike! In all the floods of the world little could feel any better than that.

With the best grace he could muster he stood his father's schemes and obsessions, the strawberries the latest of them, but all was not well.

I've lost my soul, he thought of telling Mecie, for on certain days it felt like it. But he couldn't say it. She would not understand. He told her often that she herself was his soul and his salvation.

It would hardly do to put her, in a way, in the same category as a fish.

Salt water and absence
wash away love.

. . . . .

Her mind tumbled over and over with chores and numbers. July was always filled with things to be done, things to be done, no time to consider anything else. And here she was with a month-old infant to nurse and care for along with everything else, tired and aching nearly all the time, with a pain in her back that would not go away.

The corn is nearly ready. Fourteen quarts of tomatoes canned yesterday. Beans broken, strung on cords, a dozen long strings of them hung up so far. Two crocks of kraut bubbling away in the cellar, ready to be skimmed. The carrots must be dug. Apples to dry later on.

Back home there would have been blackberries to pick in the upper field above the stone outcroppings near where John shot the bear long before they were married.

Fifty beautiful clear jelly jars on the shelves, brown paper neatly tied with string over their paraffined tops, each kind indicated in ink on the paper. Milking, churning, cottage cheese in the bag hanging on a nail, the bluish whey dripping into the pan.

No time to read, sew, knit, or think. Good. She did not want to be thinking just now.

Her mother, how had she done it, Anna wondered again. Magic the way Tina could heal cold sores with her salves, calm the most violent headaches with horseradish scrapings put on one's hands, ease toothaches and sleepless nights with cloves, chamomile, hops, willow bark, and valerian. She thought of her mother coming across the land with her baskets of apples, grapes, potatoes and cabbages, and, in her pockets, odd, strange, lovely things found along the path that she was bringing home to show her children.

Anna's dahlias, overblown, lush and indecent, nodded to her from beside the picket fence, their colors, pink, red, a deep blue-red, lavender, and yellow. They tossed their heads, challenged her with their color, their size and roundness. *What have you to equal this?* they taunted. It made her feel pale to look at them.

"You should see my flowers," she wrote to her mother.

. . . . . .

They went down to walk in the garden after supper. The summer was getting far on. Already they had cleared out peas and onions, would soon plant the fall cucumbers and greens, the late cabbage. The air was still hot from the day but she had pulled a shawl around her.

"Are you cold?"

"I've been cold for nearly a year."

The beans were being eaten up by the beetles. She had not cleaned them as often as she usually did and John didn't think it was fit work for the boys. "You could train a couple of Roby's girls . . . well, Janie anyway," he had told her, "if your back hurts too much." But she hadn't gotten around to it. She stooped, swept back some of the rough, papery-feeling leaves, found a few larvae, fuzzy yellow things the size of rice grains. She smashed them with her fingers, staining her hands with the juice from their insides.

"The sweet potatoes. We need a better place for curing. Lost too many last year." He was always planning ahead.

"Sweet potatoes, that's months away."

"Could be weeks. We've had killing frosts in early September many a time."

"That was in the mountains."

She was giving him that look, the one he didn't understand, the one he sometimes thought might mean that she felt he was now too old for her, that somehow he had gotten out so far ahead that he could not get back to her the way he should.

He gave her his hand and helped her up. They walked to the end of the rows, she still holding on to him. They leaned on the fence and she pulled a stem of timothy with its little cattail head and chewed the watery end of it. Timothy was always her favorite. He'd never seen her pull anything else.

The expression that had challenged him faded. He felt close to her, standing there in the early-evening light, the insects starting up and the heavy smells of dirt, animals, and plants still steamy from the day. She was right. It was much hotter here to the west side of the mountains. Back home it would already be cool, a little damp with dew by this time. Yes, back home.

He looked toward the house. But this was a fine place, big and brick, finer than he had ever hoped to have. And the land was like butter, richer than any he or any of his kin had ever farmed.

One of the boys walked around the porch to the door. His vision was not what it had once been. He couldn't tell which one it was. Back in the kitchen someone turned on the electric light. With a surprising pang he thought of lighting a lamp and setting it on the table, making a warm ruddy glow in the shadows of the room. This was a cool firefly light that left no shadows.

"We work too hard. We don't have enough time for . . ."

What was he going to add? He didn't quite know what was the most important thing he didn't have time for. Her? She wasn't happy, he knew. If he had more time perhaps he could change that. But did she really want more of him?

His words were a key to something in her. Something came out that she'd obviously been putting in order in her thoughts. She gave him a grateful look, probably because he had provided the right opening.

"A staff," she said, and laughed.

He didn't understand.

"That's what we need to give us the time. Servants. Somebody else to do it. We could sit back in the rockers and tell them what to do. I have it figured out."

And she told him. One man for the vegetable gardens and the

orchards. One for the yard, the flowers, shrubs, repairs around the house. A cook in the kitchen, a maid to clean.

"And a nursemaid for the children," he put in and immediately wished he hadn't. After this baby there would probably be no more need of any nursemaiding. It was a painful point between them.

But she was happy in her subject for the moment and didn't take offense. "I'll do all the nursemaiding."

They went out the lower gate, walked in a big circle around the garden and climbed toward the house. She put her arm through his and they went along in silence and an ease unusual for them these days. At the rock walk he stopped.

He couldn't let it go.

"You took good care of yourself with all that staff, but how am I ever going to get a minute to sit down with everything in the fields to be done? What will I do, reinstitute slavery?"

Her face darkened suddenly and the good time was gone from it like a candle blown out.

"That's what you're trying to do with the boys." She pulled away. "I must get to the dishes." The back door shut, not quite slammed, behind her. He knew Maudie was probably already doing the washing up, standing on her little box in front of the sink.

The smell that came to him was of rotting vegetables in the waste bin.

BY THE TIME John had finished outside and gotten back to the house the supper things were cleared away and the boys had their Latin books and papers out on the dining table. Another electric light was on though it was not yet dark. Latin was the only subject they would study over the summer. They said it was because it was difficult, but he challenged them that they did it to annoy him because he thought it useless study and had said so.

"It's the basis for everything," Leonard had said. "French, Spanish, Italian, scientific and medical terms."

"What about algebra, geometry? It strikes me learning like that would be much more useful, especially on a farm or in business." Those happened to be the subjects John wished he knew more about himself.

"They teach those, but I don't see myself as much of a mathematician."

"Maybe you should learn to look at things differently," John had said, "from a practical point of view."

As he came into the room Roland and Leonard were speaking to each other, slowly and deliberately, as if rehearsing insults that he wouldn't understand.

"Gallia est omnis divisa in partes tres," Spencer sang out.

So Spencer was in it with them. "I'll divide *you*," said John. "I know what that means and a bit more of that old tongue besides. I'm not so easy to mislead." He glared at Spencer. He knew he was egging on his bad-tempered boy, but he didn't care. "Don't think you can condescend to me simply because you're going to a state high school. I myself once had the privilege of studying with a true scholar who singled me out as promising."

"Nolite te bastardes carborundorum," Roland whispered to Spencer.

"What's that about bastards? You can't fool around with your father like that. By god, I'll yank all of you out of that confounded school and get you back behind the plow in a trice if you try to talk against me behind my back. See if I won't." He fumbled with his belt buckle, then figured that he couldn't take on all three of them. "Study something of use, like I told you."

"I told you I would take algebra," said Leonard, "but I don't know what I'll do with it. Besides—"

"Besides nothing. You've got no besides that I'd listen to. Finish up here and do the rest of the chores." John started for the door. The talk went on behind him.

"Besides, I want to teach Latin," Leonard said.

"Non dividimur," said Spencer.

"Non sumus dibii." Leonard corrected him.

Roland laughed.

"Boys," yelled John from the back porch.

. ˙ . . ˙ .

QUEENSBURG, 1915

The back pain that had returned after Milton's birth was a sullen, dreary sensation that came and went during the day and woke her at night. Perhaps it was guilt she felt. She looked into Milton's little round face, his dark brown eyes and did not truly know whose child he was, besides hers alone.

She might have put a cuckoo in John's nest after all. She had not gone to Martin with that intention, but perhaps if that had happened she should think payback rather than guilt. She smiled grimly to herself to think that it was so, but there was a nagging fear behind the smile, an uncertainty, as if all she knew could in a blink pass away as if it had never been. And again it seemed to her that everything that was ever going to happen had already happened and she was seeing shadows of what had passed.

Then the pains became acute, sharp, searing, as if she were being cut by hundreds of razors. She could hardly get her breath when they sliced into her and she began to scream whenever they struck.

It was not guilt after all.

THE NEW DOCTOR in Elizabethton was worried, she could tell. He sent them to the hospital in Bristol where a specialist in women's disorders examined her.

There was nothing he could do, he told her.

"So it's been longer than a year, then?" asked Anna.

"Oh, yes, much longer. It's very slow-growing, but you have had it for, oh, six or eight years maybe. If it had been diagnosed earlier, maybe surgery could have bought you some time. The way it is now, it is quite inoperable."

When she came out of the doctor's office the expression on her face was remote and strange. Years after she was gone, John remembered the look, not one that claimed any sympathy from him. He had thought, *Saints on fire in the square, suffering hell and glimpsing heaven.* He did not know quite what he meant by that, or, if he did figure it out, whether she would have agreed with him or not. For her part she had been thinking of the loneliness of a climber on a distant and terribly cold mountain peak.

John took her to the drugstore and bought her her first ice-cream cone. He didn't know what else to do. Vanilla. He thought chocolate would be too strong for someone who was ill. Already he thought of her as an invalid.

No hope, they said, no hope at all.

It would take months and months, almost two years, and the only treatment was morphine.

. . . . . .

It was a bad place in which to be ill. The bare glaring bulb in the bathroom would show day by day the progress of the disease. Lamplight, firelight, candlelight might have disguised the truth a little longer. A house with lamps, or with Tina's tiny candle moving through it, sweet little light that had shone true as true, generous beyond need.

She stood looking out the dining room window, her elbows on

the deep sill. The walls of the house were so thick the water bucket and dipper could sit on the sill with room to spare. John wanted water there winter and summer, even with the faucet in the kitchen. Walls. Bare chinked logs in the cabin, planed boards in the first house, covered in newspapers for insulation. Balloon framing, so open the snow came in upstairs. The second house had had tongue-and-groove beaded ceiling downstairs with wallpaper upstairs. She had never gotten used to the plaster here, the hard, cold, stonelike feel of it, like bone.

And at the McCain place—even named for someone else, never called "the third house"—she had had no time to learn the woods and hills the way she did as a child at Deerfield, no time to name the places, Jack-in-the-Pulpit Hollow, Hawk Cliff, Moss Cove, Laurel Chapel, no time to see the bloodroot, the yellow violets, trillium in spring, pipsissewa and running cedar in winter, the asters, golden glow, and ironweed of late summer and fall. She had at least been able to search out the plants she needed in Faith. Was there something she had never learned that would heal now? In Queensburg she had had to rely on what she could grow herself, or what the boys could bring in. They knew about some things, but not all of it, and did not have the interest women took in the natural sources. She should have taught Maud all that she knew, should have passed the knowledge on. What did the gypsies do for wild knowledge, always on the move as they were?

John considered little of the wild. He was for beating it back, killing off the predatory. He was interested in doing well, concerned with keeping up the place, what it was costing him to have now more than a hundred fifty acres of prime land and a fine brick house with real plumbing. And he could not bear to see anything "going back to nature," growing up in sumac, haw, box elder, and locust. Every foot of ground was meant to be of use, turned to field, pasture, cropland, garden, feedlot, woodlot, or timber reserve. She thought sometimes he begrudged her the plant and flower beds. She knew how he felt about what he termed "too much lawn," running the pasture up so close to the house as to be almost unhealthy.

"You should see my flowers," Tina wrote.

"You should see my flowers," Nell had written back way when.

You should have seen my flowers, my herbs and medicinals, how they rioted and fell all over themselves, out of control. Flowers are so alive and shameless, screaming to bugs and bees with their color. I had poppies. I had lilies. And fragrant yellow roses. Phlox, pansies.

Outside a terrible birdcall, full of distress and warning.

How odd. What bird? John would know. Roland too. I don't. Plants, oh, yes, I'm brimful with knowledge of their names and uses, but for all my love of music I have never learned the birdsongs, calls and cries. A pity.

In Queensburg she had never once blown the steerhorn that hung by the back door.

. . . to taste our salt sorrow . . .

．　．　．　．　．　．

Anna had two of the coverlets done, three more to go, one for each child. Perhaps she could do one for Roby and one for Art as they had come to be her children too, and their children like grandchildren of her own, fortunate since she would never see any of hers.

She would not live to sit by the fire, doing nothing but smoking a pipe or dipping and spitting into the flames like John's mother. But then she also wouldn't get peculiar like Hannah who didn't care to eat, would barely take a bite, and didn't like to see anyone else eating. Her mother-in-law had been that way ever since she'd nursed John's stepfather through his last illness, sitting by his bed for so long that after he died she was seized in every joint and couldn't get around anymore. And she would never have to live in the house of a despised son-in-law the way Tina had had to do since she came out to look after Anna.

The coverlet designs were a wonder, how someone thought them up. Tall graceful baskets with high arched handles, brimming with intricate and fantastic flowers, other baskets wide and low, filled bountifully with fruits, skies of butterflies and humming birds, strolling peacocks, ivy garlands braided and beribboned, the trellised rose, a garden gate, worlds of light, color and scent, refined away to white, white, white. A pattern of white dots on a white surface, only the textures of the cloth and cord, shadows of knots on the sheeting for contrast.

She would work the knots, putting a charm into each one she pulled through the cloth, that those sleeping under these white fields of beauty would good and wise and happy be. Sometimes she almost wept when she worked but more often she was completely absorbed. Kate, the hired girl John got to help with what Tina couldn't do, would bring her tea and look at the designs intently when Anna spread them out for her.

She tried not to think of getting them done in time but of doing them beautifully. The last would be a special design of her own, a garden path, blooms to either side, leading to a great fountain in the center, its shape that of a blooming tree, spurting white and high, the water curling like the edge of waves as it fell back into the pool. Even as she worked on other patterns she was blocking out that one in her mind, exactly how it should go. And there was yet another that came to her when she thought of Martin, a rendering of a great tall-masted ship in full sail. That one she knew she would never do. He had never come sailing in any fashion to claim her, but then she had never believed that he would. Still she wished it at odd and troubling times.

The sensitivity of her hands had increased, the skin seeming thinner. She knew most of the patterns as she worked them now, could do them in dusk and dim light. The blind were taught to read that way, running their fingers over dots raised on paper. And she could change, refine, or add to the established shapes as her fancy took her, making each coverlet her own. Her children must remember to turn the coverlets back to preserve them and so as not to be marked. If you lay down on one it would print its pattern on your skin.

"They're a wonder," said Kate. She had a round, ruddy face, a sweet voice, and hands as chapped and work-worn as Anna's had been. She reminded Anna a bit of Bina as she had been singing and dancing on music nights. The dance, the dance. How light and quick they had all been back then.

"I'm always amazed that you can do that so beautifully." Tina stroked Anna's hair. "Like a real artist. I have no such skill in my hands at all. Can't think where you could have gotten it from."

"It comes to me," said Anna. "Sometimes I dream patterns of things. Or I start with one pattern and it just turns into something else. I don't have to go and steal them, not like some I've heard of. Did you hear about the woman who came upon her cousin's coverlet soaking in the creek, hauled it out, and copied it right there with her own sheeting and bluing?"

"She must have been going about prepared then."

"Had been lying in wait, maybe." Anna rethreaded her needle. "But I don't know as I would mind if someone copied me. It would be flattering."

"It's a certainty no one will ever so flatter me," said Tina. "Remember those pillow shams I did with the cats in red thread? I draw worse than Spencer."

"But no one can cook like you, Mama. That's where you're an artist, in the kitchen."

"Maybe. But what you set on the table doesn't hang around long enough to be much admired, now does it?"

· ˙ · · ˙ ·

A parcel came for Anna from Faith, brown-papered, tied with four extra knots on each side and addressed in Bina's neat, childish hand.

A pair of lace curtains.

In her absence they had carried on, taken in someone to round out the number of *Comfort* subscriptions needed, allowed her the lucky draw, and sent her the curtains.

When she pulled the delicate white panels out of the paper and unfolded them she could hardly admire the beautiful rose design for her tears. Eventually all is forgotten, she knew, but in that moment she was being remembered with love and care. She would never see them again. Perhaps they did not even know that she was ill. But they had cared enough to give up a turn for her when all she had done for them was to desert them, leave them behind for her own reasons. Queensburg women she had not taken to or gotten to know well. They looked down on the folk who still lived in the mountains. They had never taken her in, had left her on the outside. Bina, Alice, Maggie, and Tempe. She said their names over and over for warmth and what comfort it could give her.

TINA HUNG THE lace curtains on the window beside Anna's bed, as she requested, instead of in the parlor. The light came through and fell in a pattern across the sheets. Anna traced the figures with her finger.

FOX BOY AND *Fox Girl loved the pool where their father had bathed, sensing perhaps that it was the place where they had been made. They would bathe there as humans, swimming and splashing in the water, then sleep afterwards as foxes because it was warmer.*

So it was that the hunter, their grandfather, found them one evening.

The man was aging, still mourning his only son, for whom he had done everything but had failed to save the boy's life. In sorrow he climbed the mountain to the very pool where Fox Boy and Fox Girl lay asleep, curled together on the rocks, which were still giving off some of the day's warmth. The hunter climbed to see once more the spot where he had last known his child in anything close to what the hunter considered the boy's right mind. And when he came and saw the foxes lying on the stones all the rage at the animal who had driven his son mad came to him with the greatest force.

Quietly, quietly, as only the most skilled of hunters can approach, he went up to the two foxes, fell on them with lightning speed and slit both their throats, each with a single stroke.

As her children writhed and bled Fox Woman appeared in her cloak and her glory, the lightning of its fringes burning and crackling in the approaching dark. And she screamed.

"Foolish, stupid, deadly man, look upon what you have done. You have slain your own, your own grandchildren."

And in the flashes of light from the cloak of Fox Woman the hunter

saw at his feet, not two dying foxes, but two human children, younger
than the son he had lost, but each with the face of his child, as beautiful
as the sun and moon, the same black eyes going blank in death.

Then the hunter knew all that Fox Woman said was true.

He cried out in anguish. He stroked the hair of his grandchildren and
under his hand with their blood on it they changed back into limp dead
foxes. At this the hunter walked to the edge of the pool. He did not stop
but went on into the water where he let himself be drowned.

When he rose floating and pale on the surface of the water Fox
Woman came down and gathered her children into her cloak.

"Is this my revenge?" she asked no one.

She took the children with her when she flung herself into the night
sky and vanished forever.

"PLEASE CALL KATE. I want her to come sing. And can she bring me
some tea?"

· ˙ ˙ · ·

She arranged the pillow for herself, brought the covers up smooth
and folded the sheet back over them. John could not stand it, could
not look at her lying still like that, so changed. The sight of anyone
covered, stretched out at full length, aroused a horror in him, eternity announcing itself once more by that position, as it had so many
times in his life, this time perhaps the worst. And the closest to his
own end. Anna would be his last.

He saw himself again on the first of those many times, a child in
a scene he knew well, but no longer freshly remembered, having
thought of it over and over again. He was standing at his father's
side in the darkened cabin, watching with his sisters as the man

burnt up alive, Martha Ann only a toddler not able to see up on the bed and wanting to climb on it. The room stank of fever and of fear and that memory always came back clearly. He could not bear that odor ever again. When Roland had been deathly ill in the first house he was not able to help the sick child except to trim his hair because of what filled that little room upstairs. Not only did he remember, he smelled the smell whenever he thought of it.

"Can I get you anything?" he asked, watching the pattern of light and shadow coming through the curtains swirl and twine over the bed. Anything rather than look at her face.

She always said, "My book," or "My work," and he would bring whichever she requested. "My work" meant she felt a little better, that the pain was less, and she might get up later. This time it was "My book."

"Do you want to paste in some more poems? There're some loose ones you haven't put in yet."

"No, never mind. I'll just read over what I have."

She took an envelope from the back of the book, pulled out some loose pages and unfolded them. John had seen her do this before and once when she had gone to bathe he had looked at the envelope. It and the pages were from the hotel in Knoxville where she had stayed on the trip out to bring Nell home. He thought them letters at first, but they were all poems that made no sense to him. He didn't recognize the tall upright hand either. Must have been something that she had found in her room and kept. She was always crazy for things to read.

He was sometimes angry at her illness. She was failing him, giving him the name again, that of a man who couldn't hold on to, or save, his women. This house, the move, might be all for nothing if she went, diminishing him, the family.

"Don't you feel like getting up today?" He wanted her to put breakfast on as usual.

Her fingers would sometimes move as if she were making knots for the coverlets even without cord. He watched her hands and not her face.

"I may come and sit in the middle room by and by."

THE PARTS OF the body that are attacked are the parts that matter most to the person. Her brother Roe, who carved those tiny animals, those delicate beautiful birds, some of them in flight, had been taken with crippling arthritis in his hands. Jenny back in Faith, who sang the bawdy song, who loved to sing and found so much fun in doing it, got a goiter and her voice changed to a rasp. Her own papa, who could outwork three men if and when he took a notion, once so hale and strong, was these days bent and barely moving. And she herself, the cancer had taken her in the womb that brought forth her children.

MARTIN. WHAT DID he look like? Sometimes I think I know, can see him. Oh, angels, he was a merry man. I had thought a fall would be somber, regretful. But such a smile on his dark tan face. Such a laugh at my ear. Merriment in his hands moving down over my shoulders, pulling at the stays. Any mourning came later.

She thought to write to him in the anguish of the first few weeks after Nell died, when she could still feel his touch on her body, tried to plan the letter as she walked round and round the kitchen table in the dead of night. She would write it all out, tell him what had happened, everything she felt, but when she tried to think of the words they seemed blank, flat, not the scream of her desire that she wanted to reach him wherever he was.

A little later and she knew about the baby and could never write.

JOHN WILL MARRY again, I know he will. He's just in his prime, fifty, and he did those other times. It'll be someone young too, not more than twenty, barely older than Roland. He'll be looking for trouble, I'll be bound. Perhaps she'll want a new house, like I did. There'll be another move and my things will be scattered, my name forgotten. Anna Maud Stockton Bayley.

Oh, please, don't forget. There're too many of us who are forgotten, Julia, Belle, all of us who never had any chances, never went anywhere, never amounted to a thing. Just tried to be good wives, get our work done, and raise our children to do their best. Except for that one time. Milton, my last, will be brought up by someone else, won't have mother or father of his own. I must tell Roland. No, not tell him all of it. Just charge him to look after Milton. See to it that in time he gets away. You too, Roland. You get away too, my first, fine and handsome. Make something of yourself. You get away from here. As soon as I'm gone. Stay till I go. I'll tell you when. An education to take you places I could never go. Get away quick, as I never could. I can't bear to think of you stuck in a mule's traces or walking the rows with a hoe all of your life. Let him buffalo you into staying and I'll come back and haunt you. See if I won't. He'll try. Don't give in, my beautiful son. And my dear baby, Milton, brown-eyed after all.

John believes that I am dying from his neglect, overwork, and not enough medical care. That is not so. I do not know why I am being taken, perhaps am dying from the effects of coming to life, but it is certainly for no reason he would ever think of.

. · . . · .

She should give some thought to dying in the faith, to making a good end of it, but whenever she tried to think of going to some heavenly home she didn't want either to go or to think. One of John's stepsisters back in Faith had seen visions of the clouds, imagined them to be just as fluffy to touch as they looked and thought that babies yet to be born were up there waiting to come to earth. Some said in her case it was the drink made her think that heaven was soft like clouds when it was hard and actual, with gates of pearl and streets of gold. There was nothing like that in the sky, Anna felt sure of it.

For us there is only this earth, to take us with it wherever it turns and for as long as it does.

SHE THOUGHT OF eternity as getting into a buggy for a ride. One climbed up, settled back comfortably, and set off, past all the beautiful places one had seen while alive, first that marvel of a spring Martin had taken her to, so big it spread out over the whole road and the buggy would have to drive through the water as their chaise had. There would be a red-winged blackbird sitting on the post beside the road. Then down a rocky lane beside a barn so old it was mossy, an orchard with John trampling the cidery windfalls underfoot, the children on a slope of daisies with the sun high behind them, the houses they had lived in at Faith. On back before she was married, to her parents' home on the mountainside with the flowers, the hemlocks in the yard, and behind the house the granite boulders overhung with roses, harboring snakes.

There are no snakes in eternity, someone said, and she replied that, oh, yes, there were, it was just like here. It was here and now, and there and then. The past was going back further and further. A trip somewhere with her great-grandmother, the one whose name she could not remember because it was foreign and she had always called her "Ganny." They were in a place where the land was flat and fields of grasses stretched as far away as one could see and someone had built a windmill that turned round and round. Her great-grandmother spoke German. They stopped and the old lady picked cherries for them.

Then on back before she was born, her father and Major DeHaven in the war. And before that, everything that ever had been, in every place. Strange countries of black gods, statues of young women with huge, perfect, rounded breasts, tiny waists with cunningly wrought girdles. The place where the Emperor had built an endless wall and tiny almond-eyed girls had their fingers burnt away taking silk cocoons from boiling water. All the way back through all that ever had been. Then around and into the future.

Yes, as she ever thought, *we belong to this earth, to all that is gone and all that will be.*

Of course she had to make herself consider it that way, the endless, endless journey to the beginning of time and back again to the place from where it went on and on. She could not think of the horror of dissolution. It was enough to be haunted by the hemorrhages, to have the dreams of flying over basins full of blood, fields of those basins.

"I SHALL BE with you in eternity," he whispered.

She turned her head on the pillow to look at him kneeling there. Oh, certainly, he was sincere, but the question of how many times he had said that before, the thought of his position in a conventional hereafter, suddenly struck her as funny. Something came out between a cough and a giggle.

"Oh, John, your life in heaven will really be complicated."

HER MOTHER CAME downstairs, flapping in those old shoes John hated so much. "One of these days," he had promised, "when she's not looking, I'm going to do away with that awful footgear. She's making us out to be paupers, not able to afford proper shoes. I don't like the neighbors thinking that."

"They're comfortable for her. And that's the main thing," she had told him.

Anna was up for the moment and in the kitchen trying to brew her peppermint tea in hopes it would stay down and settle her some. She would put in milk and sugar, make it like cambric for children.

"Want some good hot bread and butter to go with that?" asked Tina.

"No. No, thank you."

Tina got out the toasting fork anyway. "I dreamed about Mr. DeHaven again last night. He was here and wanted me to go away with him." She sliced a thick slab of bread, picked up all the crumbs with her fingers and ate them. "He said he had come to speak to me in all the forms of being alive."

"What on earth does that mean?" Anna sipped her tea. It was sweet and weak.

"I haven't the least idea. He hasn't been alive since he was nineteen."

"I thought he was twenty."

"He lied about his age. And they gave him a commission because he had a pistol and his own mount. Your dad never got over Mr. DeHaven being a major and himself seven years older and not getting past corporal."

Mr. DeHaven, her mother's first young husband, killed long ago and early on in the war. Mr. DeHaven. Tina always called him that and Anna realized she had no idea what his first name had been.

Tina glanced out the window. She turned the bread carefully in the flame from the open stove eye. "Charles," she said. "He's always asking me to leave with him. Charles that was."

· ˙ · ˙ ·

She tried to tell them each night when she talked to them one by one.

Listen, you may ask me anything. I am hiding nothing from you. Death is not an awful thing. It is release and peace.

But all the while she knew and understood what it would do to them, remembered how Gage's death had changed everything for her when she was about Roland's age, the bleak, despairing time that had lasted until she met John and fell into that sudden, overwhelming, reckless, unjudging passion. The earlier darkness from that time had come back to her now and again, taking her sleep and good spirits. Then after Nell on the train she had wondered if she should throw herself down between the cars. The young, she considered, should not have such experiences, lest they color the rest of their lives.

She hadn't known what to do then, so long ago when Gage went. She didn't know what to do now, how to make it less difficult for them all. She did the best she could with a terrible fear that at the end her best would in no way be strong enough to spare them.

"Mama," Maud asked each evening, "are you going to die tonight?"

"No, dear, not yet, not tonight."

"Mama, can I write you a letter after you are dead?"

All of her children had been eager and excited about mail, sending and receiving, especially Maud and Roland.

"Of course you may."

John would think her mind was going as well as her body, or blame the drug, if he heard her say such a thing. Comfort, somehow it was comfort, and that was important.

Comfort Magazine. The exquisite lace curtains. There, on the windows just over there. Perhaps her mind was a bit shaky, but not gone. Milton came in for his good night kiss. "Grow to be a good man," she whispered in his tiny soft ear, "and don't let Spencer kill anyone with that awful temper of his." Milton brushed at his ear where her breath tickled it and kicked to get down off the bed.

She wanted Kate to come and sing with her about the angel band coming to take one home. She missed the music and singing from their years in Faith. There had been no music nights in Queensburg, the people who did gather being given to more formal things, cards, conversation, recitals and recitations, from which she and hers had been excluded. Oh, for the stamp of lots of lively feet in a small house, near shaking it off its foundation, giving it life as little else could.

"Margaret will fix you some tea. You remember Margaret. John hired her when she was let go at the factory. Remember, she was one of the ones who wanted the five-and-a-half-day week. They've got the foreigners there now, working six days and keeping quiet."

"I remember. But Margaret can't sing. I want Kate."

"Remember. You aren't to ask about Kate again."

Maud was screaming. John's first thought was that she must stop at once, not disturb Anna. He should give her a good swat on the rear. Then he thought how careful the child was in that regard, how she took Milton away from the house whenever he was upset so that Anna would not hear him cry. What now?

The sound came from the woodlot. He rushed out to see Maud stuffing her fist in her mouth and heard her wail as Tina took one more kitten, laid it on the block and struck its head off with the ax. He stood there, counting the tiny bodies at her feet.

It was the ninth.

The scene was surpassing strange, not any usual farm routine of getting rid of unwanted animals, not drowning, shooting, or clubbing, but a sort of bloodletting, a sacrifice of some kind he sensed, but did not at all understand. And it seemed to him an act hopeless to accomplish any intended purpose, but relentlessly performed anyway.

"Why?" he asked.

"One," wailed Maud, "just one. Why couldn't we have kept at least one?" He noticed that the all-white deaf kitten, her favorite, was among the dead.

"You have too many cats, John Bayley." Tina wiped the blood off the ax on her skirt tail and walked back toward the house. Maud ran away to sob behind the woodshed, leaving him to gather up the little broken bodies and throw them down among the trees. Tina's face had been as blank and her back as stiff as if she had been a carving of wood, a figure from the great far past, carrying huge breasts and hips on her small frame, an implacable object in his life that he could not control. He could come up to her, but could not set her aside or go through her, had to go around her.

After he disposed of the kittens and calmed Maud somewhat, he went in the house to find Tina sitting in one of the rockers by the fireplace in the dining room, staring straight ahead, her feet dangling above the floor.

"It had to be done," she told him, "and it was not something you would or could do. I am losing both my girls, my least ones, in less than three years. Both my babies, who meant more to me than all the rest. Not that you would understand that, never having buried a child."

Do wives and fathers count for nothing?

Was she also losing her mind to grief and old age? She was older than his mother and had sons older than he.

"Good god, Tina. What does one have to do with the other? This won't help that, can't help it one bit."

She looked at him then, a glitter in her eyes. He noticed that, oddly, her eyes had gotten darker as she aged, not paler, as was usually the case with someone so old. They were as black and rusty as her dress.

"I thought she would live to bury me."

"So did I," he said.

There had been times when he had wanted to throw himself on Tina's mercy, if she had any, speak to her, say, This must not be. I can't survive it. But they could not join together and share their grief. If he spoke she would look at him with those cold black eyes, believe he was seeking pity, which he would have been, and scorn him for it.

She will never die, but will always be there, for all my days, sitting dark, solid, and threatening in some shadowy corner of my soul.

Her little feet in their floppy shoes swung at him like the angry kicks of a child in a tantrum. How much did she hate him? And why? Did she blame him for the disease? Most certainly she did for the unhappiness. But none of it was his fault. He would have had it otherwise if possible, but he and Anna had not belonged together. They were not suited to each other. It was simple as that.

Once he thought of asking Tina how it had been for her and

T.A. all those years ago when they first met, about the rash trip through bad country that T.A. had made up to Meadows of Dan to claim her for his prize. What ever happened to joy and passion? But he hated his mother-in-law too much to ask. Yet, in all honesty, he could not do without her at this time and had to honor the love she bore her daughter. He saw Tina often in the light from the old lamp she had put beside the bed, studying Anna's face as if it were a map of someplace to which she had not yet been.

Tina wiped her eyes. He had not noticed that she was crying. "I have done a terrible thing and, I fear, done it for nothing. Ask Maud to forgive me."

She climbed down out of the rocker and went off upstairs, as rigid as a stumpy, solid little pagan idol, hauling herself up by the handrail and puffing all the way. She usually rested in Maud's room in the afternoons and evenings, then sat up with Anna through the small hours. He hoped she would wait to have a heart attack until after Anna was gone. Mean and difficult as she was, he had need of her.

Anna called, her voice still strong. "Mama . . . John. What's wrong?"

"Nothing," he called back without going into the bedroom. "Nothing's the matter." He left the house with its smell of carbolic and of cloves burning on the bare stove lid.

· ˙ . . ˙ .

Who, she wondered, since she had been ill, was going into the yard with Maud to pee before bed? Tina? She tried to remember when Tina had stopped taking her and Nell out every evening, except for stormy and freezing ones, and let them go on their own. Maud had gone out with her nearly every night since she was out of diapers.

There was ritual, a unity, in it, waiting till dark, choosing a slightly different spot, the squatting, feet apart so one didn't wet them, listening to the streams falling on the grass. They'd always had an outhouse, of course, but it stank in spite of the lime she put in it. There did seem to be something traditional and appropriate about doing it out of doors, as if returning waters directly to the earth. John and the boys pissed off the porch on the other side of the house into her flower bed.

Then she remembered. Her mind was unclear. She had been thinking about Faith. No outhouse here, indoor plumbing, faucets in the kitchen and a flush toilet in the bathroom. How could she have forgotten? No further need to slip out into the dark, no joining with animals and the wild. But somehow she would be willing to bet that Tina still kept with the old ways. Some evening when she was not so groggy and tired, and not in too much pain, she would stay up and check on her mother to see. She smiled a little to think how Tina didn't like or trust that whirling flush. She herself was glad of it now, of disease and possible contagion being carried away.

Her mind could be more than strange. It said crazed things to her, like *The ribbons are in the soup,* and immediately she would see a bubbling bowl of stock full of limp and ruined colored ribbons covered in grease. She could not help herself and had to ponder what it might mean when all the while she knew very well it meant nothing at all.

She considered not taking the morphine, but the pain was too much for that.

SHE HAD WAITED in the summers for the smell of fever, an odor like that of a fetid swamp slowly rotting and drying at the same time, but the smell that came now was the smell of her own death. All of the burnt spice in the world couldn't take it away.

When she brushed her hair in the mornings she wondered if it would fall out the way Roland's did the summer he was so sick. She remembered how John had gathered Roland's curls, the ones that fell out and the ones he clipped off, made a packet of them and put them in his box so they could be of use if their child died. That way they would not have to bury a bald-looking little boy. Would he even care if she were about to be buried slick as an egg? She stood in the bathroom and thought of washing her hair, what a shampoo would do to it. Did she have the strength? Did she have much time left?

Her face in the mirror said, no, not much left. She touched the glass. Whose face had been reflected there before hers? Some of the departed McCains now up the hill in the little fenced plot, surely.

John hates that fence. He'd have it down, would let his cows crop and plop over the graves if removing it wouldn't give him a worse name than he already has.

What if mirrors could store the images that they had reflected, a kind of immortality? Seven years' bad luck to break one. Whoever thought that up perhaps did believe mirrors could hold on to you. She might still somehow be in Lucille Alba's triple mirror, the many selves of her. Or in the clean, cold oval one with a white frame and beveled edge in a hotel room in Knoxville. That mirror could contain Martin also, with that jaunty, reckless, confident look he had about him. Say that fancy could be true, what would it take to get one out? Bad luck for seven years for someone else?

She leaned against the silvery surface, pale forehead to pale forehead. "Hello in there," she whispered. "Is anyone else there?"

They'll think I'm crazy for sure.

She reached up for the cord to pull off the light and saw the reflection of her hand high up in the glass, thin and graceful as a white bird. But it was also like the hand of the drowning, reaching up from the depths. With a swift tug she turned the room to darkness and went back to bed.

I WALKED OUT once on deep new snow and the dark blue shadows of the trees trembled. I said to the shadows, How did I ever lose my way, thinking the track so plain, that is, assuming I had a way to lose?

The shadows had no answer.

"WHAT ARE YOU doing?" asked one of the angels.

"I am counting."

"What are you counting?"

"All the things that wring my heart."

I SHALL WAIT for the wild to return, for the wolf to come, leave track in snow above my dust, to howl in summer over my bones. I'll wait for John and his kind to be bested. Forever.

AT THE END she had time to reflect, but did not. The pain was too intense, the smell too disgusting. She gazed on her hands, once so hard, red, and gnarled that she had sometimes hidden them. They had grown pale, soft, and elegant. They caused her a great sorrow.

. . . . .

After breakfast and before going to the fields he went in to see her. These last three weeks she had gotten so much worse that Tina slept in the room with her and he bunked in the barn alone. He took her fragile hand, the flesh mostly gone, not only pale but nearing gray. Her ring, too large to stay on anymore, lay in a little white nicked saucer on the dresser.

"How are you, Anna?"

Her eyes turned toward him but focused somewhere beyond, as if she saw what was on the other side of the room, the other side of the world, and not him at all. The eyes were still beautiful though, the lashes long, and often full of tears. Then the corners of her mouth lifted slightly as if she wanted to smile at him after all.

"I am very well, thank you. Yes," she said, her voice as distant as what those eyes saw. Then she came back, momentarily, from wherever she had been, or wherever she was going to. She did smile, finally.

"John, I am so glad you could come by. Thank you." Her eyes suddenly had a light in them that he remembered from long ago. He had no idea what to say, or if he could even speak. Finally he managed. "You're welcome."

"You are not the conductor," she said.

He looked at her closely and quickly left.

He went into the kitchen. There's been a change, he started to say to Tina but stopped himself, for she would ask, What sort of change? and he would either have to lie and say he didn't know or answer, Your daughter is dying, you mean old witch. And he might feel he should add, You should fear for her, for she has a heretic soul. He had even told Anna this, that he counted her among the lost.

"That makes two of us," she had said.

"But I pray that you repent, lest I not see you in the next world." She had closed her eyes then. "Fine, you do that."

At that moment he thought of Anna only as Tina's daughter, not as his wife, the way he had felt from time to time ever since his mother-in-law had sacrificed the kittens for some salvation not to be. His heart said, *At last,* not because he wanted it to happen, but because Anna had said so often, "Not yet," and now it was "yet." He poured the coffee for himself since Tina was washing up. A full cup, strong and scalding hot, but he drank it down quickly and went out.

By the time he returned for the noonday meal Anna had slipped into a coma.

. ˙ . ˙ .

The bearded man sat in a straight chair across the room from the bed, his carved cane across his knees. He took off his delicate little glasses.

Twelve years old the first time she saw him, in the fall, just after the equinox.

He was saying something to her. His lips moved but there was no sound. "Time after time," she thought he was saying.

"Who are you?" she finally asked.

"You know," he said, speaking for the first and only time. "My words. By my words you know me."

. ˙ . ˙ .

Then she was hiding, hiding away upstairs, trying to stay away from what she knew was coming. She heard the scrambling all around the outside of the house as it tested the doors, the latches, windows. Can I go higher, she wondered, into the attic away from it? She plotted climbing, pulling up the ladder behind her, anything to keep herself safe, to avoid the jaws, those teeth, the huge blackness.

Then it came to her what the beast was, that it was nothing she could avoid, nor should she. She went down the stairs and opened the front door to the presence.

Bear, she-bear, mother bear, enormous silent bulk in the darkness before her. The bear had a smell, strange and feral, yet familiar, like blood, like childbed. It reared up, towering over her. Then it dropped to all fours and turned, inviting her, she realized, to mount its broad back.

The black fur was so long and thick she sank into it. It covered her hips, her thighs. She twisted strands of it around her hands so that she could hold on as the great animal began to climb.

They forded a stream she could not see, but she heard the stones roll aside under the enormous claws, heard the water splash. Then she knew they were climbing more steeply and she had to hold on tighter to keep from sliding back over the great furry rump. All night long the bear climbed with her on its back. There were no stars, no moon. The wind as it rushed past struck sparks from her hair and the fur of the animal. Looking back over her shoulder she could see a path of white fire behind them in the night.

They reached the top of the mountain at the very moment the sun came up.

· · · · · ·

For three days and three nights her breathing had filled the house and in the sound her firstborn, Roland, heard a wind that ground and scoured everything into dust, even the pyramids, even all the mornings of the rest of his life.

Early on the fourth day Anna died. John wrote in the McCain county tax register he used for an account book.

Anna Maud Stockton Bayley Died June 14, 5:30 A.M. 1917

Later he added "Thur." between "Died" and "June," and still later, over in the margin, someone else wrote "40 yrs. old."

He made this notation on a page opposite a list of what he was owed for seed wheat and hay and what he had to pay out to have timber cut and logs hauled.

. · . . · .

QUEENSBURG, 1917

It is hot. The night has been close and heavy. The dark and the day hold so much water in the air there wasn't even a cooling dew on the grass at daybreak. The women of Queensburg came in the early afternoon and washed her for her grave so that Tina would not have to do it. They have wrapped her in the friendship quilt with the picture of the wanderer over her heart, loosed her hair from sickroom braids and spread it on the pillow, wildflowers all around, a ministry to make up for their slights, perhaps.

"She wanted to wear the dark red dress," Mecie told them, but the Queensburg women decided red was hardly fitting and they have dressed her in a long white nightgown.

"Like an angel."

This morning they are back laden with food, enough for all of the bereaved family and more.

The family, even T.A., are all too warm in their good Sunday clothes. Maud has Milton by the hand. She wears the blue dress trimmed with the white crocheted lace with blue diamonds that her mother made for her. They all wilt quickly in the sultry heat, though the walk with the coffin is not long, up the rough, tangled lane beyond the sheds, above the barn. John always lets these banks grow up to keep them from washing. Briars dip, holding their berries barely beginning to turn, Queen Anne's lace is blooming like tiny lacy halos for very small saints. The tangle of vines and grasses shade bird nest, toad, and snake.

JOHN, ROBY, AND Art have dug the grave themselves late in afternoon and into evening. Some of the Queensburg men came and offered to help.

"Why didn't you take them up on it?" Roland had asked. "How could you do that yourself?"

"There was no need," said John.

The grave is up on the knoll in the McCain family burying ground but higher than any of the graves already there, all decided beforehand. Anna had wished to go back to the mountains, but that was not possible. Nor was the churchyard, a hearse, a regular funeral, what with the expense.

Roland is the first to leave the graveside, then Leonard carries Roby's youngest down to the house since Mecie is pregnant again and can just manage for herself. Spencer has been crying, but wants no one to know it, and Maud's bonnet is wet from sweat all across her forehead. She is far too old for those big starched things. They're for little children to shield them from sun but she loves them so. She has not let go Milton's chubby hand the whole time. The last to leave is John. He does not speak. Then, when he thinks no one is looking, out of his pocket he pulls the white whorl of a Queen Anne's lace bloom and throws it onto the coffin.

The hands from the next farm come and fill in the dirt.

The family eats the cold, brought-in things for the noonday meal, sits the afternoon away indoors, still in their good clothes, in the heat. Roby breaks down once. "I've lost the best friend a man ever had," he says. No one answers or disputes him.

In the house Tina has stopped all the clocks and wants John to stop his watch but he says, "Not yet."

About five o'clock by that watch the sky goes suddenly dark. Thunderheads have been mounting up all afternoon like the haunches of fierce horses and the wind starts to whip up the silvery gray-white undersides of the maple leaves. When the rain begins the wind is still high and the water splashes against the windows and pours in sheets off the eaves. Thunder rolls all around. Spencer begins to moan, "She's going to get wet." At this moment he does not look quite rational.

"Shut up, shut up," says Roland, looking out the window, but not in the direction of the burying ground.

John and the boys change into work clothes, come back from the chores soaking wet. Maud stands in the kitchen watching the water come down the lane, running brown as laundered blood.

"Torn away," Tina cries suddenly. "My child has slipped away from me and died. My babies, my babies, both of them." She rocks back and forth, her feet kicking in the new shoes John bought her. She is sitting in Anna's chair. Suddenly she leans over, takes off the shoes, and carries them into the kitchen. She is lifting the stove lid to cast them into the fire when John comes through the door.

"What in the hell are you doing?"

"If I have to go barefoot the rest of my life, I'm not wearing anything you bought me, John Bayley, to replace what you stole."

"Tina, I thought it was for the best. Your old shoes . . ."

"Were my comfort and your embarrassment. They were cut and padded to ease the pains my bulk has brought upon my feet. You bought me new ones for your stupid pride, not for my good. Didn't want anyone, Queensburg people, coming in here seeing me flapping around like a rag and bone person."

"Please, Tina, let's not quarrel. Not today, of all days."

Tina puts down the stove lid. She stands as if her feet are cold on the floor in spite of the heat of the day. "All right," she says, "just ask next time." Under her breath she mutters, "At least she never had to live in a son-in-law's house."

"The best friend a man ever had," Roby says again from the dining room.

"SHE TOOK SUCH good care of her teeth," John says. "Never lost a one of them." He is thinking how his own mother has hardly any left in her head and the ones she has managed to keep are stained from the pipe she smokes and the snuff she dips.

"Good god." Roby hits the door frame with his fist and the glasses rattle in the cupboard. A plate jumps. "Here I've lost the best friend a man ever had and all you can talk about is her teeth?"

John looks puzzled. "But I always thought she had a beautiful smile."

"Bet it's been a while since you saw it," says Roland.

No, not a while, only five days.

IN THE LATE evening the house sits peacefully under dripping trees. Light coming from inside gleams on the wet maple roots furrowing up the yard. Drops cling in a row to the clothesline.

From an upstairs window Tina looks out, not speaking, not crying, but with an unsettled expression, as if she would cast some sort of spell if she could.

IN THE KITCHEN very late John eats another cold drumstick in the dark. He has been wakened by the thunder of another wild storm, watches its wrath, and keeps an eye on the barns. By one bright flash there seems to be someone up at the cemetery, a stooped figure with a cane.

For some reason for the first time in years he is reminded suddenly of that odd storekeeper back at Faith, the heavyset young fellow with that shabby little place. What was his name? Interesting how decent the fellow had been about getting Rocket back to him. But he can't think how there could be any connection.

He can account for everyone in the house and when he looks out to the burying ground again no one is there.

THEN WHEN ALL is calm again and every light is out something wraps itself about the house, pours into every room, crosses each still or sleeping face. Mother, father together under this roof for once, husband, children, their quarrels, trials, and difficulties lie before and behind of them.

Those without breath are also without pain, lift away from the living, off into night, the dark, the newly washed and pure air, going back to hills and forest, earth.

. . . and say all you
devils behind me, here's salt
in your eyes.

· · · · ·

"I've made the inquiries and then went for a visit," said Tina.

"And?" Roby did not even pause in his filing. He sat sharpening the shears, his feet dangling off the edge of the porch. The grinding wheel didn't put the finest edges on tools, took off too much of the metal for his taste. And even rough-ground things could use touching up.

Tina stood with her toes nearly touching his thigh. He felt her looking down on him. He guessed it wasn't all that often she got to see the top of a man's head. She would be taking note of the fact that he was already starting to lose his hair.

"The child is sound, healthy, and will probably survive. Pretty little thing. She looks like . . ." He heard her take a deep breath. "She looks like Maud did when she was little." Tina paused again. "And Kate is agreeable. She may have been a silly, careless girl, but she seems a devoted enough mother. It will make things easier for her, money-wise, I mean, if it goes like it ought."

She sounded more sure of their plan than he was. He was not sure, not at all. Of course it needed to be done. Of course he wanted to do it for Anna's sake, for all that he owed her, but when he thought of going against his own father, even in such a case as this, something in him nearly balked.

"Do we have enough money for it?" he asked. The edges on the shears were bright as could be, but he went at them again, for the sake of having something to do while they talked. His file rasped like a hurt or angry animal.

"Barely. It will have to suffice."

"Who do I go see?"

"Not you. You don't go. It must not be known you had anything to do with this. Surely he'll think it was Kate's folks, even stony poor as they are. God knows what he'd do to you if he found out you came up with the lawyer's fee. He might take it in his mind to shoot you, son or no son. And me, since he'd figure I put you up to it, he might string me up by the toes. It has to be someone he wouldn't touch even if he did come to some different knowledge. Mecie."

"No. I won't let her. You don't need to be looking out for me. It's my place. I'll do it for Anna."

She wants me to. He didn't know how he knew that but felt it was so.

"Mecie will do it for Anna. She has already agreed. He'll not dare harm her—that is, if he should find out. He'd have to deal with her folks if he did anything and those Thomases, even from all the way over there on the other side of the state line, can put the fear in John."

So this conniving old woman had already talked to his wife behind his back. He could imagine Mecie, pale, sweaty, and ghostly when she said yes. But even so he knew she would want to do it. Mecie had never cared for John overmuch, but when his father had said that Kate's name was never to be mentioned in his house again she was as angry as he had ever seen her.

"I curdled with the wrong, the unfairness of it. I have hardened my heart against him, your father or no," Mecie had told him, the words rushing out as she paced around the table. "Think of what he was about while his wife lay dying and how he blamed the girl when he was the source of all her wages, so what else could she have done?"

When he thought on it he knew Tina was right, that Mecie was the best choice, but he was surprised Tina had asked her. Anna's mother had had little use for Mecie, what with her wild Thomas relations and what Tina called her old-wifely ways, like biting each baby's fingernails off and not cutting any of its hair until it was a year old. Perhaps she had seen at last how good Mecie was to Anna, what a friend she had been in a lonely, strange place. And when Mecie agreed to getting back at John, Tina must have been proud of her, perhaps could even have loved her, had that been required.

Roby laid the shears and file aside and took out his switchblade and the whetstone. "He's going to be sore as a hornet when he finds out. He's never been lawed over any of his bastards before now."

Like I almost was, would have been too, if he hadn't stepped in. Do you remember that, Anna? Remember who and what I'm owing? Pulled apart over this, that's what I am.

He spat on the stone. "He'll have to move on. This isn't Faith, where they mostly wink and blink at such, if that. The Queensburg folks aren't likely to stand for it. They don't care much for us anyway. Remember how the doctor thought Roland wasn't good enough to court his daughter?"

Tina almost smiled. He knew she was remembering how his father had sent back hot words to the physician to the effect that his girl wasn't fit for his son. John had never gone out of his way to ingratiate himself in the community, in fact often did the opposite.

The switchblade was long, bright, and keen. "Yes, he'll have to give this place up." Roby held the knife before his face to see if he could make out a part of his reflection in it, note if he himself had gone pale over all of this plotting. "Move on. And I'll have to go with him."

"Of course you won't. No one is going to blame you."

"That's not what I mean. I'll have to look after him. Art's gone and Roland will be leaving soon, mark my words. And the others are too young to take it all on."

"You're not obliged to, you know. Besides, he'll probably marry again. I bet he's out there looking around already." Tina sounded sure and spiteful.

"Even so, he'll need me. New wife, new family, but he's going to be getting old. He'll need me. He's Dad."

What else can I do?

He thought he saw her foot move under her skirt and he would have bet that she had had the urge to kick him, kick him hard. She was an old woman with lots of loss and lots of anger, vinegary. She probably was warmed by the sour thought of getting back at the son-in-law she hated for what was likely the worst of his infidelities. But once she did this, how cold and alone would she be? If she looked down her own way to see who might go with her when she had to move on, would there be anyone?

"What did Kate name the baby?" he asked.

He thought she might have lied, said she didn't know, but this time she didn't even try to spare either of them the wrongfulness of it all.

"Anna."

. · · · · .

QUEENSBURG, 1918

John bought the car as a wedding present for Sarah. The first two times he had lost a wife he had waited to remarry. Now time was short and he had searched out Sarah in much less than a year. She was far younger than Roby or Art, younger even than Roland. She was solid, ordinary, and competent, lacked Anna's looks, but also her darkling moods, her airs, and occasional temper, the way she wouldn't look at things as they really were.

"But what do I want with a motorcar?" Sarah had said.

"Ride two hundred miles without fatigue," he answered with the quote from the advertisement, wondering if that were really the case. "It's not any buggy or wagon."

She laughed, knowing he'd really bought the car for himself, that the occasion was only an excuse. Then, to his surprise, she learned to drive after all and went into town by herself once in a while.

Roland was furious.

"As if it weren't bad enough that you go and remarry six months and seven days after Mother died, then you have to go and buy yourself a car with the money she wanted me to have to go to college."

"Eight days," said Leonard. "O tempora! O mores!"

John ignored Leonard for the moment. "Forget about that college, boy," he told Roland. "I agreed to see you through high school and that was all. I never said yes to any college. I need all you boys right here helping out. You're plenty educated enough to farm."

"You'd have the money for enough hire if you hadn't put it on that car. If Mother were here . . ."

"But she's not, is she? Now I want you to mind Sarah anytime I'm gone."

"Mind Sarah? Mind Sarah!" Roland nearly screamed. "I'm older than she is by almost a year. I'll be damned if a girl younger than I am is going to boss me around, stepmother or no stepmother."

"You will mind. She is my wife and she is in charge if I'm not here. And you will apologize."

"Oh lord, for what?"

"Your bad language."

"Good god, when did you get so goddamned puritanical that you care about stuff like that?"

"I could knock you down, boy, for taking the Lord's name in vain. Perhaps I should. Sarah doesn't like to hear it, wasn't brought up that way. She's a regular churchgoer, not a cardplayer and so on, not like your mother."

"Damn you, you try it, just you try taking me on."

"Take care, boy. I see that now I shall not have to smite ye. The Lord himself will strike you down for cursing your own father."

But he did not feel like waiting for any action from the Lord. He first raised his fist, then looked around for something to grab hold of and strike with.

Roland tore out of the room with John yelling after him to get right back there now, that he was for sure and certain going to beat some sense into him after all.

They should understand. He had worked them hard, beaten

them when necessary, not for his sake, but for theirs, that they might know hard labor and not sloth, and that their estates would grow by their own sweat, a lesson they must remember when they had farms of their own.

He would not concern himself with whether or not they could do it, only concentrate on the fact that they must. They would be the measure of his success or failure so he must double his efforts and not allow himself to admit any enfeebling doubts on that score.

BY THE NEXT night Roland was gone. Leonard and Spencer stood silent before their father when he asked them if they knew where their brother had gone. When he cursed and threatened they said they didn't know. It was the truth. For their protection, and his, Roland hadn't told them.

When he came back some months later Roland had the money for his first year of college, earned working double shifts in a hot, dusty plant that made coke for the steel mills. He had stayed in the city up North with Art and Leah and returned to Queensburg late one night, but not to his father's house. His brothers heard someone whistling, going by the road. The tone and tune were known, familiar, a signal.

"It's him," said Spencer. He sat up in bed and hugged himself in relief.

"Yes." Leonard grinned in the dark, listened as the sound grew stronger and then fainter. "It sure is."

The whistler did not stop but went by and on up to Roby's place.

"What's that tune? I should know."

"It's one Mama made up. She used to play it on the organ."

Roland stayed with Roby and worked for him until his first college term began in the fall. He never returned to the McCain place nor slept under John's roof again.

MOUNTAIN CITY, 1918

John parked the car in the garage and ran for the house in the rain. He had taken Tina into town to catch the train for Deerfield. His former mother-in-law's trip back to stay at Dan's among her own had begun, and he felt as if he were suddenly pounds lighter and years younger. Not even being caught in the sudden thunderstorm lowered his spirits.

He had come to dislike having Tina at the new place in Mountain City more than he would have thought. They argued over everything, even the butter money. She had no real call to be there except that Sarah had had no one else to help when her baby came. It felt odd and uncomfortable, as if Tina were bringing a part of Anna along with her, but his own mother was long past being hale and hearty enough to come and assist—indeed, needed nursing herself. And Tina was a widow now with no fixed home of her own, free of any last responsibilities to her husband and on call to go where she was needed.

T.A. had dropped dead suddenly in the dining room of the McCain house on his way to the water bucket in the windowsill. It was a luckless thing to wish for anyone's death but the old man had been useless and demanding. He couldn't remember that Anna was gone and would ask for her, thinking he had seen her out in the yard. And he'd had no use at all for Sarah.

"That heavy-stepping woman was through here again, woke me up and wouldn't fetch any free water."

Maud was in the room when it happened and John worried

about her, this death so soon after that of her mother. But in truth, they had all seemed relieved.

TINA DISTURBED HIM, as always. With the present war and all he had wondered if her German blood would bring something down upon her, but nothing had happened. She would say now that she remembered not one word of her first language. He had no way of knowing whether that was true or just some ruse to distance herself from the enemy nationality.

If he had been a superstitious man he would also have said that she truly did bring some of Anna's spirit with her when she came. He hoped she'd not marked his new son in any way and that she'd taken her ghosts with her when she left. They belonged elsewhere. He had started over. Sarah had gotten rid of all of Anna's things, even the clock.

"Wouldn't they sadden you?" she had asked when he found that they were gone.

Of that he was not certain, one way or the other, but now he'd be hard-pressed to come up with so much as a slip of paper in that clear, graceful hand. It was probably for the best. But why did some of the dead rest easy in one's mind and others not?

Spotted wet with the big warm raindrops, in an unreasonably happy mood of relief and more than ready to think of other things, he burst through the back door and into the kitchen, to find the room in shadow, no lights yet on, though the clouds of the sudden shower made it seem near twilight.

His wife sat at the table, his table, with another man. Another man, who sat in one of John's chairs, with John's own cup, the thick, white heavy-bottomed one, before him. They were having coffee. He smelled the beans that had been freshly ground for this man.

And, oh god, they were both young, their faces soft and misted in the room's shadow and the steam from the coffee. He was stunned, frightened suddenly, then angry, fighting angry. What was this?

The young man stood up. He was tall, taller than John, and wearing brown. An army uniform. He spoke.

"Dad?" said Roland.

It is not salt I mean to burn
but my true love's heart I wish to turn;
wishing him neither joy nor sleep,
till he come back to me and speak.

. · . . · .

FAITH, 1925

John saluted Rufus instead of waving as he drove off, a gesture left
from when they were boys. Rufus saluted back and John drove the
car down the lane that really was his, the one he had dug out and
graveled with creek rocks. The house John had built for Anna was
considerably changed. Rufus had added a large kitchen across the
back, turning Anna's old kitchen into the dining room, and replaced
the gabled stoop with a porch that went all the way across the front.
There were two bedrooms upstairs now for the four little Colvard
girls, with a long dormer to bring in more light. Rufus was even
talking of building a millrace with a wheel to run a generator so
they could have electric lights.

John had told Rufus it was a shame that he begat only girls and
had no son to leave the place to since he'd done so well by it.

"I have a son," Rufus had said, without any further comment
and not even seeming to realize that he had mentioned it. And it
was something he had never said before.

Who might the mother be? John wondered. Probably something
had happened since he left Faith that he'd never know the straight of.

JENNY.

In that house, behind that window there, he had lain with her for
one last time and hadn't seen her since. Now he would be driving by
the store where she most likely was. Was she the reason for this trip
back to Faith? If so, he didn't seem to learn much from that sort of
experience. Women. That hired girl, what was her name, yes, Kate,

· · · 331 · · ·

in the house while Anna was ill, didn't count, pregnant or not, didn't count. But how she had gotten the money to take him to court for upkeep of a bastard was still a mystery to him. Some of his hostile neighbors in Queensburg must have gotten up a collection. That situation had cost him the McCain place, but he was not of a mind to consider losses but concentrated on advantages instead.

Roby found two adjoining farms outside Mountain City and it hadn't taken much to get him in a ready mind to move. He had another brick house now, smaller, but newer, and well built, and even more acreage, most of it flat. And he had had the new wife, Sarah, at the ready to go with the new house, new land. She had been as eager as he to leave Queensburg.

A good thing Jenny had never gotten with child. Though no one other than Kate had ever lawed him, Sherwood might well have called him out but good, made a legal accusation if that had happened to Jenny.

When Anna fell ill Jenny had written to him in sympathy. While it had excited him to hold her letter in his hands, he suspected the sentiments expressed. For a moment his little wren bird seemed more like a scavenging crow. The pages of her letter flapped like wings circling. This conduct, while Anna still breathed and had her being, had been unseemly. He had wondered, and not for the first time, about Jenny's lack of wits and judgment. But her slender arms and shoulders were so sweet. He remembered her small high breasts, like little apples, so neatly round under his hand. Anna's when she nursed had been huge and veiny. They had thinned as she did, sagged on either side of her when she lay in her sickbed.

He had kissed Jenny's letter and put it away in the locked box with his bottle of good bourbon, and the faded copy of *John Halifax, Gentleman,* the latter still the total of his literary collection. He knew she must have been thinking up ways to get him to marry her when he was free. While that single-mindedness was flattering, it also unnerved him. He had been of no mind to ever marry Jenny, no matter how much she made his blood go to fire and thunder. He was, after all, a practical man, knew she would never have done for the wife he needed. She was simply not bright or able or strong enough. And there was that streak in her that was close to fiendish.

HE COULD EASILY have walked from Rufus's house to where he was going, but he loved the car, loved to drive it, loved to show it off. If it had cost him a son for a time, well, that had been too bad, but the relationship was now at least partly mended.

"It's a new age," he had told Sarah after he got used to driving it most places.

"You're going to have a wreck, kill yourself, and not see much of it if you're not careful. And leave the babies fatherless."

The babies had been Milton, whom Sarah had taken to raise as her own, and his and Sarah's two little ones. Now she was pregnant again. The new family had made him feel strong once more after all of the weakening darkness of Anna's long illness.

Milton, too young for those memories, was happy with Sarah, but Anna's other children remaining at home were sullen, miserable, and full of blame. He thought that somehow they believed he had caused their mother's death, and at low moments from time to time he had a guilty terror that they were right. Illogical, of course, for that could not be.

His remedy was, as always, to drive them as hard as he could, his theory being that if they were worked until they could barely stand they would have less time to think about who was guilty of what, or for any other such reflections. But when he looked at their faces around the table over the fresh and steaming food Sarah and Maud had fixed, he thought that perhaps this time it would not work. This time it would drive them all away, not just Roland and Art. This time they would flee from him as soon as they could, the boys to work away from the land, up North or in the mines, Maud to marry the first man who would ask her.

Roland had perhaps done all right after all, had escaped the great European war, though just barely, finished college, and was off teaching school, trying to save what he figured was enough money to marry on. Roland's intended was nice-looking, but not a real beauty, a tall girl with a vigorous walk and a strong handshake. Still, she was no mountain woman and looked as if she might have a mind of her own, might like to run things. Oh well, Roland would never have made a farmer. He lacked the grit.

HE SAT IN the cemetery watching Jenny come to him. The lane was too steep and washed out for the car so he had parked at Cherish Church and walked up. He looked down on the plain white building, nothing to compare with the brick church he went to now in Mountain City, but it moved him. He had stood in that little churchyard all those years ago with Julia holding his hand as the first Cherish Church building burnt to the ground through the act of an incendiary never caught, she pregnant with Roby at the time. After the baby was born she would strip and examine him again and again to see if the fire had marked him anywhere. It was strange how very seldom he thought of Julia anymore.

Jenny had followed him.

She must have seen him pass the store where she now clerked for her uncle nearly full-time. The turn to go up to Cherish was right by the store building and the only motorcar in Faith at the moment would have been hard to miss. He wondered if she had locked the store, pulled down the shade, or simply walked out and left the door open.

He saw her coming along the road in her brown dress with a white collar, her hair still dark and in a knot on top of her head. Then he looked away to the ridge opposite, the upper portion against the sky crowned with naked gray skeletons of the chestnut trees that once had made enough mast for whole herds of swine, and had supplied enough timber to fill the county with schools and churches. A foreign blight invaded and in a short savage time their bark fell away and they were living no more. Chestnuts were a funeral food, someone had said and now all those great old trees had had funerals of their own. The long shape of Rich Mountain rose beyond that first ridge, with the deep cut of the gap at one end of it where the shepherds used to stay the whole summer long. There were not near as many sheep as there once had been.

He did not look at her again until she stood before him among the graves on the steep weedy slope.

"Well, Jenny."

"Well yourself. How could you ever? I said I'd marry none but you and now I'll not be marrying at all."

He had been afraid she'd make this claim again, though he had not broken a promise because he'd never made one. He looked at her. She was past thirty-five, still slender and quick, but she was pulling her hair up tighter and tighter and the tendrils that used to escape no longer did so. Her thin, pointed face was beginning to line and her throat showed the bulge of the goiter. Her voice, no longer light and clear, had gone harsh, raspy. For the first time ever he saw tears in her eyes. He had seen her before in great wrath but had never seen her weep.

"Jenny, Jenny. Don't cry. I was always too old for you. Perhaps I shouldn't have done you the way I did but I was never the man for you. Marrying was always your idea. I never thought we were suited that way."

"Ah, so I was good enough to bed but not to wed?"

"Don't talk about yourself that way. I thought it was something we both wanted at the time."

"At the time, at the time? That's some joke. What are you doing back in Faith? Come to show off and rub my face in it? And why are you sitting up here in the graveyard?"

He told her. It was still only half-formed in his mind until he spoke, but when he said the words it was clear as could be and as if it had always been his wish and the purpose of the whole trip.

"I've come to pick out my final resting place."

"Lord, John, you're not sick, are you? Do you mean that? Not just playing for my sympathy, are you?"

"No, I'm just older. Years and experience have taught me that one needs to make these decisions ahead of time."

But it had been decided in Anna's case and she had been buried not once, but twice, taken from the McCain family plot to the Baptist churchyard in Elizabethton. The home burial had not mattered to the immediate family, but Anna's brothers and sisters-in-law were adamant that she should be in a holy place and not practically out in a field with a bunch of folk who were not even kin.

"So you will be back here after all."

"If my wishes are respected."

"Why shouldn't they be?"

He could think of a number of reasons but didn't want to mention any of them. He did not tell Jenny either that it was his intent, also suddenly arrived at, to bring Anna back with him. He wondered how she would feel about lying beside him through all eternity in the cemetery of a church she had refused to attend. Or about lying in a third grave, for that matter. Three houses, three graves. The symmetry of it pleased him. Of course he didn't count the cabin. It amused him to think that she could do absolutely nothing about it. And that he would always know where she was.

"Why wouldn't they respect your wishes? What are you smiling at?"

"Nothing, nothing, it's nothing." He looked at her. She was no longer crying.

Then she knelt down before him as he sat there, scooped up earth with her hands, sprinkled it over the toes of his boots. She bent over stems of daisies and yarrow till they touched the leather.

"Guess what, John? Guess what I shall do? When you come to lie here I will walk up every day, throw myself on your grave and cry and cry till my tears soak down to you. That's for all the wrong you've done me. I hope the salt water makes you cold forever, the way I feel now."

She got up, brushed the dirt and grass off her skirt, turned and walked off down the hill. He watched her go until she had crossed the grass and reached the lane. Oh, she broke his heart. They were young no more. He got up and went after her.

"Jenny, wait. Wait for me."

He caught up with her and took her arm. She did not pull away and, after a few steps, took his hand, raked her finger across his palm.

. . . . .

Martin Daniels eventually submitted a poem to the weekly newspaper from which he remembered Anna clipped some of the pieces for her scrapbook. It was a sonnet, carefully made. He would work for months on it, put it away dissatisfied, then go back to it again and again. In the poem one lover urged another that they should run away together, but instead they made their farewells beside a spring with cattails fraying out in the wind and redwings flying overhead. He hoped it wasn't sentimental.

Martin's poetry submission was opened by the literary editor of the paper, a short, heavyset, foreign-looking man, an outsider with no family and no past in the small midwestern city where the paper was published, and with a name no one had heard before, Princeton Wrightangel. But he had a flair for his job, a taste for good writing, and was pained by what passed for poetry in many papers and most of what was submitted for his. He was determined to raise the quality of what appeared on his page and would turn to printing Elizabethan lyrics, the Romantics, or Thomas Hardy when no submissions met with his approval.

In his ire over some of the work he examined he composed rejection notices in an injudicious vein.

"You are wasting the time of the world's intelligent readers!"

"How dare you sully the elevated name of Keats with this pallid imitation!"

"The sacred is unknowable to us all. What you write is sheer pretense."

"Powerful imagery cannot redeem cloying sentimentality but you will doubtless be published somewhere, to the detriment of literature everywhere."

The notices that were actually mailed out, however, were all identical, printed on small cards in a neat newspaperlike typeface:

Dear Sir or Madam: Thank you for considering our publication. Unfortunately, your work does not meet our needs at this time.

The editor sat for a long time holding the sheet from Martin's envelope. The dilemma in the sonnet, that of one lover pledged to someone else, was familiar from many a ballad and story, but he was stirred by a sense of connection he would have found impossible to explain.

The poem was not perfect, was at once raw and overworked, yet the passion in it, the earnestness of the plea, moved him profoundly, and in the editor's peculiar and checkered career not all that many things had had such an effect. This offering, flaws and all, deserved to see the light of day.

The poem was accepted and published with, as Martin requested, only his initials at the bottom. But he felt sure Anna would recognize it.

"I dream sometimes," went the last line, "that we did never part."

It was to be his only publication.

By the time the poem appeared in print, Anna had been dead for years.

. · . · · .

He was alone. It was time. Almost. He was alone in the room. Or was he? Sarah? Sarah was off somewhere else in the house. He was alone. Or was he? It was time. He lay under the white counterpane, the tall oak panels of the headboard above. It was time. He was alone.

The room filled with blowing snow so thick and white he could see nothing. He was cold with more than mortal cold.

He called out to her, his beautiful girl of golden hair, chestnut velvet, and bright water drops.

And she came to him. By milkweed down and snowflake, she came.

Oh, John, come with us, she said. Oh, please, and held out her arms. He went straight to her.

. · . . · .

BOONE, 1939

Roland had his wife scrub and dress both their daughters for the visits as if they were going to church or to a family reunion, not just a short call on the other side of town. Their hair was waved with toilet paper rolls and straight pins and they both had to wear their strap shoes, good socks with no holes, and fluffy, starched clothes.

"The seams are poking me," said the little one. "I itch."

"But don't you scratch," said his wife. "Oh, Roland, we have them fixed up like curly little lambs for the slaughter."

"Slaughter?" shrieked the older girl.

"Metaphorically speaking," he told them. "She doesn't mean that. In fact, she probably meant to say *sacrifice* and doesn't mean that either."

"And all this over and over to go see that undeserving old woman." His wife puffed the children's hair. "A monster. She's devoured her own daughter."

"Now, Martha, be charitable. She's aged and dependent. Besides, you know that a social visit is only a part of it."

But he had to admit to himself, in spite of his hopes, that going through a formality was usually all that it amounted to. His questions, spoken and unspoken, were likely to go unanswered.

"ARE WE GOING to the house with the naked man on top?"

"Not quite naked. He's got sort of a towel."

The children both bounced on the backseat.

"The house with the mouth and teeth in the red hall? Where the old lady and the old, old lady live?

"Yes, we're going back again," he told them. "Barb, keep your shoes on."

He always took his children with him, thinking they could disarm their hostess, or that an aspect of their young faces, perhaps a family resemblance, might recover a memory long forgotten.

The old lady let them in and, as always, told them to sit in the parlor, then went away.

Please stay.

To his repeated disappointment she never took part in any of his visits and seemed to be totally immune to the charms of his pretty little girls. He often wondered if she might remember more than her mother and withhold it for reasons he could not guess. She began to play hymns off in another room and the music, sometimes punctuated by loud chords and occasionally a falling hymnal, would go on the entire time they were there.

When the old, old lady came in walking with her cane, she offered all of them candy from the dish of mints on the piecrust table and said what beautiful children he had and so well behaved. She noticed they did not swing their feet while sitting on the sofa and asked when would they be starting school.

"Janet has just finished the first grade."

"Really, so soon? How time does go! You must have said so before and I forgot."

"Oh, I'm sure not. I probably forgot to mention it or you'd remember."

Roland took a breath, paused, then asked once more about his mother.

"Anna? Of course I remember her. Such a dear, bright, good girl. And so pretty. Happy too."

He waited, wanting to ask if that long-ago girl sang as she worked, what she wore, what she read, where she went, whom she knew, but he realized anything more must come by itself.

"Now, when did you say your girls were starting to school? Ah, yes, your mother was always happy here. All of the girls who worked for me were happy. Those times were the best."

In what way were they the best? In what way was my mother, Anna, happy here? Or unhappy? For whom might she have mourned the way I've mourned for her?

But after some more conversation about nothing very much, Mrs. Alba signaled that the visit was at an end by letting Roland's daughters smell her potpourri and giving them some mints to take home to their mother. The hymn playing ceased and the old lady came to show them out.

"She's no better, as you see," said Lucille Alba. "It's not worth your time. But if you insist on coming . . ."

BACK IN THE car he had the pain and frustration he felt whenever he wanted to cry but didn't. And he was angry with himself for yet another failed search. Those letters to his mother that he had torn and tossed away. He had wanted to call them back the moment they were washed downstream. Perhaps he should have tried to trace them. He could never ask anything of his father, and after both of her daughters died, his grandmother never said their names again and did not suffer anyone else to mention them. If his aunt Nell had lived to come back home he might have talked to her about his mother, but as it was he was stalled and hobbled.

Barb and Jan took off their shoes and socks and tossed them into the front seat beside him.

"Cut that out, girls. And don't eat all the candy. Save some for your mother."

THE CHILDREN TOOK off their good dresses as instructed as soon as they got inside, but instead of hanging them up, they spread them out on their beds and ran outside without putting anything else on. There they were, skinny little tan bodies out in the side yard in their underpants and vests, pretending to play a game of croquet.

"Let them be," he said when his wife started out to get them. "They're covered enough. You know, I wonder if it is completely hopeless. She's ancient now and increasingly frail. I don't know if she really remembers the little that she says or is only speaking by rote. I keep hoping something more will come to mind, but it's so . . ."

"Grieve for the world and you'll die young," said his wife.

But he did grieve.

. . . as many fresh streams meet in one salt sea . . .

······

FORT LAUDERDALE, 1987

On his one-hundredth birthday Roby received a special telegram of congratulations from the president and celebrated by going pier-fishing near his daughter Jane's retirement place in Florida.

His son-in-law went with him and helped with the hooks and lines.

"So I'm back to bait-fishing," Roby said to him. "What are we using?"

His son-in-law had to stick the hook through the bait.

He's an old man too.

Roby wondered how much longer either of them could do this. He could not see the fish in the surf, and they were very different fish. Still the tug on the line was familiar and timeless. He loved its feel in his hands again. Not nearly so sporting as fly-fishing, but at this stage in his life it would do well enough.

And he loved the sea. After a lifetime in forest and field he had come late upon its magnificence. It sparkled and shimmered, awed and beckoned. He had no to wish to venture out upon it, yet when he looked at the vastness he knew why men did so.

Sailing sailing, over the bounding main
For many a stormy wind may blow ere Jack comes home again

A firm, sturdy strike and he landed a good-sized bass.

There was a strong breeze threatening to tear off his cap and cause him to get a sunburn on his head. The white foam of the waves went out as far as he could see with his indistinct vision, even farther than he could ever have seen.

Ah, Mecie. Aged, but still blooming and bustling, she had left him years ago, without any warning, out in her garden. He had a sudden regret that she had never seen this shining sight. Nor had Anna either. And it was fully as fair as mountains, in its own way. He thought of how it would be to have them both there with him, of how he would tell them what to look for along the coast, the rivers, the swampland, the sounds, sandbars, and shoals. But most of all, he wished to have them discover at his side the mighty boiling up of the great water itself.

Oh, my darlings, look at this.

He had them so clearly in mind that he almost spoke the words out loud to them. He caught himself in time before his son-in-law could think him touched in the head, or senile for sure.

He caught two more fish and could make out their quivering in the cooler. That was enough. He put down the rod and walked slowly to the end of the pier. The light on the water reminded him of wheat and chaff falling through a beam of sun in the mill or the diamonds after an ice storm on a bright day. He stood for a long time looking eastward, leaning on the railing till the edge of the timber cut into his forearms. The only birds he heard were those with low, harsh voices and he could not see them, but he thought he noticed a darkness on the water that might be their shadows as they went flying by overhead.

Out there somewhere, where he could never see, was a great fine fish swimming free and it was a blessed thing that neither he nor anyone else would ever catch it. He had mentioned the fish to his daughter Jane and she teased that she knew all about it, that it had a jewel in its head and was older than old.

"Ready to go, Robert?" said his son-in-law at his shoulder. He already had the cooler and the rods in hand.

"Sure, we don't want to fish out the whole ocean, now do we?"

The rest of his family would be coming on the weekend to celebrate his birthday. He would get Janie to go over their names with him before they arrived so he could remember. There would be an enormous amount to eat, including a huge sheet cake with his name on it in letters big enough for him to read. It would probably say *Robert,* or *Dad,* or *Great-great-granddad,* but not *Roby.* And surely it would not have a hundred candles!

Tonight Janie would fry their fish for supper.

SOURCES FOR EPIGRAPHS AND VERSE

223   There is salt between us.
            Arabic proverb

244   O, Western wind, when wilt thou blow . . .
            Anonymous

249   . . . in a salt land and not inhabited.
            Jeremiah, 17:16

261–262 Here is the ancient floor . . .
            Thomas Hardy, "The Self Unseeing"

263   He will not accept any food you give him . . .
            George Waldron, *Description of the Isle of Man*

277   Salt water and absence . . .
            English proverb

289   . . . to taste our salt sorrow . . .
            Christopher Fry, *The Lady's Not for Burning*

317   . . . and say all you . . .
            Kathryn Stripling Byer, "A'ma," *Searching for Salt Woman*.
            Used with permission.

329   It is not salt I mean to burn . . .
            Spell to be spoken while throwing salt on the fire

345   As many fresh streams meet in one salt sea . . .
            William Shakespeare, *Henry V,* Act 1